P9-CRW-994

The
LAST GRAND DUCHESS

Also by Bryn Turnbull

The Woman Before Wallis

The LAST GRAND DUCHESS

BRYN TURNBULL

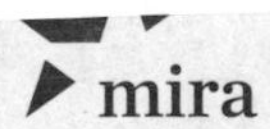

Recycling programs for this product may not exist in your area.

ISBN-13: 978-0-7783-8636-0

The Last Grand Duchess

This edition published by arrangement with Harlequin Books S.A.

For questions and comments about the quality of this book, please contact us at CustomerService@Harlequin.com.

Mira
22 Adelaide St. West, 41st Floor
Toronto, Ontario M5H 4E3, Canada
BookClubbish.com

Printed in U.S.A.

To Gran

The LAST GRAND DUCHESS

CHARACTERS

Romanov Family

Grand Duchess OLGA NIKOLAEVNA,
eldest daughter of Nicholas and Alexandra

Grand Duchess TATIANA NIKOLAEVNA,
second daughter of Nicholas and Alexandra

Grand Duchess MARIA NIKOLAEVNA,
third daughter of Nicholas and Alexandra

Grand Duchess ANASTASIA NIKOLAEVNA,
fourth daughter of Nicholas and Alexandra

Tsarevich ALEXEI NIKOLAEVICH,
fifth and youngest child of Nicholas and Alexandra,
and heir to Tsar Nicholas II's throne

Tsar NICHOLAS ALEXANDROVICH ROMANOV (NICHOLAS II),
last emperor of Russia

Tsarina ALEXANDRA FEODOROVNA,
last empress of Russia

Dowager Tsarina MARIA FEODOROVNA,
dowager empress of Russia and mother of Nicholas II

Grand Duchess OLGA ALEXANDROVNA,
sister of Nicholas II

Grand Duchess XENIA ALEXANDROVNA,
sister of Nicholas II

Grand Duke MIKHAIL ALEXANDROVICH,
youngest brother of Nicholas II and Nicholas II's chosen successor following the abdication

Grand Duke ALEXANDER "SANDRO" MIKHAILOVICH,
husband of Grand Duchess Xenia

Grand Duke PETER ALEXANDROVICH,
husband of Grand Duchess Olga

Imperial Household

ANNA ALEXANDROVNA VYRUBOVA,
companion and confidante of Alexandra Feodorovna

GRIGORI YEFIMOVICH RASPUTIN,
Russian mystic and trusted advisor to Alexandra Feodorovna

PIERRE GILLIARD,
Swiss academic and French language tutor to the Romanov children

SYDNEY GIBBES,
British academic and English language tutor to the Romanov children

Doctor EUGENE BOTKIN,
court physician to Nicholas II and the imperial family

Officer NIKOLAY PAVLOVICH SABLIN,
aide-de-camp to Nicholas II

Count PAUL BECKENDORFF,
Minister of the Palace

Count WOLDEMAR FREEDERICKSZ,
Minister of the Imperial Household

JIM HERCULES,
arap to the court of Nicholas II

Imperial Russia

Colonel NIKOLAY KULIKOVSKY,
second husband of Grand Duchess Olga Alexandrovna

Grand Duke DMITRI PAVLOVICH,
first cousin of Nicholas II and friend to Olga Nikolaevna

Prince FELIX YUSUPOV,
Russian aristocrat and wealthiest man in imperial Russia

Princess IRINA ALEXANDROVNA,
niece of Nicholas II and wife of Felix Yusupov

Officer PAVEL VORONOV,
naval officer and Olga Nikolaevna's romantic interest

Officer DMITRI ARTEMEVICH SHAKH-BAGOV ("MITYA"),
ensign in the Thirteenth Yerevan Grenadier Guards and Olga Nikolaevna's romantic interest

Officer DMITRI YAKOVLEVICH MALAMA,
officer in the Imperial Russian Cavalry and Tatiana Nikolaevna's romantic interest

Officer VLADIMIR KIKNADZE,
Russian officer and Tatiana Nikolaevna's romantic interest

RITA KHITROVO,
Sister of Mercy and friend to Olga and Tatiana Nikolaevna

ANYA VORONOVA (née KLEINMICHEL),
Sister of Mercy and wife of Pavel Voronov

Princess VERA IGNATIEVNA GEDROITS,
senior resident physician at the Tsarskoe Selo Court Hospital and the Annexe Hospital

Countess MARIA DMITREVNA NIROD,
Sister of Mercy and life partner of Vera Gedroits

Prince CAROL OF ROMANIA,
prospective love interest of Olga Nikolaevna

Crown Prince FERDINAND OF ROMANIA,
Carol's father and Crown Prince of Romania

Crown Princess MARIE OF ROMANIA,
Carol's mother and Crown Princess of Romania

Revolutionary Russia

ALEXANDER KERENSKY,
Minister of Justice (Provisional Government)

Colonel EUGENE KOBYLINSKY,
commander of the Special Detachment (Provisional Government)
at Tsarskoe Selo and Tobolsk

VASILI PANKRATOV,
commissioner (Provisional Government) of
Freedom House in Tobolsk

Ensign PAVEL MATVEEV,
temporary commissar (Bolshevik) at Freedom House

VASILI YAKOVLEV,
commissar (Bolshevik) tasked with
transporting Nicholas II from Tobolsk

YAKOV YUROVSKY,
commandant (Bolshevik) at the House of Special Purpose in
Ekaterinburg and lead executioner of the Romanov family

VLADIMIR LENIN,
leader of the Bolshevik Party

In 1896, Prince Charles of Denmark took it upon himself to read the horoscope of Grand Duchess Olga Nikolaevna, Tsar Nicholas II's infant daughter. Based on the relative positions of Jupiter and Neptune at the moment of Olga's birth, Prince Charles felt confident that the child would grow to be a woman of medium height, with a round face and chestnut hair. He predicted several "critical periods" in Olga's childhood, noting that if she reached the age of eight, she would enjoy "twelve years of peace." This period of happiness was to be cherished, Prince Charles concluded... "for it is certain that she will never live to be thirty."

PROLOGUE

November 1907
Alexander Palace

The air in Mamma's reception room was thick with smoke and rumors, unsettlingly quiet despite the crowd of people gathered within. Flanking the double doors, two footmen stood at the ready, their glittering livery bright against the marble walls. Olga's aunts and uncles gathered near the immense windows, waiting for dawn as light from the ruby chandelier pooled bloody shadows on the parquet floor.

From down the hall, Olga could hear cries of pain, the hurried tattoo of feet along the corridor mirroring the frantic thrum of a distressed heartbeat. She winced, wishing she could drown out the noise. By the fireplace, Aunt Olga paused midsentence, gripping Aunt Xenia's fingers as they waited for the noise to subside. Uncle Sandro, his arms wrapped around Tatiana and Maria as he read to them from a book of fairy stories, pressed his eyes shut, his face lined with grief; Anastasia, playing on the carpet with a set of building blocks, looked up uncertainly, pushing ringlets from her cheeks with pudgy fingers. At six years old, even she seemed to understand the significance of their younger brother's screams.

Still. In its own ghoulish way, the noise was reason to hope.

If Alexei Nikolaevich—Olga's only brother—was able to cry, it meant that Russia still had an heir to the throne.

Seated beside Olga on a cream-colored love seat, Grandmamma turned, her lips pursed into a thin line. As dowager empress, Grandmamma had long learned the art of concealing her emotions from view, but today she, too, looked beaten. She ran a hand along the diamond necklace that hung low on her breast, grasping the jewels as if they were beads in a rosary.

"Courage, child," she whispered, allowing Olga to snug closer to her side. At twelve, Olga knew she was too old to crave the comfort of her parents—too old, certainly, to require their attention while they dealt with the doctors. It was her job, after all, to be strong for her younger sisters. They'd need her, in the weeks to come. But for the moment she let Grandmamma comfort her as though she were as small as Anastasia, and wordlessly crawled onto her lap.

Grandmamma placed her hand on Olga's head, letting her fingers fall over Olga's unruly braid. "This is a difficult day, my girl," she said, her voice creaking with sorrow. "Perhaps the most difficult day we will ever face."

Olga could feel her grandmother's diamond necklace digging into the bony ridge of her shoulder blade. Today had indeed been difficult, the long hours of prayer an inadequate distraction from the dread that awaited any news about Alexei.

Hemophilia. Olga's sisters didn't yet know the word, but Olga did: she'd been told never to utter it aloud, never to hint to anyone—not even to family members outside this room—that her brother was ill. Because he'd been born without the ability for his blood to clot, any chance accident risked leaving Alexei in terrible, life-threatening pain. A fall or bump that any other child might laugh away would result in days of agony as blood coursed to places in Alexei's body where it didn't belong: joints, muscles, his blood a tidal surge beneath his skin.

Olga wished there was some way to relieve her brother's pain, but she'd been told that his condition was incurable, irreversible in its finality. For what was blood, after all, if not finite? There was only so much of it coursing through her three-year-old brother's body—only so much pain he could stand to endure.

"What will happen if we lose him?" asked Olga, whispering to conceal her fears from her sisters.

Grandmamma sighed. "We will grieve," she replied simply, pulling Olga closer into her arms.

Grief. Olga had seen too much of it already in her short life: grief beneath the shine of Papa's smiles; grief in Mamma's relentless prayers. Though Olga knew that her parents loved her and her sisters, grief had attended each one of their births—how could it not, when Mamma and Papa's most important job was to secure the Romanov dynasty with the birth of a son? Three times, Olga had listened to the church bells ring out in St. Petersburg, announcing the arrival of her sisters—grand duchesses, like herself. But she had never seen such joy—such relief—from her parents as on the day the bells rang ceaselessly to herald the birth of Alexei.

Her parents had been grieving ever since.

"But what will happen to Russia?" Olga whispered.

"Russia…" Grandmamma let out a deeply held breath. "Russia will endure," she said. "It has weathered the storms of succession in the past; it will do so again."

Lessons flashed through Olga's mind: her family tree, reproduced in her tutor's elegant script; branches cut short by disease, by revolution, the golden thread of the dynasty running into the blooming abundance of another son's heirs.

"Could they not have another baby?" she asked. "Another boy?"

Grandmamma hesitated, and in her silence, Olga could tell she was weighing the balance of what to say. "A woman reaches an age when she can no longer bear children. I'm afraid it's too late for your parents to have another child."

Olga knew she was pushing past the bounds of propriety—that such questions were impertinent at the best of times. The fact that Grandmamma was willing to discuss such matters at all was surprising to Olga—but then, perhaps Grandmamma was too weary to object.

"If Alexei is—if he's taken into God's arms..." Olga paused. Voicing the possibility aloud was enough to make her feel as though she was falling, but she took a breath and continued. "If the worst is to happen, tell Mamma and Papa not to worry about Russia. I will carry on. For Alexei. For Papa. I will become the tsarevich."

Grandmamma's eyes welled with tears; she looked across the room, blinking them back as best she could. "Bless you, my dear," she said. "You're a good girl, and I know you mean well. But that's simply not the way of things."

"Why not?" asked Olga, trembling. Much as the prospect terrified her, she knew it was right: it would ease Papa's burden, if she were to take on the heavy mantle of his succession. "If they can't have another son, someone needs to do it. Someone needs to inherit Papa's throne. I'm his eldest child; I can be his heir."

Grandmamma kissed the crown of her head; across the room, Aunt Olga lifted a sleeping Anastasia into her arms. "I'm afraid it's not that simple. There are laws in place that prevent a woman from becoming tsar."

"But Grandmother Victoria was queen of England."

"That's true," said Grandmamma. "Russia, however, is a very different country."

"Catherine the Great?"

Grandmamma sighed. "They changed the law after Catherine. It would have been much easier for your parents if that hadn't been the case, but it's God's will. When you and your sisters are grown up, you'll marry into other royal families. That is the destiny of a grand duchess: to bear children, and to build a life in a new country. Like your mother; like me before her."

The idea was unthinkable: Leave her family to carry on without her? Leave Russia without a tsarevich? Olga's future loomed before her, bleak and terrible: Alexei, constantly battling this incurable disease; Olga herself, cast out of Russia, out of her family, because she was born a girl. Mamma and Papa, locked forever in their grief, watching the dynasty crumble in their hands while Olga was too far away to help them, powerless to save her brother, powerless to save Russia—

"Courage, my dear," said Grandmamma. "God may yet provide."

Olga let the tears she'd tried so hard to hold back fall, unconcealed, down her cheeks. "How can I have courage when I'm so scared?"

Grandmamma gathered Olga close, enveloping her in the comforting scent of lily of the valley. "My darling girl. Courage does not mean a lack of fear," she said. "It means meeting whatever the future may hold with grace."

Grandmamma looked over Olga's shoulder at the sound of approaching footsteps, the tension in the room ripening as Olga slid off of Grandmamma's lap.

The footmen pulled open the doors and Papa strode in, his expression enough to break Olga's heart.

Grandmamma rose to her feet, clutching her necklace. "Alexei?"

Papa's chin quivered beneath the chestnut brown of his beard. "The doctors have told us there's nothing more they can do," he said, his eyes darting around the room as though he was looking for something he'd lost; he rummaged in his pocket and lit a cigarette with trembling hands. "My advisors tell me we can no longer conceal his condition from the people. They're drafting a—a statement for the newspapers..."

Olga turned away as Grandmamma wrapped Papa in a hug, the sight of Papa's anguish too overwhelming, too final, for her to bear. How could the doctors have failed? How could

God have turned His back on her family? Olga pressed her face into the hard fabric of the sofa cushions, thinking of every harsh word she'd ever said, every unkind action and uncharitable thought she'd ever had. Had she brought it on them, in some way—had she been too short with her sisters, too resentful of Alexei?

Someone rested a hand on her back and Olga shook her head, pressing further into the cushions. If she could stay here, like this, perhaps she'd never have to hear the words she dreaded. Perhaps Alexei might survive.

"Olga." Papa's voice was low but steady once more, his hand a comforting weight as he squeezed her shoulder. "My dear, it's time. You and your sisters must come to say goodbye."

Olga gripped Tatiana's hand as they walked into the enveloping dark of Alexei's bedroom, careful not to let her steps falter as she passed over the lintel. *Courage*, she reminded herself as she breathed in the spiced incense. Candlelight glittered in the gilded alcoves of the iconostasis that had been pulled in from the chapel, making the painted faces of saints and angels on its panels dance in the light of the flame: they watched, impassive, over the small assembly that clustered around the listless figure in the bed.

Mamma knelt at Alexei's bedside, gripping his hand in hers as she strove to keep him tethered to life. Behind her, nurses circled the bed, carrying bowls of water, bandages—with a jolt, Olga realized that they'd stuffed cotton in their ears to block out the worst of Alexei's screams, but Alexei was no longer crying. In the silence, Olga could hear the dry rattle of his shallow breath.

Mamma closed her eyes. "My baby," she whispered, lifting Alexei's limp hand to her lips.

Papa crouched beside her. "The priest is coming to perform the last rites," he murmured as Mamma gazed at Alexei. "And our girls are here," he continued. "To pray."

Mamma blinked, as though stirring from a trance. "Of course." She pulled the covers up to Alexei's neck, but not before Olga caught a glimpse of the bruise that blackened his chest from collarbone to waist. *Courage*, she told herself once more as she drew up to the bed, hoping that she would find within herself the grace she so desperately needed to face him.

Olga looked down at Alexei, swallowing her panic at the sight of him lying so still. How could this be happening? He was her little brother, her lovable little brother, who laughed when she played with him in the nursery, who tromped across the dining room at teatime to offer her his cookies. How could she go on without him? There would be a hole at the center of her family forevermore, a void that would drown them all in the enormity of his absence.

She pressed her lips to his forehead, alarmed to feel fire beneath his skin.

"Don't go," she pleaded; behind her, Mamma let out a ragged sob. "Please, Alexei, don't go, not when we love you so much—"

Mamma buried herself in Papa's chest. "How can we live without our little boy?"

A knock sounded softly from the door—the priest, Olga supposed, as she stepped away from the bed. She turned as a nurse opened the door, letting a stream of light from the hallway flood into the candlelit bedroom.

A man stepped forward and bowed. Tall and slender, he wore a rough-spun tunic and bagged trousers, a wooden cross swinging from a leather string around his neck. Though he'd attempted to smooth back his unkempt hair, the man's ragged beard and mud-caked boots made him look as though he'd arrived at the palace having crossed the length of Russia without rest. But his eyes were what made him truly distinctive: they glittered, green and restless, beneath his heavy brow.

"Where is Father Vasily?" Papa barked, pulling Mamma close

before addressing the nurse who'd opened the door. "Get him out of here. Get out!"

"I am a friend," the man replied, holding his hands up in supplication. "Summoned by a higher power than you or I alone, Little Father. A friend sent in your hour of need."

Mamma's breath hitched. She looked up, her tearstained face slack. "What did you say?"

"I am a friend, Little Mother." He inclined his head, and despite his alarming appearance, Olga found herself soothed by his gentle voice. "A priest; a wanderer. A simple pilgrim seeking the Lord's grace." He paused. "A healer, some have called me."

"I asked for Father Vasily," Papa began as the priest sidled farther into the room. "The last rites; they're all that remain..."

"I'm not here for last rites." The priest stepped closer to Alexei's bed; Papa made as if to stop him, but Mamma held him back.

"Let him approach," she breathed.

The priest stared down at Alexei, his fingers threading through his unruly beard. "This earthly realm has failed you, child," he said, pacing slowly to the side of Alexei's bed. "Medicines, machinery...these are solutions borne of men. But what use are man's weapons against an evil such as this?"

Mamma broke free from Papa's grasp. "You can heal him?" she said, clutching the priest's arm. The priest looked at her with surprise; Mamma stepped closer still, tilting her chin to meet his gaze. "You can save the tsarevich?"

"If God wills it," the priest replied.

"Please," Mamma whispered, her face lined with desperation, "please, save my son. I will give you anything—anything at all, whatever you wish. You simply have to say the word, and it will be yours. Whatever is in my power to give... Please, I beg of you."

Olga watched the priest's smile broaden, his eyes glittering as though lit by an inner fire. He studied Mamma a moment longer, his green eyes locked on her blue ones, and Olga felt the emptiness in the pit of her stomach twist—with hope or in dread, Olga didn't know.

PART ONE

1

March 1917
Tsarskoe Selo

Shots rang out across the twilit grounds of Alexander Park. Sitting on the window ledge in her father's study, Olga turned her head toward the sound. She'd heard gunfire in the days and weeks since the riots had broken out in Petrograd, though they'd never sounded so close, so final. Incongruously, she thought not of advancing troops, but of her brother, Alexei, and his cap-gun, firing at imagined enemies in the grounds where, at this very moment, true monsters stalked between the trees.

Across the room, shrouded in the darkness that had cloaked the palace since the electricity lines were cut days before, Olga's mother pulled a shawl across her shoulders. Candlelight sent dark flames up the cavernous bookshelves that lined the walls, illuminating her weary face.

"Abdicated?" she whispered.

Panic gripped her by the throat, and Olga turned to face the window once more. In the deepening gloom, she fancied she could see the orange glow of bonfires. "I don't understand. In favor of Alexei?" She glanced at Mamma: Alexei's chronic poor health had always made him seem older than his age, but at twelve, he was still very much a child, and far too young to take on the heavy burden of ruling.

Standing in front of the tsarina, Major General Resin, the commander who'd taken charge of the garrison of troops that protected Olga's family, cleared his throat. "No, Your Majesty. It's more complicated than that. We're still receiving information from the front, but it seems His Imperial Highness was most insistent on the matter. He offered the crown to his brother, Grand Duke Mikhail, but the grand duke refused it. The Duma has formed a provisional government to determine what will happen next, but as I said, we will learn more once His Majesty returns."

Olga turned her attention back to Mamma, shutting out the continued rattle of gunfire—no closer to the palace walls, but no farther away, either. Having spent the last several weeks nursing her siblings through a fierce bout of German measles, Olga had not had the time nor the energy to keep abreast of political developments, but she'd heard enough to know that unrest had been boiling in the capital. Protests in the coal plants; riots in bread lines. Rolling blackouts, hitting tenements and palaces alike; rallies and calls for change, growing ever louder as the war against the Central Powers continued to leech provisions from households and businesses.

But abdication?

From within the white folds of the Red Cross veil she'd worn since the start of the war, Mamma's face fell, her pale eyes darting around the room. "I don't understand," she said. "I simply don't understand."

She reached out a thin hand, waving her fingers insistently; recognizing the movement, Olga stepped forward and took it, searching for a logical route through her own confusion. She could hear a buzzing in her head: an insistent roar, the sound of surf crashing against the hull of a ship. With Papa's abdication, the situation had become everything she'd feared, the sickening finality in the word itself enough to keep it from passing her lips: *revolution*.

She squeezed Mamma's hand, watching as Resin's fingers tightened on the flat brim of his cap. "Where is Papa?"

"He's coming here, Grand Duchess," replied Resin, "but in the opinion of the Provisional Government, the palace is not the safest place—not for His Imperial Majesty, and not for you, either. I'm afraid they can no longer guarantee your welfare."

Mamma looked up sharply. "We have three hundred loyal Cossacks at the gate—the finest soldiers this country has ever produced," she said, sounding for a moment like her old, fierce self. "They're loyal to my husband. I fail to see the danger."

Resin shifted his weight from one foot to the other. "With all due respect, Your Majesty, Minister Rodzianko disagrees. The barracks in Tsarskoe Selo have begun to riot; they're singing the 'Marseillaise' as we speak."

Mamma paled. Olga recalled visiting the garrison less than a year earlier, trotting on horseback past 40,000 troops all sworn to protect the tsar and his family. How could 40,000 minds be so easily turned?

"And what of my children?" Mamma persisted. "Tatiana can hardly walk. Maria and Anastasia are delirious, and the tsarevich is in a very delicate state—"

"With all due respect, Your Majesty." Resin met Mamma's gaze directly. "When the house is in flames, one carries out the children."

The room fell silent. Despite her attempt at composure, Olga began to shake, a thin, uncontrollable trembling, which, given the darkness of the study, she hoped Resin couldn't see.

Mamma gripped Olga's fingers in a silent plea to keep calm. Though her poor health would make it appear otherwise, Mamma's Victorian upbringing had given her a stiff upper lip which Olga and her sisters lacked. She'd been instrumental in running the government since Papa went to command the front, overseeing the distribution of relief aid to soldiers' families, orchestrating shipments of food and provisions, reining in the government ministers whose political agendas risked the country's success at the front. Despite what people said about her—despite her German roots—Mamma had led Russia through the worst of the war years, relying on her faith in God and in Papa to make the decisions others would not.

How had things gone so wrong?

Mamma stood. "We will stay," she said finally, lifting her chin. "I won't leave the palace without my husband."

Olga walked through the playroom, the cloying scent of illness lingering in the air. Four army cots lined the back wall: within, Olga's siblings dozed, their flushed complexions showing various stages of the virus's progression. In the cot closest to the fire, Alexei writhed in discomfort as Mamma laid a cold compress against his forehead.

Olga knelt beside Tatiana's bed and felt her forehead, inspecting her sister's face for the slowly dissipating rash. Tatiana had been the first to contract measles; to Olga's intense relief, it appeared that she'd be the first to recover, too.

Tatiana's eyes fluttered open at Olga's touch. Even in the throes of illness, Tatiana was beautiful, her usually luminous face pale but lovely, nonetheless.

Olga smiled. "How are you feeling?"

"Better," Tatiana sighed, "though I don't think I'll be dancing the *kozachok* anytime soon. How are the others?"

Olga looked down the line of beds. In the next cot over, Maria slept soundly, her cheeks still covered in spots; between Maria and Alexei, Anastasia was curled into a ball, her disheveled blond hair cascading over the side of her pillow.

"They're on the mend," she replied.

Tatiana's smile grew. "Good," she said, closing her eyes. "And Mamma?"

Olga hesitated. After Resin left, Mamma had stood defiantly by the door, candle in hand, watching him retreat down the hallway. She'd closed the door, then circled back to sit at Papa's desk.

"Abdication," Olga had whispered, sinking into the cold leather of the sofa. Though she could feel the weight of unshed tears behind her eyes, she was too shocked to cry. "Did you know?"

Mamma opened the desk drawer and pulled out a stack of Papa's letterhead. "No." She searched the crowded desktop, pulling a candelabra close as she ran her hand along the leather blotter for a fountain pen. "I wish he'd consulted me first. I wish—dear Lord, I wish Our Friend was here to guide us." She unscrewed the lid of the pen with shaking hands and began to write, her script loose and fluid as she raced ink across the page. Since Papa had gone to the front, Mamma had taken to using his office as her own. Over the past few months, Olga couldn't count the number of times she'd watched Mamma follow Father Grigori into this room, closing the door behind them as they discussed the country in hushed tones.

Father Grigori. What would he say, if he were here now? If he weren't cold under the Russian soil, his mutilated body barely able to fit into a casket?

If you want him gone, say the word. Simply say it, and I will make it so.

"What will we do?" said Olga. "What do we tell the others?"

Mamma shook her head. "We tell them nothing." She pulled a bottle of veronal from the folds of her skirt, not bothering to mix the crystals into water before setting them beneath her tongue. "They don't need to know a thing until they're well again. Circumstances might be different by then." She closed her eyes as the opiate took effect, then resumed writing, her pen scratching across the page: *Dearest Nicky, if what they're saying is true…*

"How?" said Olga. She could see her mother slipping into the mania that had driven her for months, the mania which had reached new heights since Father Grigori's death. "Papa has signed his crown over to Uncle Mikhail. There is no going back."

Mamma looked up, her pen pooling ink as it stilled on the page. "Your father is the tsar. It is a God-given responsibility; it cannot be taken away."

They'd gone down to the courtyard shortly afterward to visit the Cossacks on duty at the front gate, their collars upturned against the cold. Mamma had spoken to each soldier in turn, grasping their hands in a show of solidarity, asking, with motherly concern, whether they were warm enough, whether their families were safe. Olga had followed, looking past the soldiers she considered friends to the blackness beyond the palace gates. Who was waiting there, in the woods, with bayonets and rifles, ready to fire on her family? Were these soldiers enough to keep civil war at bay?

"Olga?" Tatiana pulled Olga from her recollections, her gentle face creasing into a frown. At the other end of the playroom, Mamma was speaking to Alexei, her voice low.

"It's Papa," Olga replied. "He's—he's coming to see us. Very soon."

2

February 1913
Tsarskoe Selo

Anastasia crouched in front of the aquarium, digging a stick through the soil that reached nearly to the top of the glass.

"If I can just get them to fall in love with each other..." she muttered, pushing a lock of hair back from her cheek.

Maria crouched next to her, attempting to fasten her sash as she watched Anastasia's progress. "Can worms fall in love?"

Olga, standing in front of the mirror, stifled a smile. Of her sisters, only fourteen-year-old Maria could ask the question and mean it wholeheartedly. "Of course, they can," Anastasia replied, lifting her mass of curls from her neck to tie them back with a ribbon. "If they didn't fall in love, how would they breed?"

Across the room, Tatiana fastened her own sash. As always, the four sisters were wearing matching dresses—high-waisted tea gowns with crimson sashes—but where Olga and Tatiana's dresses showed the scantest hint of décolletage, Maria and Anastasia's were high-necked. Tatiana finished dressing, then turned to help Maria.

"Worms don't fall in love," Olga said patiently. She glanced at Tatiana, the faintest smile playing on her lips. "They make dynastic marriages based on political expediency."

Maria's eyes widened and she peered closer into the tank, but Olga glanced down at her watch. "Speaking of expediency, we ought to get going," she said. "*Shvybzik*, top button. *Top button*," she repeated, watching as Anastasia, glaring, fastened her collar properly.

They walked down the hallway, still arguing over Anastasia's worms. She was determined to create a worm empire, Anastasia told them: a race of worms so intelligent they could unlock doors… Olga, linking arms with Maria, smiled. With her irrepressible energy and wild ideas, Anastasia had long since earned her nickname, *Shvybzik*: The Imp.

"Should we tell her that no amount of breeding will make a worm unlock a door?" said Maria in an undertone.

"Of course not," Olga replied. "Just because it's not been done before doesn't mean it can't. Maybe *Shvybzik* is destined for a life of scientific discovery."

They slowed when they reached Mamma's boudoir. Though the door was open, the room was dark; within, she could hear a rhythmic voice, low in prayer. Olga led her sisters in, quietening as her eyes adjusted to the gloom.

In the daylight, the boudoir was light and airy, a comforting, modern space utterly unlike the cluttered bedrooms or formal drawing rooms in the rest of the palace. To Olga, it was a refuge, where she and her sisters spent their evenings with their parents: to share their small victories and defeats, to laugh at those problems which seemed too great to fix. The room was dominated by an immense chaise-longue covered in silk damask, its muted lilac hue giving the room its formal name: the Mauve Room.

Tonight, the electric chandeliers were turned off, the job of illumination given over to candles and low-wicked paraffin lamps that lent the opalescent walls a glimmering, peaceful glow. As Olga's eyes adjusted, she could see Father Grigori sitting at the table closest to the fireplace, his eyes closed as he rocked back and forth in prayer.

She didn't dare breathe as she picked her way across the room, sidestepping clustered groupings of furniture: the table with the half-finished puzzle; the bookcase, overflowing with popular editions of Sherlock Holmes mysteries. As she approached Mamma and Papa, Father Grigori bowed his head and swept his hand from side to side, three fingers raised as he made the sign of the cross.

"Girls." Father Grigori looked at each of them in turn, his electric gaze making Olga's stomach leap. "Come sit with us."

Olga sat down as Anna Vyrubova, Mamma's companion, relinquished her chair to Tatiana. To Olga, Anna was more amusing than authoritative: too young to be considered a lady-in-waiting to Mamma, but too old to have anything in common with Olga and her sisters. With her plain features and doughy figure, Anna, who tried to imitate Mamma's wan-faced sophistication, was simply an anomaly: Mamma's ever-present shadow, who hung on Father Grigori's words as though they were laced with gold.

"We've been discussing the tercentenary," said Mamma by way of welcome. She and Papa sat side by side, their bodies turned toward each other like twin sunflowers. "Father Grigori will be joining us in St. Petersburg for the thanksgiving service."

"Three hundred years of Romanov rule," Father Grigori said, nodding slowly. "A fine thing to celebrate. Three hundred years of power; three hundred years of peace." He knelt forward and placed his elbows on the table, shoulders rounding as he toyed with the wooden cross strung around his neck. "It is a chance to join in prayer with all of your children, Little Father, from the most powerful prince to the poorest beggar. For just as all of us are God's children, so all Russians, Little Father—rich and poor, powerful and helpless—are children of the tsar. But these events bring out the devils as well as the angels hiding among us. How can you know which is which?"

He paused to stroke his unkempt beard, and Olga glanced at her parents. From anyone else, such poor manners would have provoked censure, but Father Grigori, with his broad face and peasant upbringing, his long years of service to Mamma and Papa, couldn't expect to be held to the same standards of propriety as others. Somehow, he always put Olga in mind of a windswept crow: a bird whose feathers had been ruffled by a sudden storm, too preoccupied to worry about smoothing them down.

And indeed, Father Grigori had more than his share of preoccupations, for who else could stem the red tide of Alexei's blood sickness? Summoned from the four corners of the globe, the world's leading doctors strode through the halls of Alexander Palace confident that they could cure Alexei of the hemophilic attacks that struck him down with alarming regularity, but it was Father Grigori's prayers that could pull Alexei back from the brink—Father Grigori, who stood vigil over Alexei long after the doctors had thrown up their hands in despair. No one could explain why Father Grigori succeeded where medical science failed, but to Olga and her family the answer was simple. It was faith—pure, unwavering faith—that allowed Father Grigori Rasputin to accomplish literal miracles.

"I will tell you now, that the true Russians are those with nothing to offer you but their devotion," Father Grigori continued, his crooked mouth twisting into a smile. "Amidst all the trappings of wealth, remember that you serve the lowest of the low, as well as the highest of the high. Whether they plow fields or command armies, those whose hearts are truly pure will find their place in the Kingdom of Heaven. All are one in the eyes of the Lord."

He looked up, taking in the trappings of the Mauve Room—its icons and trinkets, its portraits. A photograph of Olga and her siblings on the table seemed to catch his eye: he picked it up, running his thumb along the gilded frame. "Such pretty things you have here, Little Mother. But as you walk out amongst your people, remember that your true wealth is measured not by gold." His grip on the picture frame tightened: with a long thumbnail, he prised a chip of gilt from the corner, revealing the wood beneath. "It lies in your children, who are more precious than rubies; purer than gold. Your children, whose souls have not yet grown base by greed or sin. When you are surrounded by saints and devils tomorrow, remember the purity of your children and trust in the word of God."

"Isn't that interesting, what Father Grigori said? About our souls?"

Lying in her bed, Olga propped herself up on one elbow. Beside her, illuminated by the glow of moonlight outside their window, Tatiana stared up at the ceiling, playing with the end of her dark braid.

Of Olga's sisters, Tatiana was the most beautiful, her sharp cheekbones and dreamy demeanor giving her the appearance of a medieval princess touched by magic. *"Pure,"* she continued. "As though our souls might cheapen over time. Fancy that."

Olga twisted onto her stomach, attempting to fluff the thin pillow that generally made for an uncomfortable night's rest. Like Papa when he was a boy, Olga and her siblings slept in camp beds, a tradition started in the reign of Catherine the Great which Mamma, with her Victorian sensibilities, endorsed. "I don't know about all that," Olga said, pummeling the pillow into compliance. "Doesn't all sin cheapen?"

"I suppose it depends on the sin." Tatiana grinned, deepening her voice to match Father Grigori's graveled tone. "Why? Have you anything to confess, my child?"

"That's not funny," Olga snapped.

Tatiana sat up. "You do!" she exclaimed. "It's a boy, isn't it? Oh, please, tell me it's a boy..."

Knowing she'd never get any sleep otherwise, Olga turned on the bedside lamp. "All right, but you're not to tell a soul," she said. "Do you promise?"

Tatiana nodded, barely suppressing her glee.

"He's a soldier," said Olga. "You recall, at Aunt Olga's tea party..."

A few weeks earlier, Olga's aunt had invited her and Tatiana to her home in St. Petersburg, along with a few dozen others: friends and relations, a few officers of good breeding. "The tall one, with the mustache..."

Tatiana wrinkled her nose, trying to place him. "Voronov?"

"Pavel Voronov," Olga replied slowly, savoring the sound of his name aloud. She closed her eyes, conjuring his dark hair and sleepy expression; his languid smile. "He's a lieutenant on board Papa's yacht."

"Voronov... I recall him now. Handsome, isn't he?"

"Terribly."

Beside her, Olga could hear Tatiana's self-satisfied sigh. "Olga's got a beau," she said wonderingly. "When will you see him again?"

"I don't know," Olga replied. Though she and her family were constantly surrounded by soldiers, opportunities for quiet conversation were few and far between. She'd see him in the parade grounds, perhaps, or on duty, but the thought was disheartening. Separated by obligation and propriety, their knowing glances would soon fade, forgotten one day, no longer wanted the next. She rolled onto her stomach, hating the prospect of losing something before it had the chance to begin. "I don't think Aunt Olga's planning another party...and even if she did, there's no guarantee he would come, is there?"

Olga could hear her sister rustle in her sheets, then heard the tidy click of the lamp switch.

In the dark, Tatiana sounded matter-of-fact. "Well, we'll just have to see what we can do, won't we?"

3

March, 1917
Tsarskoe Selo

Sunlight gleamed off the howitzer in the courtyard at Alexander Palace, the attending gunners' breath rising like smoke in the winter air. Standing outside the front door, Olga hugged her elbows to her sides. Though she was wearing a thick sable coat, she couldn't help shivering, less from the cold than from the oppressive presence of the soldiers that stood silent in the courtyard, their bayonets held to attention as they awaited the arrival of the former tsar of Russia.

Olga had always put her faith in the military, priding herself on her diligence in getting to know the soldiers in her regiments: The Third Elizavetgradsky Hussars. The Second Kubansky Platustunsky Battalion Regiment. She'd learned, as far as possible, the names of the officers and their wives, the latest on new recruits and recent skirmishes. Over the past few years, Olga had used her position as a Red Cross nurse to learn even more about the soldiers under her care, using the moments when she wasn't rolling bandages or changing dressings to ask about their homes and children, to play cards or sneak them cigarettes. *Build relationships with the people*, her father often told her. *They're children of Russia, just like you.*

Olga made a point of remembering the faces of every man in uniform she'd ever met. But now, as she looked out over the faces of the new Revolutionary Guard, their red armbands a jarring addition to the familiar Russian Army uniforms, Olga didn't recognize a soul.

Beside her, Anastasia bounced on the balls of her feet, her hands concealed in a white fur muff. "Where is he?" she muttered under her breath. At sixteen years old, Anastasia was quick-witted and insolent, but her recent illness had softened her rough edges, carved hollows into her cheeks.

"He's coming," said Olga, but the delay, supposedly caused by interruptions on the railway line, unsettled her. The imperial train had never, in Olga's memory, been late.

"Are you sure?" Anastasia whispered. "What if they've thrown him into prison?"

Olga shook her head. "They'll want to bring Papa to us," she said. "They have no reason to keep us apart."

Anastasia exhaled, condensation swirling in the air. "And what a change he'll find when he gets here," she replied, switching easily to French. She stared at the howitzer, narrowing her eyes. "Ever think you'd see one of those where we used to play Ali Baba?"

Stationed at the top of the steps, Alexander Kerensky, the new minister of justice, turned his head. "In Russian if you please, Anastasia Nikolaevna."

Anastasia glowered. "Not smart enough to follow along in anything else, I suppose," she muttered in an English faintly accented by a Scots brogue.

Olga glanced up at Kerensky's unsmiling face; his threadbare jacket and unpolished shoes. In the frenzied days following Papa's abdication, few, it seemed, wanted to take over leadership of Russia: Uncle Mikhail, Papa's chosen successor, refused the crown with almost insulting haste, leaving the State Duma to cobble together various political parties to form a provisional government tasked with leading the country until a permanent government could be elected. As the new regime's minister of justice, Kerensky had taken charge of Alexander Palace and the Revolutionary Guard stationed in the courtyard; and though he was more moderate than the militant Bolsheviks and their odious leader Lenin, Kerensky was still a socialist, and no friend to Olga's family. Olga felt his presence like a cancer in the walls, his orders cutting away her family's freedom piece by piece: orders barring them from leaving, then restricting them to a handful of rooms; orders cutting off the palace's supply of electricity and running water. Whether Kerensky could speak any language other than Russian was, to Olga, irrelevant: educated or not, he held her fate in his hands.

Next to Kerensky, Mamma, seated in her wheelchair, shot a warning glance at Anastasia, who immediately quietened. At least Kerensky had enough decency to give their mother a heavy woolen blanket while they waited. For a brief, horrible moment Olga's mind flashed to the possibility that this was a trick: making the family stand out in the courtyard for hours only to tell them that Papa wasn't coming—or worse, that he'd been torn apart by bloodthirsty soldiers in Petrograd. She paled at the vision of a bacchanal of soldiers, dancing into the courtyard with Papa's head on a pike...but then she shook her head free of such ghoulish thoughts. Russia wasn't France, even in the throes of revolution. Her countrymen, she knew, would behave with at least some degree of civility.

Finally, Maria, standing next to Anastasia, stiffened. The soldiers, whose postures had somewhat slackened after so long standing at attention, straightened too, and Olga went still. There, over the whistling wind, she could hear the faint sound of an approaching motorcar.

Tatiana gripped her hand. "He's at the gate," she whispered. "Why aren't they letting him in?"

She was right: though Olga could hear the motor, it wasn't

coming any closer. Was this some sort of insult on the part of the revolutionaries? If so, how many other petty indignities had Papa endured on his journey home from the front?

After several tense moments, they could hear the gears shift, and soon the motorcar passed the marigold walls of the palace and came into view. Olga tightened her fingers around Tatiana's; Anastasia, pulling her hands free from her muff, took Olga's free hand in her right and gripped Maria's in her left. Olga noted with some relief it was one of the imperial limousines—a closed-cab Mercedes—but while the revolutionaries had allowed Papa to retain this symbol of his station, it didn't escape her notice that they'd made him travel in a German-made car, as opposed to one of his French touring vehicles. *Another attempt to align Papa with the forces that seek to tear Russia apart*, she thought grimly, *even as he gives up everything he has to keep it together.*

The motorcar rolled to a halt beyond the white pillars that separated the courtyard from the driveway; through the window, Olga could see the peak of Papa's military cap. He sat facing forward as soldiers lined either side of the car's doorway—worried, perhaps, that Papa might try to dash across the lawn in a bid for freedom. But Olga knew there was no need for such diligence: with Mamma waiting at the foot of the stairs, Papa would do anything, withstand anything, to be back at her side.

Kerensky cleared his throat. "Open the door for the former sovereign," he called out, and the officer closest to Papa's door placed a gloved hand on the door handle. Mamma let out an involuntary noise as Papa stepped out of the car and Olga turned, lifting her gaze to the palace: above Mamma's head, in the bottom quarter of a windowpane, she could see Alexei's face pressed to the glass.

Papa walked into the courtyard flanked by two revolutionary officers. He glanced left and right, raising his hand in a salute that was not returned by a single member of the onlooking regiment. Though he'd only said goodbye two weeks earlier,

Papa had aged: deep shadows had settled under his tired eyes, giving him the look of someone haunted by a lifetime of sleepless nights. Beneath his shining epaulettes, his shoulders were rounded, the braided aiguillette on the front of his uniform sagging against his slumped chest. As his footsteps echoed on the marble, Olga could see that his beard, permanently brown in her mind's eye, was now shot through with silver.

From a lifetime's habit, Papa touched the brim of his cap as Kerensky stepped down to greet him.

"Colonel Nicholas Alexandrovich, welcome back," Kerensky said, not bothering to observe the formalities attendant on greeting a tsar.

Papa didn't seem to mind. "Minister Kerensky, I presume," he replied. "Thank you for keeping my family safe during this difficult time." He turned, his cheek twitching as he met Mamma's gaze. "My dearest."

Mamma's china eyes welled with tears. "Praise God you're safe," she whispered. Then, as though recollecting the company she was in, she looked down, playing with the blanket covering her knees. "Inside, I think," she said, raising her voice. "Your son is waiting."

"And my daughters." Papa looked at Olga, and her heart broke at his pale attempt at a smile. "I give thanks to God that I find you all safe and healthy." He turned his attention back to Kerensky, who was waiting at the doors to Alexander Palace. With one hand clenched behind his back, he held out his other as if to usher Kerensky indoors—to a game of cards, to a dining table. Wordlessly, Kerensky led the family into the gloom.

Even with the lack of electricity, Alexei's playroom was bright, sunlight pouring in from the corner windows. The natural exposure was one of the reasons their family's physician, Dr. Botkin, had insisted upon using it as the sickroom; now that everyone had recovered from the measles, the playroom had been restored to its original purpose. The cots that had lined the wall were gone, replaced by Alexei's model ships and toy soldiers, his windup trains and cap-guns. His balsa-wood airplanes had been left strung up from the ceiling on fishing wire throughout the crisis: had they fueled strange dreams, Olga wondered, as her siblings looked up in feverish delirium during the worst of their illnesses?

When she was younger, it had irked Olga to watch her parents give Alexei the biggest rooms in the children's wing: the immense playrooms, the music room and the study, a private reception room. By comparison, Olga shared a bedroom with Tatiana, and her chambers—classroom, dining room, reception room—with all three of her sisters. It had always made her feel temporary, somehow, as though her parents were waiting for her to choose a foreign suitor and move out from the home she'd always known.

But, as Mamma reminded Olga whenever her resentments bubbled to the surface, Alexei had larger rooms because he was the heir: the chosen one; their only son.

And their sickly child. Olga looked at the walls of the playroom, decorated with paintings of sailing ships and adventure; the authentic Cherokee teepee, brought back by Jim Hercules, one of their American retainers. Next to the teepee, Alexei sat in his wheelchair, which was more scuffed and worn from use than any of the toys. He longed for the freedoms enjoyed by other boys his age: the ability to skate on the canals surrounding the palace; the exhilaration of jumping horses over hedgerows. But how could Mamma and Papa condone such simple pleasures when the slightest slip could result in catastrophe? Olga's parents had tried their best to accommodate Alexei's childish whims, knowing that Alexei would never have the chance to experience the adventures he so desperately sought. Here, in this room, Mamma and Papa had tried their best to bring adventure to him.

Papa deposited Mamma in a wicker chair next to Alexei. With his dark hair and mournful eyes, Olga's brother was a carbon copy of Papa—though unlike Papa, who prided himself on maintaining a strong physique, Alexei was frail, his thin arms hidden beneath the billows of a sailor's shirt.

Alexei stared at Papa, his sallow face impassive. Until recently, he had been with Papa at the Eastern Front, shaking hands with soldiers in an attempt to buoy up their courage. When Papa had left, Alexei had been tsarevich; upon his return, Alexei's birthright had been abandoned to rebels and traitors. What must he think of it all?

Dr. Botkin dropped to his knees. "Your Imperial Majesty," he said, bowing his head. With his double-breasted uniform and closely shaven head, Dr. Botkin looked more like a soldier than a doctor: all bulk and muscle, with dark eyes and a thick black goatee.

As Botkin rose, Papa gripped his forearm. "How can I ever repay you for your service?" Papa said. Botkin nodded, his expression tight.

Finally, Papa knelt in front of Alexei's chair. He placed his hands in Alexei's lap, palms open. Alexei took them. As one, they sighed, staring into each other's eyes without speaking.

Standing at the door to the nursery, Kerensky cleared his throat. "Now that the family is back together, perhaps we can discuss your future."

Olga turned, blood hot in her veins. "Can you not give us a moment alone, for pity's sake?" she said—but Papa, still kneeling, quietened her with a gesture.

"Of course, Minister," he said, giving Alexei's hands one more squeeze before straightening.

Olga followed Papa and Dr. Botkin into Alexei's classroom, seething at Kerensky's lack of tact. Weren't they permitted the chance to grieve together for what they'd lost?

They sat around a large oak table, several maps—of Russia, of

Europe—half-unfurled on its surface. Alexei's geography lessons, Olga thought, eyeing the ochre stain that made up the Black Sea. She could see Yalta, represented by a small black dot, and a hand-drawn circle that approximated the location of Livadia, their summer palace.

Kerensky remained standing, his hands clasped behind his back. He shifted from foot to foot as Mamma settled herself at the head of the table, turning to examine the objects in the glass-fronted bookshelf behind him: a leather-bound set of encyclopedias; notebooks, worn from overuse. Insects, trapped in pieces of amber; the articulated jaw of a brown bear.

"Our government has received word from the Danish court," Kerensky began, shifting his attention back to the table. He threaded his fingers together, rushing his words. "Queen Alexandrine has inquired about the state of the former tsarina's health. Dr. Botkin, would you be able to provide me with an accurate diagnosis of her physical and mental condition?" He looked past Mamma and Papa as though he and Botkin were the only two in the room.

Botkin glanced at Mamma. "Her Imperial Majesty—her former Imperial Majesty…" He hesitated, then cleared his throat. "Her Majesty suffers from an enlarged heart, which is the cause of the majority of her physical complaints. She is prone to sciatic pain and poor circulation in her legs, which makes her incapable of sustaining normal physical activity. Furthermore, she experiences regular inflammation in the inner ear, which causes frequent migraines."

Kerensky nodded. "And psychologically?"

Once more, Botkin hesitated.

Mamma sighed. "Dr. Botkin, you may as well say what you mean to say," she said. "We're past the point of polite company."

Dr. Botkin looked pained. "Her Imperial Majesty is of an overly compassionate nature, which makes it difficult for her to shoulder the burdens of state," he said carefully. "Because of this, she is vulnerable to the nervous illnesses that plague the House of Hesse—although the stress of what she has endured over these past months," he continued, his voice strengthening with indignation, "has certainly contributed to a state of mental anguish. As it would any other woman in her position." He lapsed into silence, and Olga felt a swell of affection for the doctor who did his best to defend the dignity of his patients.

Kerensky lifted his chin. "Thank you for your candor, Doctor," he said. "I believe you've been caring for one of the ex-tsarina's attendants over these past few weeks, a Madame Vyrubova…?"

"Anna Vyrubova," Mamma glanced at Kerensky, frowning. "What about Anna, what's wrong?"

Dr. Botkin, too, frowned. "Madame Vyrubova is a devoted friend to the imperial family. I don't see why it's relevant—"

"Answer the question, please. Madame Vyrubova, is she well?"

Botkin colored. "Madame Vyrubova contracted the measles while caring for the children and has since recovered," he replied. "While complications from a train accident she sustained two years ago necessitate the use of a cane, she is, I believe, physically capable—"

Kerensky turned and nodded at one of his attendants, a soldier with a bayonet held at his shoulder.

"Madame Vyrubova was recently caught burning correspondences in her bedroom," said Kerensky as the soldier slipped out the door. "As we are currently conducting an investigation into the former emperor and empress's links to Germany, whether they actively worked to thwart the success of brave Russian soldiers at the front—"

Olga and her sisters erupted into protest, but Kerensky held up a hand. "As our investigation is underway—" he continued more forcefully "—such actions indicate a direct attempt at subverting the course of justice. Madame Vyrubova will be arrested and sent to the Peter and Paul Fortress."

Olga gasped. Anna—simple, dull-eyed Anna—locked in prison?

"It's not possible," said Mamma. "She's my friend—"

"A friend to those under investigation for their links to the German government. As I told you earlier, madam, the Provisional Government will not be dissuaded from pursuing all avenues of inquiry into your actions."

Olga felt as though she'd been kicked in the chest. If Anna could be pulled from Mamma's side, were any of them really safe?

"I see," said Papa. "Thank you, Minister, for informing us of this unfortunate turn of events. Is there anything else we should know?"

Kerensky reached into his fraying jacket to pull out a cigarette and a box of matches. He fitted the cigarette into the corner of his mouth and struck a match against the side of the box—a flame roared briefly to life, then sputtered before it reached the cigarette. With shaking hands, he tried again, and failed, to light the cigarette. With a noise of disgust, he pulled the cigarette from his lips, and Olga realized he was as anxious as she felt.

"Colonel Nicholas Alexandrovich Romanov, you and your family are under house arrest for the duration of our investigation into whether you and your wife undermined Russia's efforts in the war against Germany. As your family already knows, this means that your movements and your correspondence will be monitored." He tapped the end of the cigarette with his thumb. "You and your wife will be separately questioned about your ties to Germany; for your own safety, you will be confined to the west wing of the palace. Within these walls, you and your family will be able to do as you wish—within reason, of course." Kerensky looked up and offered a perfunctory smile. "I have no desire to make this difficult for you, Colonel. You and your family will be permitted to walk within the palace grounds, and you will retain your household." He lifted the unlit cigarette to his lips as if to smoke, then lowered it once more. "Your retainers will, naturally, be subject to the same conditions of quarantine as your family. If any of them wishes to leave, they must do so before five o'clock this evening, at which point the palace will be sealed off. Do you have any questions?"

Papa didn't smile back. "As long as we're together," he replied. "That's what counts. Thank you, Minister, for your efforts." He glanced at Olga and her sisters. "Perhaps you and I can continue this conversation in private?"

Kerensky nodded again. The soldiers behind him opened the classroom doors, and Olga and her sisters filed out.

The mood at dinner that evening was somber. After leaving Papa to his meeting with Kerensky, Olga had stood with her sisters as Mamma spoke to her retinue—the family's ladies-in-waiting and valets, their tutors and doctors and nurses. To Olga's relief, most of them elected to stay, despite Kerensky's restrictive new policies: only a handful of household members—people who had been part of their lives since Olga was a little girl—left, unable to look at Olga or her sisters as they followed Kerensky's revolutionaries out of the palace.

"...Mother's in Kiev, praise be to God," Papa was saying. "Xenia, too. They're continuing on to Crimea. Apparently, the government is permitting them to go into exile." From the other end of the table, Mamma crossed herself, almost automatically, as she stared down at her plate. Olga, too, sent up a prayer of thanks. Grandmamma and Aunt Xenia, at least, were out of harm's way. But what of her other aunts and uncles—her namesake, Aunt Olga? Her uncles, Sandro and Mikhail?

"And what about us?" said Maria. Even in the dim light, Olga could see the fear in her eyes; Olga felt it too, though she hoped she was hiding it better, for her sisters' sake. "What will we do, now we're all back together?"

Papa shrugged. "I'm afraid it's out of our hands. We'll remain here for the time being, but I'm sure the Provisional Government will see its way to letting us join your grandmother." He sawed through his pheasant, juice pooling beneath his knife. "Kerensky assures me that asylum in England is a distinct possibility. He's been in contact with Cousin George." He bit down, chewed, and swallowed, looking pleased at the prospect of moving to England. "I wouldn't worry. The government has no interest in keeping us in Russia."

From the other end of the table, Mamma nodded, her eyes darting to the closed door of the dining room. While Kerensky had allowed them to dine *en famille*, Olga knew Mamma was thinking of the soldiers stationed outside—listening, no doubt, to their hushed conversation. "And if they don't?" she asked, her mouth hardly moving.

"I've been treated with nothing but decency through this whole sorry business. I see no reason why that shouldn't continue." Papa paused, setting down his cutlery. He looked at Olga and her siblings in turn, his gaze steady. "Now, I know this is an inconvenience to us all, but I expect all of you to conduct yourselves with the utmost decorum. It's important that we cooperate with our hosts."

Olga let out a breath. Without looking up, she spoke, using English to conceal her question from the footmen. "What did he mean when he said you and Mamma are under investigation?" she asked. From the corner of her eye, she saw Tatiana look around, her cropped hair brushing her cheekbones as she glanced at the footmen. Olga knew what she was thinking: while each of the men in the room had long been in the family's service, there was no guarantee that one of them wouldn't relay Papa's words to Kerensky's men.

"The Provisional Government feels it's necessary to investigate any possibility—however implausible—that your mother or I might have worked against Russia's interests," said Papa. "Of course, they'll find no such evidence. It's a patent falsehood. To think we would try to sabotage Russia's success in the war is ludicrous."

"Then why even say it?" said Tatiana. She looked from Papa to Mamma; beside her, Alexei pushed up the brim of his sailor's cap. "There's no way the government can believe such a thing. You *are* Russia! You've been at the front for months, commanding our soldiers—"

"It's not your father they're worried about," Mamma cut in. She set down her cutlery, rested her elbows on the table, and threaded her fingers together above her plate. "It appears this government thinks more of my German birth than it does of my lifetime of service to this country." She looked down, reaching, absently, for the double strand of pearls at her neck. "Despite everything I've done for the Russian people, I'm still under suspicion."

Papa looked uncomfortable. "Come now, Alicky," he said. "They're just going through the motions. They have to put on a show for the people. Nothing will come of it. There's no evidence; there's nothing to argue."

"They think I sold out our country to Germany," said Mamma. "Father Grigori and me. We did everything we could to keep Russia on an even keel while your father was at the front." She shook her head. "Everything we did… It seems the stain of German blood doesn't wash out so easily."

Alexei reached across the table and took Mamma's hand. "Your blood is my blood—Russian blood," he said quietly, switching the conversation back to Russian. "You're the mother of all Russia, as Papa is the father. Children rebel—I know I did." He smiled, stroking Mamma's hand with his thumb. Olga watched Alexei, admiring his poise. When had her little brother grown up? "Have faith, Mamma. Russia's children will come back to you. Have faith that they'll recognize your loyalty and return it with their own."

4

February 1913
Baryatinsky Palace, St. Petersburg

She didn't know how Tatiana had managed it, but a week after their midnight conversation, Olga and her sister were standing at the front door of their aunt's St. Petersburg town house, staring up at the lighted windows.

Olga tugged her fur closer around her neck, seeking to block the billowing snowflakes from finding their way to her skin. "And you're sure she doesn't mind?"

Tatiana grinned. "She was practically sending out invitations before I finished asking," she replied, but still Olga hesitated, watching shadows move behind the netted curtains of a second-floor window.

"And he'll be here?"

"I'm not going to answer that," Tatiana replied. She lifted the heavy brass knocker as Olga glanced back at their motorcar, idling in the cobbled street. "Really, Olga. It's a party. At least pretend to be excited."

Aunt Olga opened the door herself, letting light and the faraway lilt of a piano concerto spill into the street.

"My darlings," she said, pulling first Olga, then Tatiana, into tight embraces. "So pleased you could come." She wore a high-necked tea gown, her dark hair pinned up in an elegant pompadour with cotton-ball wisps escaping at her temples. She carried an elaborately embroidered black shawl with an endlessly trailing fringe, and she repositioned it in the crooks of her elbows as she met Tatiana's admiring gaze.

"Magnificent, isn't it?" she said, holding out her arm to let the light sparkle on the jet beading. "Made by blind nuns. But I keep tripping over the ends of the silly thing, it's far too long. I'll take my own eye out if I'm not careful."

She led Tatiana and Olga up the staircase toward the sound of voices and music.

"I've seated you at separate tables, I hope you don't mind," Aunt Olga continued as they walked down the long hallway. "I love Tsarskoe Selo as much as anyone else, but you seem so far *away*, there… I keep hoping your parents will change their minds about coming to St. Petersburg for the season, it's been too long since they've had some fun." Aunt Olga turned without stopping, giving Olga and Tatiana a sly grin. "But at least we've got the two of you! What Nicky doesn't know can't hurt him."

She led Olga and Tatiana into a small ballroom, where twenty or so young people sat at round tables clustered beneath a glittering chandelier. On the ceiling, detailed plaster moldings melted down the walls, encroaching on mint-green silk; at the end of the room, a fire crackled in an immense marble fireplace flanked by tall mirrors. Framed by casement windows that looked out upon the deepening twilight, a pianist played a Glinka composition on a grand piano. To Olga, it felt as though she'd been invited to one of St. Petersburg's supper clubs, rather than a tea party hosted by her stylish aunt.

She surveyed the room and her heart lifted: there, at the table closest to the fireplace, Pavel was deep in conversation with an officer from Papa's Guards regiment. Aunt Olga deposited Tatiana at a table with two young women and a pair of gallant-looking soldiers and then, with a knowing glance, steered Olga toward Pavel.

Both Pavel and the other officer rose to their feet as Olga and her aunt approached, clicking their heels together with tidy deference. Pavel bowed, and Olga's stomach leapt at the brief, thrilling pressure of his lips on the back of her hand. He was as handsome as she'd remembered: broad-shouldered, with a trim beard and a sharp, sloping nose.

"I believe you've met Lieutenant Voronov," said Aunt Olga, "and I'd like to introduce you to Captain Nikolai Kulikovsky, my husband's aide-de-camp."

Captain Kulikovsky was tall, with even features and a full mustache, its ends waxed into tidy points.

"I'm pleased to meet you, Captain Kulikovsky," she said, as Pavel pulled out a chair for her. The table was dominated by a tall silver samovar; within, she could smell the deep and comforting scent of coal. She looked around the room before addressing Aunt Olga once more. "Where is Uncle Petya?"

Aunt Olga shrugged. "With over two hundred rooms, it's easy to lose track of him." She reached across the table, her arm briefly, delicately, resting against Captain Kulikovsky's as she poured hot water from the samovar into a teapot. "He knows we're here; he'll join us if he wants to. But luckily for us, we've got dear Nikolai to fill his place at the table."

Olga waited for Captain Kulikovsky to move his arm away from Aunt Olga's, but he didn't—with an odd jolt, she realized Aunt Olga didn't want him to. She threw a final, flustered smile at Captain Kulikovsky as he handed her a cup of tea before glancing around, certain she would see disapproval in the eyes of Aunt Olga's guests—but they were all immersed in their own conversations, eased along by the gentle, steaming aromas rising from their own samovars.

Across the room, Tatiana was already speaking to the guests at her table, laughing and smiling as she doctored her tea with milk. She looked so at ease: though the rest of the table was dressed in the latest finery from Europe, Tatiana's plain dress accentuated her beauty, making her fit in amidst their casual elegance. How did she make it look so easy?

Beside Olga, Pavel held out a sectioned dish filled with jam, sugar cubes and slices of lemon.

"I don't know how you take it," he said. "I prefer tea with jam myself, but your tastes might differ..."

Olga smiled: this, at least, she knew. "My mother was raised by Queen Victoria," she said, plucking a sugar cube from the dish with silver tongs. She dropped it into her teacup, finishing it off with a splash of milk. "We learned to drink tea the way the English do: no jam, no sugar cubes caught between the teeth. No sipping out of saucers."

Pavel grinned. "We Russians and our backward ways," he said. "Do you make fun of us when you have your tea and crumpets?"

"Of course not," she replied. She glanced at Aunt Olga, worried she'd said the wrong thing already—but Aunt Olga was leaning closer still to Captain Kulikovsky, her dreamy smile utterly unbecoming of a married woman. "I would never presume to make fun of Russia's people."

Aunt Olga tore her gaze away from Kulikovsky. "Lieutenant Voronov was only teasing," she said, and Olga realized how clumsy she sounded, how young and provincial she felt in this room full of sophisticates. *Flirting*, she told herself. *This is what flirting looks like.* "I should warn you, my dear, not to take a single word he says seriously."

"Not one word?" said Pavel, his smile broadening. "Do you see, Grand Duchess, how your aunt slanders me?"

"Slander is as slander does," Olga replied, her heart quickening. She glanced at her aunt and Captain Kulikovsky, hoping to score a point in this strange game. "Lieutenant Voronov, your own reputation might be quite beyond repair, but I don't intend on harming my own."

She smiled, but nobody laughed; finally, Pavel let out an uncertain chuckle, and Olga knew she'd missed her mark. "Well, let's just get through tea first, shall we?" he said, not unkindly, and Olga looked away, her cheeks burning. He offered her a second tray—cakes and meringues—and lowered his voice. "Do you not spend much time in St. Petersburg, Grand Duchess?"

"Is it so obvious?" she replied as Aunt Olga turned to speak to the couple at the next table over. She was grateful for it: Pavel alone seemed easier to talk to. "My parents prefer Tsarskoe Selo. But Aunt Olga's been good to Tatiana and me. We're hoping we might be able to spend more time here, get to know some new faces before we come out formally."

"I'm glad," said Pavel. "It would be difficult for me to get to know you behind the walls of Alexander Palace."

Olga straightened in her chair, resisting the urge to look at Pavel as she sipped her tea. "And would you like to get to know me better?" she asked, striving to match her aunt's nonchalant tone.

He smiled, his brown eyes crinkling at the corners. "I would, Grand Duchess."

After the tea trays had been cleared, Aunt Olga invited her guests into an oak-lined sitting room, where a crackling Parisian record spun on a gleaming gramophone.

"She'd better not have any more food in there," said Pavel, offering Olga his arm as they walked through to the sitting room. Her heart lifted as she curled her fingers around the pristine sleeve of his naval whites. She could picture walking with him, arm in arm, down the tree-lined pathways at Alexander Park—meeting Papa, charming Mamma. He patted his flat stomach. "They'll have to roll me onto the horse for the next parade."

Olga laughed. Pavel had gotten his wish: though there weren't any more tea sandwiches set out, Aunt Olga's staff had set up a cocktail bar along the far wall. Guests milled nearby, pouring glasses of champagne or vodka before setting themselves up at sofas scattered throughout the room.

"I can't believe I'm saying it after all that tea, but I'm thirsty," Olga replied, eyeing the champagne bottles on ice. Mamma and Papa practically abstained from alcohol at Tsarskoe Selo.

"Shall I get us a glass?" said Pavel, but before Olga could respond her aunt had come to steer her away.

"Sorry, Lieutenant!" she said. "You've monopolized far too much of my niece's time. Let someone else have a chance to talk to her."

Olga looked over her shoulder with an apologetic shrug; Pavel, smiling, threw his hands up in mock defeat.

"Enough," Aunt Olga muttered, squeezing Olga's elbow. "You don't want to seem overeager."

Olga glanced back once more and saw that Pavel had already struck up a conversation with Felix Yusupov and Dmitri Pavlovich. Dmitri clapped Pavel on the back, and Olga watched, hoping that Pavel didn't share her handsome cousin's proclivity for carousing: together, Felix and Dmitri had gained a longstanding reputation as St. Petersburg's chief troublemakers.

Aunt Olga led her to an empty love seat in the corner. "So nice to take a break from official business," she said, fanning herself with one hand as they sat. "Champagne? Don't tell your father." She waved at Kulikovsky, who nodded from across the room and made his way toward the cocktail table.

"Now that I've got you to myself," said Aunt Olga, once Kulikovsky had delivered their drinks, "I've been meaning to ask, how is my dear brother?"

Olga watched Kulikovsky thread back through the room to join Tatiana and a dark-haired girl at one of the other couches. "Papa's fine, I suppose. He's busy with the tercentenary celebrations coming up. He's finalizing the guest list for the church service, I think."

Aunt Olga leaned against the sofa cushions, crossing her legs at the ankle. "Surely that's work someone else can see to?" she said. "A secretary, perhaps?"

Olga smiled. "Papa won't have one. He says it's the tsar's duty to oversee every detail."

Aunt Olga exhaled, and Olga suspected she'd had this conversation with Papa before. "Every detail in Russia is a job too large for anyone, even the tsar," she replied. They lapsed into companionable silence for a moment, then Aunt Olga leaned closer. "See that girl sitting with Tatiana? Anya Kleinmichel. Her mother's one of the empress's ladies-in-waiting. And that young man beside her," she said, nodding, "is the Duke of Leuchtenberg." Aunt Olga took Olga's hand, searching the room for more faces. "Zia de Torby—descended from Pushkin, you know. Of course, she's only visiting from Luxembourg." Olga watched her with interest. Olga had read Pushkin's work, of course, and had long been fascinated by the story of Pushkin's great-grandfather Gannibal, an African slave to whom Peter the Great had taken a shine, adopted as his godson, and elevated to a prominent position at court. More recently, Zia's parents had been banished from Russia following their scandalous elopement, but Zia looked unruffled by the whiff of infamy that had no doubt followed her on her trip to St. Petersburg.

"There are so many exciting people in the world, my dear, and I want you to meet them," Aunt Olga continued. "Find some excitement for yourself. I don't mean to be critical of your parents, but living in those summer palaces, with those summer people... You don't experience much of life, out there."

Olga was silent. Given Alexei's condition and Mamma's ill health, Olga's parents preferred to keep to themselves: a decision which, by extension, meant that Olga and her sisters spent more time alone than in the company of friends. Friendship was a risk: friends might take notice of Alexei's frequent illnesses; friends might let slip that Russia's heir was less than robust.

Her aunt wasn't wrong—but agreeing with her didn't feel right.

"Tell me, my dear. That priest. Rasputin. Does your mother still invite him to the palace?"

Olga frowned. "Father Grigori? I suppose so, why do you ask?"

Aunt Olga took a sip of her champagne. "No reason. Curiosity, I suppose. He's quite *intense*, isn't he? Those eyes." Aunt Olga shivered, almost imperceptibly. She lowered her voice. "Tell me—*entre nous*, of course—what do you think of him?"

Olga watched Dmitri Pavlovich drain a glass of champagne. She ought to have known that Aunt Olga's generosity came at a price: if Mamma were to be believed, rumors about Father Grigori served as a long-established currency amongst the St. Petersburg set. She could hear Mamma's voice echoing in her ears: *Your brother's condition is not to be discussed*, she'd said, her warning as frequent as a prayer. *Father Grigori does God's work. It is not for us to criticize his methods.*

"He's a true help to my brother," said Olga carefully. "And to Mamma, of course."

Aunt Olga smiled, the gramophone blanketing their conversation with a tinny accordion track. "Well, we'd all like to be a help to your mother. But that's not really an answer to my question, is it? Do you take confession from him, you girls? Alone?"

Olga bristled. "He's a priest. What would be wrong with that?"

Her aunt raised her eyebrows, her tone delicate as she followed Olga's gaze across the room. "It's a matter of propriety. A man of his *reputation*..." She lowered her voice, her merry eyes uncharacteristically serious. "I worry for you, my dear. They say he takes *liberties* with women in order to bring them closer to God."

Olga turned away from her aunt's inquiring gaze, annoyed, suddenly, at her presumption—at her snobbish disdain. She looked again at the crowd through Mamma's eyes: at Kulikovsky, whose gaze kept shamelessly straying toward Aunt Olga; at Dmitri and Felix, who'd started a game of dice. At Tatiana, who was clutching an almost-empty glass of champagne, the color high in her cheeks as she spoke to the Kleinmichel girl. Was this what Aunt Olga meant by excitement?

"Well, if it will put your mind at ease, Aunt, I will tell you that Father Grigori is nothing but proper in his dealings with us," Olga retorted. "But if you want to concern yourself with propriety, perhaps you'd be better to start at home." She set down her glass, her temper rising like a cork in water. "I may not spend much time in society, Aunt Olga, but I know what's said in a marriage vow. And the way you've been carrying on with that—that captain—"

Aunt Olga's expression closed quickly as a garden gate. She smiled, but it was a gentle, pitying thing that made Olga wish she'd never spoken.

"I keep forgetting how little you've learned," she said, without heat. She put her hand over Olga's, and Olga, amazed, let her. She'd been so ready for a fight that she had no response. "Look around this room and you'll see a thousand forms of love—not all of which fit within the bonds of marriage." She leaned back in her chair, and Olga followed her gaze: across the room, Captain Kulikovsky was watching Aunt Olga with a tender expression.

"Not that it's any concern of yours, but my husband and I have a very satisfactory arrangement. Most couples do, when you look past the surface," Aunt Olga continued. She met Kulikovsky's gaze with that same soft look, and Olga could see why she'd chosen to respond to Olga's insolence with pity, rather than anger. "You think you know everything—it's a trait shared by all eldest siblings, I'm afraid," she said. "But live a little, my dear. Fall in love and out of it. Build friendships and break them. Live a little and earn the right to criticize others."

She patted Olga's hand once more, reassuring. Then she stood and tapped the edge of her glass, her wedding ring chiming against the crystal.

Olga scuttled off to join Tatiana, her cheeks burning as the hum of a dozen conversations fell quiet. Her aunt's gentle rebuke wasn't lost on her: the afternoon had, in the most fundamental way, been a disaster. Had she really expected to dazzle Pavel Voronov with her simple Victorian manners, her quiet country existence? What did she have to contribute to any conversation other than the little details of court life that her aunt had pressed her for, tidbits about Mamma's holy man, about Papa's work? Her life, far off in a country palace, had ill prepared her for an afternoon amidst St. Petersburg's elegant shadow court. She'd been foolish to think that, here, anyone would care about meeting her; that Pavel, for all his flattery and kindness, could really yearn for the touch of her hand.

Tatiana shifted onto the couch to make space; beside her, Anya Kleinmichel leaned forward, her brown hair falling over her shoulder. She was pretty, in a plain sort of way, and Olga smiled back.

"Your mother is one of Mamma's ladies-in-waiting, isn't she?" Olga asked.

Anya nodded. "A lady-in-waiting to Her Imperial Majesty, yes, Grand Duchess," she said, but Tatiana swatted her hand.

"None of that here," she said. "We're Olga and Tatiana, yes?"

Olga grinned. "The whole ceremony of it. So stiff, don't you think?" she added, and Anya's face relaxed, as though she'd been waiting for Olga's approval. Olga looked at the girl, her foul mood lifting slightly. Was this all it took to make friends?

At the end of the room, Aunt Olga tapped her ring against her glass for silence once more. Standing near the fireplace, Pavel, playing with the stem of his champagne coupe, caught

Olga's eye. She smiled at him, her heart lifting further still. Even with little experience in the complicated language of romance, a smile was an easy thing to give.

"The game," said Aunt Olga, pausing for a delicious moment of suspense, "is called 'Sardines.'"

Immediately, the room broke into excited chatter, but Aunt Olga held up a hand, her black shawl falling behind her like a wing. "One of you will hide somewhere in the house—east wing only, I should say—and the rest of us must find him and hide, too. The last one to find everyone loses the game. Felix, would you like to do the honors?"

Leaning back against the pillows with his long arm stretched across the top of the sofa, Felix Yusupov lifted a cigarette from his lips with thin, elegant fingers. "There's more fun in the seeking than the hiding, surely?" He smiled, bestowing upon the room the full effect of his rakish charm. "I'd rather be the hunter than the hunted."

The room erupted into whispered conversations once again, and Olga watched Felix lean closer to Dmitri, clasping him by the back of the neck as he whispered something, close enough for his lips to graze Dmitri's cheek. Her heart pounding, she turned her attention to Pavel, daring to hold his gaze.

Tatiana nudged her side. "Is this entirely proper?" she whispered. "Running through the house, hiding… What would Mamma—"

Olga smiled, borrowing an ounce of Felix Yusupov's confidence. "Mamma isn't here," she breathed, feeling suddenly, wildly, invincible.

Aunt Olga held up her hand again. "In that case, Alexander, would you care to…?"

The young man who Aunt Olga had pointed out earlier—the Duke of Leuchtenberg—stood up, straightening his tailcoat. "Give me a fighting chance, Grand Duchess, before setting the hounds on me," he said as he took off down the hallway.

Anya Kleinmichel stood as the guests began to break into search parties. "Where do you think will he go?" she said, her cheeks flushed with excitement. "I don't know the palace very well."

"The library, I should think," said Olga. "The false wall, remember, Tatiana? With the staircase?"

Tatiana grinned, and Dmitri clapped her on the shoulder in passing as he and Felix set off down the hallway at a run. "Olga and I used to know this palace like the backs of our hands," she said, taking Anya's arm.

Tatiana and Anya set off for the door, but Olga remained on the sofa, playing with the loose strap of her shoe. By the time she looked up, Tatiana and Anya were far down the hall, their figures shrinking as they reached the staircase.

Behind her, someone cleared their throat.

"I have a feeling you'll be good at this game. Might we join forces?" said Pavel. He stepped closer, brushing his thumb along the delicate skin at the base of Olga's wrist and sending up a wave of gooseflesh along her arm.

Olga hesitated, the better to let Tatiana move even farther ahead. "The bedroom wing," she said. "There are more wardrobes up there than I can count."

Pavel smiled. "The bedroom wing it is, then," he said. "I'll follow you."

They had lingered long enough in the sitting room that Olga and Pavel were the last two down the hallway, and Olga maintained her hold on Pavel's hand without looking down, as though to acknowledge the connection would be to break it. They started up the staircase; from below, they could hear the sound of laughter.

"Should we be up here?" said Olga, breathing lightly as they reached the upper landing. The long hall was deserted; the doorways in dark alcoves were closed, light pooling from the chandeliers onto the heavy carpets.

"She said the east wing, didn't she?" Pavel stepped ahead, tugging Olga's hand playfully. Olga's pulse quickened, spurred in equal measure by excitement and terror. She'd never been spoken to so informally; she'd never been alone, completely alone, with someone. She knew she ought to turn around—that Mamma would be horrified if she ever learned Olga had gone off with a man unchaperoned—but Olga tightened her fingers around Pavel's, savoring their solitude.

They paused in front of a closed door, and Pavel grinned.

"Shall we?" he said and twisted the knob.

The room was nearly pitch-black: in the dark, Olga could see the outline of a vanity and the bulk of a wardrobe, light from the hallway tracing a line down to the end of a four-poster bed. There was something thrilling about the prospect of an unlit room; something magical in the half moonlight that made Olga want to close the door behind them.

Pavel turned on the light and opened the wardrobe: inside, three dresses, long since out of fashion, turned on hangers. He pushed them aside as though to verify the wardrobe's contents, then got on his knees and lifted the bed skirt. Olga walked to the window and shook the heavy curtains, sending a cloud of dust swirling into the air.

"Well, we know the maid isn't hiding in here, at least," said Pavel, coughing. Olga waved her hand to dissipate the cloud and Pavel stood too, a half smile on his face as they watched the dust dance in the light.

"My parents used to make me clean my own room," said Olga. "They only allowed us a maid once we'd learned to empty the fireplace ashes for ourselves."

"Really?" said Pavel. He straightened his jacket, brushing a mote of dust from his arm. "I somehow didn't think you the type for manual labor."

"They wanted me to learn the value of hard work."

Pavel stepped closer and Olga was struck by how much taller

than her he was; his hand enveloped her own, the span of his shoulders twice as broad as her corseted waist. Her stomach turned: now that she was alone with him, she couldn't believe the extent of her scandalous actions. She glanced back at the open door, unsure whether to pull Pavel back into the hall, but Aunt Olga's rebuke echoed in her mind. Were she to leave now, she'd be doing the proper thing—but her life would remain half-lived.

"And did you?" he whispered. "Learn?"

Olga leaned in closer, letting Pavel run his hand up her arm—but then they heard voices.

"Quick!" Pavel beckoned her toward the wardrobe and Olga climbed in, all her fears flooding back. What would be said about her if she were discovered here, in the company of a man she barely knew?

The voices grew louder and Pavel, too, stepped into the wardrobe, pulling the door shut. The interior was cedar-scented and cramped; Pavel needed to bow his head to fit. Unconsciously, it seemed, he put an arm around her waist and pulled her close, one hand gripping the small handle inside the wardrobe door.

Olga pressed her cheek against his chest, breathing in his heavy cologne, resisting the urge, suddenly, to laugh.

"Aren't we supposed to be seeking, not hiding?" she whispered, and she could feel Pavel's chest rumble with laughter. He ran his hand up her back and into the crush of her hair, letting his smiling lips rest on the top of her head.

From the other side of the wardrobe, they heard the voices once more.

"This one's open!" Olga opened her eyes at the sound of Dmitri Pavlovich's voice; on the floor of the wardrobe she could see a sliver of light, quickly eclipsed before the door to the wardrobe rattled, alarmingly. Olga pressed closer to Pavel in terror; she looked up to see him squeezing his eyes shut as he gripped the tiny doorknob.

She watched the sliver of light on the wardrobe floor: Dmitri's pacing shadow, his huff of disappointment.

"Locked," he said. "Anyone under the bed?"

"No," Felix Yusupov replied. "Nor in it, sadly." Olga could picture Felix's downturned mouth, handsome even in defeat. "It would be a better way to while away an afternoon than these silly parlor games."

Dmitri sounded devilish. "Depends on the group," he said, his voice drifting farther away. Through the crack in the door, she watched Dmitri slow on the lintel before he and Felix drifted back into the hallway. "If we were to lose the chaperones for a little while, perhaps, we could have some fun…"

Olga let out a breath: she and Pavel were safe. Belatedly, she realized she'd been gripping him by the waist; she looked up, unwilling to move away. In the darkness she could see the outline of his face; his mouth, dark and soft; his eyes inscrutable. His expression, in the gloom, unreadable as she lifted her lips to meet his.

5

April 1917
Alexander Palace, Tsarskoe Selo

Olga pushed Mamma down the hall, wheels skimming against marble as they approached the guard-flanked door of Papa's study. Slowing, she glanced through the open door of a vacant room opposite: within, a soldier was nodding off on a chaise lounge, his booted feet resting on a tasseled pillow, a lit cigarette clamped loosely between his lips.

"You'd better put that out," Olga called. The soldier started, nearly swallowing the cigarette, and Olga smiled with grim satisfaction. "Wouldn't want to start a fire, now, would you?"

Emerging from the study, Papa chuckled softly. "Steady now, darling," he said. Much as she wanted to run into his arms, Olga knew the soldiers would prevent it: what if he slipped her some illicit message for Mamma? They'd been separated from Papa for three weeks now—a measure intended to keep Mamma and Papa from colluding as Kerensky and his team parsed through their correspondences, looking for evidence of pro-German treason.

Papa looked tired but serene enough. "Hello, darling," he said, and Olga watched Mamma's shoulders slacken with relief at the sight of him. For a couple as close as her parents, Olga knew it was torture for them both to live in separate wings of the palace, so close and yet so far away, meeting only at mealtimes in the presence of Kerenksy's armed guards.

"Nicky," she whispered, her voice so low that even Olga had to lean forward to hear. "I don't want to do this, Nicky."

Papa crouched, taking Mamma's hands in his; she gripped them, her fingers white. "We both know that you must," he replied. "He's a reasonable man, my dearest; there's no need for concern. Be strong. Tell him what he needs to know, and the rest will follow. I'll be waiting out here when you're done."

"Right, Colonel," said one of the soldiers, stepping forward. "That's enough. Let the commission get on with their work."

Papa straightened, and it irked Olga to see how passive he was in the face of the soldiers' perpetual aggravations. Mamma looked up at him, her blue eyes welling with tears.

"Be strong, Alicky," he repeated as Olga wheeled her through the door.

Olga had always found Papa's study a comforting place. With its overstuffed bookcases and walnut walls, the room had a gleaming, golden air suffused with the scent of old books and furniture polish. Even in the harshest days of winter, when the wind howled down the palace's white corridors, the study remained cozy, its heavy curtains blocking out the billowing snow. On more than one occasion Olga had fallen asleep on the divan while keeping Papa company as he worked, the crackling fire and scratch of pen on paper lulling her into gentle, beeswax-scented dreams.

Today, Olga entered hesitantly, half expecting to see the justice minister lounging, like his soldier, with his boots atop Papa's desk, but he was standing by the bookcase, staring down at a folio of cream-colored notes. In years past, only Papa had a key to the study, satisfied that the room and its contents were under his sole purview: no servants misplacing his papers while they cleaned; no errant ministers casting a well-timed eye over classified documents. Upon his return to Alexander Palace, Papa had forfeited the key to Kerensky, who had taken to using the room as his base of operations. Day after day, his soldiers carted in boxes of Mamma's correspondences—notebooks, letters that she and Anna Vyrubova hadn't succeeded in burning—and Papa's diaries; their Bibles and books inspected page by page for concealed messages. Lamp bases, unscrewed in the expectation of finding German cyphers hidden beneath the brass; portraits, removed from walls in their hunt for secret telegraph machines.

Kerensky closed the folio, looking up. "Good afternoon, madam," he said. He circled to Papa's desk: devoid of its usual clutter of photographs and icons, it now held a typewriter, a pad of paper and a single stack of letters written in Mamma's languid hand.

Kerensky followed Olga's gaze to the topmost of the letters, frowning. "Thank you, Grand Duchess. That will be all."

Mamma's voice was faint but steady. "What I have to say can be said in front of my daughter."

Kerensky exhaled heavily but he didn't respond, and Olga could feel her mother donning the chilly, imperious persona she wore in public—the one which armored her all-too-fragile soul, which allowed her to fulfill her duties as empress while her son lay, dying, in bed. It allowed her to withstand the snickers of Russia's elite without breaking down; it gave her the strength to stand up to the ministers who dismissed her as a lesser-born German princess. With a tilt of her chin and a straightening of her shoulders, Mamma's shyness turned into austerity, her reticence into steeled resolve: she transformed from Alix, wife and mother, into Empress Alexandra Feodorovna, beautiful and bejeweled. In too many ways, it was a persona better suited to the high colors and passions of an oil painting rather than to flesh and blood; but it was also the persona which, Mamma believed, bestowed upon her the all-important advantage of infallibility.

Finally, Kerensky conceded. "It's no concern of mine whether she's here or not, so long as she remains quiet." He looked up at Olga, a hint of amusement playing on the edge of his down-turned lip. "If you're capable of silence, Grand Duchess."

Olga reddened—still, she'd accomplish more by being within the room rather than without. Vowing to pass on everything she heard to Tatiana, Olga sank onto the divan. "Of course, Minister."

He nodded, rummaging in the pocket of his collarless jacket before holding out his cigarette case. Neither Mamma nor Olga took one, and he crooked them in once more, setting the open case on the desk as he reached for his lighter.

"Thank you, Empress, for taking the time to meet with me today," he began, and Mamma huffed. He looked up in surprise.

"Not that I had much choice in the matter, Minister. But by all means," she smiled witheringly as she settled against the wicker back of her wheelchair, "how kind of you to have me."

Kerensky raised an eyebrow, and Olga couldn't tell whether he was irritated or impressed by Mamma's sharp retort. Like Mamma, Kerensky seemed to have retreated behind a façade; but whereas hers was crafted of hauteur, his was politesse. "I understand how difficult this all must be for you."

"Do you?" said Mamma. "Accused of betraying my own people? My own countrymen?" She shook her head, arranging the hem of her sleeve with brisk indignation. "Paying for hospitals out of my own pocket; nursing our soldiers with my own hands…and I'm the traitor! Truly, Minister. It beggars belief."

Kerensky drummed his lighter on the folio. "With all due respect, Empress, your recent conduct has thrown that admirable sentiment into question. Given that your early years were spent amongst the very Germans we have been fighting since 1914—given that your brother, Empress, is marshalling German troops as we speak—it is not outside the realm of possibility for your allegiances to lie in two places at once."

"It has been incredibly painful to watch Germany and Russia

at war, but I know where my allegiance lies," Mamma retorted. "It lies with my husband and my son. With Russia. My loyalty to Germany ended the day I married the emperor."

"If that is the case, then you have nothing to fear from our conversation." Kerensky leaned forward, his forearms resting on Papa's desk. "I do hope you can appreciate my position, Empress. Your conduct as regent was unorthodox at best, and treasonous at worst. Appointing and dismissing ministers at will, disclosing confidential military information to unauthorized individuals, relying on the advice of a dissolute priest... These actions, Empress, have without question harmed the country you say you love."

Mamma colored as Kerensky lit his cigarette. Smoke plumed in the room, and the scent was sharper, more acrid, than Papa's eagle-headed Benson & Hedges. "This is an important conversation," he continued. "We must establish the logic of your actions. If it is all as innocent as you claim, this testimony will be of benefit to you and your husband. But make no mistake: there are those within the Provisional Government who would see you hanged for the chaos you created. I have no wish for our government to follow the French example, so I will do what is in my power to establish due procedure." He balanced the cigarette on the edge of a Fabergé ashtray, the blue enamel gleaming in the afternoon light. "So, let's not waste any more time. When your husband, Nicholas Alexandrovich, formerly tsar of Russia, appointed himself commander in chief of Russia's army in August of 1915, he named you regent in his stead. In this capacity, you—"

"No," said Mamma quietly.

Kerensky looked up, his fountain pen poised over a fresh sheet of paper. "I beg your pardon?"

"That's incorrect." Mamma shifted in her chair. "There was no formal designation, no true regency. I was tasked with overseeing the appointments of government ministers and with ensuring that the domestic affairs of our country were handled in the tsar's absence. I was to speak with my husband's authority and maintain order amongst our ministers in the state Duma."

"And this didn't strike you as odd? A wife, standing in for her husband? An empress, taking on the God-given duties of a tsar?"

"Of course not," Mamma replied, and Olga was surprised by her sanguinity. Weeks earlier, such a challenge would have provoked fury in her, but perhaps Mamma was better at diplomacy than Olga had suspected. "The tsar and I are one flesh; we share the burden of leading our country, just as we share the task of raising our children. We have no secrets from each other. Is it not right that I, knowing my husband's mind best, would be tasked with carrying out his wishes while he defended our borders?"

"But you didn't just carry out his wishes, did you? You made decisions in your own right. You appointed and dismissed ministers based on little more than impulse." Kerensky looked up, his expression impassive. "Forgive me for being blunt, but you have no practical experience in governance. Why should the tsar have trusted you over his own ministers?"

Mamma stiffened, her voice icing over. "I was guided in my decision-making by a man of God, Minister."

"Father Grigori Yefimovich Rasputin—a man with even less experience in governance than you. A peasant with nothing to recommend him to the highest post in the land beyond your assurances of his competency. You might be able to appreciate, Empress, why such an advisor raised questions amongst the Duma."

Mamma's gaze didn't waver as she pulled out a cross from the folds of her skirt—one Father Grigori had given her, carved from the branches of a larch tree in his home village. *An instrument of God doesn't need gilt and finery,* he'd said when he handed it to Mamma, his low voice rumbling through the Mauve Room: *God's spirit lives in the humble, as well as the grand.*

"You know, Father Grigori didn't care what people thought of him," Mamma said, the corners of her mouth downturned as she ran her thumb along the soft wood. "A prophet is never acknowledged in his own time—look at what the Pharisees did to Christ. The tsar is God's emissary on Earth; it stands to reason that He would send a man of God to provide His guidance in times of strife."

Kerensky scratched his pen across the page. "Men of God still have earthly preoccupations, Empress. What's to say Grigori Rasputin wasn't using your faith as a means of wielding influence over the tsar?"

"How would that benefit Father Grigori? He never asked for payment. He spoke for the people of Russia—the peasants, the villagers." Mamma looked past Kerensky's shoulder, her expression soft: she'd spent hours in here, days, with Papa, with Father Grigori; she'd sat in Kerensky's seat, balanced her own cigarettes on the dainty ashtray as she worked out matters of policy. "My husband was an autocrat, once. Before the October Manifesto, the tsar simply needed to wave his hand and his will would be done. Now, we must take ministers into account...all of them squabbling, all looking for ways to curry advantage, to push their own agendas." Her expression hardened, and Olga pictured a flock of rooks descending on the desk, cawing, flapping their wings in a bid to be heard. "Such a system was difficult enough in times of peace, but with the war... I gave the tsar the courage he needed to make decisions worthy of his station. Worthy of the limitless power that had been bestowed upon him by God."

"All decisions that strengthened Father Grigori's standing in court. All decisions that enfeebled any voices in the government that contradicted your own." Kerensky tilted his head to one side, his cordiality poorly concealing the steel edge of his questions. "You tell me Rasputin was a forgiving man, but dismissing his enemies strikes me as retribution, rather than compassion."

Mamma's smile sharpened; she leaned forward, the wheels of her chair creaking as they shifted with her weight. "Father Grigori was a forgiving man, Minister, but I do not share his tolerance. To find myself second-guessed at all turns; to be publicly undermined by ministers more interested in feathering their nests than doing what was right. Powerful men make powerful enemies; powerful women even more so. Why distract Nicholas when what was needed was a strong hand?" She sat back, a hard glow of conviction suffusing her cheeks, and Olga could see, in her eyes, the fears that had unmoored her in the final days of Papa's reign. Mamma had seen enemies on all sides, then. Had they been real, or had she willed them into existence through her own actions?

"My husband is a sensitive soul. I'm afraid he can be quite suggestible. With the added responsibility of the war, he was vulnerable to those who sought to wrest away his influence. But I knew what was more important: passing my husband's crown, intact, along to my son. With Father Grigori's guidance, I did what I could to strengthen my husband's hold on Russia."

Kerensky's hand flew across his note pad; Olga leaned forward but the minister's scrawl was illegible from where she sat. Was he a man of God, this bloodless revolutionary? In his own way, Olga was sure that he cared for the common people—but he had been appointed from within the ranks of a political party, composed of men who grappled for the power that Papa's abdication had left unchecked. These ministers felt they could throw chains upon that power and wrestle it to earth; that, with enough grasping hands, no one figure would rise to the exalted position Papa had once held. The Provisional Government claimed that it would better circumstances for all Russians—that, like the Duma before them, they could write out their lofty ideals in a manifesto, a blank page made black with promises. But promises could be broken. How could Kerensky be sure that his colleagues, with their dark suits and calculated smiles, would adhere to the ideals that had brought them together, rather than wield power for their own purposes?

But then, perhaps Kerensky's growing influence over Russia was God-given, too.

"Let me ask you, Empress: What defined Grigori Rasputin as a man of God?" Kerensky drummed the barrel of his fountain pen, sending flecks of black ink across his notes. "His faith? His charity? Doubtless you know that Grigori Rasputin was a talented dissembler, a saint within the palace walls, but a satyr without. A *khlyst*, some say. You've seen the police reports, I trust. Women in and out of his apartments at all hours; drunken fights with cuckolded husbands. Hypnotism, hypocrisy."

Olga listened, uneasy. She knew the price Father Grigori had asked in return for his service; she knew that Mamma would have paid it, a thousand times over, for what she received in return.

"Without sin, there can be no redemption; without redemption, there can be no salvation. Believe me, Minister, Father Grigori was aware of his own shortcomings. The devil tempts each of us in his own way. Who among us can claim that they've never succumbed?" She smiled, though it was a cold, merciless thing. "Minister, I expected more from you than cheap rumors. Father Grigori was a good man."

"What good man takes advantage of young women?" Kerensky snapped. "What good man engages in midnight orgies?"

"*Lies*, Minister!" Mamma's cheeks glowed with outrage, and she clutched her shawl close around her shoulders. "I'll remind you that my daughter is present, I'd thank you not to use such language—"

Kerensky ran a hand through his oiled hair, and Olga could feel his patience thinning. "What hold did Grigori Rasputin have over you? Why was he a frequent visitor to the palace?

Please, Empress—anything you can tell me; anything at all. I implore you. Can't you see what you've lost because of him?"

"It was my understanding, Minister, that I'm the one under investigation, not Father Grigori." She paused. "Are you a man of faith, Minister?"

"Not particularly," he replied. "I believe in action, Empress: action and outcome. I believe in building a better world for the Russian people; in winning this war so that we can turn our attention to providing at home what so many people already have in Europe. Religious freedom. Workers' rights. Full larders and hope for a better future. I believe in working for change, rather than praying for it."

Mamma leaned back in her seat once more. "Then we are in agreement on one thing, Minister Kerensky. In our own ways, we've worked toward what we believe to be a better future." She smiled, and it felt more genuine, now, than before. "What you need to know is this: with my husband's blessing, I appointed ministers who I believed would be of service to the tsar. I acted in accordance with my faith. I put my faith in God, in my husband, in Russia—and in Father Grigori."

Kerensky was silent a long moment. Then he tapped his cigarette end in the ashtray. "For what it's worth, Empress, I believe you," he said. "But our country needed more than your faith in Father Grigori. Russia needed competent ministers, munitions, food, stable supply lines—things that you, in dismissing competent ministers, denied it. It needs those things now, if we are to prevail against our foes."

For a split second Mamma's armor broke as she flinched. Kerensky's words, it seemed, had finally hit home—but then she steeled once more.

Olga knew what she would say next. Mamma had always been one for religious recitation, reciting psalms to underpin her conviction in her faith—in love and duty. But in recent months, a more militant psalm had replaced the rest, eclipsing her once-frequent entreaties toward tolerance.

"More numerous than the hairs on my head are those who hate me without reason," Mamma intoned. "*Many are those who would destroy me, my treacherous enemies.* Minister, faith is the bedrock on which actions are taken. If you don't have faith, then I'm not the one who's lost."

6

February 1913
Winter Palace, St. Petersburg

With its jade-green columns and gilt ceiling, its parquet floor as ornate as a piece of poetry, the Malachite Room was one of Olga's favorite places within the Winter Palace.

It was here where Mamma had prepared for her wedding to Papa: where Grandmamma had lifted the family's diamond nuptial crown onto her head; where she'd been dressed in jewelry and robes so heavy she'd needed help walking into the cathedral. It was here where all Romanov brides dressed for their weddings; here, where Alexei's future bride would one day don that same imperial mantle to become a Romanov herself.

Olga bristled. What of her own wedding: where would she dress, who would lift a crown onto her head? She'd be in a stateroom at some foreign court, wearing someone else's imperial jewels. She looked around the Malachite Room, picturing herself on a dais in the middle of the sunburst floor, the train of her wedding dress pooling around her feet like an ocean current. The Winter Palace was the most splendid royal residence in the world; no foreign prince's court could possibly compare.

Not that her family used it much as a residence: Olga had only slept here a handful of times, during grand state occasions when

Mamma and Papa were too tired to journey the fifteen miles back to Tsarskoe Selo at the end of the night. As a result, the Winter Palace, with its museum stillness and outrageous opulence, felt frozen in time, a place where duty and ceremony—Russia's history, its mythic figures—took precedence over comfort and warmth.

Today, the Malachite Room was filled with people: Papa's aides-de-camp, clustered at the far end of the room; Grandmamma and Aunt Olga, sitting with Maria and Anastasia by the fireplace with cups of tea in hand. Whispers echoed from the gilded ceiling as Olga walked in, all discussing the day's tercentenary celebrations. Three hundred years of the Romanov dynasty; three hundred years of Olga's family holding the reins of Russian power. An unbroken line, stretching through history.

Attempting to make her tardy entrance inconspicuous, Olga sidled up to Tatiana. Like her, Tatiana was wearing a square-necked white dress with a red sash, her hair tucked under the brim of a sun hat laden with silk flowers.

"Where's Papa?" she asked.

"In the gardens," Tatiana replied. "He wanted one last chance to stretch his legs before the day gets away from him."

"And Mamma?"

Tatiana gestured through the open double doors. "Sitting room," she said. "She wanted a moment alone. Nerves, I think; it's going to be a long day."

Olga nodded at Tatiana before walking down the hall. In the empty sitting room, Mamma was standing alone at the window, hands clasped as she looked down on the garden below. Though it had rained throughout the early morning the sun had finally broken through the dark clouds, bathing Mamma's weary face in sunlight. She'd changed the simple necklace she usually wore for a heavy diamond-and-pearl choker; Olga could tell it was straining Mamma's neck already, the lines on her forehead creased in pain.

"Good morning, darling," she said. She caressed Olga's cheek in a rare moment of maternal pride. "How beautiful you look."

"Thank you, Mamma," she replied. "How are you feeling?"

"I've never liked St. Petersburg." She glanced down, straightening her ivory gloves at the elbow, her face hidden by the salt-spray of feathers that topped her hat. "A *bog*, your father calls it… why Peter chose to build his city here, I'll never understand." She looked up, turning her gaze to the window. "But Papa insisted—the Duma insisted—on this whole pageant. Shaking hands, making small talk… I'll rest easier when this tercentenary business is over and done with."

Olga knew what Mamma was thinking about, but like Mamma she was loath to say it aloud: the last time Papa had shown himself on the balcony of the Winter Palace had been in 1905, after the bloody events of the revolution that had transformed Papa from an absolute monarch into a constitutional one. He'd signed the October Manifesto that day, ratifying the creation of the State Duma which limited his ability to rule as he saw fit. Even now, Papa sighed at any mention of the Duma.

"It's going to be fine, Mamma," said Olga. She stepped closer, resting her chin on Mamma's shoulder. "It's an opportunity for us to see the people. To remind them of the bond between them and the tsar."

"You sound like your father." Mamma stepped closer to the window, tenting her fingers on the glass; below, Papa's small form paced through the garden. "He's very trusting, your father. Such faith in the people."

Olga watched as Papa paused midstep and looked back at the palace as though someone had called to him from within. He was dressed in a simple blue tunic with red epaulettes and thin, gold lapels that slashed down his front to fasten at his hip. It was the uniform of the Fourth Imperial Rifles—the oldest regiment in the Russian Army. How very like Papa to choose today to honor the men who'd served his family the longest.

"Don't you have faith in the people?" she asked.

Mamma turned away from the window. "I put my faith in God," she replied. "But listen to me, carrying on. You're right, my dear, of course. Today is a good day. You'll take care of your sisters for me?"

"Of course," said Olga.

"Then there we are: something else I have faith in," said Mamma as they started back to join the others. "You."

At noon, Olga and her family went down to the inner courtyard of the palace. There, a retinue of Cossacks on horseback waited in tidy rows, followed by three carriages: a calèche for Papa and Alexei, a carriage for Mamma and Grandmamma, and an open, low-slung landau for Olga and her sisters. From beyond the palace gates, Olga could hear the sound of cannons and church bells, the cheers of the waiting crowd, and she skipped toward the landau, her heart lifting with anticipation.

Papa was already in his calèche, shielding his eyes from the sun as he watched one of his retainers carry Alexei to join him. Olga sent up a prayer of thanks that her brother was well enough to join the festivities. He'd suffered a bleeding attack only a week earlier after twisting his knee in the garden. Olga watched as Papa assisted Alexei into the calèche, the gold on his uniform glinting as he pulled Alexei into a one-armed hug, but Alexei shrugged off Papa's attention, wincing as he shifted to the opposite side of the gleaming carriage. Though he'd regained enough strength to join the procession, Alexei's knee was still too swollen for him to walk: he would have to be carried into the cathedral, and Olga could see the strain in Alexei's jaw, his bitter resignation to being seen as an invalid. *Still*, Olga watched Alexei twist in his seat to watch the Cossacks, thinking of Father Grigori's fervent prayers over Alexei only days earlier. *At least he's able to witness the tercentenary at all.*

The landau was bedecked with hothouse flowers, four white

horses pawing the ground as they waited for the signal to move forward. A Cossack offered his hand as Olga stepped up into the chassis. From the higher vantage point, she could see beyond Papa's calèche to the Winter Palace's golden gates. She could see, too, the small cluster of people gathered beyond the parade route. They were holding up placards bearing Papa's face, splashed with red paint. She raised onto her toes, using the soldier's hand for support as she tried to make out what the placards said.

"You look beautiful today, Grand Duchess," the soldier murmured.

She nearly lost her balance as she looked down, surprised—elated—to see Pavel Voronov smiling from beneath the brim of his cap.

"Pavel! How did you manage—?"

Pavel grinned. "I had to call in about a hundred favors." He held her hand a second too long, stroking the back of her palm with his thumb, and for a split second, the commotion around them melted away. Still standing in the landau's footwell, she was half a head taller than Pavel: were she to shift, ever so slightly, he would be able to wrap his arms around her and lift her out of the carriage.

"Hello," she whispered, sitting as close to the edge of the landau as possible. Beside her, Tatiana leaned forward to ask Maria a question, tactfully drawing their two younger sisters into conversation.

Pavel closed the landau's half door and ran his hand up to rest on the sash as though checking to confirm it was properly shut. "I can't stay long, I just..." He trailed off. "I had to see you."

Olga leaned forward, resting her hand on the landau's frame as well. Softly, quickly, he let his hand stray across the polished wood, coming to rest atop hers. Dressed in the uniform of his regiment, he looked the same as a hundred other soldiers in the square—yet how could she have mistaken him for anyone other than himself?

Anastasia crawled onto the seat and looked over the coachman's shoulder.

"Did you see all the people?" she said excitedly, plunging her hands into the flowers that trailed along the landau's edge.

"*Shvybzik*, sit down," said Olga. She looked up: behind Pavel's shoulder, she could see Nikolai Sablin, Papa's trusted aide-de-camp, watching carefully. She jerked back in her seat and grabbed Anastasia by the arm, pulling her into her seat with a thump. "Dignity, yes? Mamma expects us to behave."

"I have to go," said Pavel, glancing up the line. "Will I see you tonight? At your aunt's house?"

"I don't know," said Olga. There was movement at the front of the cortege, a rustling as everyone—horses, soldiers, nobles—readied themselves. From beyond the gates they heard the trill of a military band. "There's a lot going on this afternoon and—"

"Will I see you there?" Pavel repeated. Behind him, Sablin stormed toward the landau, his face like thunder. Sablin was a stickler for decorum. He would write up Pavel for insubordination if Pavel wasn't careful.

"You're going to get in trouble!" said Olga. "Go!"

Pavel grinned. "Not until you tell me you'll be there," he replied as Sablin shouldered past the honor guard.

"Yes!" she whispered, thrilled and terrified in equal measure that he would make such a spectacle of himself. "Yes, I'll be there! Go!"

Pavel clapped his hands together, giving Olga one final, insouciant wink before tearing off. Olga looked down, suppressing the sudden urge to laugh.

A shout went up from the front of the cortege and, like a ripple in water, the Cossacks began to move. The landau lurched forward, and Olga straightened in her seat as the procession slowly made its way out the palace gates.

Beyond a double line of soldiers, crowds had gathered ten people deep, the square behind them empty as they massed near the cortege route. The people had cheered as Mamma and Papa's carriages passed, but it seemed they'd saved their loudest applause for Olga and her sisters: as their landau made its way down the road, they lifted their arms in welcome—hundreds of them, standing shoulder to shoulder, sitting on the tops of motorcars and on shop steps, waving yellow and black streamers.

Olga lifted her arm in the air, and the cheering reached a new pitch. She watched, amazed, as women pushed into the soldiers' arms, holding their children aloft, weeping with happiness at the sight of the grand duchesses. Beside her, Anastasia and Maria, beaming, began to wave, bouncing up and down in their seats like twin puppies.

Tatiana laughed. "Can you believe this?" she said. "They love us, Olga!"

Olga, too, laughed. She'd never seen such adoration; she'd never experienced such an outpouring of happiness. They belonged to the people, Olga and her sisters, and she'd never felt such a sense of joy; such a sense of love. For the first time, Olga understood—truly understood—Papa's insistence on the bond between the tsar and his people: they'd lined the streets to see Olga and her family, to share in the celebration of their life, of their lineage.

As they passed the adoring faces, Olga lifted her arms higher, no longer caring about decorum as she waved to the people: one with her sisters; one with them all. Unbidden, she could feel tears, falling like a benediction, down her cheeks, and she didn't bother wiping them away: the people who saw would understand. They were her family, each and every Russian soul.

7

May 1917
Alexander Palace, Tsarskoe Selo

Olga opened her eyes and stared at the ceiling, the clock on the mantel betraying, with its mournful ticking, the fact that she'd slept long past breakfast. She detangled her feet from the covers, unsurprised to find that Tatiana had gotten up and dressed without waking her. A year ago, the thought of sleeping in would have been anathema to Olga—impossible, too, she thought, recalling the maid who used to bustle in at first light to start the fire as Tatiana and Olga changed, yawning, into their nursing uniforms. Back then, it had felt like there were never enough hours in the day to do everything Olga had pledged to do: assist wounded soldiers and wrap bandages; oversee the distribution of food and provisions to war orphans; buoy up the spirits of the men headed for the front. A year ago, Olga would have chastised herself for falling victim to the sin of idleness but now, there was no reason to wake early. Olga's work ethic meant nothing anymore: not to a palace frozen in time.

She dressed in a long skirt and white blouse, pinning her hair up in a low chignon before fastening a gold chain around her neck. She hesitated at the door, goose pimples rising beneath her silk sleeves, then turned back to the wardrobe to pull on a long woolen cardigan—a gift from Aunt Olga years before, brought back after a trip to Paris. She turned one way and then the other, inspecting her reflection in the mirror as her mind ran over the inevitable argument the cardigan would prompt in the dining room. Though it had the name of one of Paris's most prominent designers proudly sewn into the label, Mamma hated the sweater, calling it too modern, too boyish, for a grand duchess. Olga bit her lip at the thought of rehashing an old argument, one which had never resulted in a satisfactory ending, then marched out of the room, her breath billowing in a cloud above her head. With the palace's heating shut off, cardigans and shawls were a necessity even as the season turned to spring—besides, it covered the yellowed stains that, without the solicitations of daily laundering, had appeared beneath the arms of her blouse.

She walked down the staircase, glancing out the window at the monotonous gray. Even the weather, it seemed, conspired to make her feel as though her family was living inside a stopped clock: though it was early May, clouds lingered over the palace, making it seem as if days, not months, had passed since Papa's abdication.

Like the rest of the adults locked within the palace—Mamma and Papa and Dr. Botkin, Mamma's ladies-in-waiting and Papa's remaining retainers—Olga and Tatiana had taken on tutoring duties, their parents determined not to let educational standards slide for Maria, Anastasia and Alexei. Olga and Tatiana had divided languages between them and Olga enjoyed the task: her talents as an English teacher certainly exceeded her meager skills as a nurse. She thought about what would happen when they left the palace—how time would speed up, whirring like a top, once she and her family were cast out into an uncertain future. Perhaps she might attend university, she thought ruefully, or train as a tutor for some British aristocrat's bratty children, in this brave new world where she'd need a workaday job to survive.

She turned down the corridor that held Papa's study. Papa all but lived in it these days: after Kerensky's investigation had concluded he'd given the key back to Papa with little ceremony. She thought with satisfaction of the moment when Kerensky had announced that his investigative panel had been unable to find even a scrap of evidence pointing to her parents' supposed attempt to undermine Russia's war effort. Subsequently, he'd loosened his restrictions on the family: Papa and Mamma were able to spend time together once more, but Papa still spent his days closeted away, emerging from his study after dinner to read a chapter or two from some English penny novel aloud to Olga and her sisters.

Though some of her family's retainers had left the palace on the day Papa arrived, a handful had remained, their loyalty taking on new significance in the echoing absence of their peers. Olga couldn't remember a time when Jim Hercules hadn't been holding the doors for Papa and Mamma, and his familiar presence amidst so many unfamiliar faces at the palace calmed her: with Jim at the door, some small vestige of her old life still remained.

As one of the *Arapy*, Jim was part of the small contingent of Black men who'd held positions at court since before the time of Catherine the Great, their resplendent outfits and dark complexions meant to convey the strength and reach of the Russian Empire. It was an antiquated custom, but Papa had always held to the traditional ways; now, more than ever, those traditions felt as though they'd long since slipped into history, made obsolete by modern customs and modern weapons, modern ways of looking at the world. In his own way, Jim himself was a sign of change: the men who'd held such positions in the past had come from Ethiopia—many of them not by their own choice, Olga knew. Jim, however, had applied for the post after leaving his home in Tennessee, preferring the sophistication of the Russian court—and the position's generous salary—to America's Jim Crow South. Did he still collect his wages, now that Kerensky had taken over management of the palace's accounts?

"Papa's at his books, I see," said Olga by way of greeting.

"For some time now, Grand Duchess," he replied, inclining his head. "It calms him, I think."

Olga glanced down the hall, listening for the unnerving clatter of boots that heralded Kerensky's soldiers. "And calm is a luxury for all of us at the moment," she muttered, her stomach twisting as her mind turned once more to thoughts of the future. "Jim, how did you find it? Leaving America? Moving here to start a new life?"

Jim's expression was inscrutable, and Olga realized she'd never asked him such a personal question before. "It was rather a different experience, if you don't mind my saying, Grand Duchess," he replied evenly. "In all respects."

"Of course," Olga replied quickly, reddening at the thought that she'd been impertinent. Jim had long felt like a friend to Olga and her siblings, bringing back guava jelly from his journeys home, and gifting Alexei with the teepee in his playroom. But he'd always been a rather private man. What right did Olga have to pry?

Jim glanced down the hall. Two soldiers had turned toward them, their bayonets held loosely over their shoulders. "I'll tell you this, Grand Duchess," he said, as the soldiers drew near. "Starting a new life takes courage. But you and your sisters—you've got courage enough to spare."

"Busy day for the colonel," said one of the soldiers, a hollow-cheeked revolutionary with a close-cropped haircut and a jacket with a missing button. Olga searched her memory for his name: Kuznetsov. He jerked a thumb at the closed study door, turning to address Jim. "Move aside. We need to verify the colonel's whereabouts."

Jim clasped his hands and lifted his chin, addressing the wall above Kuznetsov's head. "If I'm out here, you can rest assured that he's inside," he said, and Olga watched with some amusement as Kuznetsov and his associate sized up Jim's considerable physique. Though Jim had never served as Papa's bodyguard, he'd once divulged to Olga that he'd been a professional boxer in New York City shortly before sailing to Russia. Would the soldiers be foolish enough to try to challenge him?

Kuznetsov stepped back, hefting the bayonet once more on his shoulder. "I'll take your word for it," he muttered. "What's he up to in there? Scrapbooking, I'll wager. Pictures of that old sailing ship of his—what was it called?"

"The *Shtandart*," Olga muttered.

Kuznetsov grinned, elbowing his companion. "Yeah, that's it. The *Shtandart*; I remember seeing it pass by my village one day. I heard you and your sisters enjoyed spending time onboard, and why would you not, eh?" He stepped toward Olga, his smile broadening further. "Four little beauties such as yourselves…and a whole ship full of red-blooded Russian sailors to keep you company? Who can say fairer?"

"That's enough of that," Jim snapped. "Find something better to do with your time."

Kuznetsov started down the hall, but his voice echoed off the high ceiling as he muttered to his companion. "I know what I'd like to do with my time, if she'd let me."

Olga paused, feeling as though she'd been slapped: even in all her time nursing soldiers, she'd never heard such filthy insinuations.

"How dare you," she spat, trailing them down the hall; Jim made as if to follow, but she waved him off. His duty was to Papa, and Olga could fight her own battles. "Apologize. Now. If my father heard—"

"Your father's got all the piss and vinegar of an oyster, love." Having gained some distance from Jim, Kuznetsov's bravado had returned: he leaned on the barrel of his gun, and Olga wished it would fire of its own accord to blow his elbow to shreds. "Besides, it's no more favor than you paid to that priest of yours, eh? Bet you had a few *oysters* with him in your day." He nudged his snickering companion. "Heard your sister was carrying his child, till the Devil realized he didn't want competition. Did you share him, you two? What a pretty sight that must have been."

"You think you're awfully clever, don't you? You and your little *comrades*, making horrible comments? You make me *sick*." Olga stepped forward and Kuznetsov jumped back, knowing, like Olga, that to lay a hand on any member of the imperial family would be a step too far, even for the Provisional Government. "Kerensky's little guard dogs. Shall I get you a bone from the kitchens? Perhaps fighting over that will occupy you better than snooping on my father's *scrapbooking*."

Kuznetsov laughed. "All right, all right," he said. "Claws in, Duchess. You've got fire in your belly, I can't say fairer than that. A dog knows better than to tangle with a feline." He turned to his companion, still chuckling as he lit a cigarette.

Olga walked back toward Jim, her fists clenched at Kuznetsov's sheer gall: one year ago, Papa could have had him shot for insubordination. They could taunt her, Kerensky's henchmen, but Olga was biding her time. Whatever Papa was up to in his study, she knew that it wasn't scrapbooking. He was writing letters, she was sure of it, to loyalists living underground in Petrograd; to the foreign governments who would sooner open up a new front in the Great War than shake hands with socialists. Olga straightened, letting out a steadying breath. No, Papa was biding his time—and when their plan came together, those worthless soldiers would see just how sharp her family's claws truly were.

8

June 1913
Yaroslavl

Olga walked along the upper deck of the steamship *Mezhen*, swaying with the motion of the waves as the ship shifted into reverse, its broadside connecting with the concrete quay of the river port. Below, deckhands threw immense coils of rope to the waiting sailors on shore; behind them, the onion-domed peaks of Yaroslavl's churches rose out of the new growth on the trees that blanketed the city in green.

She gripped the ship's railing, smiling at the sea of people who waited to welcome them. Hundreds of townspeople had turned out to watch the arrival of Olga's family: dressed in reds and blues, they sat on the steep banks of the river, on picnic blankets and bedsheets, mothers with babies in their laps and husbands holding their caps in their hands. They held yellow and black streamers, waving and shouting as a military band, stationed at a gleaming white pavilion, struck up the national anthem.

Standing beside her, Papa lifted his arm in a greeting; behind him, Nikolai Sablin sighed.

"Half as many as in Kostroma," he muttered. "The Duma will have something to say about that."

Papa continued waving, his cheery expression undimmed.

"They're my people, no matter how many turn up," he said. "Olga, go check on your mother. Let her know we'll be docking soon."

Olga set off toward the staterooms, the route familiar after nearly a week on board the ship. They'd set off on their tercentenary tour two weeks ago, traveling by train and trolley and steamship along the pilgrimage their ancestor, Mikhail, had taken upon being named the first Romanov tsar. Here, at Yaroslavl, they would be transferring from the steamer to their imperial train for the last leg of the journey to Moscow.

She knocked on the door to Mamma's stateroom then entered, breathing in the heavy incense Mamma burned day and night. The room was large and bright—brighter than the deck itself, and Olga saw that Mamma had pulled delicate white curtains over the window: the fine fabric refracted the sunlight, making it feel as though Olga had walked into the center of a cloud.

"Have we arrived?" asked Mamma, setting down her needlepoint. She was sitting near the window, dressed for the day's activities in a white dress and sun hat, its gauzy veil floating in a puff around the brim. Lying atop the daybed, Maria set down the Bible she'd been reading, holding her place in the pages with her fingers.

"Ten minutes, I think," Olga replied. "How are you feeling?"

Mamma flicked back the curtain, revealing the green flash of the riverbank; through the window they could hear the military band and the hum of spectators. "Tired," Mamma murmured. "This headache's been plaguing me since Nizhny Novgorod; no doubt all this noise won't help it." She twitched the curtain back into place. "Still, I am looking forward to visiting the Church of Elijah the Prophet. Can you see it from the port?"

"Not very well," Olga replied.

Mamma smiled. "I'd be lying if I said I wasn't looking forward to getting off this ship," she said, shifting on her cushions. "It's not quite as comfortable as the *Shtandart*, is it?"

Olga knew what she meant. Sailing on their imperial yacht through the Black Sea on their way to Crimea or Finland was a trip Olga looked forward to every year—one the whole family enjoyed, with its release from official duties, its wide-open horizons and endless sunsets. The *Mezhen*, by contrast, was a long and low-slung riverboat, its rooms cramped compared to its oceangoing counterpart, a traveling cottage where the *Shtandart* was a mobile palace. On the Volga, the shoreline was always within sight, the landscape ceaselessly green and rolling, beautiful but monotonous. People, too, were always there on the banks of the river, watching as the ships passed, silent but for the scheduled stops where, like here at Yaroslavl, a military band played them into port.

"How long will we be here?" asked Maria, shifting to the end of the bed. Her feet dangled above the floor before she hopped down, tucking the Bible in the crook of her arm.

"Just today," Mamma replied. She planted her hands on the sofa arm and rose, her breath tight as she spoke. "Long enough to have our things moved to the train and to meet up with some more members of our household. I'm sure you girls will be pleased to know that Anna Vyrubova is joining us here, so you won't have to take turns sitting with your poor mother."

Olga smiled, though Mamma's relentlessly wearying attitude irked her. She would be pleased to have Anna take over some of the constant effort of caring for Mamma. But why did Mamma have to make her feel guilty for it?

"Don't be silly," she replied. "Maria, you ought to get ready. Mamma, have you got everything you need?"

"My parasol," Mamma said, as Maria slipped out the door. "Help me find it, will you?"

Olga searched the room as Mamma checked her reflection in her vanity mirror, pinning a stray lock of hair back into place.

"Nikolai says the crowds aren't as large as they should be for a city this size," she offered, fluffing a couch cushion.

Still looking in the mirror, Mamma patted her hat to ensure it was properly secured. "Nikolai's a fearful old goat," she huffed. "Always one to look for the cloud instead of the rainbow."

Olga opened the wardrobe and pulled out Mamma's parasol. "Shouldn't this be an occasion for the town, like it was in Kostroma and St. Petersburg? They have the day off to see us, don't they?"

Mamma pulled a small cut-glass bottle from the drawer of her vanity and tucked it into the sash of her dress—veronal, which she took to calm her nerves. "That was the case in Kostroma and St. Petersburg, but who knows what the local authorities decided to do here?" she said. "You know how tempers can run high. Perhaps a larger gathering was deemed inadvisable."

Olga turned the parasol in her hands, feeling the weight of it shift as the silk fell with the movement. "If tempers are running high, isn't that something Papa should be concerned about?"

Mamma sighed. "Nikolai worries too much, and so do you," she said. "He's been spending too much time with those state ministers who pull faces every time your father so much as sneezes; they're looking for any excuse to limit your father's influence. They're the ones who need popular support to remain in power, not the tsar. It suits them to think your father is on the back foot, when it's their government and their policies that are unpopular."

Olga handed her the parasol. It was clear that Mamma felt she was acting foolish, and perhaps she was: Papa and Mamma shared everything with each other, including the burden of ruling. Surely they knew, better than anyone, the people they governed.

She offered Mamma her arm as they walked through the door. Outside, a wave of noise washed over them: music and singing and shouting. At the front of the steamship, Papa waited with Tatiana, Maria, Anastasia and Alexei: they all waved down to the crowd as the boat finished docking. On shore, people rushed to the edge of the river in a frenzied mass, tears streaming down their faces as they caught sight of the tsar.

Mamma smiled. "You see? We need only show ourselves and their hearts are ours." She drew closer to Olga, using the stem of her parasol as a cane as they walked down the narrow deck toward Papa. She turned to face the crowd, straight-backed as she lifted her hand in the air. "We have something the government will never have," she continued. "Loyalty."

They joined the rest of the family at the top of the gangplank, where Sablin, along with the captain of the *Mezhen* and the ship's officers, stood at attention. Below, an official greeting party waited beneath the shade of a striped awning.

Though all of Yaroslavl was looking at him, Papa only had eyes for Mamma. "Shall we?" he asked, before leading Mamma down the gangplank as steadily as if they were going on a picnic. Olga positioned herself behind her parents and followed them down to shore. Her heart lifted as she stepped on dry land: there, in the tsar's escort that lined either side of the gangplank, was Pavel.

She'd not expected to see him until after the tercentenary tour—they'd said their goodbyes to each other after Aunt Olga's last tea party, Olga playfully berating him for his earlier antics at the parade. What if Papa had seen the spark between them; what if he saw it now? She could already hear Mamma's shocked censure, her disapproving tone ringing in Olga's mind: *You're meant for better things than a mere officer, my darling.*

To Olga, it felt as though Pavel existed only within the confines of her aunt's tea parties: to see him here, so close, so publicly, was wonderful and unsettling, all at once.

"Olga," Maria hissed, prodding her from behind. She hadn't realized she'd stopped walking; Pavel winked, and Olga, tearing her focus away, continued on down to the pavilion.

★★★

Olga unpinned her hat, glancing out the window one final time as the imperial train lurched away from Yaroslavl station. The day had been a success, albeit an exhausting one. Olga's cheeks ached from the polite smile she'd worn for hours. She longed to kick off her narrow white shoes, but even here in the privacy of the imperial train's saloon car, such a lapse would be highly improper.

She closed her eyes, letting the rhythm of the carriage and the low lull of murmured conversation ease her into a daydream. Elsewhere on the train, her family was recovering from the day's strains in their own ways. Mamma would be in the traveling chapel with Anna Vyrubova, giving thanks for their safe departure from the city. Papa would be exercising, no doubt, pulling himself up on the chin-bar he'd had installed in his office while one of his aides-de-camp read him reports. Maria, surely, would be writing letters, keeping up with the few correspondences she had outside the palace; Anastasia and Alexei would be in the guards' compartment, peppering the soldiers with impertinent questions.

The dry crack of a lighter pulled Olga's attention back to the saloon: across the table, Tatiana inhaled.

"Cigarette?" she asked, but Olga shook her head. Both Tatiana and Olga preferred the activity of the saloon car to the solitude of their private compartment: officers from Papa's escort congregated here, along with any of the ladies-in-waiting looking for more diversion than could be found in Mamma's quiet quarters. Tonight, the saloon car was quiet: a cluster of officers, Sablin and Pavel amongst them, sat at the far end of the car, their heads plumed in cigar smoke as they played a hand of poker.

Tatiana tapped the end of her cigarette into a heavy crystal ashtray, her attention fixed on her novel. "Tell your friend to stop staring." She glanced up at the group of officers, her blue eyes glinting over the cover of her book. "He's being terribly obvious."

Olga's heart leapt, though not with pleasure. "Do you think so?" she asked. "I must say, I enjoy his company when we're at Aunt Olga's, but it feels somehow…different to see him here."

"Different, good?" said Tatiana, raising an eyebrow.

Olga straightened. Under the pretense of adjusting the pillow on the back of her chair, she chanced a glance at Pavel. He met her eyes, holding her gaze for a beat too long over his fanned cards. "I don't know," she said carefully. "Are all men so…passionate? I thought for a moment he might have tried to take my hand as we were walking into port, I thought I would have died of embarrassment. What if Mamma were to see? Or Papa?"

Tatiana shrugged. "He would be dismissed, I suppose," she said, setting her book aside as she settled into the banquette. "What of it?"

Olga hesitated. "But what would they think of *me*?"

"Oh." Tatiana exhaled, tapping her cigarette once more. "I see what you mean."

"When we're alone at Aunt Olga's parties it's one thing, but here…"

"Quite another." Tatiana nodded, looking stern. "Perhaps he needs to be reminded of what's at stake."

"Don't say that," Olga said hastily, dreading the idea that he might lose his position. "He's lovely, really. Forget I said anything."

9

June 1917
Tsarskoe Selo

The grounds of Alexander Park were nearly silent, but for the sound of insects buzzing in tall grass as Olga and Papa walked along the overgrown pathways. Only last year, these trails had been carefully tended, manicured to smooth perfection, any dips or rises in the landscape made gentle enough not to jar Alexei and Mamma if they were riding in a sleigh.

During the winter, Olga had been able to fool herself into thinking that Alexander Park hadn't changed as a result of the revolution: that the park's deer had simply gone into the stables to wait out the cold; that Alexei's pet elephant was in its cozy enclosure, dreaming of warmer days. Now, though, the long-awaited spring had brought with it an explosion of green that, without the steady influence of gardeners, had begun to take over: hostas burst beyond the bounds of their tidy beds and the lilac blooms that flanked the dusty pathways drooped heavy on their stems, perfuming the grounds with their intoxicating scent. Along the banks of the canal, cattails choked out the shallow waters and imprisoned the miniature ferry at its dock; in the courtyard, weeds grew between flagstones, wrapping their thin tendrils around the base of the howitzer. Even the trees had gone wild: in her bedroom, Olga could hardly see past the branches that scraped against her windowpane in the night.

By unspoken assent, Olga and Papa turned before they reached the Chinese Pavilion. In the distance, Olga could see the meadow that had grown up on an uneven mound of soil: a mass grave, dug for those who had perished during the rioting that had followed Papa's abdication. It was a ghoulish, haunted thing—built for the victims of Papa's tyranny, so the revolutionaries said—and Olga shuddered at the thought of her beloved park filled with the souls of the lost.

The palace, too, felt haunted. Olga glanced behind her, meeting the hard stare of the soldier who trailed them. They were always there, with their rifles—in the park and at the entrance to the palace, reeling drunkenly through the palace's parade halls, kicking their booted feet onto the furniture.

Papa lifted his face to the sky, basking in the warmth of the sun. "A beautiful day," he said, lifting a cigarette to his lips. "Will we get rain later, do you think?"

Olga could feel the soldier's eyes on her; she could practically hear his fingers tightening over his heavy rifle. "No," she said. "I don't believe we will."

Papa raised his voice. "Captain Yakov, I'd be grateful if you could mention to your senior officer that there's a tree, just here, I'd like to take care of. Would you be so kind as to supply me with an axe for my walk tomorrow?"

The soldier shrugged. Given the heat of the day, he'd unbuttoned the top few buttons on his uniform. Papa glanced at the disheveled collar, his mouth tightening into a moue of disapproval.

"If it will keep you busy, I don't see why not," Yakov replied, flicking his cigarette butt onto the gravel.

Olga took Papa's arm. "Always the woodsman," she said. In the absence of anything else to do, Papa had taken to chopping down trees in the park himself, laying firewood down to season. In January, he'd broken ice on the canal; now that spring had come, he'd helped create the immense vegetable garden that took up the lawn behind the Semi-Circular Hall. Though the plots were still in their infancy, the smallest sprouts had begun to push through the soil, helped along by the persistent, grubby hands of Alexei and his tutors, Pierre Gilliard and Sydney Gibbes.

Papa tucked his hand in the pocket of his jacket. "Just making sure we're warm for winter."

"Do you think we'll still be here by then?" she said. Though the immediate danger Olga had feared following Papa's abdication seemed to have passed, they'd only been promised refuge at Alexander Palace until everyone recovered from the measles. "Where will we go if they say we're to leave?"

Papa shrugged. "I've thought about it, of course. I expect we'll be sent into exile—England, most likely. But the final decision lies with the Provisional Government."

England... Olga recalled the holiday they'd taken to the Isle of Wight; visits with Uncle George, who looked so strikingly similar to Papa. England, with its quiet stone villages and rolling hills; England, hemmed in on all sides by the sea.

"What would we do there?"

Papa looked down the path. "I've always wanted a farm," he said. "Just a small one, with room for our horses and a herd of cattle... Somewhere with woodland, where we can make paths for sleigh rides." He glanced at Olga, smiling. "Scotland, perhaps. What would you say to that?"

"And we'd just...live there?" Olga tried to picture it: a quiet country existence, far from the intrigues of government and politics. Tromping across muddy fields in wellington books; taking communion in a damp stone church.

They walked on in silence, passing the vegetable garden, where Gibbes was helping Maria, Anastasia and Alexei weed a bed of leeks. Nearby, Mamma sat beneath the shade of a willow tree, working on a piece of needlework.

Captain Yakov fell behind for a moment to speak to a comrade, and Papa leaned in.

"Of course, I don't expect we'd stay in England forever," he continued, his voice low. "I expect we'd return to Russia at some point, but I won't do anything to destabilize the country further until the war is won."

"But you think we'd be allowed to return?" said Olga. Behind them, Captain Yakov clapped his friend on the back and shrugged his bayonet higher on his shoulder.

"We would," said Papa. "I have it on good authority that we will be permitted to live in Crimea after the war is over."

Captain Yakov caught up to them, cutting off Olga's next question: *And what would we do there?* Crimea, with its hot summers and long vistas over the sparkling Black Sea, was the place Olga loved most: to live there permanently would be a privilege, rather than a punishment. Would the Provisional Government allow them to live at Livadia Palace? Her heart lifted at the prospect. The grounds would be bright with color at this time of year, the courtyard palm trees blooming. Even if they were never allowed off the palace grounds, Olga would be grateful to live out the rest of her life in Crimea.

The captain shared an even glance between Olga and Papa. "Ten more minutes," he said.

Papa nodded and they continued around the side of the palace, where, beyond the palace gates, they could see people watching them: onlookers, with scraps of red pinned to their coats. She'd expected the crowds in the early days following Papa's abdication but had been surprised when they continued coming long after the news had grown stale: every day, people gathered at the gates to catch a glimpse of Papa working the gardens or cutting ice on the canals. As with the Chinese Pavilion, Olga avoided the gates when she could, her daily walk becoming shorter and shorter with each passing week.

The crowd around the gates closed in as Olga and Papa drew nearer, jeering through the gaps in the fence. From inside the fence, a handful of soldiers faced the crowd, their rifles held at attention.

Olga kept her head down.

"Here he is! The former emperor!"

"Little Nikolashka, locked away in his ivory tower!"

Hatred emanated from the onlookers like heat, and Olga turned away, unable to look any of them in the eye. She'd seen them huddled outside the Winter Palace in the darkest days of the war, begging for food from empty windows, unaware that Papa was at the front and that Mamma was in Tsarskoe Selo. Her parents had been unaware of the scale of despair in the capital, dismissing the food shortages as a temporary problem borne from the logical challenge of feeding an army of millions alongside the civilian population. *It's a question of distribution*, Mamma had said, airily lifting her chin. *The railways will sort themselves out.*

But *temporary* was hardly a relative term to someone who was starving.

"How can you stand it?" Olga whispered.

Papa smiled blandly, lifting his arm in acknowledgment. "They're still my people," he whispered back.

"Little Father! Look at you now!" Olga looked up as a sharp voice cut through the clutter. A red-faced man pushed his face through the gaps in the fence, ignoring the soldiers who took a menacing step forward. "Look at you, locked away. Do you know what was happening to us while you were feasting at the front? While you let the mystic fuck your wife?"

Captain Yakov turned sharply. "That's enough!" he shouted, and one of the soldiers stepped up to the gate, brandishing his bayonet. The man jerked back, lost his balance, and fell into the crowd.

Papa let out a breath; Olga put a hand on his arm, alarmed to feel him trembling. "Thank you, Captain," he said. He held out his hand. "I'm grateful for your protection."

Yakov stared at Papa. He tightened his grip on his rifle and looked down at Papa's hand as though he'd been asked to handle something dead. "Why would I take your hand," he said, "when the Russian people reached out to you for help and you turned away?"

Olga felt as though she'd been kicked; from beyond the fence, the crowd began to laugh, cheering on Captain Yakov's insolence as though he'd done something truly heroic. Papa balled his hand into a fist, knocking it against the side of his leg as he attempted to gloss over the moment.

Captain Yakov jerked his chin in the direction of the palace. "Five more minutes."

10

July 1913
Baryatinsky Palace, St. Petersburg

Olga sat on the upholstered arm of a sofa in her aunt's sitting room, her toes just barely brushing the floor for balance. As always seemed to be the case, Aunt Olga had invited more people to this afternoon's tea party than there were seats in the room: Felix Yusupov was sitting on the floor, a silk cravat hanging loose around his neck; behind the potted palm tree, Dmitri Pavlovich was conversing with Princess Irina Alexandrovna, a rakish grin on his face as he stood a shade too close. Aunt Olga was holding court with a group of soldiers clustered near a table piled high with sweets, her beloved Captain Kulikovsky at her side as the afternoon's indulgences transitioned from caffeine to alcohol.

"Book title—a book title!" shouted Tatiana. In front of the fireplace, Anya Kleinmichel nodded, then tapped her forearm to denote syllables.

"Seven!" Olga shrieked. Giddy, she overbalanced on the sofa arm and tipped to one side; thankfully the Duke of Leuchtenburg, standing behind her, caught her before she tumbled to the floor.

"Thank you," she laughed. With the tercentenary celebrations over, Olga was glad to be back in her aunt's sitting room, grateful for a momentary pause before moving on to Crimea for the summer. A few weeks away from her official duties—bliss, to Olga, who'd shaken more hands and made more small talk during the celebrations than ever before in her life. She'd enjoyed it, the nights out to the theatre with Papa, admiring the women in their gowns—but Mamma's ill health meant that Olga had been taking on more of the duties of an empress than a grand duchess. And after her time in the limelight, she could better understand her parents' preference for a peaceful country life.

Not that tonight was particularly peaceful, she thought, watching Anya Kleinmichel grow increasingly agitated as the hourglass on the mantel counted down her turn in grains of sand.

Across the room, Pavel leaned against the back of his chair, balancing a champagne coupe on his knee, watching Anya act out her clue without participating. Despite her misgivings about Pavel's indiscretions on board the imperial train, now that they were back in her aunt's home Olga felt that the ebb and flow between them had righted itself. On tour, they had been the grand duchess and the officer; here, they could simply be Olga and Pavel, two guests at a party.

"*The Death of Ivan Ilych*!" shouted Felix Yusupov, and Anya threw up her arms, her plain face merry with triumph.

Olga clapped along with the rest, then took advantage of the momentary pause in the game, as Tatiana took Anya's place, to sidle toward the back of the room.

As she'd hoped, Pavel joined her.

"How many syllables," he said, leaning close enough for his lips to brush her ear, "for a word meaning *dull*?"

Olga smiled and held out her coupe; Pavel filled it, bubbles roiling.

"Not enjoying the game, then?" she asked.

Pavel shrugged, replacing the bottle in ice. "Charades, sardines… Aren't you tired of games?" With everyone's attention fixed on Tatiana, Pavel took Olga's hand and pulled her out of the sitting room.

"Pavel, they'll miss us," Olga whispered as they raced through the ballroom and into the hall, her aunt's footmen tactfully raising their gaze to the ceiling.

"No, they won't." He grinned, pulling her into the alcove of a locked doorway. "Charades will end in five minutes and they'll move on to catch-me-if-you-can. We'll all end up in the same wardrobe and laugh and laugh like simpletons when it falls apart."

"I like catch-me-if-you-can," Olga replied, stung by the derision in his voice—but then he pressed his lips to hers, sending her mind spinning as she relished the feel of his kiss.

"I've missed you," he murmured, his hands heavy against her shoulders, her arms, her waist. "All those weeks watching you from across the parade grounds…it's enough to make a man go mad."

He kissed her again, with such force that her back dug into the molded wall behind her and her desire turned to irritation. She pushed him away, Tatiana's voice ringing in her head: *He's being terribly obvious.*

"Pavel," she hissed. Was he truly so beholden to his desires? "I want to go back inside. They'll be moving on to sardines, we don't want to miss that."

He stepped back, breathing raggedly. "Is that all I am to you, too?" he said. "A game?"

Olga didn't answer.

"I don't understand," she said finally. "We're together, aren't we? We're here—"

"Together? Is this really how you think couples are when they're together? Sneaking about at your aunt's house? Attending the same party, over and over and over? Pretending we don't know each other when we leave?"

"I hardly think that's fair," Olga retorted. She glanced down the hall, wishing Pavel would lower his voice. "We just got back from a tour of the country."

"A tour where we couldn't even *speak* to each other, Olga! How can this be enough for you?" He broke off, his arms loose at his sides. "Is it enough for you? Truly, is it?"

Olga's heart was beating furiously now, with fear and frustration. She wished she could offer him more—she longed to, more than she'd admitted even to herself. What would her life look like if her title didn't stand between them? A ring, a promise. Children; a life. She could see it all, there for the taking, in Pavel's brown eyes.

"It's all I can offer," she said finally. "You know that."

Pavel closed his eyes, the last vestiges of composure stripped away by the look of anguish on his face. "It's not enough," he whispered. "Not for me."

They leaned against opposite sides of the door frame. From within the sitting room, a roar went up as Tatiana's turn came to an end.

Olga could feel the pinprick of tears behind her eyes; determined not to let them fall, she looked down, wishing she could grasp at the edges of the gulf that was growing between them, pull the threads that had bound them close back together again.

"If you truly feel this way, perhaps we should take some time apart," she said finally, in a poor attempt to conceal her distress. "To think about—to think about what we want."

Pavel raked his hand through his hair. "Yes," he replied, avoiding her eye. "Yes, perhaps we should."

"Well, we're both in Crimea for the summer. Maybe we ought to keep our distance. Decide what's best for each of us," she said, though she felt sick at the thought of it. Pavel would be on tour with them; he would be there, at dinners and dances; at Aunt Olga's parties and at official functions. Unavoidable.

She lifted her chin, determined not to let her lip tremble as

Pavel nodded once more; down the hall, the door to the sitting room swung open with an echoing bang. "I think that would be for the best, Grand Duchess," he replied.

Aunt Olga and Tatiana came toward them, Aunt Olga's black shawl billowing behind her like a sail. "You're needed back home," she said, and the expression on Tatiana's face was enough to make Olga's heart stop. "It's Alexei."

11

July 1917
Tsarskoe Selo

Olga leaned on the handle of her spade, wiping the sheen of sweat from her brow with a gritty palm. Over the past several weeks, the vegetable garden behind Alexander Palace had ripened considerably, pushing bright green shoots through the tilled soil, which, to Olga, felt a little like hope. Though Olga still shuddered when passing the guards in the halls, here in the garden they became less than the jailers they purported themselves to be; here, she could ignore them as she bent over her work, dismissed as so many trees in a forest.

She looked out, breathing a sigh of satisfaction. The garden now stretched nearly the entire length of the palace, dozens of vegetable plots that were yielding fat cabbages and carrots for the kitchen table. She thought back to Crimea, in the days before the war: flowers used to grow, bright and magnificent, outside their doors, prized for their scent and color and beauty. Vegetables, Olga could now see, had beauty of their own: the solar system of lines inside a sliced beet; cabbages, unfurling their outer leaves like rose petals.

Along the avenue of grass between the plots, Tatiana, her hair bound up in a crimson kerchief, trundled by with a wheelbarrow filled to the brim with lettuce; behind her, Alexei jogged to catch up.

"Careful!" Olga called, as Alexei snatched a head of lettuce from the wheelbarrow. He grinned as he jumped into Olga's plot, tossing her the lettuce; she dropped the spade and caught it easily, laughing.

Alexei picked up the spade. "Need help?" he said brightly. Over the past few weeks, Alexei had finally recovered from the measles that had kept him bedridden for so long. Pale though he'd become, Olga was relieved to see him in the garden, ready to stretch his growing muscles. He began turning the earth, his gaunt cheeks flushed with effort but his expression serene, his movements steady as he braced himself against the spade.

He paused. "What?"

Olga smiled. "Nothing," she said. "You just—you look so like Papa, just now."

Alexei flushed, transforming once again into the gangly teenager he'd become, and Olga climbed out of the plot, soil clinging to her boots.

She collapsed next to Mamma, who was sitting in her wheelchair at the base of her willow tree, a quilt nestled comfortably over her legs as she embroidered initials onto the corner of a silk handkerchief.

"Don't let him overexert himself," she said.

Olga reached for the jug of water resting on a folding camp-table, dismissing Mamma's concerns with a wave of her hand. "He's been inside too long. The exercise is good for him," she replied. "Dr. Botkin said he needs to build up his strength."

Mamma sighed, her fingers twitching over her needlework. In the garden, Alexei threw a clump of dirt at Anastasia, who was weeding a patch of carrots nearby; she shot up as the soil hit her leg, shouting outrage.

"I suppose you're right," said Mamma, as Anastasia began to chase Alexei through the garden. "But keep an eye on him regardless, you know how easily he can—Olga, you really shouldn't be lying on the ground, darling. What will people think?"

Olga leaned on her elbow, relishing the feel of grass beneath her fingers. People still lined up by the fence in the hopes of seeing the former imperial family, but Olga had stopped worrying about what they thought of her. She thought back to the tercentenary: back to the performance of it all, the outfits and the pageantry, the displays of emotion from peasants and nobles alike. She'd been playacting the part of a grand duchess that day; how many of them had been playacting their devotion toward her father? No, Olga didn't think anyone would care if they saw Grand Duchess Olga lying on the grass, or Grand Duchess Tatiana rolling a handcart. She was done selling a story, just as the people were done buying it.

"Anastasia!" she called out, pulling a piece of grass from the earth. She bit the white end, pulling what sweetness she could from the blade. "Any new revelations on the love lives of worms?"

From across the field, Anastasia, now back at her carrot patch, shook her head, her blond curls gleaming in the sunlight. "My studies are focused solely on *domesticated* earthworms," she called back, "though I am considering the possibility of expanding my field of research to caterpillars."

Olga laughed: from the palace, Papa and Maria, along with a handful of men in dark uniforms, were walking toward the garden.

"Is that Kerensky with him?" Mamma asked, shielding her eyes.

Olga stood, knocking dust from her skirt. "It is," she replied. "Alexei! Tatiana, *Shvybzik*, come here!"

Olga hadn't seen Kerensky in weeks: he preferred to leave the day-to-day operations at the palace in the care of his lieutenants while going about his other duties for the new government.

She watched him walk toward them, his threadbare jacket and unkempt hair marking him as a harbinger of the new order. She shifted her gaze to Papa's tidy appearance with a surge of pride. Despite her family's reduced circumstances, Papa always looked the part of a true gentleman.

They reached the willow where the rest of the family had joined Mamma and Olga. Kerensky, hands clasped behind his back, smiled as Mamma set aside the quilt that had been covering her lap.

"Please, madam," said Kerensky, nodding his head in a motion near to deference as Mamma got to her feet, "don't stand on my account."

Mamma paused, staring coldly at Kerensky as she gripped the arm of her wheelchair. Tight-lipped, she took one step, then another, toward Papa and sank into a curtsy.

"Your Imperial Majesty," she muttered, casting one final, withering glance at Kerensky before returning to her chair.

Olga stifled the urge to laugh as Kerensky visibly colored.

"To what do we owe this visit, Minister?" Mamma asked, settling the blanket back in place as Anastasia shifted on the grass to sit at her feet. "It must be something important indeed, to interrupt our family time."

"Now, Alicky," said Papa, his tone conciliatory. He walked behind the wheelchair and rested his hands on Mamma's shoulders before addressing Kerensky. "Now that we're all together, we'd be most interested in what you have to say."

Kerensky looked up at the palace, rummaging in his coat pocket for his cigarette case. "I'm afraid the Provisional Government has decided that in the interests of your own safety, you are to be moved to a more secure location."

Papa's cordial smiled dropped. "Leave the palace? Why? Where will we go?"

Kerensky lit a cigarette. "The government feels that the recent uprisings in St. Petersburg pose too much of a threat to your family," he said, and Olga looked at her parents in alarm, but they stared at Kerensky, impassive. "Given that your children's health has improved—"

"Praise be to God," Mamma interrupted.

Kerensky hesitated, taking a perfunctory puff of smoke. "Quite," he replied. "Given that your family is healthy enough to work the grounds, the government has concluded that it is time to move you all to safer quarters."

"And where might those quarters be?" asked Papa. "We told you, I believe, of our preference for Crimea—"

"I'm not at liberty to say," Kerensky replied. He tapped the end of his cigarette, ash drifting onto the hem of Anastasia's skirt. "I can tell you that you'll need to pack winter clothes."

Olga's heart sank, the picture of Livadia Palace fading from her mind. She raced through a map of Russia in her mind. If winter clothing was involved, Crimea was out of the question—did that mean England was, too? They'd be staying within Russia itself, that much was clear, or else he would have told Papa that another country had offered them asylum.

"You'll be traveling for five days," he continued, addressing Papa. "Take what you need for warmth. Everything else will follow."

Papa nodded. "Thank you, Minister." He stepped forward and held out his hand. "I know you've done the best you can for us."

Kerensky hesitated, then took Papa's hand in his own. "You won't be returning here, so take all the provisions you think you might need," he said. "You leave in a week's time."

12

July 1913
Alexander Palace, Tsarskoe Selo

Olga sat with her sisters and aunts in Alexei's playroom, his scattered toys incongruously joyful despite the gloom that pervaded the palace. Three days had passed since she and Tatiana had received the summons at Aunt Olga's party; three days of anxiety and uncertainty, three days of praying for Alexei's recovery. He'd fallen off his pony in Alexander Park while trying to jump a hedgerow and for the past several days he'd lingered between life and death, his shoulder swollen and black where he'd rolled onto the hard-packed earth.

Anna Vyrubova walked in, and Olga looked up. "How is he?"

Anna's eyes were red-rimmed; clearly, she'd sat up all night at Mamma's side, sharing in her mistress's vigil over Alexei. "They've given him last rites," she said, and Olga, in a moment of unexpected clarity, realized that Anna's concern went beyond her duty to Mamma: her anguish over Alexei's condition was for Alexei himself, as a boy—as a sort of brother—rather than as tsarevich. Beside Olga, Aunt Xenia bowed her head. "The tsar has asked for you, Dowager Empress."

Without a word, Grandmamma stood. Leaning against Aunt Xenia for support, she followed Anna slowly out of the playroom.

Aunt Olga shifted across the daybed. "You'll need to be there for your parents, should the worst happen," she said quietly, taking Olga's hands in hers. "Your father, particularly. He tries so hard to be strong."

Olga's chest ached with an all-too-familiar tightness. "We've been here before and he's pulled through," she said. Memories of past days like this, spent in agonizing uncertainty, flashed through her mind: waiting on couches, threading her fingers together in prayer; distracting Anastasia and Maria as priests and doctors flitted through the palace halls. Making excuses for Alexei's frequent absences, telling officers in the Tsar's Guard that Alexei had taken ill with a stomach complaint or a broken leg. Making childish bargains with God in the dead of night, to spare Alexei for another month, another year, in exchange for doing her homework. For being nice to her sisters. For her own happiness. "He's going to pull through."

"His recovery is in God's hands. We need to be prepared for the worst."

Olga pressed her hands together, wishing she could do something—anything—to take away Alexei's pain. "We've been prepared for the worst his whole life," she replied.

They both looked up at the sound of footsteps down the hall; through the open door, they watched Father Grigori pause in front of a mirror to tamp down his wild hair.

Aunt Olga stiffened, as though she was a dog catching the scent of a rabbit. "I thought Alexei had already been given last rites," she said as Father Grigori slipped into Alexei's bedroom. "What's he doing here?"

Olga barely looked up. "He's been here every day to pray."

Aunt Olga's grip on her fingers tightened. "He shouldn't be," she replied. "You know what they're saying about him."

Olga looked up. To her surprise, Dr. Botkin and all of the nurses had shuttled out of Alexei's room, huddled together as they walked, muttering, toward the staircase.

"He's a *khlyst*," Aunt Olga whispered. "A mystic. A deviant."

"A what?"

"It's in all the papers, he was denounced by several members of the clergy." Olga could feel her aunt's eyes on her. "Have you really not heard?"

Olga didn't respond. She'd known that Father Grigori didn't have many friends, but Mamma tended to dismiss the more outlandish accusations levied against him: that he was a cultist, a hypnotist; that he could read minds. *A prophet is never understood in his time*, Mamma would say, employing her oft-repeated argument in defense of Father Grigori's actions.

Olga turned away from her aunt's inquiring gaze. She stood, her cheeks burning. "I'm afraid you must excuse me. I'm needed by my parents."

Aunt Olga looked mortified. She too, made as if to stand, but then sank back into her seat. "I'm sorry if I offended you," she said, but Olga turned on her heel. She didn't have time for her aunt's gossip-mongering.

She walked into Alexei's bedroom. Someone had drawn the curtains against the afternoon sun; candles suffused the room with golden light, flickering gently on the ledge of the iconostasis, breathing life into the gilt icons that hung within.

Alexei moaned and turned in his bedsheets, his face slick with sweat. He'd taken on a sickly yellow pallor, the color made more dire by the dark circles beneath his eyes; he kicked off the sheet and Olga could see his left shoulder, swollen beyond recognition, so distended that the doctors had put him to bed without a shirt on. Above the elbow, his arm was bruised black, but the swelling had traveled, transforming his entire arm and chest an angry, boiling red.

Father Grigori was sitting at Alexei's bedside, eyes closed, hands clasped. He was speaking, but his voice was too low for Olga to make out the words; there was a rhythmic quality to them, a deep, musical pulse that seemed to seep into the corners of the room, causing him to sway gently in his chair as though he was being buffeted by running water.

Mamma and Papa knelt at the foot of the bed, Mamma clutching the iron footboard as if it were an anchor against the tide. Behind them, Olga's sisters knelt in prayer, their eyes closed as they whispered, buoying up Father Grigori's chanting on a steady current of breath.

Olga inched farther into the room, careful not to disturb the sense of purpose exuding from Father Grigori. Whereas Papa had closed his eyes against the sight of his son, Mamma was watching Father Grigori, desperation clear in the blue of her eyes, the set of her jaw. She leaned forward, her focus on the priest so complete that she didn't so much as blink as Olga edged past her to take up her place with her sisters.

She knelt, bringing her hands together in prayer. From over Mamma's shoulder, she studied Alexei, watching his chest rise and fall too quickly. She looked at the icons hung throughout the room: gilt portraits of Christ and the Virgin Mother, carried in from Mamma and Papa's bedroom; the heavy crucifix hung above Alexei's head. The iconostasis, with its votive candles and gilded saints, was rendered in such exquisite detail that they, too, seemed to breathe in anticipation of Alexei's recovery. Items given to Mamma by Father Grigori over the years had also found their way to Alexei's bedside: napkins and pencils and used teaspoons, stuffed beneath his pillow, under his mattress. Did they truly have power, those keepsakes? Mamma certainly seemed to think so: residual grace, imbued by Father Grigori's steady hand.

Olga didn't know whether she shared Mamma's faith in icons, but she had faith enough not to disturb what Mamma had placed around Alexei's room with such painstaking care.

But prayers—those, she knew, had power. She watched Father Grigori, his fingertips fluttering, jerking as if he was receiving static shocks. Her mind turned in a flash to Victor Frankenstein and his gruesome creation, inanimate limbs jerking on a gurney, lightning passing through veins, flooding the body with blood, blood rushing to the brain, to the heart, blood that was choking Alexei from within—

Father Grigori's eyes snapped open.

"Alexei," he called softly.

Alexei stirred, eyelids fluttering, his cheeks damp with perspiration as Father Grigori fixed Alexei in his unblinking stare.

"Such suffering in one so young," he murmured. He reached forward and wrapped his fingers gently around the back of Alexei's neck, easing him closer still. "God sees how you suffer, as Christ suffered on the cross. There is pain in suffering, Tsarevich—but there is wisdom in suffering, too. God sees the light you will bring to the world one day, but He also sees the darkness. For you cannot rule with wisdom if you do not see the suffering of your people."

Father Grigori smiled. Was it Olga's imagination or did Alexei seem to be breathing with a little more ease?

"When you are tsar, you will rule over not only the highest of the high, but the lowest of the low. How can you measure their worth without knowing their hardships? Their suffering? This is a test sent by Him, my child—a test that will bring you closer to your people. Closer to God."

Alexei closed his eye, and Father Grigori eased his head back onto the pillow. Within moments, his chest was rising and falling steadily.

Mamma, still crouching at the foot of the bed, looked up, gripping the iron footboard harder still.

"Father—?" she said in a whisper.

Father Grigori turned to her. "Do not trouble yourself, Little Mother. I have spoken to God and He is not ready to take the child just yet."

Mamma cried out, her shoulders sagging with relief as Papa collected her into a hug.

"Do not let the doctors poke and prod him; do not let them give him their medicines. God will heal him in His own time."

Mamma shuffled forward on her knees, her arms outstretched; she took Father Grigori's broad hand and pressed it to her lips. "Thank you," she said, trembling. "Thank you, Father. You are truly one of God's chosen."

Father Grigori helped Mamma to her feet. "I am but a messenger," he replied.

Papa held out his hand and Father Grigori took it. Mamma turned away, wiping her eyes as Maria handed her a glass of water. She drained it, watching Alexei as she wiped a sheen from her lips.

"Let him sleep," said Father Grigori. "The Little One needs rest."

Olga marveled at the change in Mamma's demeanor. She looked peaceful now, beatific, even, as she circled to Papa's side, the twin tracks of their drying tears glinting in the candlelight. The weight of faith had always laid heavily on Mamma, but it was as though a burden had been lifted from her: as though Alexei's fate was now sealed, more completely than when the doctors had said there was nothing more they could do; more completely than when Alexei had been given last rites. "I'll sit with him," she said, her voice steady once more. "The worst is over. We have Father Grigori to thank for that."

Olga stood, lining up with her sisters to give their thanks to Father Grigori. As Anastasia threw her arms around his middle, Olga thought back on her aunt's words: *Mystic. Deviant. Khlyst.*

Anastasia left the room, and Olga stepped forward, pressing Father Grigori's hand into hers. As she met his eyes, Father Grigori smiled, sending a jolt of electricity to Olga's core.

"Thank you, Father," she said quietly.

13

July 1917
Alexander Palace, Tsarskoe Selo

Alexei sat atop a packing crate, his fingers tight on his spaniel's lead as he brushed his feet along the parquet floor in the Semi-Circular Hall. Pushing the brim of his sailor's cap back from his forehead, he twisted in his seat, looking at the mountain of luggage that had been piled by the family's remaining staff—suitcases and steamer trunks, rolled canvases and wooden boxes with labels affixed to the side bearing a large letter *R*. Mamma had spent the last week overseeing the removal of as many family heirlooms and personal items as they could carry into exile. Now, looking at the possessions that would be moved with them, Olga wondered about the fate of everything they'd had to leave behind. She had little doubt that the revolutionary soldiers would bayonet the priceless portraits of Romanov ancestors that they'd not been able to take; that they would pilfer the keepsakes in Papa's office, pocketing her family's trinkets as trophies.

She pictured the Semi-Circular Hall at its best: a thousand dinner guests seated at round tables beneath the glittering chandelier; the echoing strains of a string orchestra accompanying Bolshoi dancers who drifted between the tables as if floating on air. She closed her eyes, affixing the image in her mind. That was how she wanted to remember it. As a place of beauty and joy, not the repository where she and her family had been abandoned to await their exile.

Dr. Botkin walked past, holding out a stopper: he'd been giving them all valerian drops, which had calmed Olga's nerves but hadn't dulled her sense of dread. They'd been waiting for hours, the soldiers moving their luggage piece by excruciatingly slow piece; if they kept on at this pace, the sun would be stretching long across the palace walls before they left. She suspected the delay was a means of throwing off any would-be rescuers.

Alexei's spaniel let out a whimper, and Ortipo, Tatiana's bulldog, tried to wriggle free from her arms. Though still weakened from her illness, Tatiana managed to hold tight: unbeknownst to the little dog, the soldiers had made too many cruel comments about using it for target practice for her to risk letting it roam free through the hall.

Dr. Botkin held out the stopper and Olga took it, squeezing drops of valerian under her tongue. "How much longer?"

Dr. Botkin let out a breath. "I wish I could tell you, Grand Duchess," he said, in the gentle tone of voice she imagined he would use if speaking to someone terminally ill. "Unfortunately, I know no more than you. We're all in the same boat now."

All in the same boat. Dr. Botkin was right: they were all at the mercy of a government that no longer supported them; all waiting for an uncertain fate. Forty-six members of the household had chosen to accompany them into exile; forty-six people who had tied their destiny to Olga's family. She looked around the room. Mamma and Papa were sitting together on a traveling trunk, Mamma white-faced and tight-lipped, Papa smoking cigarette after cigarette. Though the retainers who were traveling with them—Dr. Botkin and Pierre Gilliard, Sydney Gibbes and the maids; Mamma's ladies-in-waiting, Trina Schneider and Nastenka Hendrikova—had done their best to maintain a respectful distance from the imperial family, they, too, were seated on traveling trunks, as though they were all in the ticket office at Nicholaevsky station.

And yet, an emperor on a traveling trunk was still an emperor. She straightened atop her crate, shoulders back, chin high. A grand duchess in exile was still a grand duchess.

Daylight was breaking through the immense picture windows when Kerensky finally entered. He was accompanied by a tall, heavily built man, his inexpertly tailored uniform sagging over sloping shoulders and a wide midriff—a soldier gone to seed. His thick hair had gone pure white at the temples, but his mustache, set beneath watery, pale eyes, was dark, putting Olga in mind of a genteel badger.

Papa got to his feet, and Kerensky cleared his throat. "Nicholas Alexandrovich, allow me to introduce Colonel Eugene Kobylinsky. The colonel has been responsible for the military garrison here at the palace and will be overseeing the military detachment that will accompany you on your journey."

Hands clasped behind his back, Kobylinsky smiled at Papa, but didn't bow.

"I apologize for the delay. There was a spot of unrest on the railway lines, but we've sorted it all out." He stepped back and raised his voice, for the benefit of those in the hall. "We'll be leaving for the station shortly," he said. "Please bring your personal possessions."

Olga walked out into the pale dawn, her suitcase bumping at her leg as she walked down the checkered steps. Beyond the white pillars, she could see four black motorcars idling, surrounded by a platoon of soldiers on horseback.

Beside her, Maria hiccuped, tears streaming freely down her face; Olga took her hand and squeezed, fighting to keep her own cheeks dry. She wouldn't cry in front of the soldiers who lined the courtyard, their fingers tightening over the triggers of their machine guns. She wouldn't cry as they kicked her out of her home: as they rifled through her empty closets, crowing drunkenly about the day they turned Nikolashka and his family out onto the streets. She met their impassive gaze, daring them to feel shame for making her mother, stumbling toward the motorcars, weep.

No. She wouldn't give them the satisfaction of crying.

Beneath the pillars, ancient Count Beckendorff—Minister of the Palace—stood in silence, his head bowed. Too old to accompany them into exile, the count, who had overseen life at Alexander Palace for as long as Olga could remember, would be staying behind along with the other members of her family's retinue who were too old to undertake the five-day journey: Lili Dehn, whose son was too sick to travel; Jim Hercules, whose wife and children lived in Petrograd; Anna Vyrubova, still imprisoned in the Peter and Paul Fortress.

Papa and Mamma drew up to the count, who sank into a deep, stiff-kneed kneel.

"Your Imperial Highness," he said, daring the revolutionaries to stop him from giving Papa the deference he was due. "I want you to know it's been the honor of my life to serve you."

"The honor has been entirely mine, my dear friend," said Papa. He held out his hand and helped Count Beckendorff back to his feet. "You know, we've worked so hard on the gardens, I'd hate to see it all go to waste. Would you be so kind as to distribute the vegetables amongst the servants? The firewood, too."

Beckendorff's face twisted with emotion. "Of course, Your Majesty."

Papa patted him on the arm. "Good man." He sighed, casting one last, wistful look up at the palace, then turned to Mamma with a smile. "Well, my dear," he said, as though they were going to the theatre rather than into exile. "Shall we?"

The drive to the train station was short and uneventful, the silence punctuated by Mamma's sobs. Olga looked out the window, committing each tree to memory. How many times had she been driven down this road, more preoccupied with the contents of her handbag than with the beauty of the breaking dawn?

The train station was surrounded by yet more armed guards, who watched with hard eyes as Olga climbed out of the motorcar. The ground was wet beneath her feet, her heel slipping in the mud as she followed Kerensky and Kobylinski into the station.

The platform was enveloped in steam, quiet but for the sound of three hundred soldiers shifting from foot to foot, coughing and muttering, throwing the ends of cigarettes onto the tracks. Through the mist, Olga could see that the waiting train wasn't composed of graceful imperial carriages. No, this was a hulking, ominous thing cobbled together from a dozen defunct train services, mismatched *wagon-lits* and an ancient black steam engine. Ragged Red Cross flags hung limply from the carriages, and Olga thought of the villages they would pass—the people who would see the flags, never realizing that their tsar was in their midst.

As they neared the train, Kerensky and Kobylinski turned to face them.

"You will all remain in separate compartments for the duration of the journey," Kerensky began, but before he could continue Anastasia raised her hand.

"Couldn't we share? It would be so much nicer to be together with Maria. It wouldn't be a trouble at all, I don't mind having less space."

Kobylinsky's smile was surprisingly indulgent. Did he have a daughter, perhaps? "I'm afraid not, my dear," he said, "but you'll see your sisters at mealtimes."

"That won't be a problem," Papa replied. "Might we know our destination? Now that we're here, I can't imagine it would pose a security risk."

Kerensky cleared his throat, looking uncomfortable. "Yes.

Well," he muttered. "You're to be taken to Siberia. The Ural Mountains."

"Siberia." Papa nodded evenly, as though he'd anticipated the destination already. Beside him, Mamma closed her eyes, swaying on her feet, and Papa put a steadying hand around her shoulders. "Thank you, Minister."

Siberia. Olga had been expecting it, but Kerensky's confirmation hit her like a wave. Was this really happening? Had she truly left Alexander Palace for the last time? Blackness swam into her vision, dizziness threatening to overwhelm her.

"If there's nothing else," Kerensky was saying, "it's time, I think, to board."

"Thank you, Minister." Once more, Papa held out his hand; once more, Kerensky hesitated before taking it.

Olga stepped up into the train, her eyes adjusting to the dark as she walked along the corridor. Her compartment was small, and she pushed aside the drawn curtain with her finger to watch the station platform, still swarming with soldiers that filed onto the carriages on either side of the *wagon-lit* that held Olga and her family. The train would be bristling with armed guards, fifty soldiers for each member of her family. So much anger; so much mistrust. So much trouble taken over one small family. Why couldn't they simply stop the train between villages and let them disappear?

As the platform emptied, Kerensky watched the imperial carriage. Wisps of steam obscured his face as he stood, stock-still, watching the soldiers board the train. Though she would never like Kerensky, she'd grown to respect his steady presence—she suspected, too, that Kerensky had tempered the more militant amongst the revolutionaries, enabling Olga and her family to live in relative peace at the palace. She rubbed her finger on the windowpane, hoping for clarity through the glass: was it her imagination, or had he worn a new jacket to mark their departure?

He glanced at his watch, then nodded to Kobylinski. They shook hands and Kobylinski stepped on board.

Kerensky clasped his hands behind his back and looked down the platform before fixing his gaze on the carriage.

Perhaps it was a tremor in Olga's finger; perhaps it was the wind. Whatever it was, Kerensky saw the movement of the curtain.

He held Olga's gaze, his expression inscrutable.

"They can go!" he called out, and the train lurched into the weak dawn.

PART TWO

14

February 1914
Winter Palace, St. Petersburg

Lamplight flickered in the bedrooms at the Winter Palace as Olga's maid tightened the stays on her corset. Olga breathed in sharply, resting a steadying hand on her bed's iron footboard as the maid threaded her in, watching with satisfaction in the mirror as her waist shrank. Tonight might prove to be an ordeal, but at least Olga would look the part of a grand duchess.

From her seat at the vanity, Tatiana, who was having her hair seen to by Mamma's hairdresser, looked up at Olga with a smile. "Come now, it can't be as bad as all that," she said. "It's our coming-out ball!"

Olga allowed herself a grudging smile as she straightened, running a practiced hand down her front to ensure that the whalebones were resting where they were supposed to. Two weeks ago, she would have shared in Tatiana's excitement at the prospect of finally coming out in St. Petersburg—of dancing in the elegant ballroom at Anichkov Palace, its parquet floor just large enough to accommodate only the very best society families. Two weeks ago, Olga wouldn't have been able to conceal her excitement as she slipped into blush-pink silk, her spectacular dress scented by the finest *eau de toilette* Coty had ever created.

But then, two weeks ago, Pavel Voronov had been a bachelor.

Her cheeks grew hot as she thought back to the ceremony: to standing in the small church alongside her parents, watching the only man she'd ever loved pledge himself to another. He'd looked so handsome up there in his naval uniform, his voice quiet but steady as he recited his wedding vows to Anya Kleinmichel, betraying no hint of his impassioned goodbye to Olga just before Christmas.

It had been doomed from the start, Pavel had said. Once Olga had stepped on board Papa's yacht last September and saw Pavel amongst the officers accompanying them to Livadia, they'd been unable to keep their promise to stay apart. Instead, the ship had become the backdrop to a five-month romance, Olga joining Pavel on watch duty, or helping him fill in the logbook; Olga, watching for Pavel on deck through binoculars once her family reached their palace in Crimea. Dancing together beneath the stars; meeting beneath the canopy of trees to walk Livadia's footpaths.

It had been foolish of them to indulge in their feelings for one another. Foolish, when the Duma was talking about the diplomatic importance of marrying Olga off to some European monarch; foolish, when all Pavel had to offer her was a soldier's pension. It was lunacy, Pavel had told her, for them to put their hearts above their duty to Russia; above their duty to Olga's father, who had stood next to Olga in church, watching proudly as one of his aides-de-camp made a match suitable to his station. But as Pavel and his new bride walked down the aisle, his arm crooked around her hand as they walked toward the open church doors, Olga couldn't help noticing the strain in Pavel's face as his eyes met hers, just for the briefest of moments, before he walked on.

That, she supposed, was enough. It would have to be enough.

Tatiana threw a pillow onto Olga's bed, pulling her out of her reveries.

"I know it's going to be difficult for you," she said, looking at Olga through the mirror as the hairdresser finished pinning her dark tresses in place, "but we have to have a good time tonight." She turned back to the mirror, pinching color into her cheeks. "He won't thank you for pining."

Olga swallowed her disappointment. She owed it to Tatiana to be excited about tonight; she owed it to Grandmamma, who was hosting the ball, to be grateful. She owed it to the people she was going to meet to be the vibrant and elegant grand duchess they were expecting. She owed it to her parents to be dutiful and kind, a Romanov born and raised.

She owed it to herself to be more than her broken heart.

When they'd finished dressing, Olga and Tatiana went up to Mamma's drawing room. Olga's parents were standing arm in arm by the fireplace, their glasses of champagne held aloft. Dressed in cloth of gold and a king's ransom's worth of jewels, Mamma looked every inch an empress: Olga admired the sparkle of her diamond choker, worn high on her neck; the gleaming pearls, cascading down her front. A tiara glittered amidst her ash-blond curls, but her weary eyes betrayed her lack of enthusiasm at the prospect of an evening out.

Papa beamed, drawing Mamma closer to his side as he looked at Olga and Tatiana. "Look at you both," he said. "As beautiful as your mother the day I married her. Are you excited?"

Olga swallowed her thoughts of Pavel as she accepted a glass of champagne from one of the footmen. *Excited*, she reminded herself. *Elegant*. *Dutiful*. "I can hardly wait. Are we leaving soon?"

"Soon enough," Papa said. "Before we go, your mother and I have something to give you."

He picked up a small box from the table and opened it: within sat a long circlet of perfect pearls, glowing in the candlelight.

She reached out, her hands trembling as she lifted it from its velvet casing.

"You've got your shorter strand, of course," said Mamma, as Olga ran her fingers along the necklace, marveling at its luminescence. "But these are to mark your entrance into womanhood."

She turned it over to look at the platinum clasp, stamped with a small double-headed eagle—her family's crest.

"May I?" Papa held out his hand and Olga allowed him to fasten the necklace around her neck; it was cool on her throat, quickly warmed by the heat of her skin. "Russian pearls, naturally…the best quality in the world. Fabergé designed the clasp himself."

"It's magnificent," Olga said, clearing her throat. "I'm quite overcome. Thank you, Papa. Mamma."

Her parents drew close together, beaming.

Grandmamma Feodorovna was waiting for them in the entrance hall of Anichkov Palace, her black dress glittering with the refracted light of a thousand different jewels that adorned her from head to foot. She'd lived in Anichkov Palace for most of her life, taking on most of the social obligations that Mamma and Papa declined in favor of quiet nights at Alexander Palace. *Society's Empress*, Olga had heard her referred to once or twice, and not without reason.

She sank into a curtsy as Papa approached.

"Mother," he said, kissing her on the cheek. "We're so grateful to you for showing such a kindness to Olga and Tatiana."

Grandmamma turned to her granddaughters. "Nonsense," she said, with a conspiratorial thrill to her voice, "I couldn't resist. I would have had a coming-out for you when you turned eighteen, Olga, but your mother insisted—"

"Insisted that such pageantry for one daughter is wasteful when we'd have to repeat it all again a year later for the next."

Mamma leaned close to Papa, not bothering to lower her voice as they began to climb the staircase. "Once around the room, darling, and then straight home. I don't think my heart can take much more than that."

Olga exchanged a glance with Tatiana, her own heart sinking. Would their evening end before it had truly begun? She willed Papa to intercede, trying to plead without saying a word—then he patted Mamma on the hand.

"Of course, if you'd prefer an early night, we can arrange a carriage for you," he said, "but I can hardly expect my girls not to enjoy their coming-out, can I? The three of us will stay until we drop of exhaustion."

They reached the top of the stairs, and Mamma placed a wearied hand on her chest. "Whatever you think best."

Grandmamma was already working her way down the hall. "It's only one night," she said testily. "It's good for the people to see their tsar—and for the tsar to see his people. They ask for so little, really."

"All the same, I'll feel better when I'm back in my bed," said Mamma. She smiled at Papa. "But don't feel you have to leave on my account."

Grandmamma stopped as they reached the antechamber of the ballroom, the buzzing of voices audible through the closed doors. "Of course, we all want you here, Alix, but if you'd feel more comfortable there's no obligation for you to stay. After all, my guests are here for the grand duchesses." She took Olga and Tatiana each by the hand, her eyes bright. "I want you both to have fun," she said, squeezing firmly, and Olga felt a rush of affection for her glittering grandmother. "Some of Russia's most important families are here, and I want you to meet them all. You belong in this room, the both of you. You belong here, with us."

She looked up at Papa, and Olga could see something meaningful pass between them—but then Grandmamma looked up at the master of ceremonies. She nodded, the door opened, and the triumphant trill of the national anthem welcomed them into the room.

The ballroom at Anichkov Palace was warm and inviting, electric chandeliers sending yellow light up the colonnades to dance along the curved ceiling. The first time Olga had been here as a girl, she'd been awed by its size, her voice echoing off the tall windows that overlooked the snowy courtyard.

Unlike the overwhelming opulence of the ballroom at the Winter Palace, Anichkov felt modern and elegant, its simplistic white walls lending the space a monochromatic beauty. Hidden above the dancers in a gallery, an orchestra played a thrilling rendition of the imperial anthem. Enormous marble vases sat in the window alcoves, displaying sunbursts of greenhouse flowers, perfuming the air with thoughts of a Crimean summer. Olga smiled at Jim Hercules, standing at attention outside the ballroom door. Like his fellow *arap* flanking the door opposite, he wore an elaborately detailed gold-and-scarlet tunic and matching turban, his hand curled around a heavy ivory cane.

Papa beamed as he opened the ball with Olga, their first dance a stately polonaise. Looking gallant in his naval uniform, his braided epaulettes gleaming as they caught the candlelight, Papa beamed with pride, his arm strong on Olga's back as he danced her down the hall. She could hear the murmured voices of those watching—the men, resplendent in their military attire; the women, wearing ornate dresses in every conceivable color.

She moved slowly and ceremonially, one arm held aloft as she danced. Out of the corner of her eye, she caught a glimpse of Pavel, standing beside his new wife, but whereas Olga had expected to feel sadness at the sight of him, at this moment—opening the ball under the admiring gaze of those lining the dance floor—she felt triumph. *Let him watch*, she thought, lifting her chin high as Papa swept her past.

The dance came to an end and Papa lifted Olga's hand to his lips. "Beautifully done, my darling," he said; out of the corner of her eye, she could see her uncle Sandro, who'd partnered Tatiana, bowing. Papa straightened, tugging the hem of his tunic straight. "Now, I'd best leave you to livelier partners. Your coming-out is better spent in the company of young friends, rather than old fathers."

"Careful what you say—you're not ancient yet," Olga replied, and Papa chuckled, squeezing her hand one final time before leaving her to her own devices. She looked round expectantly as the orchestra struck up a waltz; however, no one stepped forward to claim her hand. Nearby, Tatiana, too, stood alone. With a sinking feeling, Olga looked down the line of couples lining up behind her. Her triumph turned to panic: she didn't know anyone—not a single young man—to dance with. She looked at the people lined along the edge of the dance floor: members of Grandmamma's set, elderly women in dark dresses and strings of pearls. They leaned toward each other, snapping their fans open, and Olga knew they were whispering about her, about her provincially dated outfit, her criminal lack of acquaintances. This was the best and brightest St. Petersburg had to offer. How was it that Olga didn't know anyone?

She thought, wildly, of Pavel—but he was already on the dance floor, holding his wife's hand.

Papa, too, seemed to have realized the problem: he looked around and nodded once, decisively. As though conjured from thin air, Dmitri Pavlovich stepped forward, his hand outstretched. Olga took it, her fingers trembling with relief; behind her, Nikolai Sablin partnered with Tatiana.

Dmitri grinned as the music struck up once more. Though he was the picture of upper-class masculinity, with his heavy-lidded eyes and slicked-back hair, his prowess as a champion equestrian and his rapid-fire wit, Olga found him too quick by half—too charming, too arrogant for his own good. Still, she enjoyed his company, if only in small doses.

"Thank you," Olga muttered. "That had all the makings of a disaster."

Dmitri laughed. "You have a very low bar for disaster, cousin," he said, sweeping her across the floor. "What must you think when the palace runs out of sweets? When you and Tatiana can't find the right dresses for a tea party?"

Olga twirled under his arm. "I would think you and dear Felix might have stolen them to play dress-up," she retorted.

"Ahh, but you forget. Felix is soon to be a married man," said Dmitri, his voice uncharacteristically tinged with regret. "His bachelor days are behind him. I'll have to find a new partner in crime."

Olga slowed. "I forgot. You'd asked for her hand first, hadn't you?"

Dmitri sighed. "I had." Olga's cousin Irina had entertained proposals from both Dmitri and Felix but ultimately accepted Felix: they were to be married here, in Anichkov Palace, in less than a week's time.

Olga glanced over Dmitri's shoulder: across the dance floor, Felix and Irina were dancing slowly, Irina laughing at something Felix had said. Though she felt for Dmitri, Olga couldn't help being pleased that Felix was engaged: perhaps marriage would settle his wild ways. With his bohemian notions and outsized fortune—Felix's family was the richest in Russia, wealthier even than Papa by far—Felix had grown up outside the bounds of propriety. Who else but Felix could walk the streets of Moscow or Paris dressed as a woman and still hold his wedding at Anichkov Palace? Who else but Felix could consort with ballerinas and fortune-tellers, and share stories of nights spent in gambling dens and Parisian nightclubs? Though Dmitri's name was always mentioned in the same breath, Felix was the undisputed ringleader of their outrageous antics. In that, if nothing else, Olga could perhaps understand Irina's preference for Felix. Dmitri was too suggestible, too willing to follow another's lead, to be taken seriously as a match.

Olga turned her attention back to Dmitri as they rotated on the dance floor, noticing his expression tighten as he caught sight of Felix and Irina. She drew closer to him, regretting her uncharitable assessment: Dmitri was suffering, that much was clear. In a few short days, he would be sitting in the palace chapel, watching his best friend marry the woman who'd rejected him. Would his heart be breaking as he raised a toast to the happy couple?

But then, Olga wasn't sure Dmitri had a heart to break.

Dmitri swept Olga around once more, giving her a different vantage point of the ballroom. Sitting on a divan beneath the gallery, Mamma was talking with Grandmamma, both looking uncharacteristically stern; Papa stood with them, his hands clasped behind his back.

"What do you suppose they're talking about?" she asked.

Dmitri followed her gaze. "Hm? Who knows? Perhaps our dear grandmamma is imparting some heartfelt advice to the empress; encouraging her to get out more, meet some new people."

"What's that supposed to mean?"

"Oh, nothing." Dmitri's hand tightened around Olga's waist. "Just that she doesn't have much patience for that mystic your mother spends all her time with."

Olga glanced up sharply, but Dmitri's expression was guileless. Had Aunt Olga been speaking out of turn? "Father Grigori? He's Mamma's priest, why shouldn't she spend time with him?"

Dmitri smirked. "He's something, all right." He jerked his head in the direction of the society matrons lining the hall. "Do you want to give them something to talk about?" He took Olga's hand in his and raised it to his chest, pulling her in with a dreamy expression to waltz cheek to cheek.

Olga couldn't help rolling her eyes. Dmitri was incorrigible. People had been predicting their engagement for years—the handsome grand duke and the beautiful grand duchess, destined to be. Both recovering from heartbreak; both leading lights for the new generation of Russian aristocracy. Could tonight be the night they finally reached an understanding? Olga looked around the ballroom—the strangers here certainly hoped so. But entertaining as Dmitri was, Olga had grown to think of him too much like an older brother.

Still, she let him have his fun. She closed her eyes, striving to adopt a similar look of romantic bliss that would send tongues wagging as far away as Moscow.

"Are they looking?" he asked.

She opened her eyes a crack to see a coterie of Grandmamma's friends watching with avid interest. "Yes."

Dmitri spun her out as the song ended but didn't break his hold on her hand; instead, he gazed at her wistfully, looking for all the world like a man in love. "You've won the hearts of everyone in this room, Grand Duchess," he said, his voice loud enough to carry. Olga fancied she could see the old women craning forward, their jewels dangling from their necks as they strived to hear. Even Irina and Felix were watching, Felix's arm wrapped around Irina's waist. "But you've won mine most of all. I hope I have reason…to hope." He lifted her hand to his lips, and Olga could almost hear the collective intake of breath in the ballroom. After an overlong kiss, Dmitri let her hand drop; with a sigh, he began to walk backward, still maintaining merry eye contact until he bumped into the foremost of the gossips.

It was all masterfully done, Olga had to concede. She could almost believe it herself, if she didn't know Dmitri as well as she did. Smirking, she turned away, only to catch sight of Pavel standing at the edge of the dance floor, watching. His wife was nowhere to be seen, and as Olga began to walk toward him he turned away, slipping out of the ballroom into the echoing corridors of the palace.

"Pavel?"

Olga came around the corner from the ballroom's antechamber, watching Pavel's retreating back as he strode down the empty hall. Olga followed, her light footsteps contrasting with the thump of his polished boots. He didn't know where he was going—he couldn't know, having not been to Anichkov Palace before. It was Anya Kleinmichel's connections which had brought him here: his wife, whose mother was one of Mamma's ladies-in-waiting; who'd once professed to be Olga's friend. She thought of Anya playing charades at Aunt Olga's home, her wide eyes, her apricot cheeks. *Quite a step up for a young naval officer,* she thought bitterly.

"Pavel," she called once again as he reached the heavy double staircase. Shame bubbled deep within her as she chased him to the landing, wishing she could walk away. "Pavel, talk to me."

But he didn't break his stride; instead, he took the stairs two at a time, his hand brushing the bannister as he descended.

"So you'll leave your new wife to get home by herself, will you?" Olga called, leaning over the railing. She was trembling at his cowardice, his insensitivity. "A fine thing to do, with the ring barely warm on her finger."

Pavel stopped. He looked back up at Olga, his cheeks flushed. "That's not fair."

Music drifted along the hallway, the faint chords of a waltz echoing ghostly off the marble. At the bottom of the stairs, Olga watched as two footmen scurried out of sight: she appreciated their show of discretion, but she was well aware that they'd only moved out of sight, not out of earshot.

She continued down to the landing; to her relief, Pavel remained where he was, his hand resting on the railing. Though the color was still high in his cheeks, he had composed himself, his expression inscrutable. It had been months since Olga had seen him up close. She'd tried her best to avoid him at his wedding, but now she could see the barest signs of strain in the crow's-feet that lined the corners of his stormy eyes; in his mouth, tightly drawn against Olga's approach.

"Well?" he said. "Don't you have enough people to talk to upstairs?"

She smiled halfheartedly. Now it came to it, she didn't want to talk to any of them—she didn't want to meet anyone new, not when Pavel was right here. She gestured to the new aiguillette adorning his shoulder, suddenly anxious. "I see congratulations are in order," she said. "When were you promoted?"

Pavel glanced down at the golden braid. "A wedding present," he replied tersely. "From your father."

Olga flinched at his tone. She held no claim on him, nor he on her. What did it matter, if the sight of her dancing with Dmitri had upset him? She looked down, playing with the silk hem of her glove. "I wanted—I wanted to congratulate you on your marriage. I didn't have the opportunity, at your wedding..."

She faltered, knowing that they both heard the false note in her voice. Pavel held her gaze, his brown eyes soft with something that resembled pity. "I never asked you to congratulate me."

She glanced down again, her pulse beating furiously beneath her new pearls. "All the same, I—I wanted to." She glanced up, meeting his eyes for only a moment. "I want you to be happy, Pavel, truly, I do. And if she makes you happy—"

She knew she'd misspoken the second she said it. Pavel exhaled, running his hand along his jawline in an old, familiar gesture that nearly broke Olga's resolve. "Don't do this, Olga," he said. "Don't make me choose between you and her."

Olga looked up, flustered. Pavel could always catch her out, could always discern her true meaning. *You have a face of glass,* he once told her, running his finger along her cheek. *It's so clear to see what's in your mind.* "I—I wasn't," she protested weakly. "I mean it. Really."

Pavel sighed. "I know you do." He stepped closer, close enough for her to tell that he was wearing the aftershave she'd given him as a present in Crimea. The realization was enough to make her hope; she lifted her hand to his chest, to feel the beat of his heart beneath his jacket.

Pavel's hands on her wrists were firm but gentle as he eased her arms down to her sides. "Go back upstairs," he said. "Go be with your guests."

"I don't want to be with them," she replied, looking up into his eyes. "I want to be here. With you."

"Please don't put me in this position," Pavel murmured. "You'll always have my friendship, Olga—but I can't give you anything more than that."

She could feel the evening unraveling as he pressed a kiss to her forehead: she closed her eyes, wishing she could stop the tears that were falling slowly, traitorously, down her cheeks.

"What will I do without you?" she whispered.

He stepped back. With slow, painful formality, he bowed, taking her hand in his. "You are the Grand Duchess Olga Nikolaevna," he said quietly. His eyes were downcast, but his fingers were tight around hers. "First daughter of Tsar Nicholas II." He looked up, his smile cracking at the corners. "Do you really think that heartbreak will be the end of you?"

He released her hand, holding her gaze a moment longer; apology—regret—in his eyes. He sighed once more, then bowed, deeply, before walking back up the stairs.

Heartbreak... Olga had been fooling herself to think that her time with Pavel could have ended in any other way but heartbreak. She wiped her cheeks with the pads of her fingers, hoping she'd not made too much of a mess of her rouge. Pavel was right. She could no longer hold on to what they'd had.

She looked up at the sound of footsteps: Mamma was at the top of the staircase, Anna Vyrubova beside her. She came slowly down to the landing, her lined face alert with concern.

"Are you well, darling?"

"Of course," said Olga. She flipped open her fan, hoping the cool air would bring down any lingering redness in her eyes.

Mamma patted her arm. "Good," she said. "I'm going home, you know how my heart—" She broke off, examining Olga closely. "Are you sure you wouldn't like to come home with me? Tatiana can make your excuses. We could go straight back to Tsarskoe Selo if you like."

Olga looked up the stairs, toward the sound of the party. Of course, Mamma would prefer for Olga to go home with her—back to their home in the country, back to Bibles and priests. Back to comfort; back to safety.

She thought of Grandmamma's welcome, echoing in her mind: *You belong here.*

"No," she replied, her smile coming more easily now. "I'd rather stay. Good night, Mamma."

Mamma sighed without anger as she resumed walking, leaning on Anna Vyrubova for support. "Only if you're certain. Good night, darling."

Olga made her way up the stairs, knowing that she'd been gone too long, wasting precious time mourning what could never be. From the ballroom, she could hear voices; the orchestra had taken a break, and laughter trilled down the hall.

You belong here.

There, in that ballroom, was the life she was destined to lead—the life of a grand duchess. Her life, if she had the courage to reach out and take it. She'd spent too long living on the margins of her parents' expectations: on the margins of her brother's illness, and on the margins of her own comfort. Her life was here, in the glittering fray. She walked toward the ballroom, her steps coming surer, steadier. She would not lose her heart to an officer again—her heart was destined for Russia, for love and for duty, both. Never again would she prize one over the other.

15

August 1917
Siberia

The wide, shallow expanse of the Tura River churned beneath the iron hull of the *Rus*, the muddy water swallowing what weak light succeeded in breaking through the low cover of clouds. As she stared down into the silt, Olga's mind turned, morosely, to the River Lethe: were they passing through those forgetful waters even now, her family disappearing further and further from memory with each rotation of the *Rus's* propellor? This morning, they'd arrived in Tyumen after three long, hot days on board the Red Cross train, the windows sealed against the driving dust of the West Siberian Plain. Though Olga had expected Tyumen, the oldest city in Siberia, to be their final destination they were escorted onto the *Rus* for another two days' travel, and as they moved farther north and west up the snaking river, the guards seemed to breathe a sigh of relief, even allowing Papa to pace the ship's deck unimpeded: they knew, as well as Olga did, that any would-be rescuers would have made their way to Crimea, expecting the imperial family to be spirited away to some foreign refuge. They knew, with a keen sense of irony that even Olga could share, that Siberia was where Russia sent those it preferred to forget.

Along the flat riverbanks, a summer's worth of drought had starved the fields of the little color that might have made the journey scenic: dust-covered *muzjiks* worked the brown lands, heads bowed over the handles of their sickles. Close to shore, fishermen cast their nets into the dark water, looking up at the steamship belching black exhaust. Olga stared back, wondering whether they were aware of the ship's curious cargo. What would they say, if they knew the slight figure pacing the deck was the Tsar of All Russia? Would they fall to their knees, as the villagers of Yaroslavl had done four years earlier, awed at the sight of their *Batiushka*—their Little Father? Or would they spit, offended that Nicholas the Bloody would dare to travel along their forgotten shores?

A cluster of tidy wooden houses came into view, arrayed atop the low ridge of a grassy dune, their shuttered windows adorned with flowers. Below, a worn footpath edged the riverbank, where a handful of shallow fishing vessels had been pulled up and out of the lapping water. Though there were no signs of villagers the town looked cared-for: cows lowed in nearby fields, and the comforting scent of wood fires drifted across the water. At the far end of the village, a bone-white church presided over the landscarpe, incongruously large next to the wooden houses. In any other place the church would have looked quaint, but here amidst the scattered single-story dwellings it loomed, spectrally, against the gathering clouds.

A movement between the houses caught Olga's eye: there, beside a low-slung building, a woman tugged at the hand of her small child. Her colorful dress and headscarf marked her as a peasant—Olga recognized the style from portraits that hung in the halls of the Catherine Palace, portraits that Papa had walked past with a gleam to his eye. *The real Russia*, he'd say quietly, and as a child Olga hadn't understood what he meant. Even now, the traditional Russian dress looked foreign to her, more accustomed as she was to the corsets and waistcoats of

European fashion. The woman glanced at the steamship and stepped behind the refuge of the wooden buildings, the village motionless once more.

"Pokrovskoe." Unbeknownst to Olga, Mamma had joined her on deck—she gripped the railing with one hand, the wooden edges of a cross peeking out from her closed palm as she stared at the town where Father Grigori had lived.

Olga's heart lurched; behind her, Papa stopped his ceaseless pacing. As one, they searched the shoreline, looking for hints that Father Grigori had left a mark on his hometown. Only one two-story house peeked over the rooftops, its window-frames painted white: Father Grigori's, perhaps? So many had traveled to Pokrovskoe to see him over the years, well-wishers and admirers, people seeking enlightenment, wisdom, comfort. In a village this small where else would they stay, other than with him and his family: his quiet wife, his three dutiful children? Olga looked away, regretting that she'd never asked him about his Siberian home.

"He told me we would visit Pokrovskoe one day," said Mamma quietly, as the *Rus* smoothly drifted past the silent village. "I wonder whether he knew it would be like this."

Olga didn't answer as the *Rus* continued onward, the gentle forgetting of the river made more painful by the memory of Father Grigori's ghost.

The onion-topped tower of the Sophia-Uspensky Cathedral came into view hours later, the city of Tobolsk revealing itself as they inched around the bend in the river. Dominated by an imposing stone kremlin that sprawled along the rise of a rocky hill, the city itself was small, its modest log houses gathering at the base of the hill like supplicants at the skirt of a saint.

Olga squinted into the drizzling mist that had dogged them the last thirty *versts* of their journey. Along the shore, loggers fished felled trees from the riverbank, strapping them by the dozen onto the backs of horse-drawn wagons. A regiment of soldiers flanked the harbor, motorcars and lorries lingering at the ready. It seemed that was all the welcome they were going to receive from Tobolsk: no open-armed town elders—no angry villagers either.

But there were church spires. That's what Olga noticed as they made their way off the steamship: tall steeples that pierced the sky, their wrought iron crosses knocked lopsided by wind or winter's snow. The sight of them was comforting as they pulled away from the gray harbor, to know that God looked to the inhabitants of Tobolsk as fondly as He did the residents of Petrograd.

Their motorcar rattled along the streets, lurching heavily as it hit grooves in the softening ground. Mud seeped from the duckboards that lined the streets, running in rivulets beneath the uneasy foundations of the houses. Prosperous until the Trans-Siberian railway rendered it obsolete, Tobolsk had faded into insignificance and the shift in its fortunes showed. The wooden houses looked unkempt, the white stone of the beautiful cathedral dingy. Huddled against the rain, a man in rags lifted a hand in supplication, hoping for a kopeck from a passerby. Olga recalled a story Pierre Gilliard had once told her about Potemkin Villages, pasteboard façades intended to conceal the sight of poverty from Catherine the Great. She recalled the towns they'd passed during the tercentenary: scrubbed stone and freshly painted railings, healthy peasants waving their enthusiastic approval of the tsar and his family. Was this what Russia truly looked like: cloud-covered and muddy, grave faces and deprivation?

"Remember, children," said Papa, watching out the window as they wheeled beneath the shadow of the kremlin, "this is a new life for us, but it is also a new opportunity. We will make the most of this."

"God will provide," Mamma muttered, her eyes darting as she took in the town's churches.

Their new house was an austere white building with little in the way of ornamentation beyond a small gingerbread trellis over the entrance. Originally the home of the city's governor, the mansion—newly christened Freedom House by the soldiers who had accompanied Olga's family from the *Rus*—was imposing, with square windows and a modest balcony: nothing like Livadia or Alexander Palace. Olga supposed they had Kerensky to thank for the fact that it was more than a hovel: Kerensky, their jailor and protector, too far away to help now. Too far to intervene, should circumstances prove problematic.

Their first afternoon at Freedom House was chaotic. Alexei and Anastasia raced through the rooms piled with tapestries and trunks as soldiers penned in the hard-packed street around the building with a high wooden fence. The second floor of the mansion was earmarked for Olga and her family; the first was occupied by a bristling contingent of soldiers who had accompanied them from Petrograd, while the family's servants and retainers took over the house across the road. Olga's parents had a modest bedroom, and Alexei a suite across the hall—Olga and her sisters, meanwhile, were housed in a large corner bedroom, their iron cots shipped and set up, camp style, in the four corners of the room.

Anastasia was already starting to make her mark on the space by the time Olga had finished exploring the rest of the house, having claimed the cot closest to the window. Her traveling trunk open, Anastasia was spilling its contents out on the bed: photographs and icons and trinkets, letters from friends and hair ribbons.

"I hope you don't mind," she said, unfolding a hastily rolled shawl. She stepped up on the bed, her dusty shoes leaving a print on the mattress as she pinned the shawl above her headboard. "You know I prefer being near a window. Isn't this exciting, sleeping all together like this? We'll stay up into the night, talking, playing cards..."

"You might regret being close to the window when it's thirty degrees below freezing, *Shvybzik*," Olga replied as she lifted her valise onto the bed closest to the iron brazier.

Anastasia turned, her smile caught behind her long curtain of hair. "When that happens. I'll crawl in with you," she said, "and when the stars are bright, you can crawl in with me and we'll watch them together. Deal?"

Tatiana and Maria walked in, their suitcases banging against their shins as Maria erupted in protest at Anastasia's perfunctory claiming of the best bed. "Deal," Olga replied as she opened the heavy clasps of her valise.

Within, an ivory chess piece sat nestled in the folds of a silk handkerchief; she took it out, her breath catching in her throat as she set it carefully on her bedside table. She folded the handkerchief and turned to face the brazier, determined not to let her sisters see her cry. She inhaled heavily, the ghost of a long-ago conversation echoing in her head. Tobolsk was the price she'd paid for the decisions she'd made: the decisions they'd all made under the assumptions that the life they'd lived—their friendships, their faith—was inviolable. Built on stone, rather than sand.

"Olga?" Tatiana sidled over, letting the argument between Maria and Anastasia mask their conversation. "Are you alright?"

Olga hastily wiped her cheeks. "Of course," she replied. "I just needed a moment. That's all."

"Look!" Maria's voice cut Tatiana's reply short. "Come to the window!"

Olga looked out onto a flat street. From the front of the house, they could hear the sound of steady hammering as the guards completed the fence, cigarette smoke marring the fresh scent of rain on grass. Directly below, soldiers milled on the lawn, their guns held loosely as they watched the road.

It was clear to Olga that word of her family's arrival had spread through Tobolsk. On the wooden boardwalk opposite, a crowd had begun to gather: old men and their wives, hats in hand as they stared up at the windows of the house.

Anastasia's voice was hushed as she clutched the windowsill. "Do we wave?"

Olga's heart swelled at the sight of the silent vigil. "No," she said. It was a peaceful gathering, but a dangerous one. What if the soldiers turned violent? There were no likely rescuers out there, not a single young face amongst the crowd. Indeed, one white-haired gentleman was looking at the house with an expression of such fervor on his lined face that Olga was sure he would sink to his knees, if only his creaking legs would allow him to get back up. It was a gathering of the old guard, watching their way of life fading into the past. "Best to leave them be."

She turned back to face the room, despair and hope fighting for prominence in her breast. They were far from home, far from the life they'd known—but they'd not been forgotten. Not yet.

16

May 1914
Alexander Palace, Tsarskoe Selo

Olga's dress was starched stiff, her corset pinching her beneath the arms as she squinted into the sudden burst of sunlight that flooded the airy expanse of the Maple Room. From across the coffee table, laden with pink cabbage-roses that echoed the plaster garden dancing along the vaulted ceiling, she could just about make out the silhouettes of the crown prince and princess of Romania; were they smirking, she wondered, at the sight of their prospective daughter-in-law waiting for the sun to retreat once more behind a cloud; or were they charmed by her moment of unscripted discomfort?

Not that there was much unscripted about today, nor anything to hint at discomfort in the court of Nicholas II. The week-long Romanian visit had been scheduled down to the minute, a long list of events nearly as rigorous as last year's tercentenary. Olga's role was scripted, too, insofar as the Duma ministers could manage it. After all, why should they care whether Olga might prefer to meet her prospective in-laws over a quiet family dinner? Why should it matter to them that she would rather experience the summer-sweet feeling of falling in love?

No. To the Duma ministers, standing together at the far

end of the room in a failed attempt at inconspicuousness, the prospect of Olga's marriage to Prince Carol of Romania was a matter of political expediency. Nothing, not the vol-au-vents nor the guest lists for a week's worth of balls and the parades through the capital, could be left to chance. Even the palace's Maple Room, with its nouveau curves and liquid moldings, its potted palms and dusty pink walls, had been chosen deliberately as the site of their first meeting—to impress the Romanians with their sophisticated style, no doubt, thought Olga. What message would it send to the crown prince and princess to see Mamma and Papa's private chambers, with their crowded icons and chintz fabrics?

She shifted along the couch cushions out of the glare, surreptitiously glancing at the young man standing across the room, his jacket so studded with medals he looked as though he might tip over with the weight of them. If Prince Carol had been overawed by the welcome from the Russian court, he'd done a good job of hiding it. He'd hardly batted an eye as Papa made a gracious little speech; he'd bent to kiss Olga's hand as if she was any young woman, and he was any young suitor. To Olga, the effect was irksome and alluring, all at once. Balancing a teacup and saucer in one hand, he smiled at something Mamma said—then, as if he could feel her staring, he met Olga's gaze.

Olga turned her attention back to Carol's parents. "Tell me," she said, "How is Bucharest this time of year?"

Crown Princess Marie smiled patiently. "Bucharest is a delight in spring." She paused as if waiting for Olga to respond; then, realizing nothing was forthcoming, turned to address Olga's sister Maria. "I hear you're something of an artist, my dear. What do you like to paint?"

Olga could feel her cheeks burning. She'd spent the small hours of the morning torn between hope she might fall in love with Carol and dread of leaving her sisters behind. Her stomach twisted with the prospect of marrying into a foreign court.

Who, if not her, would temper Anastasia's tendency toward self-aggrandizement? Who would coax Maria out of her shell?

Across the room, Papa rested his hand companionably on Alexei's shoulder. Like Papa and Carol, Alexei was dressed in a military tunic, his thin frame bolstered by narrow epaulettes. Clearly disinterested in what Carol was saying, Alexei rocked back on his heels, glancing listlessly up at the ceiling. Without turning his attention from Carol, Papa tightened his grip on Alexei and eased him back down with a resounding thump.

She thought of sailing to Romania, where she'd only be able to correspond with her sisters by letters—worse, of receiving word of Alexei's attacks by telegram. Her heart plummeted at the prospect of hearing about her brother's death secondhand, not being there for a proper goodbye. Did love have to come at the expense of family? Was it a trade Olga was willing to make?

Papa released his hold on Alexei, nodding politely as he lit a cigarette. His expression was inscrutable as he responded: was he taking the measure of Carol as a son-in-law, or as a political ally? Olga couldn't tell: her father had the ability to conceal his thoughts as easily as closing a book.

Still, it wasn't Papa's opinion that mattered—he'd made that very clear.

"You might like him," Papa had said earlier as he accompanied Olga on a morning stroll through Alexander Park. Thin sunlight dappled the oak leaves, casting the pea-gravel walkway into light and shadow. From beyond the palace, Olga could hear the sounds of Tsarskoe Selo waking up: motorcars backfiring on the street; horses' hooves, ringing brightly on the cobblestones. Papa tapped ash from the end of his cigarette. "From what I understand, he's considered quite a *catch*."

Olga smirked at her father's attempt at camaraderie. "Maybe in Romania," she replied. "Whether he holds a candle to an honest Russian man remains to be seen."

Papa fitted the cigarette between his lips, making a noncommittal sort of grunt in the back of his throat. "Well, I don't know about that, but the Duma seemed quite set on arranging a meeting… And I must admit, I can see why. Romania would be a formidable ally, in the coming years." He trailed off, letting Olga set the pace of their stroll. "You are comfortable, aren't you? Meeting this man? Getting to know him?"

"Getting to know him, yes," Olga replied, but Papa turned, his eyebrows raised in a silent interrogation of her hesitant tone. "I know it sounds petty, but—Romania? Why would I want to be there when everything in the world is here?"

Papa nodded. "I would advise you not to set your views in stone just yet. Your mother joined a foreign court, as did your grandmother. They both fell in love with their adopted country; you might, too."

They continued on down the path, Olga playing with her strand of pearls as she mulled over Papa's words. Within the palace, she watched curtains being drawn back in the family's quarters. Mamma would be awake now, sorting through correspondences from her ladies-in-waiting. "How did you do it?" she asked suddenly. "When you met Mamma? What did you talk about?"

Beneath his chestnut beard, Papa's lips tugged upwards in a smile. "The first time I saw her, I swear my heart began to beat faster," he said. "We talked about all the sorts of things young people do, I suppose. Our lives. Our families and friends. She was…utterly enchanting." He paused; farther down the garden path, Olga watched a gardener look up from his work in surprise at the approach of the tsar, then scuttle quietly out of the way.

"And you knew you'd marry her? After that first meeting?"

Papa squinted up at the palace windows, the morning sun smoothing the creases from his face. "I knew there was no other woman on earth who would make me as happy as her," he replied, his voice full of quiet pride. He stared at the palace a moment longer before turning his attention back to Olga. "Your happiness is more important to me than anything else, my dear. When you marry, let it be for love. These—these pageants, this government—" he waved his hand at the palace with impatience "—they don't have your best interests at heart. But I do. If you do fall in love with him, no one will be happier than I. But if your heart doesn't beat faster at the sight of this young man, you mustn't feel obliged to pretend that it does."

"How gallant," said Olga lightly, but she was touched all the same.

"I mean it," Papa had insisted, tucking Olga's hand into the crook of his arm as they resumed their morning wander. "God blessed your mother and me with a happy marriage. He will bless you as well."

Candlelight flickered along the round dining tables in the Semi-Circular Hall. The room was buzzing with excitement at the prospect of a rare evening's entertainment in Tsarskoe Selo. To celebrate the final night of Prince Carol's visit, Papa had invited Antonina Nezhdanova, Russia's leading soprano, to the Alexander Palace to perform for their guests. Partway down the table, Maria and Anastasia were telling anyone who'd listen that they'd overheard her warming up in the White Hall: "She's wearing *pearls*!" Anastasia was saying, self-importantly. At the far end of the room, members of the Duma sat clustered together, casting hopeful glances in Olga's direction; beneath the glittering chandelier, Grandmamma conversed jovially with the crown prince and princess over the tail end of their dessert.

At Olga's table, Prince Carol held out two clenched fists. Alexei, his wan face solemn with concentration, hovered his fingers over one, then the other, before decisively tapping the back of Carol's left palm.

Carol opened his fingers. There, sitting in his hand, was a miniature soldier dressed in the gray serge and peaked cap of a Romanian infantryman.

"I won!" Alexei cried.

Carol handed him the soldier. "For you to remember me by," he said, grinning as he drained the last of his riesling.

Olga watched them, smiling at Carol's generosity. Although she'd spent the last week escorting him around St. Petersburg—to the ballet and balls and museums; through the manicured gardens of Alexander Park and on parade with Olga's own Hussar regiment—she still hadn't entirely made up her mind about the Romanian prince. The government would be eager for news of an alliance; whether Olga would be ready to give it was another matter.

She knew what Papa would ask at the end of the night: Did Carol make her heart beat faster? To Olga the answer wasn't quite so simple. She'd come to admire Carol's cleverness and wit, but she disapproved of the dismissive tone he took around the palace servants; and though she supposed him decent-looking enough, he did have an unsettling tendency to stare. She looked at Carol, waiting for the telltale quickening in her breast—but was it nerves that made her stomach drop as she watched him drain another glass of wine? Were Carol to ask for her hand, Olga wasn't sure what her answer would be.

From the center of the table came a commotion as Papa set down his napkin and stood. Like a ripple in water, the rest of the guests followed suit, starting with the crown prince and princess. Papa offered Mamma his arm and together they walked into the adjoining Portrait Hall, where the chairs had been lined up in preparation for the concert. Crown Prince Ferdinand, too, offered his arm to his wife but she refused it, a slight curl to her lips as she resumed her conversation with Grandmamma.

There, too, was another cause for concern: the lovelessness between Carol's parents was palpable. An air of indifference colored their every interaction, hanging between them like a miasma: only now, talking to the dowager empress, Crown Princess Marie seemed to come to life, animated without the ditchwater dullness of her husband. Ferdinand also seemed livelier as he followed Mamma and Papa, Alexei catching up to show him the toy soldier. Was this the sort of marriage Carol would expect from his wife—a union of expediency rather than affection?

Carol rounded the table. "Would you care for some fresh air before the concert?"

Olga took his arm. "The balcony, perhaps," she replied, leading him against the current of people gravitating toward the concert hall. Walking with Dmitri Pavlovich, Tatiana winked as she passed in the opposite direction. "We'll be able to hear if Madame Nezhdanova begins without us."

They walked out onto the long terrace that lined the Semi-Circular Hall, the crisp evening air a welcome change from the stuffiness of the dining room. Beyond the terrace loomed the inky blackness of Alexander Park, leaves rustling gold in the light of the palace.

Carol leaned against the railing, loosening the knot of his tie. "Cigarette?" he offered, but Olga declined. He shrugged and lit one for himself, breathing deeply in the dark. "It's so quiet, out here in the countryside," he said. "So...quaint. Why live here when you've got St. Petersburg and all its glories only fifteen miles away?"

Olga shrugged, bristling at Carol's portrayal of Alexander Palace as *quaint*. "My parents prefer it," she replied. "It's peaceful here. Away from the strains of the city. Away from intrigue."

Carol chuckled; in the darkness, she could hear a metallic scrape as he opened the lid of a flask. "I imagine I'd feel the same way, given 1905." He turned to face the palace once more, his face illuminated by the light from the windows as he gave a theatrical shiver. "Bloody Sunday. A thousand dead at the gates to the Winter Palace... I'd be happier in the country too. Although," he grinned roguishly, "there are benefits to city living. Give me a quick exit to Lipscani Street any day of the week. Oh, are you cold?"

He took off his dinner jacket and draped it over Olga's shoulders, then returned to his vigil at the terrace railing. Olga pulled the lapels close around her neck, breathing in the spiced scent of his cologne. It was comments like that which made Carol so difficult to read: his throwaway observation about the most tragic chapter in Papa's reign, followed by concern for Olga's comfort.

"What's it like?" she asked, leaning beside him on the railing. "Bucharest?"

Carol released a breath of smoke as he handed her the flask. "You'll see it for yourself before too long," he said. He smiled down at her and adjusted his footing, his arm coming to rest against hers.

Olga's heart skipped then, properly. Was this why he'd brought her out here—to ask her to come back to Romania? From within the Portrait Hall, she could hear the swell of orchestral music and the first high, clear note of the soprano. She lifted the flask, letting the heat of an unfamiliar liquor burn her throat. "You want me to come to Romania?"

Carol's smile tightened. "Well, my parents have arranged for a reciprocal visit. It's only proper, given their hopes."

Olga nodded, her heart sinking back into her chest. His parents. Of course. "And what are your hopes?" she asked, handing him back the flask.

He jerked his head toward the window. "They've made their wishes fairly clear, wouldn't you say? I'm surprised I don't see my mother watching us through the glass. Your mother, on the other hand… Would she even notice if you got engaged tonight?"

"I beg your pardon?"

Carol shrugged. "It's just that she's got her hands awfully full with that brother of yours." He took another swig from his flask before holding it out again.

Olga hesitated before accepting it; her head was swimming enough as it was. "I suppose so, but what mother doesn't?" she answered carefully.

Carol snorted. "Yours more than most." He inhaled, the cigarette's ember inching closer to his lips. "I hope you understand why I won't be proposing to you. Tonight, or any other night. Not with the condition your brother is in."

Olga nearly dropped the flask. Within the palace, she could hear the strains of Antonina Nezhdanova, her voice soaring in triumph atop a burgeoning crest of strings. "I don't know what you mean," she stammered.

"Of course, you do," he replied. "You think we didn't know about the tsarevich? It's quite common knowledge." He threw the stub of the cigarette behind his shoulder and Olga watched it plummet into the grass. "I think we'd had our hopes it wasn't true, but I'm afraid it's all too obvious what's ailing him. You're not the only royal family to have tainted bloodlines." Carol rested comfortably against the railing, as though he was discussing a weather phenomenon, rather than Olga's family. "As I'm sure you can appreciate, I won't bring something like that into my lineage. My mother spoke to our physician before we came, and he confirmed that such diseases run through the wife." He smiled, and patted Olga on the hand. "Like the original sin. So, you see, there can be no union between us. But I'm happy to go through the niceties, show our parents we're really considering this. You're a nice girl, all things considered. It's nothing personal."

He tucked his flask back into his pocket; Olga, thunderstruck, clutched the terrace railing, afraid her trembling knees would give her away. *Look at your decision through love*, Papa had advised, *and the politics will follow.* She'd never, not once, fathomed that her decision would be made for her by the inevitability of blood. If Carol knew about Alexei's condition, what else was being said about her family by the other crowned heads of Europe?

Carol straightened, cracking his knuckles. "Listen to us, out here missing the show. Shall we?"

He offered her his arm; automatically, Olga took it. Together, they walked into the Portrait Hall, Olga too shocked, still, to hear the audience's applause as the soloist took a sweeping bow.

17

November 1917
Freedom House, Tobolsk

Despite what she'd been led to believe about Siberian winters, Olga found Tobolsk to be surprisingly bearable in the waning days of the year. Though several layers of sweaters were a necessity by the end of October, it was still warm enough to sit on the balcony and look out at the town gardens across the road, where the oak trees stubbornly held to their browning leaves and horseback riders, wearing their lightest furs, rode sedately along the grass.

Without the usual complement of housemaids to keep on top of cleaning, the sunlight that streamed through Freedom House's picture windows caught on streaks in the unwashed glass. Dust, tracked inside from the hemmed-in courtyard, settled into the crevices of every room, clouding up when they sank into cushions and fading the blankets and carpets they'd shipped in from Alexander Palace, fine materials that ought to have glimmered in the fading season's sun.

Still, Olga was grateful that the shipment of furniture from Tsarskoe Selo had reached them in the first place: she'd doubted, upon their initial arrival, that anything would. The pieces—sofas and tapestries, Mamma's silver tea service and Papa's books—

felt reassuring, even set amidst the unfamiliar surroundings. As a means of entertainment, Mamma had allowed Anastasia and Maria to oversee the dispersal of furniture throughout the house, and the result was delightfully bizarre. Pieces that had no business being together had been arranged cheek-by-jowl, empire-style lamps set atop art nouveau desks; Chinese folding screens positioned behind English chintz.

News came slowly to Tobolsk, when it come at all—in week-old newspapers and ripped-open letters that hinted at further correspondence deemed too sensitive to pass on to Olga and her family. Still, clues slipped through, in the form of gossip from members of the household who were allowed to run errands in town, as well as from a few of the more candid guards: war still raged on Russia's borders; Lenin, leader of the Bolshevik radicals, was trying to stir up discontent with the Provisional Government. A shipment of wine had arrived with the furniture from Alexander Palace, and it had nearly started a riot amongst the soldiers—Pankratov, the commissar in charge of Freedom House, had tipped the casks into the river rather than start trouble with the local soldiers' soviet.

In the absence of news, Olga still had prayer—that, at least, was a certainty. Since arriving in Tobolsk her family had been given regular services at the small field chapel they'd set up in one of Freedom House's reception rooms, and while the services themselves were a spiritual comfort, they lacked something in the way of ceremony. In a space built for business rather than religion, the priest's voice sounded flatter, more earthbound, than it would have surrounded by the solemn beauty of a house of God.

But today, Pankratov had arranged for them to attend a private Mass at the nearby Church of the Annunciation. Though the church was only a stone's throw from Freedom House across the town gardens, the change of scenery was enough to make Olga weep: the comforting glow of icons illuminated by candlelight, arrayed in a thousand different hues of gold; the intoxicating scent of incense, permanently laced in the air. Amidst God's familiar trappings, Tobolsk felt almost friendly, and as she stepped back out into the chilly sunlight after the service, the day felt greener, warmer, than when she'd gone in. Even the soldiers lining the route back to Freedom House seemed less intimidating than before. As she walked through the town gardens with Alexei, she chanced smiling at the redheaded guard who trailed their footsteps.

"Isn't this lovely?" She breathed in the sweet scent of autumn leaves, the collar of her fox-fur coat brushing her chin as she listened to Maria and Anastasia, racing down the footpath; Tatiana, laughing at some comment Pierre Gilliard had made. A few paces ahead, Mamma discussed the service with Papa as he pushed her chair, its wheels creaking on the pavement. Beyond the distant rooftop of Freedom House she could see the gold-topped spires of the kremlin, gleaming in the sunlight. "Who would have thought a walk could make me so happy?"

Alexei grinned. "In that case, tell *Shvybzik* to slow down," he said. "The slower we walk, the more time we'll have to savor it."

Olga sighed, noting, with some surprise, that Alexei's legs had grown long enough to match her stride. "If only we could keep this little park," she said. "I think I could stand the house if we were allowed to walk here every day."

"I wonder whether they'd let us." Alexei glanced at the soldiers; though most were stationed far enough off the path to give the family some privacy, they still carried rifles. Beyond the confines of the garden, which had been closed off for Olga's family, couples walked along the duckboard sidewalks: they winked in and out of sight beyond the trees, little figures coming home from their own church services. "All I know is that it would give me something else to do other than split wood. I'm sick of playing the woodsman."

"I'd split all the wood in Siberia if it will make Papa happy."

She paused, watching as Papa stopped to say something to Pankratov. Pankratov, unarmed though flanked by two of his officers, tilted his head in a sort of acquiescence, and Olga guessed that Papa was thanking him for the outing. "He's grown so quiet lately."

Alexei shrugged. "What is there for him to say? It's not like he's got much to occupy his time. Did you know he's started talking to the guards?"

"Really?" Olga squinted into the sunlight as one of the soldiers called out, warning Maria to stay on the path. "What about?"

Alexei shrugged. "The war; where they served before coming to Tobolsk. He's going down to play cards with them after dinner tonight."

"And Pankratov doesn't mind?"

"I'm not sure he knows," Alexei replied. "But I can't imagine he'd care. It's their job to keep an eye on Papa…playing cards with him would make it easier, I suppose."

"I suppose so." Papa always had been better at connecting with people one-on-one. Perhaps in time his efforts might lead to further privileges for the family, like walks through Tobolsk's city center, an evening at the opera. "Have you spoken to him much? Pankratov?"

"A little," Alexei replied. "He sometimes visits with Papa while we're in the yard." He leaned close, his sleeve brushing against hers. "He's a criminal, did you know?"

Olga scoffed. Short little Pankratov, with his milk-bottle glasses and puppy fat? "A bookkeeper for criminals, perhaps."

"No, it's true," Alexei insisted in a whisper. "He was a member of *Narodnaya Volya*—the radicals that assassinated Great-Grandfather. He killed a gendarme in Kiev in some argument about a woman. He's dangerous, Olga."

Olga looked up. Pankratov had fallen a few steps behind Mamma and Papa, his hands clasped behind his back. But for his military attire, he could have been one of Papa's courtiers—a local official, taking Papa on a tour of some far-flung corner of his empire. "He seems fairly harmless now," she replied. "What does Papa say about it all?"

"He says we need to be careful. With Pankratov and anyone else who's gone over to the revolutionaries."

Olga nodded, picturing Papa descending into the guards' room on the first floor of Freedom House, a bottle of cognac in hand to help loosen their lips. Perhaps one or two might divulge their growing dissatisfaction with the new regime; perhaps Papa could convince them that he wasn't the bogeyman they'd imagined him to be.

We might win them over, she thought. *One or two—that would be enough.*

They'd nearly reached the end of the park and Olga slowed her steps. Across the street, the soldiers on guard at Freedom House had opened the barricade and Olga could see the house beyond: the dark vestibule, the unlit windows. The small balcony; the short, dusty courtyard. Her sisters had already passed through the park's kissing gate, but Olga's heart sank at the prospect of returning to endless letter-writing and needlepoint. She turned, prepared to ask Pankratov whether they could linger a little while longer in the green, but then from the far end of the garden, church bells began to ring from the tall tower of the Church of the Annunciation: a steady, sonorous peal.

Alexei frowned. "What are they ringing for? The service is over."

As if in response, bells began to ring from a neighboring church, the sudden explosion of noise sending a flock of pigeons scattering into the sky. Within seconds, some far-flung spire across town began to peal, too; then a fourth struck up a high, discordant clanging.

Olga looked up, midstep, as another church joined the chorus of bells, the sound resonating in her chest as warm and joyful as a song. She glanced around: through the thin line of trees that marked the edge of the garden, the people who had been strolling along the sidewalks had stopped walking. They silently turned toward the park, their caps doffed as they watched Olga's family.

Olga blinked back tears. "They're ringing for us," she said.

Papa didn't acknowledge them directly—that would have been too obvious, Olga knew, too clear a statement for Pankratov to ignore. Slowly, tentatively, he touched the brim of his cap with his thumb as if adjusting it, fingers stiff in a silent salute.

At Papa's movement, the soldiers began to close in, and Olga's heart quickened. Ahead, Maria, Tatiana and Anastasia were clustered together in the middle of the road, glancing back uncertainly at Mamma and Papa. The soldiers moved closer, Pankratov bringing up the rear with a face like thunder, and Olga saw the quiet little man for what he was: criminal. Dangerous. She froze, her elation dissolving into fear. How could the town be so obvious in its support? In her mind's eye, she watched the privileges they might have been given slip through her fingers as the guards moved closer still, circling the family—

Suddenly, a soldier shot out of Freedom House. He sprinted toward Olga and Alexei, a telegram in hand.

"What is it? What's happened?"

The redheaded soldier behind Olga stepped forward as the messenger darted past, glancing nervously at the street. He closed his hand over Alexei's upper arm.

"Get inside," he said, and chivvied Alexei and Olga past the fence.

In the courtyard, soldiers lined the short stretch of ground up to the vestibule, shoulder to shoulder; they hurried Olga and Alexei along as Papa wheeled Mamma toward the steps.

"I don't understand," Papa was saying, as two soldiers lifted Mamma's wheelchair up the stairs; behind him, Pankratov had fallen behind to talk to two of his lieutenants. "What's happened? What's going on? The church bells—"

"It's nothing to do with the church bells," said the closest officer. "Inside, Colonel, if you please."

They led the family into the upstairs ballroom, where armed soldiers stood sentinel at each of the windows. Still wearing their furs, Olga and her sister sank onto the closest sofa; their morning teacups were still on the coffee table where they'd left them before church, brown rings staining the china.

"What's happening?" Papa repeated, resting his hand on Mamma's shoulder. "What's going on?"

No one responded; for several moments, the only noise Olga heard was the thud of the grandfather clock; the sound of footsteps and shouts from below. Soon, Pankratov entered, holding a telegram.

"I apologize for the confusion, Colonel," he began. He glanced down at the telegram, adjusting his wire-rimmed spectacles. "I'm afraid this will come as a shock. We just received word that the Bolshevik Party, operating under the leadership of Vladimir Lenin, has seized power in the capital. Red Guards have stormed the Winter Palace and overthrown the Provisional Government. They've elected Lenin as Chairman of the Sovnarkom and Leon Trotsky as the People's Commissar."

The room was silent, and Olga looked from Mamma to Papa. The Bolsheviks were a fringe movement of upstarts and radicals; they'd only organized as a political party five years earlier. Though the Provisional Government had its share of socialists, the fact that it had been cobbled together from various political factions meant that no one ideology held too much sway. Unlike Kerensky and Pankratov, who could put their leftist ideals aside to focus on the day-to-day business of governance, Lenin and Trotsky were hard-line revolutionaries, who advocated the complete overthrow of Russian society. To Olga, the implications of what Pankratov had told them were clear: the Bolsheviks' actions amounted to a second, shocking revolution, turning Russia even further from autocracy than it had already come.

Still seated in her wheelchair, Mamma reached out. "Alexei," she said, "Alexei, come here."

Though he was far too old for it, he rose from his seat beside Olga and sat on Mamma's lap; she wrapped her arms around him, as if worried that Pankratov's soldiers meant them ill.

Olga's heart was beating fast. *Overthrown*, Pankratov had said. Such a word implied violence: riots in the streets, firebombs and gunshots, women and children taking cover behind the broken rubble of buildings. Hadn't the upheaval of Papa's abdication been violent enough?

"I see," said Papa quietly. "What news of Minister Kerensky?"

Pankratov glanced down at the telegram. "It appears he's fled the capital," he replied. "If the Bolsheviks had arrested him, we would know."

Papa nodded once more. How could he be so calm? "And what will this mean for my family?"

"I don't know," Pankratov replied grimly. "As far as I'm aware, they've made no definitive plans concerning you."

"I see," Papa repeated. "Well, Commissar, seeing as there's little to be done for it, I think we're best not to worry ourselves. I'd like to thank you again for authorizing our little outing today; I believe it's done wonders for our spirits. Now, if you'll excuse me, I've work to do."

Papa shook Pankratov's hand; Pankratov, looking as stunned as Olga felt, nodded. He exchanged a glance with his soldiers, who filed out of the room.

Outside, the bells continued to ring—for Papa or for Lenin, Olga couldn't know.

18

August, 1914
Alexander Palace, Tsarskoe Selo

Olga walked down the hall, marveling at the sudden explosion of activity. Until yesterday, Alexander Palace had been a quiet, restful place, where servants whispered along the parquet floors and one could enjoy the sound of wind caressing the trees in Alexander Park. Before now, the only real commotion that ever broke the stillness of the halls was caused by Anastasia and Alexei racing on their roller skates, Maria running behind them in an attempt to slow their chaotic games.

Today, however, the palace was a veritable hive. From their post at a second-story window, Olga and Tatiana watched a procession of motorcars and lorries circle the courtyard, men striding down the halls in all manner of military dress, government officials and workmen surging in and out with the steady regularity of tidal swells.

Tatiana gripped her arm as, below, two men lifted a heavy-looking wooden box from the back of a lorry.

"Papa's new telephone," she whispered. "He's finally given in!"

Olga smiled. Her father had resisted installing a telephone in his study for years, grumbling that instantaneous communication was a nuisance more than a luxury; that anything he needed to know could reach him just as easily by telegram. But two days ago, he had received news which meant that time, for the foreseeable future, was of the essence.

Olga's family had been sitting down to dinner when Count Freedericksz, Minister of the Imperial Household, had walked into the room. Kindly Count Freedericksz, with his placid expression and upright bearing, was often a source of amusement to Olga and her sisters, who whispered that if one were to wax his spectacularly long mustache just right, the ends would meet at the back of his neck. Today, however, he looked unusually grave.

"Your Imperial Majesty," he said, bowing at the waist.

Papa, his knife poised over the venison on his plate, set down his cutlery. At the other end of the table, Mamma inhaled sharply. Alexei, still wheelchair-bound after a recent fall on the *Shtandart*, leaned back, his wheels sliding with the shifting weight.

Olga's heart plummeted. She knew what Freedericksz had come to say, and for a brief, childish moment she pictured herself pushing the minister from the room, as though preventing him from giving his message would keep it from becoming real.

Freedericksz's hand trembled as he held out a small envelope. "I received word from the foreign minister only moments ago, Your Highness. I regret to inform you that, despite our best efforts to the contrary, Germany has declared war on Russia."

Anastasia's mouth dropped open; Maria let her fork clatter onto her plate. From their stations against the wall, Olga could feel, rather than hear, the footmen stirring as they, too, absorbed the news. Would they be sent to the front, she thought, picturing the palace servants exchanging their silver trays for bayonets? Sent to fight the Germans, their blood washing over Prussian fields like summer rain—

"Nicky..." Mamma stood, looking stricken. Pale-faced, she

gripped the table for support; in an instant, Papa was at her side, pulling her into a close embrace. "Nicky," she whispered again, her eyes welling with tears. "God help us."

"I know," he murmured as Mamma rested her head against his shoulder. "My love, I know. We can't pretend we didn't know this day would come." He looked up, then gently eased Mamma back into her chair. "Alexei, I need you to be strong for your mother. Can you do that for me? Count Freedericksz, if you would be so kind as to summon the foreign minister..."

"He's already on his way," said Freedericksz, falling into step with Papa as they left the dining room.

War. Inevitable, inexorable war. Russia had been on the brink of mobilizing for months, Papa shut away in his study sending increasingly urgent letters to Cousin Willy in Berlin, hoping to stem the flood before ministers with martial ambitions prevailed over cooler heads. Only hours before that fateful dinner, they'd prayed for peace in the family chapel—now, watching from the window as Maria and Anastasia ran through the courtyard to accost the workmen with the telephone, Olga realized that the die had already been cast when she'd been pleading with the Almighty to spare Russian lives.

"What do they want with Serbia anyways?" said Tatiana, looking past the white columns that demarcated the courtyard from the park.

"It's bigger than that," Olga muttered. "Cousin Wilhelm seeks to expand Germany's borders at the expense of our allies. If we let him, the world will think we're weak." She turned to face Tatiana head-on. "And after Manchuria, we can't afford to let that happen."

"Very good, Grand Duchess." Olga turned at the sound of her tutor's voice: Pierre Gilliard was walking down the hall toward them. "You've been following the newspapers, I'm glad to hear it." He bowed his head in a leisurely, genteel greeting, looking for all the world as though the commotion below was nothing but a tempest in a gilded teapot. "Your parents need you. It's time to go to St. Petersburg."

Hours later, they were in the Winter Palace, congregating in the vast expanse of Nicholas Hall. Beyond the closed balcony doors, Olga could hear the steady hum of the people who'd gathered in Palace Square. Most days, those who lingered beneath the balcony in the hopes of seeing the tsar were disappointed—unaware, perhaps, that Olga and her family lived in Tsarskoe Selo. With the announcement of war, they'd come in droves to witness the tsar's historic address: crouching on the Alexander Column's broad pedestal in an attempt to get a better vantage point; massing along the Neva River in skiffs and rowboats, making the family's arrival by boat from Peterhof nearly impossible. They carried ribbons and banners, waved immense flags and lifted portraits of Papa, saved from the tercentenary, high in the air. It felt to Olga as though the inhabitants of St. Petersburg were more inclined to treat the declaration of war as a public holiday than a national emergency. More than one fight had broken out amongst the rowboats that jostled near the stone embankment, tipping unwary passengers and belligerent spectators alike into the brown water.

They'd even joined Olga and her family in the Winter Palace itself: courtiers, officers, ministers and attendants, anyone with the scantest credentials had slipped inside, filling the echoing halls with a joyful din. Five thousand of the city's most luminous inhabitants had come together in Nicholas Hall for a thanksgiving service, praying fervently in front of the ancient icon that had helped General Kutuzov turn back Napoleon's armies in 1812. Olga prayed as ardently as the rest, her heart swelling with pride as Papa, his voice ringing against the marble, vowed to keep all Russian enemies from setting foot on imperial soil.

After the service ended, Olga lingered with her family as the worshippers filed out of their seats. Of course, Olga was used to seeing officers, the reds and blues and whites of their parade uniforms so joyous, so bright, as they danced through ballrooms or performed exercises on horseback during parades. Today, the colors had taken on something of a different tone. In the reds she saw violence; in the blues, mourning. Russia's army had always been a source of pride to Olga, but she had never dreamed it would be put to use—not in the twentieth century, not in a world of diplomacy. Staring at Kutuzov's icon, it felt to Olga as though Nicholas Hall had been plunged back in time, the officers wearing the same illustrious jackets that their forefathers had worn to their deaths in 1812.

"How long do you think it will last?"

Olga turned around; Dmitri Pavlovich was standing behind her, in the white jacket and red epaulettes of the Life Guard Cavalry Regiment.

"A year, maybe less," Olga replied, her throwaway tone belying her uneasiness. "There's no chance Germany has the manpower to overcome our army." She indicated Dmitri's uniform with a nod of her head. "Will you be joining your regiment right away?"

Dmitri looked past Olga at the sea of uniforms filing out of Nicholas Hall. "It's as you say: if it's all over within the year, I wanted to do my part," he replied. "Can't let the French have all the fun, can I? Besides, someone's got to rescue Felix."

"Oh?" Tatiana drifted toward them. "What about Felix?"

"He and Irina are in Berlin—they got stuck there on the way back from their honeymoon. The kaiser won't let them leave, apparently, so it's all quite fraught." Dmitri fiddled with the sleeve of his jacket. "It's not as if Felix plans to enlist, so it's hardly a problem if we don't get him back for a while yet. He and Irina are staying in the Hotel Adlon; they might not even realize there's a war on."

"I thought all noblemen would enlist," Tatiana replied. "We need as many officers from our best families as we can get."

"Not Felix. He's found some loophole: because he's an only

son, he's not required to join up." Dmitri looked amused and frustrated in equal measure at his best friend's capriciousness. "Still..." He glanced at Papa speaking with the cassock-clad Metropolitan who'd overseen the service. "We've enough manpower without him. I pity the poor farmers we'll be up against."

He sighed, then turned his attention back to Olga and Tatiana. "And what about you?" he asked. "What will you do for the duration?"

Olga took Tatiana's arm. "We start our training with the Red Cross tomorrow. Mamma's setting up an officer's hospital."

Dmitri reached into his jacket and pulled out a flask; looking around surreptitiously, he raised it in a mock toast. "Well, here's hoping you won't have much to do," he replied, and took an abbreviated swig. "And I mean this in the best possible way: I hope you don't see me until the war's over."

Olga shivered at the thought of her handsome cousin, unconscious and bloodied on a stretcher. "Dmitri, are you... Are you quite prepared for all this?"

Dmitri let drop his breezy demeanor as he pocketed the flask. "Riding into battle? Yes. Overseeing a battalion of troops? Less so, if I'm honest. But I've trained to be an officer my whole life. It's what we're meant to do, all of us. Defend Russia from its enemies. Fight for the tsar.

"The rest of it..." He took a deep breath, his gaze fixed on some distant point beyond Olga's shoulder. "I am ready to die for my country—for your father—if God wills it. I like to think I've made peace with the idea of it. But who knows what runs through a man's mind in his final seconds on earth? Who knows what will happen when the moment comes?"

"*If* the moment comes," Olga replied, and Dmitri's troubled smile warmed.

"If," he conceded, then shook his head. "Death is death, regardless of whether I deal it by my own hand or direct it from the back of the battlefield. The toll that will take on my soul...

perhaps that will be the most difficult part of it all." He shook his head again, more brusquely, like a dog shaking off water. "Listen to me: this is hardly a subject to raise in the company of ladies." He smiled, sounding once more like his old self. "Shall we join your parents?"

Olga and Tatiana took Dmitri's proffered arms; with the ceremony over, only family remained, clustered by the windows in preparation for Papa's appearance on the balcony. Aunts Xenia and Olga had come with their husbands; Grandmamma was fanning her flushed face as they listened to the waiting crowds. Olga watched Anastasia and felt a pang of regret for Alexei, left back home in the Alexander Palace. He was still too weak after a recent attack to show himself in public. *What message would it send,* Tatiana had whispered, *for the people to see the tsarevich in a wheelchair?* Farther along the immense room, Uncle Mikhail, who'd returned from exile in Europe, stood with a handful of Duma ministers, casting dark looks over their shoulders at Father Grigori, sitting alone in the farthest row of chairs.

He should have remained behind with Alexei, thought Olga, observing the blue shadows beneath his eyes. He shouldn't have left Pokrovskoe at all, not after he'd been brutally attacked barely a month ago. Papa hadn't made his daughters privy to the ghastly details, but it had involved a madwoman and a knife—and Father Grigori's abdomen, judging from the way he was sitting stiffly upright, his hand curled on the head of a cane.

Olga watched him, both out of pity and clinical interest, and though she felt woozy at the thought of someone sinking a blade between the priest's ribs, she tried not to look away. She would be starting her training with the Red Cross tomorrow, after all; she needed to steel herself to the sight of pain.

Mamma sat beside him, the gauzy veil of her sun hat floating around the brim. She, too, was watching Father Grigori—the attack had come as a shock, and Mamma had sat up for hours waiting for word of his recovery: in the end, Dr. Botkin had prescribed a strong opiate to calm her nerves. Olga thought of Mamma's sleeplessness, knowing that her concern was for more than the priest's well-being: who could protect Alexei in Father Grigori's absence?

Mamma stood and beckoned to Maria. "Come away from the window," she said, and Maria dropped the curtain through which she'd been peeking.

"I've never seen a crowd that big," Maria said wonderingly, as Father Grigori rose unsteadily to his feet. He made his way to Mamma and Papa, his cane tapping heavily on the floor. "It looks like all of St. Petersburg is out there."

"Father, you should be sitting down," said Tatiana, abandoning Olga and Dmitri to offer Father Grigori her arm, but he shook his unkempt head, waving aside her solicitousness with a sweep of his black-cloaked arm. By the window, Papa, dressed in a simple infantry uniform, was speaking with Nikolai Sablin, making last-minute adjustments to his remarks. He looked up at Father Grigori as if surprised to see him.

"Little Father, I must say again to you—this war will be the end of all things." Father Grigori's voice was low, his expression stricken; yet his words carried through the room with enough clarity that Grandmamma looked up sharply, her fan stilling in her hands. "It will mean the end of Russia, the end of all we know—"

Papa shook his head, looking more amused than alarmed.

"You've made your feelings on this matter quite plain, my friend," he replied, "but I'm afraid that war is a necessary evil."

Father Grigori bent over his cane, anguish clouding his features; beyond the palace windows, they could hear the errant drift of a brass band. "Your people will suffer, Little Father," he continued. "It's not too late for you to change course, to find peace with the warmongers—"

From across the room, Sazonov, the foreign minister, spoke up. "That's quite enough, Father," he said sharply, looking down at Father Grigori through heavy-lidded eyes. "Your Imperial Majesty, I'm afraid I must insist. This is far beyond the purview of a *cleric*..."

Papa smiled. "Father Grigori, the foreign minister is quite correct. Your realm is faith; mine is policy. We must go to war." He laid a hand on Father Grigori's crooked arm and lowered his voice. "I want you to support me in this."

Father Grigori's eyes flashed—with pain? With anger?—but then he bowed his head. "You'll always have my support, Little Father," he said. "But do not forget that it is the people who will carry out your wishes. They will fall on their swords for you, Little Father, but remember He who told His people to beat their swords into plowshares, who urged peace amongst all nations—"

"And were Germany and Austria-Hungary intent on peace too, I would agree with you," Papa began, but he was cut short when Father Grigori gripped his arm and drew close, unblinking as he peered into Papa's eyes.

Sablin started and Sazonov let out an exclamation of anger, but Father Grigori clung to Papa's arm, his voice low, rhythmic. "I speak with the voice of the people, Little Father, and the people do not understand what they mean when they tell you they want this war. It is bloodshed, Little Father, bloodshed for Russia—"

Papa pulled away. "You mean the people standing out there?" he said, and swept out his arm, letting the muffled cheers from Palace Square speak for themselves. "You may speak with the voice of the people, Father, but I speak with the understanding of God's will. And it seems to me that the people and the Almighty are aligned in their support of our cause."

With a final smile at Father Grigori, Papa turned back to the foreign minister, who positioned himself in such a way as to block Father Grigori from Papa's view. As Father Grigori shrank back, his shoulders rounding in defeat, Papa stepped toward the balcony. He straightened his tunic, then nodded at the footmen holding the doors.

The footmen opened the doors in unison, and Nicholas Hall was flooded with the full force of sound as Papa stepped out onto the balcony. It was overwhelming: at the sight of Papa, the people in Palace Square cheered with an abandon that Olga had never heard, not even at the tercentenary; it was a wall of noise that shook the windows in their panes, reverberating in Olga's chest and filling her with the warmth of conviction in the war that, until this moment, Olga had lacked. Wars were terrible, yes, but necessary, in the face of aggression: how else could Papa protect Russia's interests in Serbia? In a few short months, Papa would have reestablished Russia's prominence amongst its continental allies, and proven Russia's strength to the world.

Papa raised his hands in an attempt to silence the crowd, but it soon became evident that his remarks had been prepared in vain. There was no stopping the sea of people from showing their support, through cheers and songs and prayer. Olga stepped forward, watching from behind Papa's shoulder as a ripple of movement made its way through the audience: one by one, they sank to their knees, holding out their banners and flags; over the commotion, Olga could make out the strains of the imperial anthem, discordantly, beautifully, as people began to sing.

Of course, Papa was right: the people's support for this war was incontrovertible. Through Papa, God had made His will known; through Papa, God would win the war against Cousin Wilhelm and his invading army. Whatever blood was spilled on Prussian battlefields was the price they would pay, willingly, for a lasting peace; it was a price they could pay, because through sheer size alone, the Russian army would silence its enemies under its bayonets.

On the balcony, Papa looked back into the room and beckoned Mamma forward; her cloudlike hat wafting above her head, she sailed onto the balcony and lifted her hand in acknowledgment, and the crowd roared once more. Olga watched her parents, silhouetted in the summer sun, as they accepted their people's love.

19

December 1917
Freedom House, Tobolsk

It took 120 steps to traverse the distance of Freedom House's courtyard: 120 paces around the perimeter, trailing close to the fence to eke out as much of a walk as possible. It was barely enough to satisfy Olga's desire for exercise, much less her desire for entertainment, but still—it was 120 steps farther than the house, with its short corridors and abbreviated rooms, provided. With their trips through the town gardens formally curtailed, every square inch of the courtyard had grown as familiar as a fingerprint: the hard-packed dirt that disintegrated into mud at the slightest hint of rain; Papa's piled logs. The small, hopeful patch that Alexei had tried to coax into a vegetable garden upon their arrival in Tobolsk, which had halfheartedly produced a few shrunken swedes before falling dormant for the winter; the forgotten debris that hemmed the bottom of the fence, leaves and cigarette butts and dust.

With the arrival of winter, the courtyard's familiar surroundings had transformed: modestly, at first, as the mud beneath Olga's boots glittered with the morning's hoarfrost; then all at once as snow began to fall in December, covering the tired patch of brown in a blanket of white.

December also brought new activity to the courtyard in the form of an immense, half-built snow fort. Started by Alexei and Anastasia shortly after the first snowfall, the fort—dubbed Snow Mountain—had become a project that occupied everyone in the household. Gibbes and Gilliard had drawn up a blueprint of sorts to guide construction of a helter-skelter several *arshins* taller than the height of a man, with stepped-back footings for stability and a short log staircase frozen into the snow.

Even the guards had joined in the construction of the mountain, bringing cut blocks of solid snow down from the steppe in wheelbarrows and helping to cart out buckets of water from the kitchen to freeze the structure solid. Their enthusiasm surprised Olga: Papa's frequent visits to the guardrooms, it seemed, had borne fruit in the guise of friendlier relations with their captors. Olga, in her own way, tried to emulate Papa's example by learning the soldiers' names and faces—something that she'd been avoiding as a matter of principle. Now, as she sank her shovel into the snow partway up the growing mound to carve out a place for a log step, she could look over the busy courtyard and know which of the guards suffered from poor circulation in their hands and feet; which ones had left children back at home and regarded their afternoons building Snow Mountain as a way of capturing some memory of time spent with their own families.

She dug the blade of her shovel into the ground, using the handle as support for a moment's rest. To many of the guards, Olga suspected, Lenin's seizure of power had come as something of a shock—and though the seizure, which was being called the October Revolution in the newspapers, had yet to make itself felt in Tobolsk, she guessed that many of the guards felt Lenin's Bolsheviks went too far in their violence. They, like Pankratov, had been appointed to their posts by Kerensky's Provisional Government; they, like Pankratov, did not necessarily share Lenin's radical ideology. Though she wouldn't go so far as to call the guards friends, they had become, in her mind, something more than enemies.

She resumed digging, thinking of the week-old headlines she'd read about the jubilation that had accompanied Lenin's rise to power. His revolution was breaking like a storm across water, but Olga wasn't naïve enough to think that it wouldn't reach their Siberian shores—to her, the Bolsheviks' lack of communication with Tobolsk was nothing more than a temporary state of affairs as they solidified their hold on Russia. She'd read about Lenin's beliefs on property and wealth: she knew that her family's stay in Tobolsk was undoubtedly a cost that this new government would not long be willing to pay. How soon before their circumstances were further reduced?

Night fell quickly in Tobolsk, and without the diversion of Alexei's collection of Pathé newsreels that had kept them occupied through the winters at Alexander Palace, Olga and her sisters had taken to crafting knickknacks and handiworks that, in years past, they sold for kopecks apiece at charity bazaars in Yalta and St. Petersburg. Here, Olga found the work to be a welcome diversion from the cold. Generally, her handiwork was tidy, but even though they'd pushed the sofas as close to the iron furnace as possible, the finger-stiffening chill made her stitches loose and uneven.

Across the room, Papa emerged from his study with Alexei in tow. "More sewing tonight, girls?" He walked over as he fixed his cuff link, a flash of white disappearing into his sleeve. "I'm glad to see it."

"Idle hands are the devil's plaything," Mamma intoned, stretching out a thread on her embroidered bookmark to snip it short. She looked up at Papa. "Will you read to us, darling?"

He kissed the top of her head. "Not tonight, I'm afraid. We've got some business to attend to downstairs, Officer Bentov has been teaching Alexei chess." He clapped a hand on Alexei's shoulder. "Shall we?"

As they started down the staircase, Tatiana and Olga exchanged a glance; as one, they stood, and made their way to the samovar beneath the window.

Tatiana poured steaming water into the teapot, addressing Olga in an undertone. "Did you notice...?"

Olga nodded as she stacked teacups. "A letter, do you think?" She glanced back at Mamma, silhouetted beneath the flickering glow of an oil lamp. "Who might it be for?"

Tatiana shrugged. "Supporters...a rescue attempt?"

Olga's heart lifted as Tatiana voiced what Olga herself didn't dare to say. "I hope so," she whispered, before Mamma called them back to the sofa.

She brought the cups over to the table so Tatiana could pour tea, suppressing a smile as she picked up the waistcoat she was knitting for Papa to inspect the stitches. *At last: momentum!* The change in government had brought increased tensions to Tobolsk, but also, perhaps, opportunity—a chance for salvation, to slip Olga and her family through the Bolshevik Party's grasp. She pictured the letter in Papa's cuff, passed along to one of his footmen, perhaps, or handed to Gilliard in a perfunctory handshake to be whisked out of Freedom House; a response brought back by the same channels, hidden beneath a dinner tray. Blueprints and guards' schedules, smuggled out to Tobolsk's monarchists, rallying them to rescue; loyalists lining the town gardens, waiting for the church bells to ring anew.

"...Another two *arshins* added to Snow Mountain today: how's that for progress?" Anastasia was saying, as she nestled next to Tatiana on the sofa. She curled her stockinged feet beneath her as she inspected her petit-point cushion cover. "Just you watch, it will be taller than the fence by the time we're finished with it."

Across the room, Mamma jabbed her needle into the edge

of her bookmark to reach for a different colored thread. "You girls and that mountain—it's a wonder none of you have caught a cold," she said, pulling out a small spool from the sewing box. "You're sure it won't be too dangerous for Alexei? You know what a daredevil he can be, and without Our Friend to pray for him..."

She trailed off, enclosing the spool in her palm. The pain of Father Grigori's death had not diminished with time—not for Mamma, whose grief felt frozen, bound inextricably to the past, present and future. To Mamma, the thought of Alexei suffering another attack was akin to the sword of Damocles hovering over his head, without Father Grigori to cross it blade to blade.

"Of course, Father Grigori is praying for Alexei—he's watching over all of us," said Tatiana staunchly. She looked at Mamma with a bracing smile as she tucked the edges of the fur coat she was using as a blanket around Anastasia's feet. "And as for Snow Mountain, it's being made with every possible safeguard in mind."

"You ought to come out and see it for yourself," offered Olga, unraveling a line of olive knits and purls. "It might put your mind at rest."

"I can see it perfectly well from the window," Mamma replied. "Besides, this close to Christmas I like to stay focused on our gifts for the household and guards. I do wish you girls would take it all a little more seriously..."

"Will we have a tree this year, Mamma?" Maria asked, half-asleep beneath a profusion of blankets and coats on a nearby divan.

"That's for your father to decide." Mamma bent back down over her needlepoint then let out an impatient huff as her lamp, which had been wavering on its final few drops of oil, sputtered and died. "Olga, dear, would you go downstairs and ask for more paraffin?"

The rooms on the first floor were much warmer than those

above, heated not only by the furnaces that dotted every room but also by the crush of guards on duty. Down the hall, she could hear the clatter of dishes and conversation in the dining room, the sound bringing her back to evenings spent with the officers in the *Shtandart's* mess hall.

The chamberlain's room—the room the duty officer used as his office—was located across from the staircase, its oak door partly ajar. Smoke curled through the crack, and Olga could hear the low timbre of her father's voice; she crept closer, listening.

"...Thank you for allowing the children to construct that silly snow fort, you can't imagine what it means to them," Papa said. She heard the crack of his lighter, a momentary silence before the metal snapped shut. "I daresay it will be the difference between a joyful winter and a sorrowful one. Children need fresh air and exercise."

"It's no trouble at all, Colonel," Pankratov replied. Olga frowned, surprised he was still at Freedom House—didn't he usually pass off command at nightfall? "I fully appreciate your position." He paused. "I hope my men are comporting themselves with the utmost decorum. Particularly with regard to your daughters."

"They're a credit to you," Papa replied, and Olga pictured Pankratov's answering smile. She heard the heavy glass thud of a decanter top; the slow gurgle of spirits into glasses. Now was the time to knock on the door and ask for paraffin—but she stood still, listening. It was dangerous for Papa to be alone with Pankratov if he'd not yet dispatched his letter; had he given it to Alexei to pass on to some sympathetic guard?

Pankratov sighed. "Colonel, I'm afraid I've invited you here to discuss a delicate matter. As you are well aware, the new government intends to replace me. I'm afraid my affiliation with the Provisional Government has put me at something of a disadvantage."

Olga felt her knees weaken. Pankratov, replaced?

"I'll be leaving in a few weeks' time, along with my men," he continued. "We'll remain here until the new government finds a suitable replacement."

And a new contingent of guards, Olga thought to herself. All those nights Papa had spent in the guardroom; all those soldiers he'd softened toward their cause. All the inroads he'd built, crumbling before her eyes—

"I'll be sorry to see you go," Papa said. "I can't imagine this has been an easy position for you, but you've done well by my family."

"I appreciate you saying so," Pankratov replied, "and I hope you can appreciate that there are still a few matters to attend to before I go. The new government has directed us to reduce the expenditure of your household." Olga heard something slide across the table; she leaned toward the door, careful not to let it creak as she peered inside. "These are ration cards for all members of your family. If you like, I can provide them directly to the kitchen."

Olga could see Pankratov and Papa facing each other across a wide oak desk, Panrkatov's dark eyes fixed on Papa as he picked up the ration cards. Between them stood the decanter and a pair of tumblers; in one corner, an immense furnace heated, no doubt, by the wood Papa had so diligently cut.

"I see," Papa murmured, the back of his neck flashing white above his collar as he looked down at the cards. "What of the provisions we brought with us from Petrograd?"

"I'm afraid those provisions have quite run out."

Papa slid the ration cards back across the table as Olga leaned closer to the door, her heart beating fast. They'd brought food from the kitchens at Alexander Palace, crates of preserved vegetables and canned food, enough to bolster whatever supplies their cooks might find in Freedom House's kitchen. Her mind turned to the bread lines she'd seen in Petrograd, growing ever longer during the long years of the war; the hollowed bellies of soldiers she'd seen in the infantry hospitals.

"Well, I suppose some measure of deprivation is to be expected," Papa continued. "I would be most obliged if you would supply these to our kitchens."

Pankratov made no move to retrieve the ration cards, his expression inscrutable as he wrapped his fingers around his glass. "'Some measure of deprivation,' Colonel? Forgive me, but I can't call your lack of caviar much of a hindrance."

Papa drummed the tabletop. "Caviar," he said lightly. "Never cared for the stuff."

Pankratov was not amused. "Have you any idea the deprivation your people felt at the end of your reign, Colonel? How much a loaf of bread cost in the capital?"

Olga could see the stiffening in Papa's shoulders; the gentle tightening of his jacket. "Of course I do."

"Then you'll know such levity is the height of callousness."

Papa tapped the end of his cigarette into Pankratov's ashtray. "I apologize; I didn't mean to sound insensitive," he replied. "It seems to me that food is plentiful enough here in Tobolsk. No doubt we have your new government to thank for that."

Pankratov didn't miss the edge in Papa's voice—nor did Olga. She was surprised by Papa's easy dismissal: surely, he'd known about the food shortages in Moscow and Petrograd? "Food supply was never in question, Colonel," he shot back. "Your government's abysmal handling of food distribution—that's what drove prices up. No trains, bringing grain to market; meat, spoiling in carriage cars because they weren't being scheduled on the railways."

"Excuse me, Commander," Papa said sharply. "But my government's priority—*my* priority—was to win the war. We were forced to make difficult decisions. Any government would have done the same."

"That's as may be," Pankratov replied. "Your soldiers might

have been well fed, but their families weren't. How could you expect men to fight knowing that their wives and children were starving? War cannot be won on empty stomachs, neither on the front nor at home."

To Olga's astonishment, Papa bowed his head. "That is my cross to bear."

They were both silent for a moment as Pankratov refilled their glasses. Olga was surprised at Papa's candor—he so rarely discussed the past. Even before the war, Papa preferred not to talk about his work. Whenever Olga would ask about the business of ruling, he would quickly, deftly, turn the conversation back to focus on her: her daily life, her cares and concerns. An inquiry about a minister's speech in the Duma would transform into a discussion about Olga's charity work; a question about Russia's educational system would turn into a conversation about Olga's marriage prospects. It had always made Olga feel important, that her father, the tsar, would care about the petty concerns of her day-to-day life.

Before the war, it hadn't occurred to Olga to ask Papa what he felt about his role as tsar; after the abdication, she hadn't wanted to pry.

But perhaps he had simply been waiting for someone to ask.

She was about to knock when Papa spoke again.

"Tell me, Commander: when did you become a revolutionary?"

Pankratov leaned back in his chair, balancing his glass on the rise of his stomach. "I'm sure you already know that story, Colonel."

"I'm afraid I don't," Papa replied. "Please, enlighten me."

"You're aware of my involvement in *Narodnaya Volya*, I suspect."

Papa nodded slowly. "I've been made aware, yes," he said. "The group's assassination of my grandfather left…quite an impression on me as a young boy. I struggle to understand why a man as compassionate as yourself would have anything to do with such violence, particularly toward a reformer like my grandfather."

Pankratov smiled as he leaned forward, setting his glass on the desk. "What a thing to say—but then, those at the top of a system of repression don't ever see the horrors at the bottom. The system under your grandfather was corrupt, Nicholas Alexandrovich; under your father, that corruption grew. But we saw the monarchy for what it was: a myth, built on crumbling foundations." He sat back, seemingly indifferent to the insult he'd imparted. "If it's of any comfort to you, I did not take part in the assassination directly."

Papa's reply was so quiet Olga strained to hear it. "I'm glad to hear it, if only for the sake of your eternal soul," he said. "The assassination of an emperor—of God's chosen representative on Earth—"

"That may be what you believe, Colonel, but faith alone can't sustain a government," Pankratov said. "I'm afraid I cannot subscribe to the idea of a God who chooses his representatives upon something so fallible as bloodlines. Nor, it seems, can Russia."

Papa's chair scraped the floor as he stood, and Olga's heart plummeted—she turned away from the door, expecting Papa to storm out in disgust at Pankratov's blatant blasphemy—but she looked back in a moment later to find Pankratov offering Papa a cigarette.

"Violence was a means to an end—it always is a means to an end," Pankratov was saying as Papa sank back into his chair. "I'm afraid we saw no alternative. Conversation, advocacy... how can peaceful means motivate those who benefit from the suffering of others? We had to be willing to seize power from those whose belief in their own supremacy blinded them to the possibility of a better future."

"And how does it feel? Now that you've achieved your ends?"

Pankratov smiled. "I do not regret my political ideals, Colonel, nor do I reject them. Just as you do not reject yours."

Papa was silent for a moment. "So. Here we sit, autocrat and revolutionary. Was it revenge, then, that prompted you to take this post?"

"No. I must confess I was reticent to accept the position." Pankratov looked almost amused as he reached across the table to light Papa's cigarette. "I don't believe in revenge. I believe in change. We're building a better world for everyone, not just for the select few who benefit from being born into privilege."

"Forgive me, but I'm well apprised of this future that Lenin and his radicals espouse," Papa retorted, his voice strengthening with indignation. "No art, no music—the death of progress. Everyone demanding a say, crippling the ability to get things done in a timely manner, rather than a single leader making decisions to the benefit of everyone—"

"But you didn't *benefit* everyone!" said Pankratov, hitting the table with his fist. "You failed the vast majority of your people. You speak of art, of music as if we're against them. Without oppression, people will have the ability to pursue those things in earnest; they'll *thrive* once the basic necessities of life are met. But right now, the people need bread and food and shelter." He sat back, decisive. "We're building a world that looks to the future, Nicholas Alexandrovich, not the past."

"I see." A thin ribbon of smoke curled above Papa's head. "Tell me, Commander. Is there room for my family in this glowing republic of yours?"

Pankratov fixed his steady eyes on Papa once again. "Did you know I was imprisoned in Schlisselburg Fortress, Colonel? Fourteen years… Fourteen years of captivity. The first few were difficult—I was a young man, after all, with a young man's restlessness—but soon I recognized the opportunity that prison afforded me. You see, it gave me the gift of time: time spent in the pursuit of an education, rather than being ruthlessly exploited by some factory owner for a pittance.

"Though I was imprisoned, I chose to liberate my mind. I became literate, and in time I turned toward geology as my primary field of focus. I know," he continued, smiling. "Geology, of all things. I studied the very stones that made up the Schlisselburg's walls. I was captivated by the natural science of the world. The earth is in constant flux, Colonel: tectonic plates shift beneath our feet, moving in beautiful synchronicity."

In a strange way it seemed to fit. Olga pictured Pankratov, the bookish revolutionary, marveling at the restless energy of a world at once moving and still. The glimmer of silver in the heart of a mountain; the firework spark of a volcanic eruption.

"I was exiled to Siberia after my release, and while others viewed my departure as further punishment, I saw it as an opportunity. I learned all there is to know about the harsh beauty of this incredible landscape. My love for Siberia grew from the hard soil of exile and flourished."

"I'm pleased to hear it," Papa interjected quietly. "I must confess, I've grown to appreciate this part of the Empire in my time here."

Pankratov inclined his head. "Indeed," he replied. "Do you know how a diamond is formed, Colonel? Through the application of pressure. Intense pressure forces the atoms in carbon to bind together to form, over millennia, something unbreakable. Something beautiful.

"Change is the natural order of things, Colonel. Change under conditions of intense pressure. In time, that change will result in something beautiful. That's what we're creating in this revolution: beautiful change. Inevitable change."

He leaned back in his chair. "I don't know whether your family has earned its place in our new system, but I hope it has," he said finally. "And if they do, they will be expected to accept change. Change, and all of the beautiful opportunity it creates."

PART THREE

20

January 1915
Annexe Hospital, Tsarskoe Selo

Olga stepped out of the operating room, leaning against the bulk of a casement window as she set down a covered bowl with shaking hands. Beneath the nunlike habit of her nursing uniform, her head ached—the pins holding her hair in place were too tight, but she didn't dare remove them. How often had she suffered through an overlaced corset at a state dinner? How often had she lifted a tiara from her head at the end of the night, massaging her aching brow? Olga was used to discomfort in the name of service to her country, and never before had her service been more vital than now. Her heartbreak over Pavel and concerns about marriage—problems that, less than a year ago, were paramount in her mind—now seemed as though they belonged to someone else; and in a sense, perhaps they did. The war, after all, had affected everyone: farmers had become soldiers, princesses had become nurses. Even St. Petersburg had transformed in the wake of the war, abandoning its Germanic name for the more patriotic-sounding Petrograd. Why, then, should Olga be immune to the forces of change?

She lifted her hand to her habit, thinking to pull one of her pins loose, then thought the better of it. More than once,

Dr. Gedroits had snapped at her after a lock of hair had fallen free while she was dressing a soldier's open wound. She pictured Dr. Gedroits' gray eyes flashing with disapproval: with her curt demeanor and preference for men's clothing, Princess Vera Gedroits had not become Russia's first female military surgeon without adopting some measure of ferocity in the way she treated her nursing staff. No, a headache was a small price to pay if it meant remaining in Dr. Gedroits' good graces.

She wrenched open the window to let in a sudden blast of night air, resisting the urge to look down at the bowl. Assisting in the operating room always made her light-headed, but to Olga the worst part of the job was this: disposing of infected tissue, shrapnel shards, bloodstained bullets—whatever the surgeon had cut from the groaning officer under her knife.

For Olga, becoming a Red Cross–certified Sister of Mercy had been easy enough in the classroom. She'd beaten Tatiana, Anna Vyrubova and Mamma in all of their exams and could recite the steps involved in excising a wound without a second's hesitation. She'd smiled at the other nurses assigned to the Annexe, committing their names to memory as they attended evening classes: Rita Khitrovo and Maria Nirod, who, like Tatiana and Olga, set aside her title as Countess within the walls of the hospital. Olga had received rare praise from Dr. Gedroits on her bandage rolling, and had attended her Red Cross graduation confident that she would quickly become the doctor's most trusted surgical assistant.

In practice, however, nursing was more difficult than she'd anticipated. Dreams of decomposing limbs wrenched Olga from sleep nearly every night, the mousy scent of gas-gangrene lingering in her nostrils long after she'd left the ward. Faced with the bravery of soldiers willing to give everything they had—health, dignity, life—in the fight against the Central Powers, Olga did all she could to bolster her failing nerves, but when tasked with passing Dr. Gedroits a sterilized scalpel over a seeping mass of flesh that had once been a human shoulder, she seemed incapable of doing anything other than freezing solid.

She closed her eyes, recalling Dr. Gedroits' snort of impatience as she wrenched the scalpel out of Olga's hand. Tatiana, also attending, had stepped forward to take Olga's place: why did the sight of blood not affect her in the same way? How did she manage to push past the suffering to do what was needed?

From down the hall, Olga heard the sound of footsteps and looked up. Rita, dressed like Olga in a habit, chambray dress and apron, came out of one of the wards, wheeling a trolley filled with sterilized bandages.

She smiled, though her expression quickly turned quizzical. "Are you quite well?"

"Of course." Olga indicated the bowl with a nod of her head. "Incinerator."

Rita let out a breath, her fingers tapping against the trolley. "If you aren't up for assisting in surgeries, you should say so," she said finally. "There's no shame in it. The rest of us are perfectly capable, and you're so good with the officers. There's plenty of work for those not cut out for the heavier tasks. You could dress wounds, sterilize instruments."

Olga smiled, appreciating her friend's candor: since certifying as nurses, the distinction between Olga and the ladies-in-waiting who'd trained alongside her had mellowed considerably. She straightened. "Truly, Rita, I'm fine. The air's a little close in there, that's all."

Rita hesitated. "If you're sure," she said before continuing down the hall.

Olga was sure: the war needed more than her nerves. It needed her hands as well as her heart; her action as well as her prayers. Alongside her nursing duties, Olga oversaw the Supreme Council for Care of Soldiers' Families, while Tatiana headed a committee for the refugees fleeing to the capital from villages along the front line. They'd given up their spare time to sit with convalescing officers and visit Red Cross trains, attend the openings of new hospitals and send off regiments headed to the front with spirited speeches. Even Maria and Anastasia were doing their part. Though too young to train as nurses, they visited the city's hospitals, circulating amongst the soldiers in an effort to buoy their spirits.

That said, all of Olga's activities paled in comparison to Mamma's. She had always worried for her mother's health, but the war seemed to have given Mamma a new well of strength to draw upon. No longer was she confined to a wheelchair, fretting about Alexei's condition: now, she assisted Dr. Gedroits in the operating theatre, conferring with the senior physician on leading medical practices; she gave over the gilded reception halls of Catherine Palace for use as a military hospital and sat by the bedsides of wounded soldiers as though they were her own children. In the evenings, Mamma prayed with Father Grigori, her fingers kneading together as she entreated God to watch over Papa's armies, to give them the strength they needed to defend the Empire.

Mamma's crowning achievement had been the renovation of a thirty-bed outbuilding in the gardens behind the palace infirmary itself. Originally built to house patients with infectious diseases, the small hospital, newly christened the Annexe, had been modernized to accommodate the needs of injured officers, and was where Olga now worked. Mamma had expanded Dr. Gedroits' duties to include full oversight of the Annexe—a tall order in addition to her other responsibilities as senior physician at Tsarskoe Selo's civilian hospital, but the doctor had proven more than equal to the task. In the short months since the war began, Dr. Gedroits had proven almost as indispensable to Mamma as Father Grigori, the sound of her spat-topped boots a heavy tread next to Mamma's light steps as they paced down the hall.

Olga closed the window and picked up the bowl, carrying it

down to dispose of its contents in the basement incinerator before hurrying back up the staircase. Basements, with their low light and damp walls, had always made her uneasy: she could never quite dismiss the sound of faraway movement as mere industry, hearing in the darkness the low whispering of voices long gone, the sweep of a ghostly hem across the rounded flagstones. As she returned to the first floor Olga breathed easier: her last ghastly duty done, she could do a final turn of the wards before retiring to Alexander Palace.

She paused as she passed the common room where the patients—those who were able—congregated after dinner. In a corner, two officers had strung a wire across the billiards table and were playing a game of table tennis. Colonel Baedmedev lunged to one side to return a wide volley and Olga was satisfied to see that the limp he'd been nursing for nearly three months had almost entirely disappeared. Lieutenant Shuriov, dealing out a game of cards, was similarly close to fighting fit, but what of the others? Corporal Yefimov, keeping score of the match as he puffed on a cigarette, wouldn't be returning to active duty—not with the false leg he'd been fitted for only the day before. Olga had attended his surgery six weeks earlier and had handed Dr. Gedroits the bone saw she'd used to remove his gangrene-infected foot. Nor would Field Marshal Orentov, who was smoking a cigarette in the corner. He'd not said a word since arriving at the hospital two weeks ago; he hadn't uttered a peep when they removed three of his frostbitten fingers.

At the edge of the billiards table, an officer seated in a wheelchair looked up as the French bulldog in his lap twisted to free itself from his grasp, falling to the ground before popping to its feet like a cork out of a bottle. It shot across the room, and launched itself into Olga's arms, wriggling with glee.

"Hello, Ortipo," she laughed, kissing the dog between the ears before depositing it back in the soldier's lap.

"Done for the day, Grand Duchess?" he asked, ruffling the dog's ears. Dmitri Malama had been at the hospital for nearly two months recovering from a fractured femur, and though Dr. Gedroits had removed the plaster cast that had enveloped his leg from hip to ankle almost a week ago, he was still too unsteady on his feet to go without the aid of a wheelchair for long. With his ruddy cheeks and perpetual smile, he'd charmed all the nurses who'd met him on their rounds, but he'd been particularly taken with Tatiana. It was a sentiment Olga's sister readily returned: it hadn't been lost on Olga that Tatiana had cooked the nursing roster so that she alone changed the dressings in Malama's six-bed ward.

Sitting in a nearby armchair, an officer with his arm bound to his chest leaned forward, his free hand outstretched as he offered the dog a piece of bread. Ortipo trotted over, and accepted the treat with a snort of thanks.

"A nurse's work is never done," Olga replied, and the officer looked up. Unlike Malama, he was dark, with olive skin and black hair, full lips curving beneath his waxed mustache. *Georgian*, Olga thought, picturing him in the elegantly flared *chokha* tunics she'd seen on Georgian retainers at court, a long line of bandoliers strapped across his chest. He must have been in Malama's ward, otherwise Olga would have remembered his warm eyes. "I'm afraid Tatiana's still with Dr. Gedroits. They just completed the last operation of the day, but Tatiana's sterilizing the operating room."

Malama slipped a lead over the dog's head. "Well, I suppose we'll just have to wait a little longer, won't we, Ortipo?" he said easily. "But we'd both be content to wait all night for the lovely Sister Tatiana to give us a pat on the head."

"It's a good thing I consider faithfulness a virtue, or else I might be offended by your preference for her," Olga replied, and Malama's friend smirked as she pulled a packet of cigarettes from her apron. "How's your leg?"

"Healing." Malama rubbed Ortipo's velvet ears as his friend offered Olga the use of his lighter. "Dr. Gedroits thinks I'm only a few weeks away from rejoining my regiment. Once I've gotten used to the stick, I'll be right as rain. You don't think your sister could be convinced to take Ortipo when I go, do you? Only war is no place for a pet, and Shakh-Bagov here is far too keen to get back to the front for him to be of any use in caring for the little beast."

Olga nodded as the other officer stowed his lighter back in his pocket, filing his name away in her constantly shifting mental roster of patients: Shakh-Bagov. "Leaving a puppy in my sister's care? One might almost think you were worried she'd forget you." She knelt in front of Malama and fixed Ortipo with a steady glare; looking from one to the other, she shook her head. "No. It would be impossible to forget you when you bear such a resemblance to the bulldog."

Malama and Shakh-Bagov laughed, but any response was cut short by the sound of tires skidding on snow. Olga went to the window and pulled the curtains open: in the glare of the field lights, she watched an ambulance screech to a halt as *sanitary* ran out from the hospital, stretchers tucked under their arms. Generally, the war wounded reached the Palace Infirmary by way of ambulance trains, the front-line medical "flying columns" having patched them up enough to survive the twelve-hour journey back to Petrograd or Moscow. The system wasn't perfect, but it had the benefit of predictability: Olga and the other Sisters of Mercy could prepare for the incoming officers and meet them at the train station for initial assessment. But war wasn't the only source of injury in Tsarskoe Selo. For an ambulance to arrive this suddenly, this chaotically, it could only mean that the incoming patients were civilians.

Olga watched as two burly *sanitary* unloaded the ambulance. Rather than conveying the patient to the main hospital, they carried her toward the Annexe, and Olga let out a cry as they passed through a curtain of light. Anna Vyrubova lay on the stretcher, animated only by the jostling movement of the *sanitary* as they conveyed her toward the door.

Olga sprinted out of the room, her exhaustion forgotten as she met the *sanitary* in the hallway.

Anna was nearly unrecognizable, but for the tangled mess of her bloodstained skirt—Mamma had given it to her years ago, having spent months embroidering the hem with gilded grape leaves. Her face was slack and bloodstained, her left cheek and eye obscured beneath a rusty bandage. Beneath the soot-stained fabric of her chemise, Olga could see an ominous bulge near Anna's neckline that looked like it might be a broken collarbone. The skirt hid any other injuries Anna might have sustained; however, it was clear the damage extended far beyond what Olga could see.

"What happened?" she asked, falling into step with the stretcher.

"Train accident," huffed one of the *sanitary*. "Derailed just outside of Petrograd. The medics who arrived at the wreckage identified Madame Vyrubova; they knew that the empress would want her here." He shook his head as Olga held open the door. "I'm afraid you must prepare for the worst, Grand Duchess. Her pulse is very weak."

Olga trailed Anna toward the operating room where Dr. Gedroits had been forewarned, it seemed, of her incoming patient. She'd changed into a clean surgical gown, her hands held aloft as she ushered in the stretcher with a nod of her head. Behind her, Maria Nirod stood where Olga and Tatiana had been only an hour earlier, ready to assist the surgeon, and Olga felt a rush of relief that Tatiana had been dismissed before she could see Anna in such an awful state.

Dr. Gedroits lingered at the door as the *sanitary* transferred Anna from the stretcher to the operating table. "Thank you, Olga," she said, watching the *sanitary* leave through narrowed eyes. "Your mother is quite distressed. Perhaps you would be more use to her than to me. Sister Nirod is more than prepared to help me with the initial assessment."

Olga nodded; from within the depths of the room, Anna groaned. "Will she survive?"

Dr. Gedroits exhaled heavily through her nose. "I can make no promises," she said finally, "but I will do my utmost."

The door closed behind her, and Olga's knees buckled with the deep realization that Mamma's closest friend might not last the night.

Dr. Gedroits' office was small and plain, a single oak desk and chair buttressed by the presence of a large bookcase stuffed with medical textbooks. Devoid of religious symbols or portraits, the room offered little in the way of comfort, and Olga wished they'd moved to the hospital's small chapel in the courtyard—but Mamma, in an uncharacteristic show of secularism, had deemed the chapel too far from Anna's sickbed.

"We'll go to the chapel once we've been given more information," she said to Anna's whey-faced parents, who had rushed to the hospital as soon as they'd been informed of their daughter's condition. "Our prayers will be all the stronger when we know what to pray for."

Anna's mother nodded, accepting Mamma's advice with brittle resignation, clasping her husband's hands over the card table that the officers had supplied from the common room for the makeshift vigil. Like her thirty-year-old daughter, Madame Tanyeva was small and doughy, her once-dark hair graying beneath the brim of her hat. She'd barely spoken a word since arriving nearly a half an hour earlier, and Olga was thankful that, despite her own despair, Mamma had been able to take charge.

"God holds all of us in His hands," Mamma said, sinking into a camp chair next to Mme. Tanyeva. She pressed a small crucifix into Mme. Tanyeva's hand, and Olga knew that Mamma's steadiness stemmed not from her compassion alone, but from her all-too-shared experience of waiting for a child to pass through peril. "He is with us, whether we attend Him in His chapel or here."

Olga set down two cups of well-sugared tea. "You'll want to keep up your strength," she whispered.

Anna's mother looked up, red-eyed. "How kind of you, child," she said, sounding as though she was speaking from the bottom of a well.

Olga straightened. Like Mamma, she knew how to handle the grief of uncertainty: that slow and dreadful counting of the minutes and hours spent waiting for news. To Olga, such moments were measured in the performance of idle tasks: the steady knitting of a scarf, the precise embroidering of a gilded bookmark. But here in Dr. Gedroits' austere office, busywork was in short supply; instead, they sat in silence, listening to the rustling of the hospital around them, the billowing of the snow that had begun to gust at the windows.

Tatiana leaned over. "It's time to do the rounds," she murmured, rubbing the bridge of her nose. She glanced at Mamma, the shadows beneath her eyes deepening; had Anna not been brought in, Tatiana would have left for the palace long ago.

"Let me do it," Olga replied, and it was a mark of her exhaustion that Tatiana didn't protest.

Thankfully, Olga's rounds were brief. Given the late hour, most of the men were already asleep and she was able to work quietly with the aid of bedside lamps—they turned beneath her hands as she checked dressings, barely waking as she inspected for bedsores. This, at least, she could do, she thought, satisfied that her touch was light enough not to disturb them while they slept. Why was changing a dressing so much more bearable than treating the wound itself?

She fluffed the pillow beneath a dozing Dmitri Malama's head; in the next bed over, Shakh-Bagov set down the novel he'd been reading.

"Your friend...how is she?" He shifted, using his good arm

to prop himself upright; in the glow of his lamp, she could see him in silhouette only, his chest artificially bulked beneath an overlarge nightshirt by his bandaged arm. Whereas in the common room, Olga would have put Shakh-Bagov's age at around thirty, now, with his hair disheveled by the pillow, he looked no older than twenty-two. "I've been worried for her."

Olga finished administering to Malama. "We don't really know yet," she replied. "We're still waiting for news." She nodded, indicating Shakh-Bagov's arm. "When was that dressing last changed?"

He smiled apologetically. "Your sister was supposed to see to it today," he replied. "I think it will hold until morning, if you don't have the time."

She pulled her stool next to his bed, adjusting the lamp so that the light fell directly on his chest. "Don't be silly," she replied. "I won't have you getting an infection on the one and only night I'm responsible for your ward. What would Dr. Gedroits say?"

Shakh-Bagov shifted; with Olga's help, he shrugged out of his nightshirt, revealing broad shoulders and a concave stomach, his one arm bound to his chest like a broken bird's wing. "Are you as terrified of her as I am?" he said conspiratorially. He leaned forward to allow her to untie the bandage's knot, fastened behind his back, and she swallowed down a sudden, absurd impulse to smooth his ruffled hair. "Do you know, I didn't realize she was a woman until after she'd wheeled me out of the operating room? Told me if I'd any objections to a female physician she could put the bullet right back where she'd found it." He chuckled. "I think she'd make a fine general, were she so inclined."

Olga began to unravel the bandage, steadily winding the cotton back into itself as she went over, under his shoulder joint, smiling. Dr. Gedroits' refusal to wear dresses had seemed strange to her too, at first, but she'd long grown used to the doctor's proclivities: in fact, her refusal to live by anyone's standards but her own seemed something worth admiring, in its own way. "Well, she's certainly the most formidable physician in Tsarskoe Selo, as well as the most skillful. She's even managed to whip me into shape—though really I ought to be doing this in the dressing room rather than on the ward. You won't tell, will you? Only your wound doesn't look to be seeping, and I'd rather not wake the rest of the ward taking you out."

He smiled. "Your secret's safe."

"Good." She indicated the patch of gauze that covered Shakh-Bagov's chest near his armpit. "Bayonet?"

He shook his head as she began to peel the gauze away, smelling for signs of infection. "Not much sport for bayonets on these battlefields, I'm afraid—hand-to-hand combat seems to have gone the way of the bow and arrow. It was a Mauser: eight-millimeter right through the joint. Hurt like the devil, but the doctor says I'll make a full recovery."

She looked up, grinning. "And if you don't, you'll still have motion enough to aim a pistol. That should do, in a pinch."

"Exactly, Grand Duchess. Needs must." He quietened as Olga inspected the wound; satisfied that it was draining properly, she reached for a sterilized square of gauze. "That accident...what happened to the other passengers?"

Olga held the gauze in place with one hand as she began to unravel a fresh bandage with the other. "I don't know. Sent to the infirmary, I suppose. I'm glad they brought Anna here."

Shakh-Bagov was silent for a minute as Olga positioned his arm once more, pinning it to his chest with the bandage. "She's already in surgery, isn't she? I wonder how long the others will have to wait. I can't imagine the ratio of doctors to patients in the civilian hospital is superior to what we've got here. But I suppose that's a perk of being friends with the empress."

Olga bristled. "It's the empress's prerogative if she wants to help a friend. And Anna is a nurse at this hospital, same as me. If that doesn't entitle her to special treatment, what should?"

Shakh-Bagov looked suitably chastened. "I'm sorry. I didn't mean to cause offense."

She finished rolling the bandage and secured it tight above the shoulder so that the knot wouldn't disturb him while he slept. "You didn't," she replied crisply. "How does that feel?"

He shrugged experimentally. "Good. Excellent. Thank you, Grand Duchess."

She lifted his nightshirt and helped to guide his free hand back through the sleeve. "None of that, Officer. I'm a Sister of Mercy, same as anyone else."

He looked down at his lap, smiling. "No special treatment," he said quietly, playing with the hem of his sheet. "Thank you, Sister Romanova. Please know I'm thinking of your friend. I'll be praying for her quick recovery."

She handed him his book. "I appreciate that," she replied. "She means a great deal to my family."

Olga shut the door behind her, the brightness of the hall jarring after the dim peace of the ward. Without any remaining duties to distract her, Olga lingered, listening for distant sounds of panic or grief, anything to indicate that Dr. Gedroits had finished in the operating room.

She started down the hall, Shakh-Bagov's words echoing in her ears: *I suppose it's a perk of being friends with the empress.* He hadn't said it with heat or bitterness, though the words themselves were enough to make Olga frown. What did it matter whether Anna was saved by her friendship with Mamma, so long as she was saved? Mamma had taken on so many responsibilities since the start of the war, and Papa even more so: Anna had been a help to them both, a distraction and a comfort. And Mamma had so few friends. She spent time with a handful of ladies-in-waiting, but no one who made her laugh like Anna—no one who treated her as an equal, rather than an empress.

Were Anna to succumb to her injuries, Mamma would surely shatter under the strain.

And who would be there to pick up the pieces?

She turned a corner, thinking of what she would say if she tended to Shakh-Bagov again. As an officer, was he not benefiting from the tsar's attention, too?

Olga rounded another corner and looked up. There, at the far end of the hall, Dr. Gedroits stood in a whispered conversation with Father Grigori outside the operating room.

Olga was gladdened by the sight—physician and priest, working together to save Anna's life—but then Father Grigori made as if to push past Dr. Gedroits, and the doctor lifted her arms, barring the door.

"I must insist! Madame Vyrubova requires rest, she cannot possibly receive anyone—"

"And what would bring her rest and solace better than prayer?" Father Grigori shot back. He stepped closer to Dr. Gedroits—too close, as he clamped his hand around her arm. "I must commend this woman's soul to God."

"I commend this woman's body to *science*," Dr. Gedroits spat, and wrenched her arm from Father Grigori's grasp. "I insist that you leave her be. It is highly improper for you to push your way into a sickroom. The risk of infection *alone*—"

"What is this?" said Olga as she reached the end of the hall. "Father Grigori, what's going on?"

Father Grigori looked thunderous. "Her Imperial Majesty sent for me directly," he said, staring daggers at Dr. Gedroits. "The Lord has not abandoned His faithful servant in her hour of need. He has called me to pray over Anna Vyrubova and commend her spirit into His hands. But I am thwarted by those who do not believe in the Lord's teachings, disbelievers and secularists, too deaf to heed His words..."

Olga hesitated. Father Grigori's heart was in the right place, but he wasn't helping his case by raging. To Dr. Gedroits, the only cross worth worshipping was the scarlet square that adorned the sides of ambulances; the only sermons worth listening to were those recited in operating theatres and lecture halls to impart wisdom upon medical professionals.

As Father Grigori paused for breath, Dr. Gedroits interjected, loosening the knot of her tie.

"Madame Vyrubova is in a very grave state, and I do not think it wise to disturb her at this critical juncture. She sustained multiple fractures in the accident, including to her cranium and her spine; should she become agitated, any movement—any at all—could prove extremely dangerous." She glared at Father Grigori, wrapping her fingers firmly around the door handle. "This is *my* hospital. I will not have my patients disturbed."

"I quite agree, Doctor," said Olga. "Why don't we all go to your office and inform the empress about Anna's condition..."

Father Grigori stepped forward once more, his heavy cassock sweeping around his knees as he took Dr. Gedroits by the forearms. Too stunned to respond, the doctor gaped, outraged, at Father Grigori's impertinence as he peered, unblinking, into her eyes. Olga made as if to break their hold, but then—

"She will live, Doctor," he said, and lifted his green gaze to the ceiling. "You may not believe in His mercy, but I know it to be true. The Lord will hear my prayers. Anna Vyrubova will live."

Dr. Gedroits stared at Father Grigori for a long moment, the lines around her mouth tightening before she pulled a key from her pocket and locked Anna's room with a resounding click.

"Thank you, Father, but *I* will save Madame Vyrubova's life. Should she recover, it will be the result of medical science. Not your prayers."

Father Grigori's smile congealed, his eyes lighting with some inner fire as Dr. Gedroits turned on her heel and walked down the hallway, Olga running in her wake.

21

January 1918
Freedom House, Tobolsk

Snow mounded in the deep casings of Freedom House's windows, piling high on the balcony where, in more temperate months, Mamma watched the clouds grow gilded in the sunset. With the arrival of the new year, the temperature in Tobolsk began to plummet, and the furnaces meant to warm the house through were impotent against the relentless cold. To ward off frostbite, Olga and her sisters had taken to wearing their winter furs indoors atop layers of sweaters and skirts, but the chill air crept mercilessly through any cracks in their armor: up sleeve cuffs to bite at their wrists; past thick knitted scarves to caress their cheeks.

In such cold, movement was a necessity rather than a luxury, and Olga was thankful for the distraction of outdoor activities: sawing wood with Papa; building Snow Mountain to ever-greater heights. Now the mountain loomed over the courtyard, as wide at the base as it was tall, with a broad, shining ice slide. Alexei, standing at the top clutching a makeshift sledge, looked precarious as he waved down at Olga, his breath clouding in the air.

Olga waved back. "Are we certain it's safe?" she muttered, leaning closer to Tatiana.

"It's too late now," Tatiana replied. "He's already up there, and you know as well as I do that he's only coming down one way."

She looked up at her infinitely breakable brother, bouncing on the balls of his feet to keep warm. The structure was solid enough—Papa and Gilliard had made sure of it—but so much could go wrong in the pursuit of joy: recklessness, carelessness, haste—

"This was a mistake," she shouted, stepping forward. "Alexei, don't—"

Before she could finish, Alexei sat down on the sledge and kicked off, launching himself down the slide with a devilish whoop. Olga closed her eyes, waiting for the sound of Alexei slipping, a scream of pain—but then Alexei was at her feet, laughing.

"Such a worrywart," he said, brushing snow from his knees as he rose. "Really, Olga. It's just snow."

Snow that can lead to ice, ice that can lead to slipping, slips that can cause bruising, she thought. *Bruising that can lead to disaster, without Father Grigori to save him.* "Alexei, I'm not sure it's a good idea to go again. What if something were to happen?"

"Come now, he's fine," Papa said, resting a heavy arm around her shoulders. "Not letting a young man enjoy the snow is positively un-Russian! Remember skiing down the hill in Alexander Park?" He looked up at Snow Mountain's three solid tiers, his cheeks pink. "This is half the height of that."

Olga recalled the gentle slope of the hillside, manicured to smooth perfection by Papa's honor guard: sliding down on wooden skis, carving long, graceful curves into the snow.

"Go on, Olga," said Tatiana. "See for yourself. It's just a bit of fun."

Alexei held out the sledge; Olga took it and started up the

steps she'd helped to freeze in place. She knew she was overreacting. The structure wasn't even all that large. It was a child's plaything, a distraction, but her legs still shook when she reached the top. She crouched low on the mountain's modest peak, trying to ward off an unfamiliar dizzying sensation: usually she was fearless when it came to heights.

"A bit quicker than that!" From down below, she could hear Anastasia's snort of disapproval. "The sun has already started setting, and other people want to try!"

With a deep breath, she wrenched her eyes open and stood. Above the protection of the fence, wind breathed life into her scarf, sending it billowing around her neck as she twisted to look over the barrier. The view was breathtaking: the setting sun's rays stretched long across the neighborhood, twisting the shadows of the guards beyond the gate into fairy-tale creatures; snow glittered in the public gardens, softening the flower beds into unfamiliar mounds as her fear dissolved on the air.

"Come on, Olga!"

She sat on the sledge, gathering her skirts beneath her before digging her heels into the hard-packed snow. She looked up to admire the view once more and caught sight of a curtain twitching in a second-story window: Mamma, her face obscured by the sunset glare.

Olga kicked her feet onto the sledge and propelled herself down the ice slide—the ride was glorious, exhilarating, over far too soon. As the sledge reached the bottom of Snow Mountain it banked and rolled; Olga tipped over onto the snow, laughing.

"See?" Alexei helped her to her feet. "What did I tell you? Nothing to fear." He grinned and snatched the sledge from Olga's grasp, darting back to the base of the mountain. "*Shvybzik*, shall we go together? Let's see if we can slide all the way to the gate!"

Olga watched as they climbed, still savoring the giddy feeling of the slide as Tatiana and Maria began throwing snowballs up at the mountain.

Papa sidled over, pulling his cigarette case from his overcoat; he held them out, but Olga demurred. "It's good to see you laugh," he said, lighting his cigarette. "You've been so quiet these past few months. I've missed that beautiful smile."

She watched Alexei and Anastasia scrape snowballs from the top of the mountain to pelt back down at Tatiana and Maria. "I suppose so," she replied. "Though there's not been much to smile about, has there?"

He let out a tobacco-scented breath. "I disagree," he replied, lifting his face to the setting sun. "It's a beautiful day, and we're all together. That's reason enough, I think."

She shifted, crossing her arms to keep her fingers warm; she glanced back at the house, where a handful of soldiers huddled by a bonfire, passing a cigarette between them. One of them watched Papa carefully, the bottom half of his face concealed in a heavy scarf, and Olga thought once more of the letter Papa had slipped into the cuff of his sleeve. "I've heard from some of the guards that we're to be subject to rationing. Is it true?"

Atop Snow Mountain Alexei and Anastasia balanced on the sledge, and Papa waved his encouragement as they kicked off. "It's no different from the rest of the country," he said finally. "It's important to show the people that we share in their hardships."

"The people don't have a household of fifty," Olga pointed out. "What are the kitchens meant to do? How can they feed our staff, the guards, and our family?"

"The monastery has offered to supplement our larder with whatever we need—eggs, fish, bread. We might end up eating simpler fare, but that's always been my preference. Better for the digestion." He looked at Olga, a smile twitching beneath his beard. "You aren't worried about our food supply, are you? You shouldn't concern yourself, my dear."

Though the courtyard was full of people, no one, it seemed, was paying attention to their conversation: the guards at the bonfire; Olga's siblings, climbing up the mountain. Mamma, her face pressed to the window. "Shouldn't I?" She stepped closer, lowering her voice to an undertone. "Why is that? Won't we be here much longer? Should we be making preparations to leave?"

Papa lifted his cigarette to his lips.

When it was clear he wasn't going to answer, Olga stepped closer still. "So, what should concern me, Papa? Because no one is telling me what's happening—no news, nothing." She reached for Papa's cigarette, her hands trembling as she pulled it from his fingers. "What's going to happen if the Bolsheviks decide to separate us? What if they put us out in the streets, or into prison? What if Alexei has another attack? What if we're never allowed to leave this courtyard again, if I don't ever get to see beyond this little patch—if I don't get to find a husband, have children..." She jammed the cigarette in her mouth, more to stop herself from crying than from a real desire to smoke. "Have you thought of that, Papa? Have you made any plans, anything at all?"

Papa lifted his arm and collected Olga close; she leaned into the strong column of his chest, tilted her head onto his shoulder.

"My dear girl," he whispered. "I forget you're not a child any longer. It's not fair for me to keep you in the dark." She pressed her face into Papa's scarf, the scent of his aftershave permeating the wool: citrus and cedarwood, putting her in mind of the greenhouse gardens at Livadia where the lemons grew as plump and large as cricket balls.

Olga drew back. "Tell me there's reason to hope." She closed her eyes, picturing Papa's letter, whisked from person to person through Tobolsk to Tyumen; enclosed in the lining of someone's jacket as they bought a third-class train ticket to Petrograd. Perhaps the return of Pankratov's soldiers to the capital could be a blessing in disguise; perhaps those who'd grown sympathetic would help rally their cause. "Tell me there's something I can do—something to be helpful—"

Papa hugged her close. "There are a thousand reasons to hope," he said finally. "Be patient. Think of your sisters. You mustn't give them cause to despair, not now. Support them; help your mother. There's always hope, so long as we're together."

22

February 1915
Tsarskoe Selo

Olga walked through her parents' apartment at Alexander Palace, the scent of roasted coffee awakening in her a muscle memory of alertness that made her steps quicken as she reached the door of the Small Library. Most mornings, Olga and her sisters breakfasted in their own dining room, their tightly regimented days leaving little time for leisurely conversation; however, as Papa and Alexei were to travel to the army's headquarters at Mogilev today, she wanted to say her goodbyes in person.

She stepped inside, smiling a hello at Nikolai Sablin, who was tucking into a lemon scone. Across the table, Alexei, dressed in a miniature version of an officer's uniform, was shoveling down a plate of scrambled eggs; beneath his chair, Ortipo, left behind by Dmitri Malama, rooted for scraps. Papa read through a stack of letters, while Mamma, dressed in her white nursing uniform, sipped at her tea, perusing a ledger of the Annexe's operating expenses.

"You won't believe it, Alicky," Papa was saying, peering down at the letter. "This is a petition from a woman who wishes to enlist in the infantry. Believes herself more than capable of holding her own against the men. *An irresistible force calls me to defend my country, and I am willing to make the ultimate sacrifice to ensure its survival…* I must say, I give her full marks for courage. Good morning, Olga, darling."

"Good morning," Olga replied, helping herself to the platter of eggs set on the sideboard between glass-fronted bookcases. "That's rather different, isn't it? A woman soldier?"

"Unusual, but not unheard of," offered Sablin. "A woman enlisted in the army during the war with Napoleon; she received a commendation from Tsar Alexander, I believe."

"It's unnatural." Mamma set down her ledger, her voice crisp with disapproval. "We all have our part to play in the war effort but it's hardly appropriate for a woman to take up arms. What message would it send to our men?"

"It might give them added incentive to prove their gallantry," said Papa, folding the letter along its well-worn crease. "You know, I'm inclined to grant her request. I don't think we ought to make a regular occurrence of it, but if she's as brave as she seems on paper, we could use that kind of spirit in our ranks. I'll talk to Nikolay Nikolaevich about it, see what he thinks."

Mamma sighed. "I wish you wouldn't. Nikolay Nikolaevich might be the commander in chief, but he isn't the tsar. If you feel this young woman's petition has merit, you ought to be the one to grant it, whether Nikolay agrees or not."

"That's a quick change in your tune," said Olga lightly as Sablin poured her a cup of coffee. "You think it's inappropriate, but she ought to be allowed to enlist?"

"Whether I think it's appropriate or not is irrelevant," Mamma replied. "Either way, it's the tsar's prerogative to decide. If he wishes to grant her request, he ought to do so without feeling obliged to consult with anyone—least of all Nikolay Nikolaevich."

Papa exchanged a meaningful glance with Sablin. "He's my military commander, Alicky; I can't make decisions that affect the military without consulting him," he said. "It's about the principle, darling. I respect Nikolay as my commander in chief; I will pay him the courtesy of asking his opinion on military matters."

"He's the one who ought to be paying *you* respect, and I don't believe he does," Mamma shot back. "I don't see why he should be making decisions about the army and covering himself in glory in the process. Father Grigori says that glory flows to the Empire from the tsar—not from the commander in chief. I know he's your cousin, Nicky, but allowing him to claim your successes for himself is a danger to your prestige and your power. I don't like it, dearest. I don't like it one bit."

Olga looked from Mamma to Papa, holding her tongue. Mamma had voiced her dislike for Grand Duke Nikolay Nikolaevich, Papa's tall and handsome cousin, before. With his forceful personality and booming laugh, Nikolay was popular not only with his soldiers but with Russian society at large—it was this last point, Olga suspected, which irked Mamma the most.

Papa stood; beside him, Alexei looked up expectantly. "He is carrying out my wishes to the letter," Papa replied, straightening his belt, "and the general staff is more than satisfied with his command. You must understand how important it is to maintain harmony amongst the generals, my dear, particularly when there are so many other pressing concerns at hand." He frowned, folding his gloves one over the other as Sablin hastily dabbed his mouth with a napkin. "What troubles me more than Nikolay's so-called glory is the state of our supply lines. Shipments of coal and ammunition are having difficulty reaching the front line. Food, clothing, medical equipment… Our troops are moving too quickly to receive the supplies they need."

Mamma stepped close to Papa and smoothed down the black-and-yellow ribbon that carried his Order of St. George. "Is that not the job of your ministers?" she asked. "Supply lines, ammunition… You're above such concerns." She shook her head with gentle despair. "I worry you've not learned from your past. You occupy your time thinking of the trivial when you ought to turn your attention to the consequential. Remember the Duma. When you give up power over what's important—even to a cousin like Nikolay—you'll never get it back."

Olga looked from Mamma to Papa. She could hear the censure in Mamma's words: the slow, steady erosion of absolute power was a goal that some members of the Duma, with their radical ideas on universal suffrage, actively sought. Every time the Duma contradicted Papa, their conviction in their own prominence—their own power—grew.

Papa looked down at Mamma, his eyes shining. "My fierce wife," he said. "What would I do without you?"

"My peaceable husband," she replied, resting her hand against his chest. "You know that I love you for your soft heart. But it's moments like this where you have to show your strength. Duty and honor, dearest! Your duty is to the country, not to your cousin's vanity. Take back what is yours and let him sulk over his bruised pride."

Across the table, Alexei spoke, his mouth half-full of toast. "Wouldn't it just be easier if you took charge of the army?" he said, employing a black-and-white logic that reminded Olga that her brother, despite his military uniform, was only ten years old.

Papa smiled indulgently. "As your mother rightly pointed out, we now have a state government that needs to be taken into consideration on such matters," he replied. "My dear boy, one day these decisions I take will be yours. You must learn to listen for the voice of God within you. He provides a clarity to my thoughts which makes me certain of my path. The Duma's counsel helps me understand the minutiae of an issue at hand, but it is God who guides me toward the actions I must take."

Alexei frowned as he fed Ortipo the crust. "But you could, couldn't you? Take over command of the army? If God told you it was the right thing to do?"

Papa leaned down to kiss Alexei on the crown of his head.

"If God illuminated that particular path to me, then of course I would heed His word," he said. "But for now, He seems quite satisfied with the ministers—and the commanders—I've chosen to help me in my task. Now, we ought to be setting off."

"So should we," said Mamma, nodding at Olga. "We'll be late to the hospital if we're not careful." She pressed a cross into Papa's hand, closing his fingers over the metal before raising his fist to her lips. "From Father Grigori," she whispered. "To remind you to be forceful in your dealings with Nikolay and the government. You are guided by God in your actions."

Mamma left Olga in the front hall of the Annexe, her footsteps light as she set off toward Anna's room. To Mamma's great relief, Anna had survived the long night of her accident, as well as the multiple surgeries which had followed—though still bedridden, she'd been moved into a private room that Mamma had done her best to make comfortable by hanging the bare walls with photographs and icons, bringing Anna a quilted coverlet from her own bedroom.

Olga paused outside the supply room, where Tatiana, whose shift had started several hours earlier, was preparing for the morning's surgery.

"She's in a state," Tatiana warned in an undertone, steel clattering on steel as she pulled a tray of sterilized instruments from the autoclave. She nodded toward the door. "Best to stay out of sight, if you can manage it."

"Consider me forewarned," Olga replied, pulling out a stack of bed linens. Dr. Gedroits' mood had steadily blackened over the past several weeks, exacerbated by the increasing number of casualties pouring out of the ambulance trains—and by Father Grigori's near-constant presence in the hospital. It irked her, Olga knew, to see Father Grigori credited with Anna's survival. Dr. Gedroits had succeeded in barring him from the officers' ward, but Mamma insisted that he be allowed to visit

Anna. More than once Olga had caught sight of him through Anna's open door, his head bowed in prayer over Anna's bed. "How many procedures today?"

Tatiana shook her head, setting the instruments down on a trolley piled with clean bandages. "Four," she replied. "Colonel Brusilov's developed gangrene in his foot; we may have to amputate up to the knee."

"Poor man," said Olga.

Tatiana shrugged. "Better his leg than his life. Mamma's made a new schedule for the week, you're to change bedsheets in the wards today."

"Bedsheets?" Olga circled to the schedule pinned to the wall. "Isn't that a job better suited to a *sanitar*? I thought I was to assist in surgery."

"You were, until yesterday's episode." Tatiana looked up. "You've been moved to ward-rounds. Dr. Gedroits can't run the risk of you losing your breakfast in surgery, can she?"

Olga reddened. "It was nothing." Yesterday, she'd been assisting in the routine excision of shrapnel from an officer's chest but made the mistake of glancing down at the open wound. She'd dropped the scalpel she'd been holding, perspiration inching down her neck at the sight of the patient's raw flesh—even Dr. Gedroits had noticed when she'd gripped the gurney for support.

Tatiana hardly looked convinced. "It was nothing that time; who's to say it will be nothing again? The fact is, we can't run the risk of a nurse collapsing mid-operation. Or dropping an instrument into a cavity." She glanced at the nearby clock. "Look, I don't have time to argue. I'm in surgery all day, then I've got committee meetings all evening. If you're upset, take it up with Mamma. Couldn't hold the door for me, could you?"

Olga opened the door, her cheeks still burning. "Tatiana, honestly, I don't know what happened," she said. "I'm trying to do what I can for the war effort—"

"The war effort—the war effort!" Tatiana huffed, her anger

boiling over as she spoiled for a fight Olga wasn't aware she'd picked. "Can't we go five minutes without talking about the war effort?" She exhaled, her shoulders rounding as she tightened her hold on the gurney. "Bedsheets, Olga. Just do it, please."

The ward smelled of contradictions, the antiseptic tang of disinfectant combined with the earthy scent of unwashed men; freshly laundered cotton of bedsheets and bandages undercut by an iron whiff of blood. In each ward, cots were lined one by one beneath the ancient eyes of Mamma's gilded icons, brought down from the palace; from the common room down the hall, strains of a string quartet echoed from the horn of an ancient gramophone.

With most of the officers finishing their luncheon in the dining room the wards were quiet: only a handful of patients dozed in their beds, enabling Olga to change most of the bedsheets uninterrupted. Beyond the rounded windows, fat snowflakes had begun to dance in the bright afternoon sunlight, buffeting the glass with increasing vigor. Several hundred kilometers south, Russian soldiers were freezing on the front lines, their breath clouding in the air as they walked along the trenches. Here in Tsarskoe Selo, they had thick brocade curtains and coal-burning boilers, potbellied woodstoves and warm blankets; on the front lines, the soldiers had nothing but what they could carry on their backs. No wonder so many arrived at the Annexe with advanced frostbite.

Here, they could recover in comfort. For most of the officers, the Annexe was the closest thing they'd had to a permanent address since the start of the war. Many stayed for months at a time, regaining their strength before being sent back to a regiment that often no longer contained the familiar faces of their brothers-in-arms. Many had made their beds a little reflection of their lives: some had been sent coverlets, gifts from anxious mothers or wives; others had crammed their bedside tables with family photographs or stacks of postcards. If she opened the drawer beside each bed, Olga was sure she'd find small flasks of contraband vodka, hidden from Mamma's prying eyes; paperback novels and playing cards to while away the idle hours of convalescence.

She stripped the sheets off a cot and kneaded the mattress, reddening at the thought of Tatiana—her shadowed eyes, her short temper. How had Olga missed the obvious fact that she wasn't sleeping? The oversight felt like yet another sign of Olga's incompetence: her incompetence as an older sister, her incompetence as a nurse. She'd thought she'd been effectively concealing her shortcomings from the rest of the nursing staff, but Dr. Gedroits' new roster had proven otherwise. Olga's failures were now affecting the other nurses, leaving them to pick up her loose ends.

If the best Olga could do within these four walls was change bedding, was she not better to spend her time elsewhere: in the administration of her war committees, in the opening of new hospitals and the welcoming of refugees? She could make speeches and smile for photographs, visit the front line with Papa. She pictured leaving the difficulties of nursing to those who were competent, retreating behind Mamma's favorite complaint of an "enlarged heart" to sidestep her humiliation.

"Can I be of assistance, Grand Duchess?"

Olga looked up. Dmitri Shakh-Bagov stood at the foot of the bed, his dark hair parted and glossed as brightly as his boots. His arm, no longer bound to his chest, was supported by a linen sling and he smiled, tucking his free hand in his pocket. At the hospital, she'd grown used to the sight of men in their nightclothes and shirtsleeves, the informality a necessary convenience for changing bandages. Close up, Shakh-Bagov made a fitting argument for the dashing new Grenadier uniform: his green *gymnastiorka* tunic was tailored close to his slim torso, the scarlet piping at his lapels matching the red and gold of his shoulder boards. At his waist, his distinctive Grenadier belt buckle glinted in the morning light, bearing the cypher of an exploding grenade.

She smiled. "With that arm? I can't imagine you'll be much help to me, Officer. But thank you for your concern."

He lifted his elbow experimentally, wincing as he tried and failed to raise it higher than his shoulder. "I suppose my services as a chambermaid leave something to be desired. Would you settle for some company?"

Olga was used to chatting with the patients—most wanted a story they could relay to their friends, an anecdote about the grand duchesses: that time they made Tatiana Nikolaevna blush; the day Olga Nikolaevna laughed at one of their jokes. With Dmitri Malama's departure a few weeks ago, Tatiana had relinquished her hold on Shakh-Bagov's ward, and Olga had grown used to the sight of him reading and writing letters. Did he relay, in his frequent letters home, anecdotes about Olga?

That time Olga Nikolaevna changed his bedsheets.

She looked down, depositing the soiled sheets in her hamper. "I hardly think that's appropriate, Officer."

He stepped back, blushing. "Grand Duchess, I didn't mean to presume, it's only…it's my bed, you see. It doesn't feel right to have you clean up after me when I'm perfectly capable of doing it myself. Please permit me to help."

Though most of the officers who passed through the Annexe maintained high levels of decorum, some occasionally descended into bawdiness, heard through the walls, in the common room. Clearly, such bawdiness didn't extend to Shakh-Bagov: he looked mortified at the thought of presuming anything inappropriate. The thought amused Olga. The grand duchess, scandalizing the soldier.

"I suppose you could pass me the clean bed linens," she said finally.

Shakh-Bagov handed her the sheets over the iron footboard.

"I must tell you," he said as the red receded from his cheeks, "I never expected a grand duchess to know how to make a bed."

Olga shook out the top sheet; it billowed in the space above the mattress before settling like a parachute on grass, and she tucked it into place with tight precision. "You might be surprised to know that my mother taught me." She stepped back, admiring her handiwork. "My sisters and I sleep in army cots just like this one. I learned my nurse's corners before I knew what nursing was."

"Is that so?" he said, and Olga couldn't tell whether he was teasing or genuinely incredulous. "No grand four-poster? No silk pillowcases?"

"Plain old cotton." She smiled, meeting the officer's dark gaze. "I'm afraid you'll be quite disappointed if you were hoping to hear any fairy tales about glass slippers and golden eggs. We're rather a boring bunch, really. We mend our own blouses and arrange our own flowers." She moved on to the next bed, pulling back the quilted coverlet. "Truly, you don't need to keep me company, Officer. I'm sure you have much better ways to spend your time."

"Hardly," he replied as she tore apart the bedcovers. "If I have to play one more round of table tennis with Captain Orlov, I'll stuff the blasted ball down his throat."

"Restless, are you?" She handed Shakh-Bagov the slept-in sheets in exchange for clean ones. "That's good. It means you're getting your fighting spirit back."

He grinned. "Who's to say I ever lost it? I can't quite believe I got myself injured so early on in combat. I'm ready to go back to the field as soon as I'm able; according to Dr. Gedroits, I should be fighting fit in two weeks' time."

"Don't be in too much of a hurry," Olga replied. "If you rush, you'll only get yourself injured again and end up back here."

"Spoken like a true nurse."

Olga looked down at the half-made bed. "A true nurse

wouldn't be changing bedsheets," she replied. She looked up. Above the door hung twin portraits of Papa and Mamma, their oiled faces surveying the room with equanimity. What would they say, if they heard Olga speaking so informally—so candidly—with an officer? She'd always strived to maintain a friendly distance from the patients under her care, but she couldn't deny that there was something about Shakh-Bagov that drew her attention. She'd tried to ignore it, knowing that there was little to be done about a flirtation—it was already such an intimate thing, nursing, without allowing attachments to form.

She sank onto the bed. "Can I tell you something? I'm not entirely sure I'm cut out for this sort of work."

He shook a pillow loose from its case one-handed. "What? Bed-making?"

"Nursing. My sister…she's so *good* at it. Watching her work, it's as if she was meant to be in hospitals. Meant to heal. Even Mamma seems to be indefatigable. But me? I nearly fainted in surgery yesterday." She picked at a thread in the bedsheet, pulling it loose from the weave. "I just wonder whether I could be put to better use elsewhere. Making speeches, shaking hands… I'm good at that sort of thing."

Shakh-Bagov set down the pillow and lowered himself onto the empty cot opposite hers, the wire springs creaking beneath the horsehair mattress. "Do you know, I've been preparing for this war my whole life, Grand Duchess?" he said. He looked up, light catching on the brass buttons of his uniform. "The 13th Regiment. Erevan Grenadiers. My father was a Grenadier; my grandfather, too, he fought at Borodino. As children, my brother and I used to sneak up to Father's bedroom and pull open the wardrobe, just to look at his uniform. We never wanted anything so much as to wear it." Shakh-Bagov chuckled, staring past Olga's shoulder at the billowing snow outside. Olga could appreciate the significance of his family's legacy: the Erevan Grenadiers were one of the most prestigious regiments in the entire Russian army, originally composed of battle-hardened Georgian soldiers who'd cut their teeth fighting invading Persian and Ottoman armies.

And Russian armies, Olga reminded herself. Georgia had only become part of the Empire over the last century.

"Anatoly stole his belt buckle once and wore it to church beneath his overcoat. Papa was furious when he found out—he gave us both a beating—but secretly I think he was pleased to know the regiment meant as much to us as it did to him," Shakh-Bagov continued. "Cancer got him in the end, but I know he would have preferred a clean death on some battlefield, somewhere. A warrior's death." He smiled, the gentleness in his eyes making him look less like a soldier, more like a poet. "As a young man, Papa had read about Valhalla. He was always fascinated by Norse myths."

Olga pictured Shakh-Bagov and his brother as black-haired children running their hands through the dark of a wardrobe, pressing their noses against the tobacco-infused wool of their father's uniform. Whispering stories about Viking warriors in bloodstained serge and khaki, telling tales of their glorious deaths amidst the barbed wire.

He looked down. "Duty. Loyalty. Gallantry. Those were the values I grew up with; they were the values I took to the regiment, when I was accepted amongst their ranks. At military college, we learned about the battles of the past: Borodino. Aslanduz. Poltava. They taught us gallantry, bred it into our bones, raising us on the stories of Russia's past in the hopes that we, too, would one day face death with open arms.

"And then I was made an adjutant. An army administrator. I was shocked. I thought I'd be made a captain, like my father—like Anatoly, like my grandfather. The appointment felt a failure, somehow. As though I wasn't good enough to lead men into battle."

Olga watched his features cloud over. "It's hardly a demotion," she said. "It's an administrative position, and an important one at that. You're the right-hand man for your commander; you're there, watching the decisions as they get made."

He smirked. "Tell that to a young man of eighteen whose brother has been decorated for bravery," he replied. "Sending men into battle while leading from behind… It felt cowardly. I could hardly look Anatoly in the eye when I took up my post."

"There's nothing cowardly about it," said Olga. "You're in different positions, that's all there is to it. You have different skills to offer."

He ran his hand along the striped mattress, his free shoulder lifting in a sort of concession. "My grandfather fought with horse and bayonet; my father, with sabers and pistols. Hand-to-hand combat—that's true heroism. Confronting your enemy face-to-face, knowing you have an equal chance at survival. But what use is bravery against a machine gun? What good are myths against a mortar blast?" He shook his head, his features clouding further. "We got caught out by the Austrians near Viskoe-Tarnovka: eighteen officers dead and thirty-four wounded. They aimed for our epaulettes. Anatoly was amongst them."

Olga let out a breath but didn't respond. This far from the front, the war bled into life in fits and starts: in ambulance trains and operations, in bandaging wounds; in burying those who didn't survive the journey north. Her understanding of the war was limited to those who'd left the battlefield breathing: she'd been spared the sight of those poor souls left behind.

"My brother was no coward, nor were the other officers in our regiment who led their men into battle. But machine-gun fire cares so little for our myths of our past. For Borodino and Aslanduz." He grimaced. "The mightiest army in the world—that's what we call ourselves. But we've rested on our laurels too long, cosseting ourselves in stories of past glory while our enemies build weapons capable of destruction without a second's mercy. Anatoly's bravery, his heroism; his expertise and his experience, his years of schooling and training and loving and living...what did it all amount to, when he died within ten minutes of entering the battlefield?" He shook his head. "A dead hero is still dead. One more gallant warrior who will feast in the halls of Valhalla."

Instinctively, Olga reached across the space between the cots, bringing her fingers to rest on his knee. "I'm so sorry, Officer."

He looked down at her hand, his face tightening. For a moment Olga worried she'd overstepped herself—but then he rested his hand over hers. "When Anatoly died, I thought I'd kill myself. But now, I'm one of the last remaining officers in my regiment. I owe it to his memory—to our men—to keep myself alive." He stared down, stroking the back of her hand with his thumb. His touch sent electricity crackling through Olga's skin, jolting her heart into motion, reminding her with each thumping beat that she, too, was alive, that despite her weakness she was strong, that despite her pain, she could feel joy

He met her gaze. "You know, I was in St. Petersburg—Petrograd, that is—during the tercentenary celebrations. I came out to Palace Square and watched you and your sisters as you passed in your carriage, waving to the crowds. You were so small: a pinprick princess, a thousand feet away."

Olga nodded. "I remember that day," she said. "People were lined up all along the parade route. I'd never seen anything like it." She glanced at the ward's open door, amazed no one had interrupted their conversation. "Perhaps that's where I'm best suited: in front of those crowds, giving them strength from afar. Like Papa."

He conceded her point with another shrug of his good shoulder. "You're a good nurse, Grand Duchess," he said. "I've seen you in the halls and the common room, sitting with the officers. Changing bandages; making them laugh. I've watched you comfort men when they wake up screaming; I've seen you write letters for those who've lost the use of their hands. Your greatest strength is your compassion.

"If you were to leave this hospital you would be replaced by another nurse. But to the men in this hospital, you're so much more than that. You're our tsar's daughter. You're the reason we're fighting." He smiled, leaning closer. "The imperial family…you're as much a myth to these men as Valhalla, if I may be so bold. But you're here, reminding them of what they're fighting for. And moreover, you're witnessing the true cost of war. You're seeing the price paid by the gallant. By the loyal. You are looking into the darkness and bringing light to those who linger there." He squeezed her hand, his dark eyes crinkling into a smile. "Perhaps that's worth changing a few bedsheets."

Gently, he released his hold and leaned back. "If you were to leave this hospital, you would become that pinprick princess once again. You'd be a thousand feet away from the people, just as you were in that golden carriage. A myth." He stood and offered her his hand; she took it and rose to her feet, hearing once more the distant sound of the gramophone; laughter, from the officer's common room. "Just be here, Grand Duchess. That is more useful to these men than you can ever know."

23

February 1918
Freedom House, Tobolsk

Olga stood by the curtains in Mamma's small sitting room in Freedom House, listening to the sound of the guards milling below, thinking of Shakh-Bagov's smile.

Shakh-Bagov. *Mitya.* She'd started referring to him as Mitya in her mind soon after that conversation in the ward, when electricity had jumped between their palms: after such a spark, Shakh-Bagov felt too formal; Dmitri, his given name, too common. But Mitya—*my darling*—suited him more than anything else, for he had been darling to her: his silhouette, unforgettable, framed by the oak door of the common room as she'd wheeled past with her supplies; his company, valued, as he'd followed her on her rounds, lightening her moods, his questions making her feel interesting, smart, kind.

As his nurse, Olga hadn't let her feelings show—she hadn't dared to call him Mitya to his face, hadn't dared let her hand linger overlong on his shoulder as she changed his bandages. But she had cherished the time she spent with him even as she dreaded his return to the front line. But his return to the front line had been inevitable, and Olga had borne his departure as best she could, for he wouldn't have been darling to her if he'd tried to shirk his duties. His courage was as dear to her as any other facet of his personality, which sparkled like a gemstone, lighting the dark corners of her mind in the long nights of his absence.

Now, she leaned her forehead against the window frame, pulling aside the muslin curtain in the sitting room to watch the snow fall.

Mitya. Where was he now, lighting the dark wreckage of Russia's ruins?

"Olga, dear, I need you." Mamma was seated at a small desk in front of the furnace, Pierre Gilliard standing behind her. "Your eyes are better than mine. What does this say?"

Olga let the curtain fall back into place, and circled to join them, Gilliard over Mamma's left shoulder, Olga over her right as they studied a thick leather-bound ledger of expenditures itemized in Gilliard's neat script. Ink bled through the onionskin paper, making the figures difficult to read atop their ghostly counterparts.

Pinned to the top of the ledger was a handwritten note, which Mamma pulled free and handed to Olga.

"It says that our monthly expenditures are reduced to six hundred rubles per person," Olga read, wrinkling her nose with distaste. Written in the unlettered scrawl of Pankratov's replacement, Pavel Matveev, neither the note itself nor its contents were to Olga's satisfaction. Six hundred rubles... How far would that stretch? "And that there will be no allowance for our servants."

Mamma closed her eyes. "Thank you," she said. At Alexander Palace, Mamma's Mauve Room had always been a place of repose. Here, she'd attempted to recreate her beloved sanctuary, bedecking her sitting room with the same gilded icons and graceful furniture, the same heavy carpets to keep out the chill. At Alexander Palace, there had been something endearing about Mamma's overstuffed aesthetic: here, the furniture looked at odds with the room's small proportions, making the space feel insistent upon its occupants' former glory.

Tatiana shifted her chair closer to the desk. "Is that on top of ration cards?" She glanced uncertainly from Mamma to Gilliard, and Olga was thankful that Maria, Anastasia and Alexei weren't in the room. "The rest of the household will have their own ration cards, won't they? Six hundred…that amounts to over four thousand rubles for the family. That's for additional expenses? Clothing, and the like?"

Pierre Gilliard leaned forward, the chain of his pocket watch swinging across his stomach. "That's to pay for the household," he explained.

"We're still receiving packages from town," she pointed out. "Bread, fish…just yesterday, we were given eight bottles of milk from the monastery. Surely that will help."

"It will help, but it won't solve." Mamma leaned back in her chair, pressing her thumb and forefinger to the bridge of her nose. "And though we only received eight bottles, I'm sure they sent twelve. Who knows what else the guards are taking off the top? I don't doubt those baskets were twice as full before they reached the kitchen."

Olga didn't doubt it either—though they'd only been at Freedom House for less than a week, the new guards serving under Matveev were coarser, more aggressive, than those who'd left. Just this morning she'd found a dirty word carved in the door frame outside her bedroom. She'd gone over it with a butter knife, attempting to gouge it out before her sisters noticed it, but the insult lingered in her mind.

When Papa had asked her and Tatiana to sit in on Mamma and Gilliard's meeting about household expenses, Olga had assumed she'd rather know what they were facing than remain in the agonizing dark about her family's circumstances. But now, looking over Mamma's shoulder at the ledger made her feel ill. She circled back around the desk to sit next to Tatiana.

"It's not just the food, it's the money," Mamma was saying to Gilliard. "We're close to the last of our savings as it is. Without access to our bank accounts, we won't be able to pay our staff."

"I'm afraid it's unlikely we'll see those accounts again," Olga muttered. "No doubt the income from our estates is lining Lenin's pockets as we speak."

"Please, Olga, I won't have that tone," Mamma replied wearily. "I appreciate you wanting to help, but bitterness is so very unbecoming. Pierre, what do you suggest we do? I don't want to reduce the household, not if we have any other options."

Gilliard planted his hands on the table, the edge of his high collar digging into his chin as he stared down at the ledger through wire-rimmed spectacles. "I'm afraid you have little choice, Empress," he said. "I'm sorry to say it, but the numbers are clear. Concessions will have to be made."

"I won't let anyone go," Mamma said firmly. "These people followed us here from Alexander Palace at great personal risk. I won't leave them destitute; I won't have them punished for their loyalty."

"I admire your sentiment, but the decision is no longer in your hands," Gilliard replied. "We must dismiss staff—at least ten people, by my count. And reduce wages for the rest."

Mamma was silent for a moment—then she opened the desk's drawer. "Very well," she said, pulling out a bottle of veronal. "Leave the list with me and I'll raise it with the emperor. He'll want to make the final decisions himself. Thank you, Gilliard."

Gilliard collected the ledger, bowing at the neck before leaving the room; Mamma closed her eyes once more, and held out her hand for Olga.

"Ten servants," she muttered, using Olga's arm to steady herself as she stood. With Olga's help she navigated the small room's cluttered furniture to her divan, bracing a hand on her corset as she sank down into the pillows; behind her, Olga could hear the sound of water tumbling into a glass. "They've sacrificed so much for us. I only wish there was something we could do."

"Perhaps it's for the best," Olga replied gently. "They'll be able to make a fresh start—find new positions—"

"And who amongst these brutes will give the imperial household a fresh start?" Tatiana circled to the divan with a glass of water in hand as Mamma uncapped the veronal, carefully measuring out the small crystals with a dainty spoon. "They're as much a symbol of the old order as we are. They'll never be allowed to forget it."

"Not to mention the bother of finding new retainers once we leave this place, God willing," Mamma added, stirring the water clear. "We'll be required to build our household up from scratch."

Olga glanced at Tatiana as Mamma drank down her concoction, but neither responded.

Already Olga could see that the sedative was taking effect, blurring the edges of Mamma's expression as she settled into the cushions. "Thank you for your help, girlies," she said. "I know it's not easy, but we must all pull together. Father Grigori would be proud of you both."

"Of course, there will be a new household," Tatiana muttered as they walked down the hall. They'd shut the curtains and closed the door to Mamma's sitting room softly, leaving her to her barbital-laced dreams. Olga had put the veronal back in Mamma's desk drawer, but not before noting how empty the bottle had become. Mamma had always relied on sedatives to calm her nervous disposition, but in the past few months her use of them had grown exponentially. "The new government may not like us, but at some point, they'll leave us in peace. Once the war is over, they'll have no reason not to let us be."

"Won't they?" Olga lowered her voice as they passed Alexei's bedroom; within, she could hear her siblings studying with Sydney Gibbes. "And how exactly would it serve them to have us move back to Alexander Palace? Or Livadia? They certainly won't let us live in Petrograd." She rubbed a hand across her eyes, trying to erase the memory of Gilliard's ledger. "What if they have something else in mind for us?"

"Don't be ridiculous." Tatiana glanced through Alexei's open door; within, Anastasia looked up and waved. "Matveev told us in that note, plain as day: they don't want us to be an expense that much longer. They're going to have to find somewhere for us to go."

Olga took Tatiana's arm; together, they continued toward the ballroom. "That's my concern: it will be *their* choice, not ours." She looked up at the sound of an opening door: two of Matveev's guards emerged from the ballroom, their uniforms slashed with red armbands, and Olga switched to English. "I don't like the idea of being so deep in their grasp."

They were interrupted by a commotion in the hallway; Olga looked up, her fear bubbling to the surface once more as Alexei shot past, howling, into the ballroom.

Olga started to run; behind her, she knew Tatiana was racing, too. They caught up to Alexei at the window and followed his gaze down into the courtyard.

Outside, Papa stood beside a bonfire next to the flat-capped figure of Matveev. His hands clasped behind his back, Matveev nodded once, curtly, and half a dozen guards advanced on Snow Mountain. Wielding flat-bottomed shovels, they began to hack at the mountain, ripping deep into its white core.

"What are they doing?" Alexei moaned. He pressed his forehead to the glass, tears streaming down his face. "How could they?"

Olga watched a second longer, fury building within her as Tatiana pulled Alexei into her embrace. She turned on her heel and ran out of the ballroom, careening down the stairs and out into the bone-chilling cold.

"Stop it!" She stormed toward Matveev, her stout heels sinking into the snow as fire coursed through her veins. "It's a *plaything*, for goodness' sake! How could you?"

Papa caught up to her, shrugging out of his greatcoat. "You'll catch your death, my dear," he muttered, placing it around her shoulders.

Olga stared at their new overseer, shaking. Small and unkempt, with something of a rodent's sharpness to his features, Matveev looked like the sort of criminal Olga expected to find in the ranks of the Bolshevik party: duplicitous and power-hungry. Obsessed, like their leader Lenin, with asserting an authority he'd never earned.

"Upsetting children, and for what? To prove yourself, is that it?"

"Olga," Papa muttered. He squeezed her shoulders, as if to remind her of the balance of power, but Olga shrugged free, channeling some of Mamma's principled outrage.

"You've no business here; this matter doesn't concern you," Matveev replied, dropping cigarette ash on the snow. "Go back inside, Grand Duchess."

"So, I'm still a grand duchess, am I? I thought you might have forgotten," Olga breathed. "And in that capacity, I demand to know: what exactly do you think you're doing?"

Matveev tore his flat gaze from Snow Mountain. "I call you a grand duchess as a mark of courtesy, nothing more," he replied. "A courtesy, I might add, that I expect to see returned. We can make this a cordial arrangement or an unpleasant one; it makes no difference to me either way."

"And it's *cordial* to tear down a child's snow fort?" Olga shot back.

Matveev turned his attention back to Snow Mountain. "You see a snow fort, do you? I see a hazard from which you or your sisters might fall and injure yourselves. Given your brother's condition, I think it a courtesy indeed to safeguard your welfare. I see a structure upon which your diminishing household might signal to counterrevolutionaries, putting my men at risk of an ambush. Worst of all, I see a pedestal upon which the imperial family might be plucked off, one by one, by snipers aiming over the fence. It is your safety I fear for, madam." He shook his head; in the window, Olga could see Alexei's stricken face as the guards continued to break the mountain down. "What Pankratov was thinking in allowing that thing in the yard, I'll never know."

Papa sighed. "He was doing something kind for the children."

Matveev's smile was more a sneer than anything else. "The kindness I will show to your family will be in keeping them alive," he retorted. "And I'm sure you won't fault me for the actions I take in that regard."

He turned on his heel and walked away, leaving a brown smudge in the snow beneath his boot.

24

June 1915
Tsarskoe Selo Station, Tsarskoe Selo

The train station at Tsarskoe Selo was silent, but for the rustling of the nurses and doctors and *sanitary* that waited at the platform—small coughs and genteel whispers, the shifting of weight from foot to foot. Standing shoulder to shoulder with Tatiana and Rita Khitrovo, Olga glanced up at the frantic sound of beating wings. Overhead, a bunting swooped beneath the vaulted ceiling, disappearing into the tangle of a nest it had fashioned in the crux of a pillar.

Farther down the line, Dr. Gedroits stepped forward, consulting her pocket watch. "There," she said quietly, and beyond the open arch of the station Olga could hear the heavy chug of steam and iron, the noise sending a frisson of anticipation and dread coursing through her veins. All around her, the Sisters of Mercy began to stir. Dressed in identical frocks and white habits, it was difficult to distinguish between them, though Olga did recognize a few faces from long-ago ballrooms. There was Princess Rayevskaya, her petite frame dwarfed by the doctor standing next to her; at the far end of the hall stood Anya Kleinmichel, her nursing habit strangely reminiscent of her wedding veil. Olga had given her a thin smile as they'd assembled in the train station, thinking of Pavel: was he well? Olga was sure she would have been sent word if Pavel had perished—still, she didn't have courage enough to ask Anya a question for which she might not want to hear the answer.

The locomotive eased into the station belching black steam, its battered carriages adorned with the red-and-white emblem of the Red Cross. Olga recalled touring one of the ambulance trains before its inaugural voyage to the front: threading through the gleaming bunks, listening with interest as some official or other detailed the work that had taken place to make the carriages useful for medical transport. Dust-covered and pockmarked, the carriages that made up this ambulance train looked as if they'd crossed through hell and back, and Olga supposed, in a very real sense, that they had. From beyond the soot-covered windows, Olga could make out the indistinct movement of hands and faces.

The *sanitary* were the first onto the train, bypassing the combat sisters who'd accompanied the train from the front line. The sisters descended, bloodied and weary, and it was clear they'd not slept for a single minute of their journey from the front. They stared at Olga and the rest of the sisters from the city hospitals as if suspicious of their clean aprons and scrubbed hands; more than one followed on the tail of stretcher-bearing *sanitar*, barking directives for a patient's care.

One by one, the *sanitary* deposited their stretchers on the marble floor of the train station and Olga, along with the rest of the sisters from hospitals around Tsarskoe Selo, stepped into action. She knelt by the nearest stretcher, which contained an unconscious infantryman. Somehow, the dust that had settled into the creases around his eyes put Olga in mind of the stage makeup she'd seen on Bolshoi dancers, nimble twenty-year-olds tasked with playing jealous fathers and aged patriarchs, their dark hair powdered with flour. Despite the jostling of the *sanitary* as they'd brought him off the train, the soldier was motionless, and Olga suspected he'd been given morphine. The smell of him was almost overpowering: it was clear he'd been injured days ago, the stench of blood and sweat and vomit commingling with such potency that Olga struggled not to retch. Instead, she lifted the blanket that covered him from the neck down.

His legs were a bloodied mess, flesh and bone and bandage stained with the browning rust of blood. Someone—a doctor or medic—had cut the man's breeches to better access his wounds: they hung in clotted ribbons, the khaki congealed and black.

Olga gasped, holding the edge of her habit to her nose before steeling herself to finish her assessment. Somehow, in the open chaos of the station, suffering seemed easier to bear than in the cloying closeness of the surgery; here, she was able to calm her shaking hands, focus on the man in front of her as she took stock of his injuries.

"Sister Romanova." Olga looked up; behind her, Dr. Gedroits cast an appraising eye over the soldier, her spectacles glinting, calm despite the confusion of soldiers, *sanitary* and sisters. "What have we here?"

"Looks like the work of an artillery explosion. He has extreme damage to his lower extremities, as well as shrapnel wounds to his abdomen and chest." Olga sat back on her heels, wiping her hands on her apron. "He's an infantryman—bound for the wards at Catherine Palace, I should think."

Dr. Gedroits nodded, the crease between her brows deepening. "Any more details?"

"According to the tag on his lapel he was sedated six hours ago. Morphine. It looks as if they've treated his wounds with potassium permanganate, but he'll likely require amputation of one, if not both, of his legs."

The doctor made a note on her clipboard. "Well, we'll leave that to the surgeons to decide," she murmured. "All right, mark him down for the Catherine Palace and move on. And Olga? Good work."

The day was far too long and frustratingly short, the stream of casualties carried out of the train so endless that Olga worried there wouldn't be space for them all in the wards of Tsarskoe Selo, created out of hastily converted summer homes provided by Papa's friends and government ministers. Between the whispers of the other nurses and the griping of conscious soldiers, Olga could tell that the war was going poorly: Russia had abandoned Poland entirely, had simply up and left a region of the Empire they could no longer defend. She mourned for the lives lost in Poland but set aside her grief: every soldier here was a life spared, a warrior who, God willing, could return to the front and one day make right the devastating loss.

After hours of assessing patients, Olga's back ached from leaning over stretchers; her fingers, so nimble and quick from years of piano lessons and embroidery, were stiff and shaking as she unwrapped dirty bandages. Most of the soldiers had been hit by artillery fire, their wounds gaping and impersonal: abdominal injuries that stank with infection, their torsos—that marvel of God's engineering—rendered so vulnerable, so fragile, by steel and bullets. Wounds to the extremities, too, were gruesome. Some had already undergone the most rudimentary of amputations at the front, leaving them with stumps where their arms and legs used to be, ragged and black with potassium permanganate; others pleaded with her, sobbing, to save their limbs. What use would they be to their families, to their farms, without arms to bring in the harvest? Few recognized her as the grand duchess she was, and for that Olga was grateful: to the soldiers under her care, she was just another nurse with a soft smile and tender hands.

The worst, though, were the head wounds: the men who came in disfigured by bullets and shrapnel, their contorted features concealed beneath the abbreviated dignity of a gauze bandage. To Olga, the physical pain of their injuries was difficult enough to contemplate but knowing what awaited them on their recovery was more overwhelming still: they would be condemned to a life in the shadows, poor devils, their faces an unwelcome reminder of a war that had already taken too many young lives.

It was over one such patient that Olga's nerves finally failed her: a young man, barely eighteen by Olga's estimation, his head swathed in a bandage so thick that the only clue to his identity was the scrub of a mustache he'd tried, and failed, to grow. She lifted the gauze to assess the damage: his skull, visible through a split in his scalp, had been crushed inwards, bone fragments pressing on the gray matter beneath. The fact he'd survived so long was a miracle in itself. His eyelids fluttered at her touch, revealing flashes of white.

She pressed the dressing back into place, but his brain, swollen beyond the constraints of his skull, had begun to bleed anew: she could feel him slipping away beneath her fingers, his pulse erratic as he began to convulse. His eyelids flickered, as if questioning the absurdity of circumstances that had led to his arrival here, now, at the end of his short life. Given time, given peace, the boy's wounds might heal—unlike Alexei, his blood might clot, giving him a fighting chance. But what matter of life would he have? Perhaps a cleaner death was what he deserved: his hand held by someone whispering comfort, someone who, in the farthest reaches of his listening soul, he might believe to be his mother, his sweetheart, the wife he'd had yet to meet.

But Olga's role was to heal, and she redoubled her efforts to stem the inevitable tide, pressing his brain back into place as if such a thing would save him—until she felt his pulse weaken beneath her fingers, sputtering like a candle at the end of its wick. Slowly, carefully, she lifted her hands. She began to whisper platitudes and Bible passages, long-ago nursery rhymes from her childhood, songs he might have known. In her mind's eye, she pictured the home she hoped he'd had: the fields he'd tilled, the gleam of sunlight on billowing wheat.

Too soon, she closed his eyes and stood. Brushing a clean

patch of her sleeve across her cheeks, she signaled for a team of *sanitary* to bear him away, to join the growing assembly of those who'd not survived the journey home.

She stepped outside, the fresh air a jarring contrast to the miasma of the train station. To Olga's surprise, dusk had fallen over Tsarskoe Selo, the dim half-light as close to darkness as the city ever saw in summer. On the street below, ambulance lorries idled in a long line, ready to bear their patients away to the comfort of a warm bed, and though the prospect of a long night's sleep was still hours away, no one would begrudge Olga a moment's peace. She patted down the pockets of her apron for her cigarettes, her heart beating dizzyingly loud in her ears.

"Light, Grand Duchess?"

Olga looked up. Anya Kleinmichel was leaning against a nearby column, looking nearly as weary as Olga felt. She held out her lighter, fingers loose around the silver and Olga took it with a nod of thanks. She inhaled, willing her shaking hands to still, but Anya didn't seem to notice; together, they leaned back against the pillar and watched the line of ambulances receive their steady stream of patients.

"We look," said Anya finally, as she tapped ash onto the cobbles, "like the only two people in the world having a bad day."

Olga looked over, incredulous. A joke, from Anya Kleinmichel? She'd always seemed so quiet…but then, Olga had never made much of an effort to get to know her.

She rested the back of her head against the windowpane, staring up at the tangle of electrical wires overhead. "We're an awfully long way from my aunt's tea parties, aren't we?"

Anya let out a billowing breath of smoke. "You know, I never thought you noticed me at those parties," she said. "You were always at the opposite end of the room."

Olga shifted, thinking of her aunt's parlor: Tatiana, holding court by the fireplace, surrounded by friends; Olga, set apart, whispering in some dark corner, pursuing romance. "Of course, I noticed you," she said finally. "You know how Aunt Olga is. Always making connections."

Anya closed her eyes. Tendrils of her hair had escaped the confines of her habit: she'd not bothered to tuck them back into place, and they lifted with the gentle breeze. "Your aunt's parties were the best I ever attended," she said, her voice soft with faraway pleasure. "Even your coming-out ball, as beautiful as it was… I preferred the intimacy of your aunt's home. She always invited such interesting people."

On the street, a pair of *sanitary* hopped out of the back of an ambulance and shut the doors; one knocked on the cab and the ambulance pulled out—bound for Catherine Palace, Olga assumed. "Did you know Aunt Olga joined a flying column at the front?" She shook her head, chuckling. "She tells me she's asked for no special treatment. She's sleeping in the same quarters as the rest of the sisters: no bathing facilities, no comforts."

"Good for her." Anya jerked her head back toward the station as two *sanitary* carried out another stretcher. "Is it what you pictured?"

Olga's fingers had stopped trembling; she looked down at her fingernails, grime showing beneath the tidy half-moons of her manicure. "No," she said. "No, it's nothing like I thought."

"Nothing ever is." Anya stubbed out the end of her cigarette. "Not nursing, not life; not marriage."

Olga was silent as she offered Anya her cigarette case. On Pavel's wedding day, she'd wished for his happiness—she'd not given a thought to Anya's. "How so?"

"Well, for one, I didn't expect we'd be spending our first year as newlyweds apart." Anya inspected the brand on the cigarette before lighting it. "We didn't know each other all that well when he proposed—it was all arranged, you know—but those first six months…after our wedding, before the war…"

She smiled. "We grew close. He's a good man, Grand Duchess. Kindhearted."

Olga nodded, astounded that it had been little more than a year since Pavel and Anya's wedding—little more than a year since she pleaded, one final time, for Pavel's affections. Had she been the ghost in their marriage from the outset? Had her presence in their house diminished, as their feelings toward each other grew?

"He is," she offered finally.

"You know, I joined the Red Cross to be close to him—or as close as I can be, given the circumstances." Anya looked down at her cigarette, the ember edging toward her fingers. "But I worry it's made me know too much of war: too much of pain, too much of suffering. Too much of what might happen to Pavel." She glanced back at the door to the train station; they would have to return soon, back into the misery of the endless stretchers. "The physical injuries, I think we could withstand, but the impact of this war on his mind, on his soul… The man I sent off to war might not be the one who comes home to me. If he comes home at all."

Olga bowed her head. The last time she'd spoken to him, Pavel had promised Olga friendship. Did she not owe that friendship to Anya in return?

"This war has taken so much from so many—husbands, fathers, brothers. Limbs, sanity…there's no telling what the war might ask of you." She glanced at Anya. "But the one thing it's taken from everyone in Russia—every single person in Europe—is certainty. I can't pretend to know what the future holds for Pavel, but what I do know is that he is a good man. Whatever the future holds, that core of him will remain."

Anya's eyes were hard. "Do you truly think so?" she said. "Even after all of the horror you've seen—all the horror Pavel will see—do you think he can withstand it and come out a good man?"

Olga squeezed Anya's hand. "I know he can."

They stood in silence a moment longer as they finished their cigarettes, though Olga didn't want to tarry overlong. The doors to the train station opened and Olga looked up, worried it was Dr. Gedroits coming to chide them for their idleness. Instead, it was another patient, the blanket trailing from his stretcher as the *sanitary* carried him down the stairs.

"Wait." Olga threw aside the end of her cigarette and jogged forward to tuck the blanket back into place. She paused, studying the soldier's face in the light from the open door.

Mitya. His face bruised and swollen, with a nasty gash on his forehead and an arm bound up in a hastily tied bandage. Olga was surprised she'd recognized him at all.

She cleared her throat. "What happened to him?"

"Trampled under a cavalry charge, Sister," said one of the *sanitary*. "He's in quite a state, I'm afraid—he may not have use of his hand again. But the doctors at Catherine Palace will do their best."

She ran her hand along his cheek, but he didn't wake; like so many others, he'd clearly been sedated. She could only imagine the circumstances that had led to his injuries, and while she felt for his doubtless pain, she couldn't help feeling a soaring, shameful relief. He was here, home.

Safe.

"Take him to the Annexe Hospital," she said.

The *sanitary* exchanged glances. "Sister? I'm afraid he's down for the officer's ward at Catherine Palace, the good doctor said—"

"The Annexe," Olga repeated firmly. "By order of the Grand Duchess Olga Nikolaevna."

25

July 1915
Tsarskoe Selo

In the Annexe Hospital, white was the color of healing. To Olga, who compared it to the riotous shades that adorned Petrograd's palaces and chapels, white had always felt unremarkable—a blank canvas on which to paint something more exciting—but in a hospital ward white signified hope. It was what she looked for on bandages as she dressed officers' wounds: the slow, tidal ebb of bodily fluids on the underside of gauze; the crisp, hard shell of a plaster cast as bone knitted back into bone. It was the comforting sign of cleanliness, starched bedsheets and bandages rolled neatly in the linen cupboard; the tail-end flash of nightshirts in the common room as officers regained the ability to lift themselves out of bed in pursuit of diversion.

At a hospital, white was the color of healing, but gray was the color of death. In the darkened room that served as the Annexe's morgue, Olga lit thin tallow candles, hoping to dispel the ashen pallor from Field Marshal Orentov's lined face. The bloom had long since faded from his cheeks, and the candles only briefly conferred upon him some facsimile of life: light flickered in the rises and valleys of his hollowed visage but did nothing to erase the bluish gray of his thin lips.

She stared down at the body, willing herself to feel something—anything—other than guilt. Though Orentov had died just hours before, he'd faded from the living long ago: in the months since his arrival at the hospital his body had healed but his mind had not, and as the other officers played table tennis and stretched their limbs, Orentov had grown ever more silent, the whites of his eyes graying as he stared at some unseen nightmare.

Dr. Gedroits had shaken her head at the sight of him. *Traumatic neurosis*, she'd muttered, pity etched in her features: time, only time, might heal the field marshal of his invisible wounds. Without the promise of a medical procedure to ease his suffering, Olga had tried to draw the field marshal out of his shell. She sat with him and read aloud, hoping that the sound of her voice might spark some latent joy in him, but her efforts were to little effect, and with so many other patients requiring her care, her time spent with him began to shorten: in these last few weeks, all she'd managed to offer him was a kind word as she sat a steaming cup of tea on his bedside table; a smile as she picked up the cold dregs later in the afternoon.

She pulled a small crucifix from her apron and pressed it between Orentov's stiffened fingers, hoping he'd found the peace that had eluded him for so long.

She returned to the ward, avoiding the sight of Orentov's stripped mattress by the door: the sight was too pitiable, too tragic, when she needed to reserve her sympathies for the living. Instead, she lifted her face to the beam of summer sunlight that streamed through the picture window, allowing the gentle hum of the ward to wash away the lingering stillness of the morgue. Someone had opened a window and the room felt brighter for the breeze: beyond the green wall of shrubbery, she could hear the errant drift of conversation. Inside, a fly buzzed lazily above the heads of the dozing officers, bumping against the glass as it searched for a way back out to the garden.

She took her time on her rounds, making more of an effort to talk to each officer under her care as she turned those who'd begun to form bedsores and made note of those whose bandages were in need of changing. As she worked, she kept the corner of her eye trained on the bed beneath the window where Mitya lay, his injured hand rising and falling atop the coverlet as he dozed.

When she'd seen to all the other patients, she set a tea tray down on Mitya's bedside table.

"Good morning," she said, pouring tea and a splash of milk neatly into a clean cup.

"For whom?" He shifted upright, the blanket sliding off of the heavy plaster cast that encased his left leg almost to the hip. "What time is it?"

"Nearly eleven," she replied. "I've only got a few minutes, I'm lunching with the Yusupovs in Petrograd once I'm done here."

"How exciting." He stared across the ward as he sipped his tea one-handed, sunlight glinting across his stubbled chin. Though the bruises he'd arrived with four weeks ago had long since healed, Mitya's stay at the Annexe was destined to be a long one. He'd gotten caught beneath the hooves of an advancing German cavalry charge in Poland, and the encounter had left him with multiple fractures to his leg and a crushed right hand.

She pulled up a stool, and glanced at the book on his bedside table, the gilt name of the author unfamiliar to her: Nikoloz Baratashvili. "Has Dr. Gedroits been in to see you?"

He exhaled heavily, casting ripples across the steaming surface of his tea. "What's there for her to see? It's all much the same as yesterday."

"May I?"

She took his injured hand and carefully guided it into the sunlight. Dr. Gedroits had performed multiple operations in an attempt to set the bones straight: immobilized on a wooden splint, his fingers bandaged over healing stitches, his hand resembled an insect pinned to a board.

He flinched, the ends of his fingers twitching involuntarily.

"I'm sorry," she muttered, lightening her touch. "Everything seems to be progressing nicely. How's the pain?"

"Bearable."

She met his gaze, hoping to coax a smile from his sallow cheeks. "Is it really? Or are you being gallant?"

He handed her the empty teacup and picked up his book. "It's bearable," he repeated dully, turning his attention to the worn pages.

Olga looked down, the painted china frivolous amidst its clinical surroundings.

"I wish you'd let me take you outside," she said, looking up at the spotless blue beyond the windows. "It's such a beautiful day, and winter will be here before we know it. Fresh air, sunshine…"

Some small muscle tightened in Mitya's face. "I'm fine here."

"It would be no trouble at all. I can find you a wheelchair, you won't even have to—"

"No. Thank you, but no."

He closed his eyes, settling back against the pillows, and though Olga knew she'd been implicitly dismissed she didn't want to leave. In their short months apart he'd grown so distant, so unlike the thoughtful man she'd known before.

"Healing takes time, you know," she said quietly.

Mitya looked up. "And what happens if I don't heal? How am I meant to be of any use to my regiment?" He stared at the ceiling, resting his ruined hand atop the pages. "It's been a month and I can barely move my fingers."

Olga leaned closer, not wanting to share his frustration with the rest of the ward. "At least you have fingers," she whispered, her concern hardening at his self-pity. "Do you know how many men I've seen who've lost their arms? Their legs? How can you sit there feeling sorry for yourself when you've still got hope?"

"*Just aim a pistol*, you told me once." He turned to face her, and in his eyes she saw the same bottomless despair that had plagued Field Marshal Orentov—that same gray, creeping into the whites of his eyes. "What use will I be if I can't even do that?"

Felix Yusupov's palace sparkled in the noon sunlight, its marigold façade set back from the steep granite embankment of the Moika River. Inside, Felix and Irina's apartments were sumptuously decorated, the monochromatic design of each room putting Olga in mind of the spectacular jewels that sat in the Yusupov family vault: citrine in the ballroom and amethyst in the dining room; emerald in the library and sapphire in the sitting room. She marveled at the riot of luxury that so perfectly suited Felix's peacock sensibilities. In contrast to the sensible furnishings Mamma had used to create the homey surroundings of Alexander Palace, Felix's excess felt almost obscene.

Side by side in their sitting room, Felix and Irina Yusupov, too, sparkled. They resembled a couple from one of Aunt Olga's fashion magazines, their world-weary expressions making them look as though their young marriage had already exhausted any novelty it might briefly have held. Olga's beautiful cousin had married Felix knowing his reputation; now, with a newborn baby in an upstairs bedroom and a heavy silver hookah placed next to the samovar on the coffee table, she wondered whether Irina had truly grown as blasé as her husband or was simply putting on a show.

Wearing a pheasant brown lounge suit beneath an ornate paisley house robe, Felix ought to have looked handsome; to Olga, however, the sight of an able-bodied man in civilian dress was enough to put her off her lunch. She thought of Mitya and bristled: why should he offer his life for Russia when the country's wealthiest man was sitting at home with a hookah pipe between his lips?

"Are you all right, Olga?" Dmitri Pavlovich asked as he reached for a toast point.

Olga glanced up. "Hm? I'm sorry, I was dreaming. What were you saying?"

"I was *saying*," Dmitri replied, "that I'm astounded Felix and Irina even got home. What did you have to tell Kaiser Wilhelm to let you leave Berlin?"

Irina rested a jewel-laden hand on Felix's arm. "Felix's father arranged it with the German authorities," she explained. "So kind of him. We were permitted to travel through Denmark and Finland… It rather extended our honeymoon, didn't it, Felix?"

"How lovely." Dmitri finished piling caviar atop the toast point and crammed it into his mouth, his eyes flashing. Unlike Felix, Dmitri was dressed in his uniform: he'd recently returned to Petrograd from an extended tour of the front lines with Papa. "But then, you were never one to turn down a holiday, were you, my friend?"

Felix arched an elegant eyebrow as he loosened his tie, unbuttoning the top of his dress shirt. The effect, paired with the incongruous robe, conferred upon him the rumpled elegance of a bohemian. "If this is about the fact that I haven't enlisted, you know full well that I've obtained an exception on compassionate grounds," he said, looking more amused than irritated at Dmitri's dig. "My mother never recovered from losing my brother—to subject her to the death of another son and heir would be unfeeling. Besides, Irina and I have little Bébé to think about, now."

"Of course." Dmitri lifted his champagne coupe, pausing just long enough that the toast could almost be construed as mocking. "My congratulations. Fatherhood suits you."

"Motherhood suits Irina more," Felix replied, sweeping an admiring gaze over his wife. "I wager I'm the luckiest man in Petrograd… Unless you've finally decided to make an honest man of our dear Dmitri, Olga. Put him out of his misery, won't you?"

Olga's smile thinned: such a comment was either hopelessly tactless or cruelly pointed, given Dmitri's lingering affection for Irina. He'd thrown himself into his military career after the wedding, even receiving the Order of St. George for gallantry, and though Olga suspected his focus was the result of heartbreak, she approved of Dmitri's renewed commitment to his cavalry regiment.

She reached for Dmitri's hand and gave it a reassuring squeeze, hoping that her feigned interest might prompt in Irina a pang of regret for choosing the man who'd opted to sit out the war. "If we have news, of course you'll be the first to know," she said smoothly.

"Tell me, Olga," Irina said as Dmitri reached for another piece of toast, "your mother's healer. Grigori Rasputin. Is it true he has the gift of prophecy?"

Felix wrapped an arm around Irina, stretching his legs out long next to the caviar tray. "You're married to a prophet, my dearest. Or had you forgotten?" He lifted the pipe to his lips, leaving the room in manufactured suspense as he sent smoke billowing through the air. "I once dreamt the train my parents were to take to Moscow the next morning would be derailed, and it was. It was a terrible mess for the authorities, I'm told; Mother wouldn't go near anything with a steam engine for weeks."

"A true prophet could have ended this war," Dmitri commented. He leaned back in his chair and lit a cigarette—to her surprise, Olga caught the whiff of whiskey on his breath, despite the fact that they'd been drinking nothing but champagne since their arrival. "Shame you weren't able to use your powers of foresight to warn Grand Duke Nikolay about the Polish retreat. You could have saved a lot of lives."

Felix shifted upright, dislodging Irina from his embrace; he lifted his coupe, and a servant came forward with an open bottle of Novyi Svet. Olga declined the offer of more, surreptitiously glancing at her wristwatch. It had been a mistake to come.

"Prophecies, healings..." Irina smiled, her attempt to calm the waters of the conversation nearly pathetic in its blatancy. "I keep hearing such incredible stories about Grigori Rasputin. Are they all true?"

"Not all of them, I'm sure," Olga replied.

"Some are all too easy to believe," Felix muttered darkly.

"I beg your pardon?"

Felix smiled: beneath his loosened shirt, Olga caught the flash of a diamond necklace. "Cousin Olga, is it true what they're saying about Nikolay Nikolaevich? Has he resigned as commander in chief?"

"Of course not," Olga replied. "Where did you hear such a thing?"

He shrugged. "I heard that Rasputin doesn't approve of his military strategy. Is it true he's trying to convince the tsar to take over command?"

"You're remarkably well informed for a civilian, Felix," Dmitri interjected acidly; between them it felt as if Olga was playing a game of doubles' tennis, the conversation lobbing back and forth too quickly to follow. Why did it matter if Father Grigori cared about military strategy? He might not have friends in government, but even his harshest critics had to see that the guidance he gave to Mamma and Papa was well meant. "I'd assumed you were too busy keeping Petrograd's social clubs in business to know about what's happening at Stavka."

"Not that I've anything to prove to you, but I'm very committed to ensuring Russia's success in this war," Felix retorted. "I've given over several of my houses to the Red Cross; in fact, we're in the process of converting an entire wing of this very palace into a hospital." He met Dmitri's glare with a smirk as he leaned back against the sofa cushion, as if daring his friend to criticize him further. "I hand-selected each and every doctor and nurse that will be working here myself. I prefer to allay pain rather than inflict it."

"And it won't be a hospital for officers," Irina added, resting a proprietary hand on Felix's knee. "Felix insisted that we open our hospital to regular enlisted men. I think it's rather exciting. He cares so much for charity."

Felix shrugged. "Of course, we removed all the valuables, but just think of the cultural education they'll receive, convalescing in a home as grand as this. I don't doubt some will leave much more enlightened than they came. Dear Irina might give some lectures if she has the time."

"Lectures." Dmitri's eyebrows shot up as he knocked the end of his cigarette against an ashtray, watching the ember fall and fade. "How magnanimous. Felix Yusupov, educating the peasants. I've given up my palace, too, by the way, to the British Red Cross."

Felix's self-satisfied grin broadened as he watched Dmitri: with his elbow perched on the top of the sofa he played with the end of the hookah pipe, tightening and loosening his grip on the silver mouthpiece.

Irina tried again. "The war effort takes all sorts," she said. "We want to do what we can with what we have. We're donating to charity; we're equipping hospitals. With the sort of resources we have at our disposal, it would be irresponsible not to contribute."

"And after the hell of the front line, who would begrudge them a glimpse of heaven?" Felix swept a paisley arm around the room, his gaze still fixed on Dmitri. "This palace will be the most beautiful sight many of them have ever seen, an architectural beauty rivalled only by nature. Imagine, they'll be telling their children back on their farms about the time they stayed in Moika Palace." He fitted the hookah pipe to his lips, looking thoughtful. "I want that for them, truly, I do. They're Russia's heroes, every last one of them."

Olga watched Felix's dancing fingers, and her mind flashed once again to Mitya. "I quite agree," she said tersely. "But not all men are cut out to be heroes. Dmitri, I'm quite ready to go, I think—"

"Have you even seen the front line?" Dmitri cut in, and Olga could feel the heat of his anger rising, brittle and curt, aimed at Felix. "Not the soldiers. The line itself. It runs through farmers' fields and forests, over swamps and rivers—truth be told, it moves so quickly these days, you're never entirely sure where you're fighting. But it often cuts through towns. Villages. Places where people can't get away…they're running before the bullets, pulling their children along as we try to defend them. We can't, as often as not; and those who do manage to escape the carnage often succumb to starvation. And that's to say nothing of the infantrymen that charge the enemy. Barbed wire and broken glass; pain and anguish."

Felix lowered the pipe, the smile dissolving from his lips.

"You can pat yourself on the back all you like about your charity, Felix, but until you've looked the devil in the face, there's nothing you can tell me about heroism."

To Olga's satisfaction, Felix finally had the decency to look chastened.

She returned to the hospital after lunch, and though she wasn't due until after dinner she walked into the wards, officers looking up in surprise at the sight of her dressed for her luncheon rather than in her nursing uniform. She passed Field Marshal Orentov's cot, unsurprised to find a new officer asleep beneath the sheets.

Mitya set down his book when Olga stopped at his footboard.

"Chess," she said without preamble. "Do you know it?"

"Not well."

"Well, I do. And you will." She smiled, her hands clasped over her handbag. "Exercise for the fingers; activity for the brain. You might not feel ready for fresh air, but chess isn't beyond you." She started for the door before he could respond, calling over her shoulder. "We'll play for an hour every afternoon. I'll bring a board."

26

April 1918
Freedom House, Tobolsk

Noise traveled far at Freedom House, none farther than Alexei's cries, and while Olga had been able to escape the sound, if not the anguish, of his pain at Alexander Palace, here there was no quarter: his screams echoed through the sitting room and Mamma's study, the ballroom and the field chapel.

Even Matveev's stone-faced guards seemed troubled, going to what lengths they could to avoid the second floor. It was clear to Olga that most had never seen a child in such pain: they stood out of the way for Dr. Botkin, not bothering to search his medical bag for correspondence or contraband as he bounded up the stairs to his young charge.

They ought to feel bad, Olga thought as she came down the staircase with a bowl of gray water—what else did they expect, when they kept the family penned up like cattle? Matveev's new restrictions on time spent in the empty courtyard were to blame, leaving Olga and her siblings with little recourse for their restlessness beyond sewing, interminable sewing. To everyone's annoyance, Anastasia had taken to doggedly walking up and down the staircase, complaining about her thickening figure—it had only been a matter of time before Alexei joined her, making a game of it by bringing in his sledge from the wreckage of Snow Mountain to toboggan down the stairs, crashing, inevitably, at the landing.

Olga walked out into the overcast courtyard, daring the guards at the door to object, but they let her pass—out of pity or negligence, she didn't care. A flash of movement caught her eye and she looked up. Papa was sitting on the greenhouse roof, staring across at Freedom House's windows. She wondered at his insistence on wearing his colonel's uniform: like Olga, Papa had lost weight during their months in Tobolsk, the buttons on his *gymnastiorka* buckling with the excess fabric. What purpose did it serve, now that Lenin had signed the Treaty of Brest-Litovsk? The treaty, which had formalized a ceasefire with the Central Powers, had been lauded as a signal of peace by the Bolsheviks, but Olga knew that Papa saw it as capitulation: a defeat which had resulted in the loss of Russian territory as well as Russian lives. Maybe he was the only uniformed officer left in all of Russia: the last one still fighting, from his lonely perch atop a glass roof.

She drained the bowl by the bottom of the fence, leaving a puddle atop the hard earth; then, in no rush to return to the gloom of the house, she leaned against the fence and knocked a lonely cigarette out of its packet.

She studied it ruefully before lighting it, wrinkling her nose at the harsh tobacco. Before shaking out the match, she held it up, allowing it to burn to the quick. What would happen, she wondered idly, if she were to let it fall on Freedom House's wooden fence, coax the ember into a flame? She pictured fire licking up the stucco walls, the house warm for once as smoke filled the ballroom; Alexei, carried out on a makeshift bier along with all the valuables. What would happen to her family if they were to lose this sanctuary? Prison?

The flame made its leisurely way along the match, the wood releasing the sweet scent of the sapling it used to be as it puckered into ash. She shook it out, disappointed at her cowardice, her lack of originality.

From around the corner, Olga could hear the sound of industry. She dropped the match and circled around to the slender patch of ground between the back of Freedom House and the kitchen outbuilding, where Anastasia was chipping away at the hard-packed earth in Alexei's garden.

But for a rough-hewn border, the garden was a small rectangle of earth that, after the fierce winter, looked no different from the gray dirt of the courtyard. Anastasia leaned heavily on her shovel, a curtain of hair falling over her face as she tried to break through the soil.

"It's too early," Olga called out. "You're wasting your time, the ground is still frozen."

Anastasia paused, pushing hair out of her eyes with a grimy hand. "What else is there to do?" She tightened her grip on the shovel and changed tactics, scraping inches of frozen soil into an anthill pile.

Olga came closer, resting her hand on Anastasia's elbow; beneath the yellowed cotton of her blouse, Anastasia's skin was warm with exertion. "You'll break it."

Anastasia passed the shovel to Olga. In the day's flat light, Olga could see how pale her sister had become, the freckles that once dotted the bridge of her nose all but gone after the winter's cold; how tall she'd grown, her stockinged ankles visible beneath the too-short hem of her skirt. "How is he?"

"No better, no worse."

Anastasia nodded again, her eyes fixed on the windows of Freedom House, made opaque by the low clouds. "And Mamma?"

Olga thought of Mamma at Alexei's bedside, pushing icons beneath his pillow, eyes glassy with veronal-laced determination. "Much the same."

Anastasia sank onto the garden's border and hugged her knees to her chest, her voice too small for someone so bright. "I didn't think… I thought going down the stairs would be like Snow Mountain, it's no higher, and he's been good for so long. I thought maybe—maybe he'd gotten over it, maybe Father Grigori had healed him properly after last time—"

The question had plagued Olga for years: why did Alexei insist on being so reckless? His antics weren't unusual for a boy of thirteen, but despite the fact that his daredevilry so often resulted in catastrophe, he continued to put himself in peril.

"I won't pretend that you weren't foolish," Olga said, "but I'm not going to blame you for things that aren't your fault. Alexei is practically an adult now; he ought to take responsibility for his own actions." She inspected her cigarette, letting the smoke plume, thin and acrid, from the ember. "It's not your fault Alexei doesn't know enough to keep himself out of harm's way. I'm sorry, but that's the truth of it."

Anastasia looked up, tears streaking down her dirt-stained cheek. "But what if he dies? What if he dies and I'm to blame?"

Olga knew she ought to be more scared for Alexei; that she ought to be upstairs, listening to his echoing groans, praying with Maria in the field chapel; helping Tatiana, tireless Tatiana, as she cleared the sickroom. But it was as if Olga was experiencing the crisis secondhand. Perhaps she'd seen too much pain during the war, too much death and grief; perhaps she'd been here too often, the narrow confines that defined her fear for Alexei grown so familiar she could push them, mold a space for herself to breathe.

Whatever the reason, Alexei's condition wasn't paralyzing her with its usual potency.

"If the worst happens, it happens," she replied. "I suppose we've been waiting for it all our lives, haven't we?" She took one final drag from her cigarette. "Waiting for Alexei to die… But then, he's no longer heir to the throne. All that care, all our secrecy. What was it for?"

She could feel Anastasia staring, her outrage palpable. "He's our brother," she replied, her voice shaking. "Heir or not, he's still our brother. I would move heaven and earth; I would shake hands with the devil himself to keep Alexei safe."

Olga thought of Father Grigori's glittering green eyes; the constant rumors, whispers that followed him like shadows. She pictured his expression, triumphant, every time Alexei ceased crying in pain; triumphant, each time Mamma grasped his hand in desperation.

Whatever is in my power to give will be yours. Please, save my son.

Olga knelt to extinguish her cigarette, stubbing it against the cold earth. "Didn't we?"

27

August 1915
Tsarskoe Selo

The summer sun in Petrograd stretched long and languid into the evening, and though Olga knew that the bright nights were time stolen from the dark winter to come, she adored the fact that midnight resembled late afternoon; that the sun, in its reluctance to set, merely dipped below the horizon at the witching hour, leaving behind an indigo sky that never truly deepened to black. In the weeks of perpetual daylight, time itself felt suspended, as if the city existed beneath the glass dome of a bell jar: the ticking clock slowed, and each magical moment felt like a gift not to be squandered by something so commonplace as sleep. Were they in Petrograd, Olga knew the buildings along the Nevsky Prospect would be washed pale by the midnight sun, the streets along the canal crowded with couples walking arm-in-arm, jewel-laden and tireless as they strolled to their boxes at the ballet.

At the Annexe, the white nights worked their wonder too. After dinner, patients streamed into the hospital garden, and though Dr. Gedroits' nursing schedule remained rigidly set for early mornings and early evenings, Olga felt little compunction in traveling down from Alexander Palace with her sisters to join the officers in quiet celebration. Walking along the gray-green wall of a cypress grove, Maria wheeled a young officer out from the common room, a book tucked beneath her arm to read aloud; nearby, Anastasia was playing badminton, amusing the assembled onlookers as she dove for the shuttlecock, her ribboned hair flying. Beneath the swaying branches of a weeping willow, Tatiana was talking to Viktor Kiknadze—with his brilliantine hair and self-satisfied smile, he was too arrogant for Olga, but Tatiana seemed to be enjoying herself: she leaned close and rested a hand on Kiknadze's arm, and Olga felt a pang of regret for Dmitri Malama, off fighting at the front.

As for Olga, she was content to sit in the garden, watching Mitya over the chessboard between them. They'd been playing for nearly three quarters of an hour, and Olga had steadily closed her pieces in on Mitya's king; now, within one move of victory, she watched as he lifted his knight and shifted it across the board with stiff fingers.

"You're sure that's the move you want to make?" Olga asked.

"Well, now I'm not." Mitya grinned, his finger still resting on the knight. "What's wrong with it?"

Olga shrugged. "I wouldn't be much of an opponent if I told you," she replied, as Mitya studied the board.

Finally, he lifted his finger. Without preamble, Olga moved her queen across the board and checkmated his king.

He shifted in his seat, resting his elbow atop his walking stick. "Well, an Emanuel Lasker I am not," he said finally, knocking down his king with a flick of his hand. "I ought to practice more."

"We've been playing almost every day," said Olga as she pulled out a wooden box from beneath her chair. "And you are getting better. Chess takes time, that's all. You'd never learn if I let you win."

She began clearing the pieces from the board, sweeping them into the box one by one. As she reached for the white queen,

Mitya's hand met hers. He ran his thumb along the back of her palm, sending fire into the pit of her stomach.

"Win or lose," he said, "I enjoy the fight."

Olga met his gaze, savoring the feel of his hand on hers.

"Sister Romanova!" Olga pulled her hand out of Mitya's grasp and turned. Dr. Gedroits was standing at the door to the Annexe, packing the bowl of her pipe with tobacco.

It was clear that Dr. Gedroits had only just finished her work for the evening: though she'd removed her medical overcoat, her shirtsleeves were wrinkled from the day's wear, the cuffs pushed carelessly to her elbows. As was her custom, the doctor was dressed in trousers and a waistcoat, her tie neatly knotted beneath the vee of a stiff collar.

"You're here awfully late," said Olga as she met the doctor at the hospital's entrance, leaving Mitya to finish clearing up the chessboard. Belatedly, she realized she was still holding the white queen, and hastily stowed it in her pocket. The doctor inclined her head in her perfunctory concession to Olga's station, and though the lack of deference might have made Mamma bristle, Olga didn't mind: within the hospital grounds, the doctor reigned with earned authority.

Dr. Gedroits pushed back a wisp of hair that had fallen loose from its bun. "Working on a paper about blood transfusion," she said, lifting the pipe to her lips. Olga glanced into the hall behind her: when Dr. Gedroits worked late, Sister Nirod usually lingered on the ward to walk her back to her palace apartment.

Olga offered her a lighter, and the doctor nodded her thanks as she took it.

"Nearly done, I hope?" Olga asked as Gedroits lit the pipe, the smell of tobacco blossoming between them. "Your hard work does you credit."

"It's not my work I wish to discuss, but yours." Gedroits returned the lighter and leaned against the hospital's brick façade.

"It's awfully conscientious of you to come on your time off, Grand Duchess."

Something in the doctor's tone made it clear to Olga that the comment wasn't meant as a compliment. "We wanted to cheer the men up. Neither Tatiana nor I had any committee meetings tonight, and Maria and Anastasia spend so much of their free time at the other hospitals…"

"I can see that," the doctor murmured, looking out across the lawn at Mitya as he hobbled across to join the onlookers at the badminton net. "And Her Imperial Majesty? Has she joined you on this visit?"

"She's at Alexander Palace." Olga resisted the urge to elaborate—to tell Dr. Gedroits that Mamma, while unaware of the visit, would no doubt sanction it, because it was to the benefit of Russia, was it not, to make the army's officers feel valued? "She's helping the tsar with important—important policies—"

"And what about you?" Dr. Gedroits' face was impassive. "How long do you plan to stay with the officers? To *cheer them up*? It's nearly ten o'clock, and you and Tatiana have an early start."

Olga glanced back at the grounds. Though Anastasia was still locked in her badminton match and Maria was bent over her book, using its cover as a lap desk on which to transcribe a letter for the officer in the wheelchair, Tatiana and Kiknadze had vanished; wandered, no doubt, around the side of the hospital.

"Not much longer, I should think."

For a moment, Dr. Gedroits was silent; she stared at Olga, tightening her grip on the pipe's bowl. "Tomorrow, I'd be grateful if you would see to Lieutenant Kiknadze's dressing."

Olga hesitated. "Of course. But doesn't Tatiana usually take care…?"

"Your sister is needed elsewhere—and between the two of us, it's not wise to form strong attachments to any one patient." She turned her attention back to the badminton game, watching as a cheer went up from the officers as Anastasia returned a particularly challenging volley. "Perhaps it's a lesson you ought to take to heart as well, Grand Duchess."

Olga, too, watched the shuttlecock's progress, her fingers tightening around the chess piece in her pocket. "I'm sure I don't know what you mean, Doctor."

"Don't you?" Dr. Gedroits fitted her pipe in the corner of her mouth, the ember flaring orange. "I don't mean to be overly familiar, but our work here is more important than our personal feelings. We cannot afford to become overly invested in the welfare of one individual. Not when so many others need our attention."

Olga reddened. As Mitya's nurse, Olga enjoyed the moments she could spend with him, even welcomed his company as she changed bed linens and delivered tea to the other officers on the ward, but she'd always let the cap and veil of her nursing uniform stand between them. She took a professional pride, even, in his increasing dexterity, his steadily improving mood—and though she'd tried to tell herself that this late visit to the Annexe, in her best day skirt and lace blouse, was nothing more than a courtesy call intended for all the officers in the blue-lit yard, she'd spent time with no one but Mitya.

She'd wanted to spend time with no one but Mitya.

"If this is about Shakh-Bagov, I've been helping him with his recuperation," she replied. "He's been displaying signs of traumatic neurosis. The chess is a means of helping him to gain strength in his hand while improving his mental—"

Dr. Gedroits pulled the pipe from her lips and knocked the overturned bowl against the brick wall; the ember fell loose, and the doctor tamped it carefully beneath the heel of her shoe. Behind her, Olga could see Sister Nirod, who'd changed out of her nursing uniform, lingering at the end of the hall. "The chess is an excuse to spend time with a handsome young officer. Don't flatter yourself by thinking anyone sees it differently," she said. She turned to go back inside, then looked once more at Olga, her expression softening. "I'm not entirely without feeling, but the fact of the matter is that we are not friends to these men. We're professionals. To give them the wrong idea is to nobody's benefit, least of all your own."

The doctor inclined her head before returning inside, but Olga remained rooted to her spot in front of the hospital door. Was it really so obvious? If Dr. Gedroits, with her countless responsibilities, had noticed Olga's growing affections, who else was whispering behind their hands, making veiled comments as they followed the trajectory of Olga's crush?

For that was what it was, Olga reminded herself as she slowly made her way back along the green: a crush. Nothing more. How could it be anything else, when her duties as a nurse—her duties as a grand duchess—would always come first? Dr. Gedroits had been right to remind her of that undeniable, incontrovertible fact. Affection was a luxury she could ill afford, an indulgence made inappropriate by the circumstances of war.

And yet, if they were living in times of peace, Olga's feelings for Mitya would still be an indulgence. *They would be non-existent*, Olga reminded herself. Were it not for the war, Olga would never have met him—she would never have grown to admire his tenacity, his soulfulness; his quiet reserve. The thought of it saddened her: to think of a world in which she and Mitya had never met.

Mitya stood at the side of the badminton net, his broad back accentuated by the spread of his shoulders as he leaned on his walking stick. He was so different from other men. Not impulsive like Pavel, nor entitled like Felix. Not impassioned like Dmitri Pavlovich or condescending like Prince Carol. Though Papa had told her once he'd never force her to marry anyone she didn't want, Olga suspected that his permissive tone would extend no further than the narrow pool of men deemed, through some accident of birth or privilege, worthy of her bloodline: sycophants paraded in front of her by the government, courtiers huddled in corners like bureaucratic cupids, whispering about dynastic alliances.

Mitya turned as she reached the badminton court, his expression quizzical as she passed behind him and disappeared across the road, into the overgrown park that abutted the hospital's west wing.

Though the midnight sun still burned orange behind the trees, the sky above Olga had finally darkened, sending the purple bruise of a sunset long across the heavens. Olga paused in a clearing, allowing her eyes to adjust to the gloom; behind her, she could hear the sound of Mitya's footsteps as he made his way through the undergrowth.

"This feels awfully risqué," he said. From beyond the curtain of cypress needles they could hear the sound of the distant badminton tournament; closer by, the thin ribbon of a gramophone record echoed from a far-off window. "What's this about?"

Before she could lose her nerve, Olga stepped close to Mitya—far closer than she'd ever dared, outside of the normal proximity of nurse and patient. She lifted her hands to his chest, her heart beating furiously as she savored the feel of him beneath her fingers: his collarbone; the ridge of his scar.

Mitya let his stick fall as he wrapped his hands around her waist. "I've hoped, but I never believed…"

She felt it in her throat, first: the anticipation, the thrill, as she succumbed to something she'd too long denied. She pressed her lips to his, knowing that he was already slipping through her fingers: that theirs was a connection built on the shifting sands of circumstance. One day, duty—his and hers—would pull them apart, but here, now, Mitya pulled her closer and the world slowed just enough for her to feel the glorious free fall of a skipped heartbeat.

28

August 1915
Tsarskoe Selo

The curtains were drawn in Olga's bedroom as she and Tatiana dressed for dinner, the single sliver of light tracing up the dragonfly wallpaper the only indication that the Alexander Palace and its grounds were still bathed in evening summer sun. Wrapping her customary pearls around her neck, Olga glanced at Tatiana's reflection in the mirror, her bony back visible as the maid helped her into her corset.

"I suppose I just don't understand why Dr. Gedroits won't let us do our usual rounds anymore," Tatiana was saying, her voice floating atop a recording of a French pianist that Aunt Olga had given to them after their last tea party. She studied her reflection in the mirror, fixing a diamond earring into place. "It seems such an inconvenience when we've gotten to know the men in our own wards so well."

Olga smiled at the maid. "Thank you, I think we can finish up on our own," she said, and the maid curtsied before collecting Olga and Tatiana's discarded nursing uniforms. "I think she just wants to make sure that all the men receive the same standard of care."

Tatiana huffed as she stepped into her evening gown. Whereas

Olga had chosen a midnight-blue dress with a lace overlay, Tatiana had opted for a berry-hued Empire-line—both were a few years out of date, as Mamma had forbidden them from purchasing any new clothing for the duration of the war, but the colors alone felt refreshing after so many long days in their uniforms.

"Same standard of care…isn't it better for us to get to know each of our patients? To learn how they behave when they're in pain; to be able to monitor their progress from the very start?" She slipped the dress's straps over her shoulders and smoothed the bodice straight. Tonight, Papa had called together a small gathering of family and friends for a dinner party. The occasion paled in comparison to the leisurely dinners, long speeches and glittering balls they had been accustomed to just a year earlier, but now it felt almost indulgent. "It seems a better system for us to learn all there is to know about a handful of men rather than to spread ourselves too thin."

"I agree, but it seems the good doctor does not," Olga replied, picking up a square bottle to envelop herself in a rose-scented cloud.

"Well, we must keep the peace with the good doctor," Tatiana muttered, inspecting her reflection in the vanity mirror one final time before circling to the door, sidestepping to avoid the lingering mist of Olga's perfume.

"Very true." Olga lifted the needle on the gramophone, the tinny sound of Erik Satie squelching into nothingness. She could hear Anastasia and Maria setting out from their bedroom next door, and took her time putting the record back in its sleeve. "One war is enough to be getting on with at the moment."

They walked down the hall, passing Alexei's suite of rooms: playroom, classroom, music room. "I suppose it's not unbearable," Tatiana continued, her heels clicking against the parquet floor. "Viktor and I will simply have to find time together outside my rounds. Perhaps we could go to the hospital after dinner, I doubt Mamma would mind."

Under the guise of adjusting her gloves, Olga slowed as they reached the staircase. "Yes, I meant to talk to you about that. Viktor...are you quite sure about him?"

"What's there to be sure about? He's fun, isn't he? Gallant, too. He's got so many good stories."

"He does," Olga tried, disconcerted at how much she sounded like Dr. Gedroits, "but what do you know about him, really?"

Tatiana slowed. "I don't know what you're on about, Olga. I know no less about him than you do about that Shakh-Bagov you spend all your time with." She stopped talking as they passed two footmen on the landing, who bowed before continuing up the stairs. "What's this about? Because I don't much fancy a lecture."

Olga paused. Even now, five days later, the feel of Mitya's lips still lingered on her skin. Though they'd not yet had an opportunity to repeat their liaison in the garden, Mitya had taken once more to helping Olga on her rounds: wrapping bandages and making beds, his smile the highlight of her hectic days. The moments she stole with Mitya were no more than any other young couple might expect. Was it really right for her to try and talk her sister out of the same experience?

"You know as well as I do, we have to be sensible about all this," Olga said finally.

Tatiana's expression darkened. "Why's that? Because you've been so *sensible* with Shakh-Bagov? I've seen him following you around like a lovestruck fool, watching you moon over those little love notes he slips into your trolley when he thinks no one is looking."

"I'd be grateful if you were to leave him out of this," Olga shot back. At the bottom of the staircase, she could hear the sound of Papa's guests arriving—too few to be considered a proper party, too many to count as a quiet family dinner.

Tatiana huffed. "And what about Dr. Gedroits and Sister Nirod? They spend all their time together, and no one seems to give them a second thought."

Olga paused midstep. "Dr. Gedroits and Sister Nirod? Really?"

Tatiana continued on, looking amused at Olga's lack of worldliness. "Though I suppose she'd say their case is different, as Sister Nirod isn't a patient."

Olga shook her head, amazed she'd not seen it for herself. *Dr. Gedroits and Sister Nirod…* It wasn't all that surprising, really. She thought of herself and Mitya, taking comfort in each other's company, the strains of war bringing them closer together than they ever would have become in peacetime. With her heavy workload not only at the Annexe, but also at the civilian hospital, Dr. Gedroits was shouldering her own wartime burdens. Why shouldn't she have a companion to help her carry them?

But she wasn't here to discuss Dr. Gedroits. She continued on down the stairs, keeping her voice low. "Shakh-Bagov and I have an understanding. A connection—"

"And you don't think I have that with Viktor?" Tatiana removed her glove and scrubbed the tears from her cheek with an impatient hand. "When I'm with Viktor, I forget my worries…" She pulled her glove back on, stretching the silk above her elbow. "He's a distraction," she said, anguish laced beneath her matter-of-fact tone of voice. "Because if I think too far into what might be, I can't focus on what is."

When Olga stepped out onto the balcony, Tatiana was already at the other end of the table, doggedly conversing with Uncle Sandro and Aunt Xenia. Given the temperate weather, Papa had arranged for dinner to be served on the balcony that wrapped around Mamma's reception room, the heavy candelabras set atop the long table providing ambiance, more than lighting. Beyond the wrought-iron railing, swans nested in the pond, flashes of white in the dark water; on shore, a scarlet-liveried footman threw them stale bread crumbs brought out from the kitchens.

Papa had arranged the dinner in honor of Aunt Olga's return from the front, where she'd been serving as a nurse in a medical "flying column." Alongside Olga's immediate family and Aunt Olga herself, Grandmamma had made a rare appearance at the Alexander Palace. She sat next to Papa, listening to Aunt Olga's stories with a thin smile.

"Let me tell you, it's been a nightmare in terms of personal comfort," Aunt Olga said airily over the soup course. She swiped a hand through the air, deterring a wasp that had been seeking to land on her wineglass. "I'm no stranger to roughing it—I've had more than enough picnic lunches on the *Shtandart* to prove it—but this is something else entirely. Do you know, I often went three days without a rest?"

"Your stamina does you credit," said Papa. He lifted his glass of mineral water, sparkling in cut crystal. "I'm proud you're doing your part for the war effort."

"Well, we must all do what we can for Russia," Aunt Olga replied, lifting her glass in response. "And we'll be rewarded for it, in this life or the next."

Olga glanced at her aunt. According to Felix Yusupov, Aunt Olga had asked Papa to grant her a divorce from her estranged husband, but her request had been denied. Did she hope, perhaps, that her good example might persuade Papa to allow her to marry her beloved Captain Kulikovsky?

"Indeed, we must," Papa replied, setting down his cutlery; wordlessly, the footmen lining the palace wall came forward and whisked away the dishes. "In fact, I've an announcement to make. I've informed Stavka that I will be taking over personal command of the military." He looked down the table at Alexei and winked. "We're leaving for Mogilev on Monday."

The group fell silent; Grandmamma twisted in her seat, candlelight illuminating her raised eyebrows. Olga exchanged a glance with Tatiana, unsure what to say. Papa's announcement was news to her, as much as it was to the rest of the table: it didn't bode well, surely, that Papa felt he needed to exercise direct control over the military.

At the far end of the table, Dmitri Pavlovich set down his glass. "Well. Let me be the first to congratulate you, sir." He placed a hand over his heart, his thumb brushing against his St. George's Cross. "Might I ask, what prompted your decision?"

"Nikolay Nikolaevich's incompetence, for one." Mamma dabbed at her lips with a napkin, leaving a pale stain on the white linen. "We'd reached an impasse, hadn't we, dearest? There was just no avoiding the facts any longer."

Papa beamed. "I'm rather looking forward to it," he said. Below the balcony, Olga could hear the swans in the pond, their wings a flurry of sound on water as they fed. "A chance to do my part properly, as it were."

The next morning, Tatiana jumped out of the motorcar as it pulled up in front of the Annexe, barely sparing a backward glance for Olga as she strode through the double doors. Inside, Olga caught sight of Kiknadze, smiling broadly as he greeted Tatiana with a bow.

Olga waited in the car, giving Viktor and Tatiana a moment alone before she traced her sister's footsteps into the hospital. She often found herself on the back foot when it came to Tatiana—somehow, her younger sister seemed so much more mature than she felt, in all the ways that counted. Whereas Olga had allowed Dr. Gedroits' disapproval to color her opinion of Kiknazde, Tatiana thought for herself, accepting Kiknadze's merits and flaws with a wide-eyed pragmatism that Olga couldn't help but admire. It wasn't right to hold her to a different standard of behavior—not when Olga herself had formed a similar attachment to Mitya.

She'd delivered Dr. Gedroits' rebuke: Tatiana would have to decide whether or not to heed it.

The dining room smelled of burnt coffee, pots of jam and

blackened toast in racks positioned like sentries along the long table. At the far end, Mitya sat hunched over a newspaper, reading intently. He curled his wounded fingers around a cup of coffee, and Olga couldn't help marveling at his ongoing recovery.

He rose to his feet at Olga's approach. "No uniform today?"

"I'm not on shift," she replied. "And I can't stay long. Tatiana and I just wanted to look in on our way to the station to say hello."

"I'm glad you did." Mitya folded his newspaper. "Do you have enough time for a walk?"

The grounds were wet after early morning rain, and Mitya's stick sank into the grass, leaving a pocked trail as they walked past the hospital's outbuildings to the park across the street. Dressed in his uniform, the gold thread of Mitya's epaulettes glinted in the September sunlight, the smell of pomade wafting from his neatly parted hair. But for the stick, he looked the picture of vigor, his gentlemanly demeanor enhanced, rather than diminished, by his lingering limp.

Once they'd reached the park, Olga threaded her hand through Mitya's crooked arm, smiling at how her hand fitted perfectly into the crease.

"You're quiet today," she commented. "Is something the matter?"

"I've received my orders," he replied, in a voice that fell just short of cheerful. "I'm to rejoin my regiment in two weeks' time. I daresay you'll be glad to see the back of me."

Two weeks... She tightened her hand around his arm, his jacket heavy beneath her fingers. "Don't say that," she said. How could he be leaving when they'd only just reached an understanding? "You know I'll be praying for you."

"And I for you." Mitya turned to face Olga head-on, his dark eyes honeyed amber by the sunlight. "I know it's presumptuous of me to ask, but would you write?"

Olga wrapped her arms around his neck, the rasp of his jaw

rough against the delicate skin of her cheek. The thought of him returning to the front line terrified her, but she knew better than to let herself get carried away: it wouldn't do to let him see the toll his departure would take, not when he needed the confidence to go.

He broke away, resting his forehead against hers. "I've been wanting to do that all day," he whispered, brushing a lock of hair from her cheek.

"So have I," Olga whispered back. "Two weeks…"

"Two weeks," he replied, his smile fading. "Will you? Write?"

She leaned into his chest. "Of course." He wrapped his arm around her, blanketing her with the scent of soap and leather. "Every day, if you're lucky."

He looked down, his lips upturned. "If I was lucky, I would be staying here with you."

"I wish you could," she replied, "but it would be selfish of me to want you here until the end of the war."

She felt the rumble of laughter, deep in his chest. "Spoken like a true Romanov," he replied, drawing away so they could continue walking hand in hand. "Much as I'd like to deny it, I'd be lying if I said I was looking forward to getting back to the front line. I'm told the shortages are getting worse."

"That will come to an end soon," Olga said, pleased that she could at least put his mind to rest on one of his concerns. "Papa is going to the front today to take over as commander in chief." She breathed in the sweet smell of needles on the forest floor; overhead, nesting birds rustled in the green. "He'll set the shortages to rights."

Mitya's hand twitched in hers. "He's doing what?"

"He's dismissed Grand Duke Nikolay Nikolaevich." Olga glanced up at Mitya. "I thought you'd be pleased to hear it."

He paused once more, leaning heavily on his stick. "I'm—surprised, that's all. What prompted that decision?"

Olga recounted last night's conversation: Mamma's pride,

Papa's determination. "Necessity, I suppose. It's hardly a secret that the war isn't going as well as he'd like. He says he must do his part."

"His *part*?" Mitya stared at Olga, his tender expression gone. "Isn't it his *part* to lead the country?"

"Of course, but the army is central to the country, isn't it?" Why did he sound so incredulous? "I think it's a mark of his courage that he's decided to go. He feels we ought to get the military back under control after our defeats, become more strategic in our approach—"

"He's not a military commander, Olga. He's got no practical knowledge of battle." Mitya shook his head, birdsong trilling in the trees. "I know he's your father, but I worry he's not thought this through."

Olga bristled. "He's my father, but he's also your tsar," she reminded Mitya, a small ember of anxiety lighting within her like a spark on paper. "Ordained by God; sworn to defend Russia from all foes."

"Ordained by God..." Mitya muttered. He ran a hand along his jawline, staring down at the deadfall beneath his feet.

"He knows what's best for Russia," Olga retorted. In her mind's eye, she ran over the end of the dinner; Grandmamma's uncharacteristic silence as she said good-night, bumping her cheek against Olga's; Dmitri, silently draining his glass of water. "His faith will lead us to victory. Can't you see that?"

Mitya continued through the trees, his stick sinking into the earth.

"Can't you see that?" Olga asked, her conviction faltering. How could Mitya not understand that Papa was doing what was best? It was a decision Papa hadn't taken lightly; moreover, it was a decision that could turn the tide, make right Nikolay Nikolaevich's spectacular failures.

Mitya paused beneath the yellowing shade of a beech tree. "The military is bleeding," he said finally, his fingers white against the head of his cane. "We're losing men at a rate that we cannot afford; we're ill equipped, both with ammunition and supplies. My men write to tell me that the army has begun rationing bullets; that the German army is a far more formidable foe than we'd ever imagined. Your father is many things, but he's not a military mind. Surely he would do better appointing someone more experienced—"

"He feels it will speak to the men—the knowledge that their tsar is with them, in the fight." Olga could feel her cheeks burning, her indignation at Mitya's stubborn refusal to see reason. "How is that any different from what you told me to do? You told me to be here, showing our brave officers that I care. How is Papa's plan any different?"

Mitya looked as sick as Olga felt; from beyond the confines of the park, they could hear the sound of motorcars; horses' hooves, clattering across the cobbled street. "And who will lead the country while the tsar is at the front? The Duma?"

"My mother," Olga replied. "She's been supporting Papa for years, she knows everything there is to know about domestic affairs—"

Mitya dug his cane into the ground, his jaw tightening on words he clearly didn't want to say.

"What? What's wrong with Mamma?"

"Please," he muttered. "Please, let's change the subject."

"What's difficult about it?" Olga could feel fire licking up her spine; anger, at Mitya's reticence. She resisted the urge to cross the small patch of grass that stood between them, to put a finger under his chin and make him look her in the eye. "You're the one who asked; you're the one who has so much to say on the subject. What's wrong with my mother—the tsarina, *your empress*—overseeing the tsar's affairs at home while he's at the front? Tell me, what's so wrong about that?"

He looked up, his dark eyes flat with some unfathomable emotion: her Mitya gone, shielded behind the cool façade of a soldier. "Is that a command or a request, Grand Duchess? Because it no longer feels like we're speaking as equals."

Olga stepped back. She could feel Mitya pulling away as they stared at each other across the sudden gulf of her position—a gulf that had always been there, invisible, as she tried to cross the breach. Pavel's parting words echoed in her mind: *You are the Grand Duchess Olga Nikolaevna.* Her title had torn them apart. Here, now, she could see that same look of defeat on Mitya's face.

She'd deceived herself in thinking that theirs was a connection built on mutual trust, mutual attraction: that her refusal to use her title at the hospital meant the rest of the world had forgotten it, too. Dr. Gedroits and the *sanitary*, the patients and other nurses, all smiling at her insistence on being called Sister Romanova rather than Grand Duchess: they'd done it as a means of placating her, in deference to the title Olga had never wanted. Was this how all of her friendships—her romances—were to end, with the inevitable, maddening reminder of her position?

"I'm sorry," she said finally. "You must know I didn't mean it like that, I think we both got—"

"Carried away." Mitya exhaled heavily. "I understand. I do. But you must try to understand, too. I'm a soldier. I live and die on the orders of those in charge. Your father is my tsar, and I will follow his orders to my last breath, but I cannot pretend to have faith in him as my commander in chief."

Slowly, he bowed his head once again, the gesture feeling like some final, horrible goodbye. What he'd said was tantamount to treason—enough, certainly, to have him stripped of his position in his elite Grenadier regiment. As grand duchess, Olga knew she ought to report him.

But as Olga Nikolaevna?

"Let's—let's forget this conversation ever happened," Olga said quickly. "We can talk of other things; forget we've had a disagreement, move on—"

Mitya looked up. "How?" He shook his head, anguished.

"How can we ever truly know each other if we can't disagree? If I'm not able to speak my mind?"

"Of course, you can speak your mind," Olga replied, taking his hand in hers.

"Even if I'm critical of your parents?" Mitya shook his head, his grip slackening. "We must face facts, Grand Duchess. Our duties don't lie with each other."

"And what if you mean more to me than my duties?" Olga turned his hand over in hers, tracing the lines of his palm with her finger: head, heart, life.

"Do I?" Mitya's smile softened further. "Will I still, when I'm back at the front?"

"Two weeks," she whispered. She didn't want to look up, to face the possibility of rejection in his eyes—but they would never stand on an equal footing if she didn't give him the option to go. "I want you to know that you're more than a—a distraction, to me. If you want me to write to you, I'll write; if you want me to pray for you, I'll pray." She lifted her head, meeting his anguished gaze. "If you want nothing more to do with me then I'll leave you alone. From this point on, I will leave you be, if that's what you want. I don't want you to feel a sense of obligation holding us together."

Slowly, deliberately, he turned his hand so they were palm to palm once more. "The fact of the matter is that you will always be above me," he whispered. He lifted her fingers to his lips, kissed them one by one. "I'm in love with you, Olga. Not with the grand duchess; not with the Romanov. With you. You have my heart. For as long as you want it, my heart is yours—but I must be free to speak my mind, even if it's something you don't want to hear."

Olga wasn't sure whether to laugh or cry; whether hers was a feeling of relief or sadness. She leaned into his chest once more, and he wrapped his hands around her waist: a soldier and a nurse, a couple set, finally, on the same footing.

"No special treatment?" she said, and Mitya chuckled.

"No special treatment," he replied, as she lifted her chin to meet his kiss.

PART FOUR

29

April 1918

Freedom House, Tobolsk

Olga opened her eyes, staring up at the white ceiling. The room was cold enough that, in the half-light of the graying dawn, she could see her breath clouding above her; in the darkness, she could hear the gentle rustling of her sisters in their beds. Outside, she heard the sound of boots on pavement, the far-off clatter of a horse's hooves on cobbled streets.

She tried closing her eyes, but sleep was beyond her now. Instead, she let her sight adjust to the gloom, searching the ceiling for the crack that stretched from the door frame nearly to the window. At the Alexander Palace, her bedroom walls had been covered with dragonflies: as a girl, she fancied she could see them dance in the half-dreaming moments between sleep and waking, looping and swirling across the ceiling with a magic only a child could conjure.

Here, no such magic existed; no such hope that fanciful creatures might take wing and fly away.

She rolled onto her side, curling her blankets close to her chin to stave off the morning chill a while longer. She'd learned long ago not to trust in magic, nor hope—not when so many of her patients arrived from the front cold, long dead after a painful journey. No fancy, no flight. No faith that waving a wand might reverse their fortunes, that they might recover thanks to the tireless efforts of a hopeful grand duchess. It was no wonder, to Olga, she'd grown increasingly disheartened after Mitya returned to the front line.

But where Olga wilted, Tatiana had bloomed: as the war went on, she grew ever more tireless, her refugee committee taking up more hours of her day as the enemy encroached farther onto Russian soil. Even the sight of wounded men seemed to affect her differently than Olga, energizing rather than depleting her, giving her added incentive to increase the number of hours she spent at the hospital.

That practice seemed to be serving her well now. With Alexei still recovering from his most recent attack, Tatiana had become, once more, a Sister of Mercy: she spent as much time in Alexei's sickroom as Mamma herself, propping up Alexei in bed to take sips of broth as the swelling gradually receded in his leg; sending Anastasia to the kitchens for fresh water. She'd even rebuked Matveev over the state of Alexei's diet, demanding that the kitchens supplement his meals with iron-rich foods.

Tatiana turned in her sheets, her breath shifting from the slow, steady lull of sleep to the hitched irregularity of wakefulness. Olga glanced out the cracks of the window at the brightening sky. The house would be stirring soon.

"Tatiana," she whispered. "How did you do it? During the war? How did you manage with the pain and grief of it all?"

Tatiana sat upright, the long rope of her braided hair hanging dark against her rounded shoulders. She rubbed a hand over her sleep-worn face and shifted the heavy blankets aside.

"Do you remember playing in the tide pools at Livadia? Before Papa had the swimming pool made...do you remember the day Anastasia got swept up by a wave?"

Olga could feel that long-ago day lingering on her skin: lying on the pebbled beach, staring up at the rounded cliffs, the light so bright it washed all the green pale. "Papa went in after her," she replied. "He didn't even take off his jacket. He dove in and didn't come up again until she was back on the shore."

In the gray half-light, Tatiana nodded. "She was too small to swim against the current. The wave just…knocked her off her feet. I remember waiting for them—it felt like hours."

Olga glanced at the small mound that was Anastasia, lying in her bed: once dawn broke through the window, they would see the mess she'd made of her army cot, the scarves and coats and small rugs she'd piled, one over the other atop the covers; the photographs she'd pinned to the wall, including the one she'd taken of herself in a mirror, kneeling against the back of a lemonwood chair, using it to hold her box Brownie steady.

Tatiana got to her feet, the springs groaning as she searched for her house robe. "That's what it feels like, I fancy," she muttered, as if to herself.

She turned back to Olga, sliding her arms through the sleeves of her robe. "You must harden your heart," she continued. "You must take all of the feelings you wish you could feel—grief, rage, love, despair—and push them deep into the core of yourself. Harden your heart. There's nothing else to do. No other way to stop yourself from falling into the tide."

Harden your heart. The advice sounded simple enough, but Olga found it impossible. How could she harden her heart at the sight of Alexei? He'd been in bed for weeks, and though he'd lost the ghastly yellow pallor that had crept up his face, his leg was still swollen—the blood not yet reabsorbed into his bloodstream. He winced, his narrow shoulders hunched as he shifted up in the pillows.

Still. Progress was progress, and with Dr. Botkin's assurance that Alexei was out of immediate danger, even Mamma deigned to leave Alexei's bedside after luncheon to join the rest of the family in the sitting room.

"It's Father Grigori's doing," she said, nodding with conviction as she worked at undoing a seam in one of Anastasia's corsets. "Still watching over us from on high; still caring for our boy."

Across the room, Papa emerged from his study, a book tucked under his arm. As he crossed to a chair beneath the window, Olga could make out the title: *The Brothers Karamazov.*

"Father Grigori…still a friend to this family," Mamma murmured, turning the corset over to see how much fabric the undone seam afforded her. Out of the corner of her eye, Olga saw a flash of something sparkling and turned to look—but it was only Mamma's ring, catching in the light. "One of our only friends, it seems…"

Maria passed out cups of tea and Olga sipped hers, wishing for a spoonful of sugar to take away the bitterness. Mamma's idle chatter disturbed her: their only friend, a dead man? She thought of Dr. Botkin, tireless in his efforts to allay Alexei's suffering; the servants who'd remained at Freedom House without pay, shuttling in and out of his sickroom with pillows and fresh water. Were their contributions so worthless in Mamma's eyes?

She was pulled from her thoughts by the sound of movement down the hall. Moments later, Matveev entered, with two armed guards at his side. He was followed by a man in a freshly pressed greatcoat—with his combed-back hair and neatly trimmed beard, he looked more handsome, more genteel, than the guards who flanked him.

"Good afternoon, Colonel," said Matveev, clasping his hands behind his back. "I won't mince words. I must inform you that recent unrest in Tobolsk means we can no longer guarantee your safety."

"I beg your pardon?" Papa closed the book, keeping his place in the pages with his finger.

"Commissar Yakovlev has recently arrived from Moscow with orders to remove your family to a more secure location."

Matveev indicated the man standing beside him with a nod of his head and Yakovlev stepped forward, his lips pressed together in a thin smile. "I trust I can count on your cooperation in this matter."

"Absolutely not." Mamma's voice was sharp; she set aside the corset, staring at the men as though they'd suggested something obscene. "Our son is gravely ill; he can't possibly be moved."

Papa stood. "I'm afraid she's right, gentlemen." He circled to the back of the sofa, resting his hand on Mamma's shoulder. "As you're well aware, Matveev, our son suffers from an illness of the blood; any movement could prove fatal. You're welcome to have your own doctors examine him to confirm it."

Yakovlev's pleasant expression hardened, almost imperceptibly. "Is that so?" He turned on his heel and stalked out of the room; Matveev and Papa followed.

"They can't possibly be serious," Mamma muttered, plunging her needle into the fabric with renewed vigor, but Olga looked at Tatiana, seeing her own dread reflected back in her sister's eyes. Unrest in Tobolsk...that could mean any number of things. Bread riots, like in Petrograd? Infighting amongst Lenin's troops?

Or perhaps the arrival of loyalists, ready to launch a rescue?

The men returned to the sitting room, and Mamma craned her neck to look at them, imperious. "Well? You've seen it for yourselves. Our son is ill. Any question of leaving this house must be put off until he's well again."

Yakovlev's fingers twitched, and though she couldn't see anything concealed beneath the bulk of his greatcoat, Olga fancied he was used to carrying a sidearm: a pistol, perhaps—something small and discreet. Easily reached, under the right circumstances.

"I agree that the boy is too ill to be moved, but it doesn't follow that I can't carry out my orders," he said. "I'm tasked with removing Colonel Romanov from Tobolsk; the rest of you may follow once your son is well enough to travel."

Mamma paled; across the room, Maria let out a small gasp.

"I'm afraid that is quite impossible," Papa replied. He circled back to Mamma and sat down, collecting her beneath his arm as though he could shield her from the news. "I received assurances from your predecessors, gentlemen, that my family would remain intact. I hope I can count on you to honor those assurances."

Yakovlev was silent for a moment; beside him, Matveev watched, almost sulking. Whoever Yakovlev was, he clearly outranked Matveev—he had to, in order to bring such disastrous news. *From Moscow, then*, Olga thought, panic rising in her throat as she eyed the high shine of Yakolvev's boots. Did he plan to take Papa back to the seat of Lenin's government?

"I am not my predecessor," Yakovlev said, finally, "and my orders are clear. I'm afraid my hands are tied."

"Where are you planning to take him?" Mamma asked.

"I cannot say," Yakovlev replied. "But rest assured, I will personally vouch for the colonel's safety."

Olga knew, with dizzying certainty, that if Papa was taken away, they would never see him again—that he would disappear within the depths of Lenin's duplicity, his bitter malice, his anger—

Mamma grasped for the cross she wore, shining about her neck. "You ask me to trust the word of a revolutionary?" she said. "You ask my children to put their father's life in the hands of a man they've never met?"

Yakovlev let the insult in Mamma's words stand unchallenged. "I'm afraid I must insist," he said. "Colonel, you will be leaving Tobolsk tonight. If you refuse, I am authorized to use force."

At the other end of the room, Maria and Anastasia began to weep. Yakovlev glanced at them, coloring.

"I must tell you, Colonel, I have no desire to make this difficult," he continued. "If you do not wish to travel alone, you may take one of your daughters with you; the rest may follow along once the boy is well enough to travel. In either case, you will be leaving at dawn. Make your preparations accordingly."

Olga slipped into the sitting room, her heart pounding as she listened for a shout behind her: a guard, perhaps, or one of her sisters, someone suspicious that Olga was going where she wasn't meant to. The room, however, was silent. Mamma and Papa were in their bedroom, packing up their suitcases. The decision had been an agonizing one to make, but inevitable, given Yakovlev's refusal to budge: Papa was leaving at dawn, with Mamma, Maria and Dr. Botkin to support him. Olga, Tatiana and Anastasia would remain behind with Alexei, waiting until he was well enough to travel.

She crossed the sitting room to Papa's study and tried the door handle, sending up a prayer of thanks when she found it open. He would be coming to clear his personal effects soon, no doubt, but for the moment the room was tranquil, sun-drenched from the corner windows. As was the case at Alexander Palace, the miscellany on Papa's green-topped desk was meticulously arranged, pens and picture frames lined in perfect rows; envelopes and sheets of paper piled in neat mounds. In the corner, a grandfather clock kept time, its steady ticking a relentless reminder of the urgency of Olga's task.

Be patient, Papa had told her. She had been patient. She'd bitten her tongue at indignities from the guards, had choked down her frustration at walking the same 120 paces in the courtyard. But now they'd run out of time, and if there was some way Olga could communicate with their would-be rescuers—to let them know that they needed to set whatever dominoes they'd placed into motion—she needed to find it.

She knelt before the desk, running her hands over it with trembling fingers. There was something here: she could feel it, something that could help them, guide them. She opened the desk drawer and emptied its contents—pens and inkwells; a pot of glue and a half-filled photo album. Photographs, neatly bundled and secured with rubber bands: the *Shtandart*; winter at Alexander Palace. Alexei, laughing in a rowboat; Olga herself, as a baby, a child, a young woman—

Of course, she thought as she turned over the photo album in her hands, *he needs an excuse for the time he spends in here.* She set aside the album and knocked on the drawer, hoping to hear the hollow ring of a false bottom, but the wood was solid.

She pulled the drawer out completely, shaking her head at her own stupidity. The drawer would have been searched for a secret compartment by the guards before they brought it into the house. She ran her hands along the drawer's cavity—perhaps he'd secured some message on the underside of the wood?—then turned her attention to the photographs, pulling them free from their rubber bands and scattering them along the tabletop, flipping them in hopes of finding some cypher written on the backs.

The album. Papa had glued each of the photographs neatly down, his tidy, slanting script detailing each photograph's contents: *Tennis in Finland 1912; Tsar's Guard on Polar Star 1908. Alexei and Maria rollerskating, Livadia 1910.*

She could hear footsteps in the next room over but ignored them. She was close, so close, to finding some hint: a letter from Sablin, Papa's trustworthy aide-de-camp, perhaps, or a note from their extended Romanov relations—something, anything, out of place. She prised a photograph from its page with her thumbnail, but there was nothing hidden beneath it: no note, no code. Nothing to indicate the album was anything more than it appeared.

The door handle rattled, and she flew upright.

"Olga?" said Papa. "Who let you in here?"

"The door was unlocked." Olga planted her hands on the desk as she stared down at the photographs, her earlier panic replaced by a sudden, dreadful calm. "What is all this, Papa? These...these photographs..."

Papa crossed to the bookcase. "I'm not sure I take your meaning," he said. "They're albums. I've been chronicling our lives for posterity… My dear, I really ought to let the servants in here to begin packing."

Olga circled the desk, taking Papa by the hands; she pulled him to the window, afraid a guard might be eavesdropping at the door. "Of course they're just albums, but your *plans*, Papa," she whispered. "Whatever provisions you've been working on, we've run out of time. You need to get a message to your supporters, let them know you're being moved. They might be able to intercept your train, get you and Mamma to safety, but only if we can alert them…"

Papa looked down, politely quizzical, and Olga loosened her grip. "I'm afraid I don't understand, my dear," he said. "My books…my photographs, I'd like to take them with me. What do you mean, provisions?"

She could have cried out. "Papa, the wolves are at the door. If they take you to Moscow, all will be lost. Don't you see that? We'll never have another opportunity once you're in the capital. We need to escape, *now*."

She trailed off at Papa's look of strained pity. Behind him, the grandfather clock thudded in time with Olga's heartbeat.

"My dear, I'm afraid you've read too many fanciful novels," he said quietly.

She was silent a moment longer. "You mean to tell me you've made no plans? No means of escape?"

"There were no plans to make," Papa replied. "I'm sorry to disillusion you."

"No…no plans?" Olga's knees trembled; she gripped the edge of the window, the glass cool against her back as she leaned against it for support. "Papa, there's unrest in Tobolsk—that means there are loyalists in the city, surely! Soldiers, good Russians, good Christians, ready to help their tsar…" All these long months of waiting; Papa's visits to the soldiers—Olga, sitting dumbly with her knitting, trusting in the imagined bravery of others. "Do you mean to tell me you've done nothing to save our family?"

Papa circled to the bookcase and began pulling out volumes, stacking them one on top of the other atop the scattered photographs on his desk. "Of course, I tried. You think I wouldn't have done anything—everything—necessary to ensure your safety? Your sisters' safety?" He shook his head. "But in the end, all of the intrigues I was made privy to were unfeasible."

"There was more than one?" Olga looked up, picturing armed guards storming Freedom House; Sablin and Mitya and Dmitri Malama, directing cobbled-together regiments in the town gardens.

"Oh, yes," Papa replied, "but they all involved splitting the family up: taking your mother and me in a first rescue attempt, with the rest of you following. Seven was too large a number to take at once..." He shook his head again, light glinting off the faded braid of his cap. "It was too risky. How could I leave my daughters behind? And poor Alexei...how could he be expected to scale down a building?"

"Too risky?" Olga stood, trembling. "Papa, we're being split up regardless! If you'd done what was needed, we'd be through this by now! We might have been rescued by now if it weren't for your cowardice!" She knew she was wounding Papa, but she didn't care—she didn't care, either, that Papa's reasons for refusing to leave were entirely justified. The gravity of their situation made her blind to anything other than her utter desperation. "They're going to take you to Moscow and try you for *war crimes*, Papa! Do you not see that? Do you not see the danger you're in?"

"Of course, I see it!" Papa shot back, dropping his armful of books. She'd hit on the core of him. Papa was red-faced, pacing the room with a restlessness that she'd never seen before—not even in their long frustrating year of imprisonment. "Why do you think I stayed, Olga? To protect *you*—to protect your sisters! I will sacrifice my own freedom if it means ensuring your safety!"

"You could have protected us by letting us go," she said finally, tears streaming freely down her cheeks. No rescue; no salvation. "If we'd been allowed to meet people, rather than spend our days with you and Mamma in that—in that *summer palace*! We might have had friends willing to fight for our cause—" Olga's heart was beating wildly. She knew she ought to stop, but she was voicing things she'd never expected to say, the depth of her anger cutting, like a wound, to bone. "Aunt Olga knew it," she said bitterly. "She knew we were being suffocated by you. By Mamma. We might have married, Tatiana and I, if we'd been given the opportunity. We might have been *safe*, we might have been able to save you, in turn—"

"Don't." Papa was ashen; he stared at Olga and she knew she'd gone too far. "Don't you dare judge me for keeping our family together."

She stepped back suddenly, ashamed but unrepentant. "You're the tsar of Russia," she said. "Despite what they say, you're still the tsar. You could have saved us all, if only you'd been brave enough to do so."

Papa let out a heavy breath. "I stopped being tsar long ago," he said, his voice cracking with effort. "My only duty that remains—the only duty I ever truly cared about—is that of a father. I could not abandon my children. I simply could not."

Olga stooped; she picked up the books and handed them back to Papa, tears falling on the leather covers. "The choice is no longer yours to make, Papa," she replied. "Through your own inaction, you've seen to that."

30

March 1916
Alexander Palace, Tsarskoe Selo

The courtyard at Alexander Palace was lined with troikas, fur-clad men and women stepping out in their finery to make their way across the glittering snow. Within, the Semi-Circular Hall was alive with the movement of three hundred couples, sparkling like china figurines as they turned in perfect unison on the parquet floor in time to the echoing strains of an orchestra.

Even in peacetime, Olga was unaccustomed to such crowds at her family home: state occasions were generally held at the Winter Palace, while society events had always been the purview of her extended Romanov relations. Wartime, however, had forced her parents' hands: they'd thrown open the doors of Alexander Palace to welcome the Romanian royal family, using a state dinner to press their case to the Romanians to join the war on the side of the Allied powers. Papa had lifted his moratorium on alcohol for the duration of the visit, and the assembled guests were reveling as much in the champagne as they were in the dancing: as Dmitri Pavlovich pulled her onto the dance floor, Olga watched Prince Carol and Felix Yusupov drain their glasses, holding out their empty coupes for more from a waiting footman.

Olga, too, had enjoyed her share of champagne, and as Dmitri whirled her across the dance floor, the bright colors of the evening ran together in a vibrant sprawl: the firelight swirl of gold; the greenhouse flowers Mamma had had sent from Crimea—violets and lilacs and white roses, wisteria tumbling from vases in a tidal sweep of purple. Pastel dresses pulled out from mothballed storage seemed to breathe with new life as the women wearing them danced in the arms of aristocrats clad in the bright reds and blues of their honorary regiments.

After spending so long in military hospitals, Olga found the sight of so many able-bodied men jarring. What would Mitya, sent back to the front with his stick still in hand, think of all these retainers in their ceremonial uniforms, carefully ironed but never pressed into service? On the fringes of the dance floor, Olga glimpsed the officers she'd nursed to their deaths, their clouded eyes narrowed at the sight of so many unearned medals.

She pressed her hand to her chest, her heart rattling beneath her ribs. "Goodness, I'm dizzy."

Dmitri steadied her. "Too much champagne?"

"Too much of all of it," she replied, as Dmitri led her out of the fray. "I don't know that I feel up for dancing…it seems inappropriate, somehow."

He shrugged. "No less so than singing in a cemetery," he replied, holding out a chair for Olga. "But we answer the call of our tsar from whence it comes. Shall I get us some refreshments?"

He threaded back through the dancers as Olga looked around the room, her pulse returning to normal. By the fireplace, Maria was talking to Prince Carol; she lifted a hand to her dark hair, her diamond-and-pearl necklace sparkling in the firelight as she turned.

Olga smiled, amazed that Maria had become so lovely, seemingly overnight—but then, that was the magic of an official debut. Of her sisters, Maria was the only one who wouldn't have been offended that her coming-out was something of an afterthought—indeed, her debut in wartime had only been possible because of the importance of impressing the visiting Romanians. Olga recalled the first state ball she'd attended: at sixteen years old, she'd found the evening to be magical, a tireless swirl of dancing unmarred by circumstance—but Maria, with her self-effacing nature and sweet temperament, hadn't given a second's thought to sacrificing her moment in the spotlight to the war effort. Even now, she looked at Carol with bright eyes, and though her interest in him was surely feigned, Olga was impressed by her sister's commitment to dazzling their foreign guests.

Dmitri returned with two glasses of champagne. He sank into the chair next to her, following her gaze to Prince Carol. "Not going to dance with the guest of honor?"

Olga watched Carol sidle closer to Maria, thinking of her last conversation with the Romanian prince. She'd bristled at news of his return to court; indeed, she'd done her best to avoid him for the entirety of his visit. But Maria tilted her head to look up at him, looking utterly charmed. "Why? You think I've some measure of influence over him?"

"Don't you?" Dmitri turned to face her, champagne sloshing dangerously toward the rim of his glass. "To hear Petrograd tell it, you're all but betrothed."

"In his case, as in ours, don't believe all that you hear," she muttered. "At least he seems to be behaving himself. Should we go rescue Maria before he says something insulting?"

Dmitri leaned back in his chair as the orchestra shifted to a Viennese waltz. "Oh, let her have her fun," he replied. "It's not as if she'll get a proper coming-out; from tomorrow, we'll be back to homespun cotton and black-market vodka." He lifted his glass, letting the bubbles catch the light. "I'll miss these little luxuries back at the front. Your father runs Stavka with a fist of iron."

"Does he indeed?" Olga shifted closer in her seat. "Tell me, Dmitri, has he done well? Have the shortages stopped?"

Dmitri watched the dancers. "He's certainly enthusiastic about the task," he replied, and Olga wasn't sure if he meant the observation as a compliment. "But I daresay our empress is taking some time to adjust to her new role as well. I gather she's taking guidance from some rather unconventional sources."

Olga didn't feel up to sparring with Dmitri. "If you mean Father Grigori, Mamma surrounds herself with those she trusts."

"As well she should," Dmitri replied. "I only hope her trust isn't misplaced."

Olga stood, her hands heavy on the armrests of her chair. "I do wish you wouldn't be so cryptic," she said. "If you've something to say, then say it."

"Very well." Dmitri looked up, light flickering in the newfound hollows of his cheeks. "Is it true Rasputin wants to negotiate a separate peace with Germany?"

"Of course not," Olga shot back. Why was everyone so preoccupied with Father Grigori? The press, the police—everyone, it seemed, had something to say about Grigori Rasputin. Olga had grown used to the sight of his black cassock sweeping around the corners of Alexander Palace, following in Mamma's footsteps. After uncovering multiple attempts on his life, Mamma had had Father Grigori placed under police protection, but the constant intrigue was wearying: they'd both grown nervous, unsettled, in recent months.

"Then why does he spend all his time at the palace?" Dmitri's charming façade dropped completely: he looked hard, sharpened by his experiences at the front. "To hear people tell it, he all but lives there, now."

"Mamma trusts him—Papa trusts him. Why is that not good enough for you?" Olga shook her head. "Given your similar position of privilege in Papa's entourage, I'd be wary of casting aspersions."

Dmitri's answering smile was empty. "Aspersions? You misunderstand me, Olga. Pay me no attention; I'm nothing but the court jester." He drained his glass, setting it on the ground before rising to his feet. "A lonely fool, hoping that someone might take him seriously one day. Shall we dance?"

He held out his hand as the orchestra shifted into a new set, strings soaring above a cushion of brass. Olga blinked. Behind him, the pale faces of dead officers lingered, half-hidden by the candlelight, watching the glittering show.

"No," she replied, disconcerted. "No, I'm done for the moment."

Dmitri bowed and melted back onto the dance floor. When had her cousin grown so maudlin? When had Olga herself become so tense? She walked along the edge of the room, hoping to slip upstairs, out of earshot of the cloying orchestra; out of sight of the guests and their hollow pleasantries. In her mind's eye, she saw Mitya, hunched over a desk behind the front line; Pavel and Sablin, their swords drawn as they faced down German bullets.

Near the door to the Hall, Mamma sat on a divan with Anna Vyrubova, the pair of them looking like playing cards—the queen of hearts and the queen of clubs—as they conversed with Grand Duchess Vladimir. In the year since her accident, Anna had recovered to the point that she no longer required a wheelchair to navigate the broad halls of the palace; she would, however, walk with a cane for the rest of her life. In some strange way, Olga rather suspected that Anna enjoyed the attention; that she saw her invalidity as a point of common ground with Mamma's frequent indispositions.

As Olga approached, Grand Duchess Vladimir rose from her cane-backed chair, a circlet tiara glimmering atop her mass of iron curls. She performed a hasty curtsy before stalking off, glancing at Olga in passing.

Olga slowed. "Goodness, what's got her in such a state?"

Mamma sighed, exchanging glances with Anna Vyrubova. "She came to discuss your marriage prospects, of all things." She looked down, playing with the long strand of her pearls as if wishing she had some task to occupy her: knitting, embroidering. "She wanted to propose her son Boris as a match. *Boris*… I told her in no uncertain terms that such a union was quite unthinkable."

Olga sat down. Boris Vladimirovich…at nearly twenty years her senior, Boris was useless: a vacant-eyed grand duke with nothing to offer Olga beyond his pedigree and a long line of mistresses. "I'm glad you declined."

Mamma leaned over to pat Olga on the knee, her rings sparkling with a life of their own. "Your papa told you you'd not be forced into a marriage you didn't want," she replied. "I'm simply helping to shorten the list."

"Indeed," Olga said. They were silent for a moment; across the room, Dmitri approached Papa and bowed, his Cheshire smile restored as he said something that made Papa laugh. With its full complement of gleaming medals, Papa's naval uniform marked his changed position within the military: he wore his sabre close to his side, a deep blue sash cutting down the front of his tunic.

"We so outnumber him," said Mamma placidly. "I think it's why he adores Dmitri so. All us women; your father, standing alone." She smiled, though even in the midst of a pleasurable evening her expression still looked strained. "Much as I miss him while he's gone, I think that's why he was so eager to go to the front—to spend some time in male company. He'd never say so, but I know he hopes you'll meet some nice, well-bred young man soon. A son-in-law would help tip the balance."

Dmitri took Tatiana's hand and led her out onto the dance floor, her arms aloft as they began to sway in time to the music. *Court jester*, he'd called himself, dancing in time to Papa's tune. The circumstances of Dmitri's life were tightly tied to Papa's favor; but Olga had never once considered whether it was a favor Dmitri had wanted in the first place. What sort of life did he lead when he slipped out of the glare of her family's spotlight? Once Olga and her sisters married, Dmitri's proximity to that spotlight would fade. What relevance would he hold, once he was supplanted in Papa's eyes by square-jawed sons-in-law?

She let out a breath, replacing Dmitri with Mitya in her mind's eye: Mitya, laughing with Papa; Mitya, dancing her across the ballroom. "Given the circumstances, nice young men might be in short supply," she replied. "Does Papa have anyone in particular in mind?"

Mamma looked meaningfully at Prince Carol, who waltzed past with Maria. "We'd hoped, of course…" she said, trailing off. "Such a disappointment—but no one blames you, darling. We simply have to be patient; wait out this ghastly war. He'll turn up. I know he will."

Olga played with her pearls. "And what if he already has?"

Mamma's smile was more understanding than Olga had expected. "Your father's officers—Malama and Kiknadze, that handsome Shakh-Bagov you spend so much time with—they're wonderful men, you know. All so gallant…it's a shame none of the foreign princes ever seem as nice. But those officers are not suitable husbands. Not for a grand duchess." She tilted her head as the orchestra shifted into the opening strains of a Rebikov waltz: a melancholy thing, all minor chords and sloping progressions. "We're content waiting. He'll come along before you know it."

Olga stilled, the pearls warming beneath her hand. "You know about Shakh-Bagov?"

"Of course, I do," Mamma replied, exchanging a knowing glance with Anna. "Your *mitya*, is that correct? I make it my business to know everything there is to know about you and your sisters." She leaned in, her tone conspiratorial, girlish. "But don't give it a second's thought, my dear."

Olga pictured the *sanitary* at the Annexe, passing information to Mamma. How could she not have realized her quiet moments with Mitya were monitored? "Who told you? Do you have me followed?"

"Naturally," Mamma replied, as though surprised that Olga had even asked the question. "What sort of mother would I be if I let you go off with some young man unchaperoned? And though I am pleased that your young officer has proven himself to be a gentleman, you mustn't allow yourself to get carried away by a wartime diversion. I know how you can be about your little crushes."

How like Mamma to misunderstand. "He's not some *crush*, Mamma. He's kind and smart, and a gentleman…and I'm in love with him, Mamma. I love him."

The orchestra swelled into the silence that stretched between them, but Olga's heart thudded with the certainty of it. She'd not said it before, not even to herself, but she'd never felt so sure of her own mind.

"My dear, you're still a child," Mamma replied finally, her certainty matching Olga's note for note. "You don't know what love is, and you certainly aren't in love with an officer." She looked across the room, a flush of red rising in her cheeks. "Besides, he's not really even Russian, darling. You know how hotheaded the Georgians can be."

"He fights for his tsar, like his father and grandfather before him," Olga retorted. "If that doesn't make him Russian, what else possibly could? Besides, you fell in love with Papa when you were younger than me. How can you say that I don't know my own heart? Mitya and I—"

"Because the moment they're gone, you turn your attention to another," Mamma snapped. "Look at Tatiana and that lovely Dmitri Malama! Or you and that naval officer you met at your aunt's tea parties! I'll not stand in the way of an innocent dalliance, but you must understand that such things can't possibly last."

Olga tensed, recalling her last moments with Pavel on the staircase at Anichkov Palace: his sudden formality; Mamma's timely arrival moments later. "What do you know about Pavel?"

Mamma pursed her lips, almost comically condescending as she shattered Olga's illusion of self-determination. "You mooned over that boy for far too long, and it was becoming a distraction. Young men reach a point in their lives where nothing but marriage will do. I simply pointed his mother in the direction of a more suitable candidate."

"You what?"

"And was I wrong?" Mamma's eyes were round, guileless. "He's happily married; you're free to spend your time playing badminton with your officers. We're not pushing you to find someone tomorrow, Olga, not until the war's over. In fact, I think your father and I are being quite patient."

"I see," said Olga, trembling. "And what, exactly, constitutes suitability? Mitya is smart and brave, kind, gallant—"

"As are a dozen other young men of better stock," Mamma replied crisply.

"Is that so? And who might those other men be? The Prince of Wales, perhaps? Yes, I can see it now: renouncing my faith in order to rule over an island half the size of Moscow; to be a figurehead with no ability to influence the country toward good. Prince Carol, perhaps? He and I would loathe each other from the moment we said our vows." She was incandescent at Mamma's presumption, at her snobbery, her blind arrogance—her assumption that Mitya was disposable, that Pavel had been disposable. That the officers she cared for were nothing more in Mamma's mind than toy soldiers, toy paramours, to be cast aside when they no longer served their purpose. "What about a Prussian duke? Or an Austrian count? I'm sure our people would love to see me married to the enemy. The truth is, Mamma, there are no better prospects—particularly not for someone with *tainted blood*, as Carol so kindly reminded me the last time he was here. The old ways are dying out, along with the noblemen who've sustained them. I doubt there will be anyone left after the war who meets your impossible standards. They'll all be dead, ground to dust on the front line, along with their titles."

"Olga!" Mamma's admonishment was as sharp as a slap, but Olga didn't care: she continued, her voice low, hard.

"When the war is over, we will be living in a vastly different world, Mamma. We can all see it coming; a world where men are judged on the merits of their actions, rather than the accident of their birth. And I will not spend my life as a relic of a bygone era."

Mamma was silent for a moment, then she lifted her chin, her tiara glittering in the candlelight. "You are ordained by God, like your father and your brother, to serve Russia," she said finally. "God will provide. Trust in Him to provide you with the husband you need to help our country move forward."

Mamma eased herself upright and held out an arm: Anna Vyrubova, summoned as a magnet to true north, was at her side.

"I think we'll make our exit," Mamma said, the matter clearly closed. "I don't think I can bear the thought of Grand Duchess Vladimir throwing dirty looks at me for the rest of the night… you'll make my excuses to Papa, won't you? Only I've an early start tomorrow." She shook her head one final time. "*Boris Vladimirovich*… What could she possibly have been thinking?"

31

May 1918
Freedom House, Tobolsk

Olga picked apart the threads holding together the hem of her beaver coat, the seam nearly invisible beneath the profusion of fur. The detailed work hurt her eyes, and she held it closer to the window to catch the light: it would be easier, she knew, to split the silk lining, but such a fix would be evident to anyone who bothered to look. No, going along the seam itself was the better course of action; furthermore, the heavy weight of the fur would conceal any signs of tampering.

She set down her scissors and pulled the seam apart; surreptitiously, she glanced at the door before reaching into her pocket and pulling out five large gemstones and a small opal brooch. The final stone—a square-cut pink diamond—had once sat nestled in an exquisite diadem, but Mamma had broken apart the setting when they left Tsarskoe Selo, reasoning that it would be easier to transport individual jewels than full sets.

Medicine, Mamma had called them, when she'd asked Olga and Tatiana to conceal the jewels in their clothing. "They'll be too squeamish to go through ladies' underthings, so put the most valuable ones in your corsets," Mamma had instructed them in an undertone whilst packing for her departure with Papa. Between the two of them, and with Anastasia and Alexei's help, they'd managed to conceal most of what Mamma had left behind. Even now, Anastasia only had a few glittering jewels left in the basket at her feet. *Medicine*, Mamma had said, to be used at some later date, in some later world, to heal their family's fortunes.

Olga shifted the coat on her lap, using it to shield the diamond from view so she could inspect it more closely. Devoid of the setting that had once made it elegant, it looked needlessly large, its beauty self-evident, but its value nonexistent. There was nothing this diamond could do, here: milk, now, was a luxury; heat was a luxury. Without the ability to exchange it for money, the diamond was little more than a trinket.

Still—its value might return one day. She dropped the diamond in the cavity and folded the hem back over, trying to make the seam straight.

Across the room, Tatiana sat with Alexei. Under her guidance, he threaded a needle, his brow furrowed as he knotted the end of the thread. He could be a frustrating student, easily stymied by failure, but just as she was a patient nurse, Tatiana was a patient teacher: she set three small rubies in the cuff of Alexei's greatcoat and folded the seam back over, showing Alexei how to stitch just beneath the crease to make it look as if the alteration was never there.

She finished sewing the seam back together, her cheeks burning as she cut the thread. Mamma and Papa had left weeks ago, and the thought of her last conversation with Papa hadn't lost its sting: how could she have been so callous? Most evenings, she sat up late into the night, endlessly rehashing what she'd said as she listened for footsteps outside the bedroom door. She'd cut her father to the core, and though she'd kissed him goodbye before his departure, she'd not forgiven herself for setting harsh words between them. Why was she so incapable of holding her tongue?

Still. She didn't regret her words, only the timing—and the timing had been anything but inconsequential. The last few hours before Mamma and Papa's departure had been torturous: the solemn family dinner, marred by the presence of Matveev's guards along the walls; the silent vigil that had followed in the sitting room, waiting for Yakovlev to retrieve them.

Mamma had cornered Olga when Papa was taking leave of Alexei in his bedroom.

"Forgive each other," she'd said, her voice aching with the strain of it all. "You'll never forgive yourself, otherwise. Don't let bitterness fester."

But though Olga had made up with Papa, the memory of her words still lingered like smoke in her mind. *You could have saved us all, if only you'd been brave enough to do so.* Was Papa, too, haunted by Olga's accusations?

In their last moments at Freedom House, Mamma and Papa had stood arm in arm in the graying dawn, neither attempting to hide their tears as they hugged their children goodbye. Outside the gate, two bow-backed tarantasses awaited, hauled into view by anemic mares. Even in the midst of her grief, Olga couldn't help noting the indignity of it: was this the best Matveev could conjure for the former emperor—a peasant's conveyance?

Even Yakovlev seemed embarrassed at the lack of consideration. He'd ordered two of his guards back into the house to find a horsehair mattress to set atop the bare boards, and Maria had unraveled her long shawl to lay atop it: Maria, as always, looking to Mamma's comfort. Yakovlev had offered Mamma his hand to help her climb atop the mattress, his eyes downcast like a schoolboy's.

His solicitousness had worried Olga as she hugged her father goodbye—was it proof of a guilty conscience? But it seemed the Bolshevik had been true to his word. Several days later, Matveev summoned Olga to give her the news that Yakovlev had delivered Mamma, Papa and Maria safely to their destination.

Ekaterinburg, Olga thought, running her fingers along the hem to see if she could feel the jewels beneath the fur. Whatever was the point of taking them to Ekaterinburg? If her long-ago history lessons were to be believed, Ekaterinburg was an industrial backwater—a mining concern set deep within the Ural Mountains. As far as cities went, it offered nothing different from Tobolsk: it wasn't even all that distant from Tobolsk, by Russian standards.

No, if Olga's memory was correct, Ekaterinburg was a speck of nowhere—a city without distinction.

But then, perhaps that was its very appeal.

She finished her inspection of the hem and stood to ease her aching back: sitting, these days, felt quite as strenuous as standing, in its own peculiar way. She crossed to the double doors that opened onto the balcony. Matveev had forbidden them from stepping out at such a height, but there was nothing to stop her enjoying the view through the windows.

Across the street, the town gardens had bloomed once more, trees unfurling their broad leaves with the vibrant first green of spring. Near the cathedral, a couple on horseback moved sedately among the foliage. Olga watched them, admiring his upright bearing; her chestnut hair. His trimmed beard, so similar to Papa's.

Don't you dare judge me for keeping our family together.

She glanced at Alexei, sullen-faced as he wrestled with his needle; Anastasia, quietly sorting through Mamma's jewels.

"The hats have changed." Tatiana stepped closer to the window, and the sleeve of the blouse she was mending trailed on the floor. "Have you noticed?" She plunged the needle into the fabric, swift as a fish in water. "The brims aren't quite as full."

Olga turned away from the window. "Trust you to notice a detail like that," she said. Without hesitating, she snatched the blouse: ignoring Tatiana's protests, she threw it over her head like a scarf, raising her voice to a comical pitch. "The *brims* aren't as full!" Anastasia and Alexei looked up, gleeful. Tatiana reached to grab the blouse back, but Olga set off across the room, allowing Anastasia and Alexei's laughter to spur her on as she jumped atop the couch, twisting out of Tatiana's grasp, the sleeve of the blouse trailing behind her. "The *brims* aren't as full! It's fashion, my dears, fashion is ever changing, always transforming to ever greater heights—"

"Excuse me!" Matveev stormed in, his rat face pinched. Olga halted, her giddiness swiftly turning to panic—had they left anything valuable in the open?—but Anastasia, it seemed, had enough presence of mind to cover their work with the bulk of her skirt.

Olga nodded as she caught her breath. "We're sorry, Commander." She thrust the blouse back at Tatiana in a ball, chastened.

Matveev cast a lingering gaze over the room. "I would have expected better from you, Grand Duchess," he said. "Aren't you a little old for playtime?"

Tatiana tugged on Olga's arm; as one, they slumped back into their seats.

As Matveev left the room, Olga picked up her coat. Anastasia bowed back over her work; Alexei threaded another needle and Tatiana resumed her darning.

They were quiet over their work for a moment, then Tatiana broke the silence with a high-pitched whisper. "The *brims* simply aren't de rigueur—" and set everyone to laughing once again.

PART FIVE

32

July 1916
Moika Palace, Petrograd

Narrow cots stretched the length of the ballroom at Moika Palace, the iron head- and footboards barely wide enough to accommodate the breadth of a broad-shouldered man, but sufficient for the purpose of convalescence. In a nearby bed, a patient rolled onto his back and Olga followed his gaze up to the ballroom's spectacular barreled ceiling, with its plaster moldings as ornate as a Turkish rug, and she recalled Felix Yusupov's words when he vowed to turn part of his Petrograd mansion into a hospital: *After the hell of the front line, who would begrudge them a glimpse of heaven?*

She was impressed that Felix had followed through on his promise; further impressed still that he was here, walking her and Mamma through the ward and displaying an impressive knowledge of the hospital's workings in the process. With his head doctor beside him to correct any factual errors in his tour, Felix, dressed in tweeds and carrying an entirely superfluous walking stick topped by an immense sapphire, had already told them about how he had handpicked his own staff, pointing out the dressing room and the small operating theatre installed in the vestibule.

"Of course, it's for families like ours to do what we can for the brave men of our nation," he said as he swept his hand over the sight of the beds. "Those of us with means must show our gratitude for the sacrifices they've made."

Olga smirked; beside her, Dmitri Pavlovich leaned close. "Always the center of attention, our Felix," he muttered. "Even when he's meant to be discussing the contributions of others."

"I don't think he can help it," Olga replied, "but I'm glad he's doing something, at least, for the war effort." Felix's refusal to enlist still grated at her, but the opening of his hospital eased some of her objections. If Felix intended to live out his war years as a dilettante, at least he'd proven himself to be useful.

She slowed, allowing herself to gain a few beds' worth of space between her and Felix before calling over a nearby Sister of Mercy.

She nodded at a patient in a nearby cot. "Shouldn't that man's dressing be changed?"

The sister flushed. "Begging your pardon, Grand Duchess, but it's a matter of supply. We're waiting on a shipment of bandages from Moscow, and even if we had everything we needed…" She curtsied once more. "We just don't have the resources to change bandages on a daily basis."

"No?" Olga looked round the hospital. "How so?"

"We're understaffed, but that's the way of things, isn't it, Grand Duchess? They keep calling us Sisters up to the front lines, and those of us left behind manage as best we can. And that's not to mention medicines: chloroform, morphine…"

"We seem to manage well enough at my hospital," Olga said, thinking of the well-stocked supply closet at the Annexe, but Dmitri cut off her line of inquiry with a smile.

"Thank you, Sister, we mustn't take up any more of your time." He waited until the nurse had trotted off down the line of cots before addressing Olga in an undertone. "These are enlisted men, Olga. They're not officers. If medicines are running short, who do you expect will receive them?"

Olga paused. "But that's horrible."

"War's horrible," Dmitri whispered, as they drew closer to the rest of their party. "These men are cannon fodder, Olga. The fact they've survived long enough to be brought back from the front lines is more than any of them expected in the first place."

They approached Mamma and Felix, Olga's mind reeling. *Cannon fodder...* How could she smile at these men knowing that they were last in line for care? She'd always assumed that the other hospitals in Petrograd—hospitals opened by other nobles with ballrooms to spare—received the same share of supplies as the Annexe.

She turned her attention back to the tour. Up ahead, Mamma was kneeling by the bedside of a dark-haired patient, his leg bound from ankle to thigh in a plaster cast. Aside from wealth, what differentiated him from Mitya? Education? Luck? He stared down at his lap, clearly terrified to look the Empress of Russia in the eye.

Mamma smiled and pressed a small cross into the man's hand. "The Lord watches over you, as He watches over us all," she said, and the man nodded rigidly, as a rabbit might in the presence of a fox.

Olga registered his uneasiness, but Mamma didn't seem to notice. "I'll pray for you," she said, as she took Felix's arm and walked away. Olga and Dmitri followed; Olga threw a final backward glance at the soldier, who'd dropped the cross into his lap, holding his hands aloft as if they'd been burned.

The tour finished shortly afterward, Felix escorting them down the opulent marble staircase. He leaned on his cane, smiling. "You'll stay for tea, won't you?"

"I'm afraid I've such a headache just now," Mamma replied, patting Felix on the cheek, "but you're such a dear for offering.

Besides, I've a pressing meeting back at the palace to prepare for. Olga, darling…?"

Olga followed Mamma outside, wishing she could stay behind to discuss the shortages with Felix in private. Felix was wealthier than Croesus; surely, he could stretch the budget he'd allocated to the hospital a bit further?

"A meeting," Dmitri murmured, as they walked out to the street; beyond the narrow lane, the Moika River churned, the water brown beneath the swirling eddies of the ferryboats. "Can I ask who she's meeting with, or will I be disappointed by the answer?"

Olga sighed as Mamma stepped into the car, fussing with her skirts as she sat. "I know you don't like him," she said, and Dmitri rolled his eyes, staring up at the yellow façade of Felix's home. "But Mamma's got so many cares on her mind at the moment…if he gives her the support she needs to take on Papa's duties while he's at the front, is that so bad?"

Dmitri reached past Olga for the door handle but hesitated before turning it open. "Tell her not to bring anything from Rasputin again," he said quietly. "You saw how it unsettled that poor soldier. It unsettles them all, to have anything to do with the mystic."

Mamma slumped as the motorcar pulled away from Felix's palace. "Forgive me for not wanting to stay for tea," she said, pulling a bottle of veronal from the folds of her overcoat. "I couldn't stand the thought of sitting there a moment longer… not when there's work to do."

"There's work to do but not enough supplies to get it done," Olga replied as Mamma shook out a pinch of crystals to place beneath her tongue. "Did you see the state of their bandages? One of the sisters told me they're low on chloroform."

"Yes, the doctor mentioned it as well," Mamma said. She tilted her head back against the leather seat. "I just don't know what to do about it all. It feels as though the ministers are doing everything they can to slow down our efforts, at the very moment we need to speed things up." She sighed. "Still, at least they're bringing their troubles to me rather than the Duma. It's important they know that I am the authority in your father's absence. I'm the only one who seems to be able to get anything done around here."

Their motorcar stopped before turning onto Obvodiny Channel Embankment to let a horse and buggy pass; on the corner, Olga watched a line of people outside a bakery, their shopping bags slack. "It's not just the medical shortages, though, is it? Grain, bread… We're running short of everything, it seems."

"We wouldn't be if the supply lines could be sorted out," Mamma replied as the car lurched across the bridge. "But that's a whole other matter."

"Can't the military be called in to help?" Olga asked. She thought of Papa on his last visit home, his face drawn as he stared down at ministers' memorandums in his office. "Surely they could step in, take over the railways for the duration of the war?"

"And have your father give up more of his power to army bureaucrats?" Mamma shook her head, her gaze fixed on the passing buildings. "No. He can't afford to lose any more authority than what he's already given away. Father Grigori has foreseen that the shortages will resolve themselves. Loaves and fishes… Water to wine. The Lord will provide."

Olga sat back, threading her fingers together as she stared out the opposite window; outside, couples walked along the narrow streets, staring at the imperial motorcar. Did Mamma really trust in Father Grigori's prophecies to such an extent? Surely there was more to governance than sitting on one's hands, waiting for a miracle—but then, they'd all seen Father Grigori perform miracles before.

When they returned to the tree-lined enclave of Alexander Palace, Anna Vyrubova was waiting at the palace door, Father

Grigori beside her. Olga offered Mamma her arm as they walked up and through the checkerboard courtyard, Father Grigori's green eyes fixed on Mamma.

Anna stepped forward, holding out a letter. "From your sister, Your Imperial Majesty."

Olga looked up. Mamma's sister—Olga's aunt Ella—was a nun: following her husband, Grand Duke Sergei's, assassination, she had all but retreated from the material world, selling off her spectacular jewelry to fund a religious order in Moscow.

She eyed the letter, with its spidery black lettering. What could Aunt Ella possibly be writing to Mamma about?

Mamma sighed. "Another lecture, no doubt," she said wearily. "Take it up to my boudoir, Anna… I don't have the strength to tackle her now."

"You have more strength than you know, Little Mother," Father Grigori said, taking Olga's place at Mamma's side. His sleeve brushed Olga's arm and she pulled back, almost involuntarily, at his touch. "Strength enough to counter your enemies; strength enough to counter the devils that plague you."

He paused to smile down at Olga. He'd always been kind to her—and wonderful with Alexei—but the slow drip of rumors that followed him from room to room had become a steady stream. Dmitri, Aunt Olga, Dr. Gedroits, even the soldier at Moika Palace…everyone seemed to have their reservations about Father Grigori, loath though they were to tell her outright.

Mamma expected Aunt Ella's letter to include a lecture. Had word of Father Grigori reached the cloistered walls of her nunnery?

"I might have strength, Father, but strength means nothing without loyalty." Mamma stared at the envelope in Anna's hand and sighed. "Loyalty is all that matters… Loyalty to the tsar, loyalty to me. It's all I ask for from my family, and it's what I never seem to get."

Father Grigori helped Mamma up the marble steps and into the darkness of the hall beyond, her hunched silhouette supported by Father Grigori's tall figure.

33

May 1918
Ekaterinburg

Olga stepped off the train, her stomach swooping as her foot traversed the unexpected distance between the carriage and the platform. Feeling as though she'd missed a stair, she stumbled onto the muddy platform, relieved to be on solid ground. Though they'd arrived in Ekaterinburg at two o'clock in the morning, their train had shuttled between the city's two stations for hours: now, at nearly nine, Matveev had finally consented to release them from their nausea-inducing crawl at the industrial depot outside the city center. Surrounded by stone-faced guards, the platform was sparse and utilitarian, hemmed in by trees bent beneath the weight of the driving rain.

She looked back up at the train, tightening her grip on her suitcase: within, Pierre Gilliard stared back at her, the glass in his spectacles glinting in the morning light. Matveev had forbidden him from accompanying Olga and her siblings onto the platform—he'd forbidden any of the remaining entourage from disembarking, though they'd made the journey from Tobolsk too, first in the same rickety tarantasses that had conveyed their parents away months earlier, then on board the *Rus*, which had brought them downriver to Tyumen. Finally, they'd journeyed by rail from Tyumen to Ekaterinburg, in a third-class carriage smeared with grime from its previous occupants.

She held Gilliard's gaze as Tatiana, Anastasia and Alexei disembarked; beside him, Isa Buxhoeveden, one of Mamma's ladies-in-waiting, dabbed away her tears with a handkerchief. Though they'd been separated from their retinue for the last leg of their journey, Olga had felt some small comfort that people she'd known her whole life—people who'd helped raise her—were only a stone's throw away, both in Tobolsk and on board the train. Now, the thought that she was taking leave of them permanently threatened to overwhelm her. Resolving not to cry, she lifted her hand in farewell before turning to face the guards that flanked their path to a waiting lorry.

Unaccustomed as they were to carrying suitcases, Olga and her siblings struggled with the weight of their belongings as they walked toward the lorry, the bad weather adding challenges to an already challenging morning. Beside her, Tatiana carried not only her suitcase, but hefted Ortipo under her opposite arm: with his bowed legs and solid bulk, the little bulldog was unsuited to the terrain, but Alexei's spaniel, Joy, bounded through the mud as if it were so much snow, her paws black as she strained at her leash.

Anastasia let out a cry and Olga turned: the clasp of her suitcase had come loose, and she stopped at the foot of the platform to try and fasten it once again. Olga let out a breath, resisting the urge to snap at her youngest sister: why did *Shvybzik* not take more care with her belongings? She rested a hand on her midsection: her corset, reinforced with Mamma's jewels, had been digging into her stomach for the duration of the journey and she yearned to remove it, yearned for a room where she could escape from the prying eyes of their guards. Escape, just for a moment.

Alexei caught up; wordlessly, he handed Joy's lead to Olga and doubled back to retrieve Anastasia's suitcase.

"Grand Duchess?" Olga looked up. Matveev was waiting at the idling truck. "Inside, if you please."

She circled to the lorry, using her suitcase to steady herself as she climbed into the cargo bed. Black and belching nearly as much exhaust as the train, it was utterly unlike Papa's elegant vehicles back in Tsarskoe Selo: his touring cars and landaus; his sleek Mercedes and striking Silver Ghost. At least the lorry had the benefit of being dry. Olga climbed in, recalling the gilded carriage she'd once traveled in for the tercentenary; Pavel's hand, lifting her up into the chassis.

Ekaterinburg was utterly different from what Olga had expected it to be. Under different circumstances, she would almost call the city, its wide boulevards and sweeping rivers visible through the lorry's open end, beautiful. As they climbed the gentle slope toward the house, Olga looked out over the river. Given the rain, the vista was hardly inspiring, but after nearly a year of Freedom House's monotonous views, Olga drank in what she could see: the long, gray neighborhoods bordering the wide river; the green forest beyond.

Ipatiev House—their new home—was immense and charmless, a heavy, hulking structure carved into the side of a sloping hill. As Olga climbed out of the lorry, she took in the building: only its top windows were visible above the double fence that had been built around the perimeter, its roof slick with rain. Her heart pounded as she walked past the barricade, the scent of the fresh-cut wood still sharp: the fence was twice as tall as the one at Freedom House, and looked much more solidly built. Out of the corner of her eye a flash of red caught her attention. A small child was standing on the roof of the house next door, his sweater a punctuation of color in the gray as he attempted to make a sodden kite fly.

She watched Matveev's narrow back as he led her and her siblings to the door. What reason did they have to bring Mamma and Papa to Ekaterinburg rather than Moscow, after all? She eyed the mansion, unwilling to look at the guards that flanked her path—with a jolt, she realized that all the windowpanes had been painted over with white.

Guards opened the double doors and Matveev ushered them into a dark vestibule and up a narrow set of stairs. Unlike at Freedom House, which always felt restless with sound—footsteps and motorcars; snatches of conversation—this new residence was silent: guards stood at attention in every room, their eyes fixed firmly above Olga's head as she passed.

They'd been allowed to bring their own belongings to Tobolsk, furniture and paintings which gave Olga some sense of constancy—some sense that Freedom House, for all its limitations, had been a home. Here, the rooms were sparsely furnished, the belongings no doubt left over by the individual from whom the home had been requisitioned.

It had been a home once, Olga thought, eyeing a stuffed brown bear as they passed through to the sitting room. Perhaps it could be again.

Within, Papa was pacing in front of an unlit fireplace. He turned as Anastasia dropped her suitcase and flew into his arms with a cry.

"They're here?" Maria rounded the corner, stopping short at the lintel. "Alexei! Olga!"

Olga gripped Maria tight, not realizing, until this moment, how very difficult the past few months had been. She'd walled away her worries for her parents, for her sister, as a means of necessity—a means of survival. She'd hardened her heart to the possibility of disaster, numbed her fears as best she could; on seeing Maria, all her fears returned as her heart softened with knee-sagging relief at their reunion.

She released Maria. "Where's Mamma?"

"In bed," Maria replied, pointing. Tatiana dropped her suitcase and ran in the direction she indicated. "Around the corner and to the left."

Olga turned to Papa, her stomach lurching as she noticed how much thinner he'd become. She'd walled away, too, her guilt over their last conversation—pushed it deep within her in a futile attempt to stop her own words from haunting her at night. There was little use for remorse: not when nothing could be done to alter circumstances; not when Alexei had needed her to be strong in their parents' absence.

But what thoughts had plagued Papa in the long weeks of their separation?

Papa released Alexei, clapping him once more, genially, on the back. "Go say hello to your mother," he murmured.

She hesitated as Alexei left the room. What if Papa hadn't forgiven her? But Papa held his arms open, and Olga crossed the space between them to fall into her father's arms.

He pulled her close, and Olga realized that there was nothing, in Papa's mind, left to forgive.

34

November 1916
Nizhny Novgorod

The imperial train chugged westwards, the countryside flashing past through the curtained windows: town, forest, frosted farmland. Along with her sisters and mother, Olga had been traveling through the night, and the sensation of waking up on a moving train never quite sat right with her: she felt queasy as she stepped into the dining car for breakfast, declining the offer of eggs in favor of weak tea.

Tatiana was already seated, poring over a newspaper.

"Have you seen?" She passed the paper over and Olga read the headline: another day, another attack by the Duma on Father Grigori. She sighed. A week earlier, Purishkevich—a staunch monarchist who'd defended Papa's policies countless times in the past—had delivered a two-hour speech to the government, railing against the "dark forces" that had infiltrated Alexander Palace. The other members of the Duma had taken up his rallying cry, calling for Father Grigori's dismissal; the uproar was such that Mamma, in a rare show of defeat, had arranged to travel out of the capital to visit several outlying hospitals and cathedrals.

"She's letting it consume her," Tatiana whispered. Olga followed her gaze down to the opposite end of the long table where Mamma sat, surrounded by documents. She'd called the short trip a holiday, but it was clear that Mamma had not left her business affairs back in Petrograd. Even now, she was going over a list of government ministers she'd marked for dismissal in the wake of Purishkevich's speech.

Olga passed the newspaper back to Tatiana. "I'd best see if there's something I can do," she whispered. "We don't want her agitated when we arrive."

She crossed to Mamma's end of the dining table, where Mamma's muttering was audible even over the steady chug of the train. "Sturmer's no good any longer, not since he stopped taking Our Friend's letters…and as for Protopopov—" She stopped scribbling notes and squeezed her eyes shut, letting out a breath of air in an impatient hiss.

"Would you like me to lower the blind?" Olga asked.

Mamma glanced up. "Oh, yes please, dearest, my head is splitting. I can't stand the glare…" She leaned back in her chair as Olga pulled the blind down, concealing the passing fields from view. "It's a nightmare, Olga, honestly…"

Olga sat down. "You ought to rest, Mamma," she said; at the far end of the car, Maria and Anastasia had joined the table, looking proper in their matching dresses. "Some quiet would do you good. You're stretching yourself far too thin as it is."

An empty bottle of veronal rolled next to the stack of state papers, shifting lazily with the movement of the train. "Absolutely not," Mamma replied. "We're at a critical juncture, Father Grigori and I… Surrounded by enemies on all sides, by those who seek to wrest your father's power from his grasp…"

"I can't believe it's so dire as that," Olga tried, pouring Mamma a cup of tea. Out the opposite window, Olga could see that they had reached the outskirts of Nizhny Novgorod, the small village enclaves replaced by squat buildings. "Surely everyone wants what's best for Russia. What's best for the war effort."

"Autocracy is what's best for Russia, and your father has already given too much to those who seek to take what's his," Mamma shot back, striking the table with the base of her fountain pen. "He's too kindhearted for his own good, too willing to compromise when what these ministers need is an iron fist." She shook her head. "He just doesn't understand that to be tsar is to be feared—to be hated, even, so long as you are acting in accordance with God's will. Well, they can hate me if they must, but I see what they cannot… I am guided by a man of God."

Olga watched her, uneasy. She'd heard Mamma's tirades before, but this mania, this agitation, was new. "I know this situation with Father Grigori is difficult for you," she said finally. "If there's something that I can do to help…?"

"Slanders and lies—it's all slanders and lies." Mamma swayed with the movement of the train as it slowed, easing its way into the station. Outside, Olga could hear the waiting crowd, roaring in anticipation of their arrival. "He's being persecuted by his enemies—enemies of the tsar, drawing ever nearer. Do you know what he told your papa? *Rivers of blood.* He's seen blood in the Neva; he's seen catastrophe." She inched her fingers toward her neck, wrapping them around the cross she wore. "If he's seen it, it will come to pass. We must pray for guidance; we must pray for the safety of our holiest men; for the safety of our tsar. We must pray that the forces of good overcome the host of evil that is massing against us."

"Your Imperial Majesty?" Anna Vyrubova slid open the compartment door. "We've arrived. Grand Duchess, perhaps you might wait with your sisters while your mother disembarks."

The mass at the St. Sophia Cathedral lasted nearly two hours, but for the first time in her life Olga barely heard a word of it: she sang along with the familiar hymns, thinking all the while about Mamma. Despite her mother's conviction that the growing outcry against Father Grigori was nothing more than slander, Olga could sense a shifting tide, a scent on the wind that had become too undeniable to ignore. Rumors, left unchecked, could gain power—power enough to destroy lives, to change the world. To topple autocracies? She looked up at the gilded angels and saints painted on the cathedral's towering walls: they told a story of faith; of hope and of persecution.

Rumor and belief…slander and lies. She'd heard the whispers in Petrograd; she'd seen the newspaper columns alleging that Father Grigori had become so influential that he needed only to murmur a name in the right circles, and their fate—for good or ill—would be sealed. Mamma was concerned about the Duma gaining powers that ought to rest solely with the tsar. Was it not as harmful for power to bleed from Papa's hands into Father Grigori's?

Olga was still mulling on Mamma's words when they reached the Destyatinny Monastery later in the afternoon. As their landau passed beneath the ivory bell tower, Mamma looked upwards.

"I've been looking forward to this part of the visit most of all," she said as the bell began to ring overhead. It seemed as though the hours Mamma had spent in Mass had done her some good, turned her mind away from the thoughts of retribution that had so consumed her on the train. "Destyatinny is home to Maria Mikhailovna, a renowned seer. She's offered to give us her blessing, girls."

Maria and Anastasia exchanged thrilled glances. "A *seer*…" Anastasia whispered, twisting in her seat to look at the monastery's modest buildings. "How does it work? Do you ask her questions?" She shot a devilish grin at Maria. "We ought to ask her about Maria's dance with Prince Carol… Will he ask for her hand?"

"I doubt that's how it happens," Tatiana replied. Up ahead, a line of nuns waited at the monastery door, their black wimples reminding Olga of her Sister of Mercy uniform. "I think she simply channels whatever the Lord wants her to hear."

"Be respectful, girlies," said Mamma, smoothing down the front of her skirt as the landau creaked to a stop. "This is neither the time nor the place for high spirits."

As they entered the small building that housed the seer, any risk of high spirits quickly dissipated: the air in the darkened hall that led to the seer's cell felt heavy, hushed; imbued with some ancient wisdom that thrilled and terrified Olga in equal measure.

They paused outside a heavy oak door, the wood grown smooth and mottled with age. "We believe Eldress Maria to be around one hundred and seven years old," the abbess whispered as she selected a key from the ring at her waist, "and she does have a tendency to speak in riddles. Don't be disappointed if you can't make sense of her words."

"And don't be distressed by her appearance," a second nun added. "She has chained herself to her bed of her own free will."

The abbess fit an iron key into the lock, and Olga and Tatiana exchanged glances. *Chains?*

The bottom of the door groaned against the flagstones as the abbess pushed it open and stepped inside; within, Olga caught a glimpse of a narrow room with wooden walls before whatever candle had been illuminating the small space was snuffed out. Moments later, the abbess emerged from the gloom, trimming the wick of an oil lamp. She smiled, and beckoned Mamma inside.

Olga lingered at the door; she could feel Anastasia peering over her shoulder and edged aside, but not so far she couldn't see. Mamma was kneeling at the side of a darkened cot, its occupant concealed by a patchwork curtain. With a clinking noise, the occupant pulled the curtain aside, only slightly; Mamma leaned closer, and Olga strained to listen.

Mamma smiled down at the seer. "Thank you for seeing me, Eldress," she said. "Are you quite comfortable?"

The old woman chuckled, her laugh crackling in her chest. "Comfort has not been my concern for many years," she replied, and her voice was reedy but strong. "What use have I for the luxuries of this world when my eyes see only the glory of the next?" She lifted her hand, palm up, and Mamma took it, leaning closer still as the seer started to whisper.

Olga watched, struck by Mamma's piety—her stillness. Compared to what she'd witnessed on the train, Mamma was a different person entirely. Earlier, she'd allowed herself to be driven by fear; here, she governed her actions through compassion. She was always at her best when caring for others: whether it was Alexei or Papa, or the soldiers she nursed at the Annexe, Mamma had a second, indefatigable source of energy that she seemed able to draw upon if it meant helping another living soul. It was only in Father Grigori's company that her desire to heal—her desire to help—seemed to twist into something uncontrollable.

Mamma bowed her head, and the seer lifted a limp hand to Mamma's forehead before making the sign of the cross. She got to her feet to leave, and Olga watched as the seer turned her shadowed face to Mamma's retreating back.

"Behold, the martyred empress," the old woman murmured—or had Olga imagined it? Neither Mamma nor the abbess seemed to notice.

Olga was next to receive the seer's blessing. She walked into the cell, her eyes adjusting to the gloom; beyond the curtain, the seer lay propped up in her pillows, chains clinking around her thin wrists. She turned at the sound of Olga kneeling next to the bed—with a jolt, Olga saw that the old woman's eyes were milky white.

"My dear child," she said, holding out a papery hand. "Come closer."

Olga took the seer's hand, resisting the urge to pull away from her clawlike grip.

"The promise of youth deceives us all," she said, strands of white hair falling over her impossibly lined face, "for it is but a fleeting gift we are given by the Lord. We mortals believe youth to be eternal, do we not? For some of us it is." She took her sightless gaze past Olga's shoulder, and though she knew that behind her was nothing but a bare wall, Olga fought a strong urge to turn around. "For others, we must accept the gifts that are offered to us by Him, whether they are ours for a minute or for eternity."

"I—I'm sorry," Olga whispered. "I don't know what you mean, Eldress."

The seer smiled, revealing a mouth with only a handful of brown teeth remaining. "What justice is there in this world, when old bones live on and the young wither to dust?"

Olga's heart stopped. "The—the war, Eldress?" She stared into the seer's white eyes, hoping for some sign of acknowledgment. "Are you talking about the war? About Mitya? Will he survive—?"

"Hm?" The seer cocked her head to one side, the movement of her chin surprisingly quick as she listened, as if to a voice on the air that Olga could not hear. Then she reached out her wizened hand and laid it on Olga's forehead. "Bless you, my child," she said. "It will all be over soon."

35

November 1916
Alexander Palace, Tsarskoe Selo

Olga finished her letter to Mitya, blotting the ink dry before folding it into an envelope. She'd described her visit to the seer in as much detail as she could muster, pleased to have something to relay to him beyond the monotonous details of her days at the Annexe. Most evenings, she wrote to Mitya, and his letters back brought to life his days at the front: the towns he passed through; the men in his regiment. She was sure that he glossed over many of the darker aspects of soldiering, but he gave her enough to fix in her mind an image of him kneeling in the snow, using the broad of his thigh to write to her.

She finished addressing the envelope and consulted the clock on the mantel: it was nearly teatime, and Tatiana would be coming home from her shift soon. She left the envelope on her desk, propped up so that her maid would notice it and take it down to post.

Though he'd been gone for months, Mitya was still foremost in her mind—foremost of all the men she'd nursed back to health; foremost of all the men she'd ever felt for. When the war was over, would she even be able to see him? She recalled Mamma's airy dismissal at Prince Carol's state dinner: *a distrac-*

tion; a wartime diversion. Despite Olga's fiery retort, she knew that Mamma was right in one thing: Olga had been chosen, by God, to serve Russia, to put the country's interests before her own. She still believed that above all else. It was the life she was born to.

For a moment though, Olga allowed the life she desired to blossom in her mind: Mitya by her side; two sons in her arms. She would give up the trappings of her position if doing so allowed her to remain in Russia, with Mitya. They would live in a farmhouse, tending to their small flock of animals; Olga would learn how to boil water, how to bake bread. Every evening, she would fall asleep in the arms of the man she loved.

She reached the bottom of the staircase, allowing herself to feel the heaviness of the tears she couldn't afford to shed. Whatever else, it was a lovely dream.

She could hear the commotion in the Mauve Room before she reached it, Mamma's voice echoing down the hall.

"You dare to question your brother's judgment—*my* judgment?"

"I question your counsel!" Olga looked in; Mamma and Papa were seated by the fireplace, watching as Aunt Olga paced before them. She'd changed out of her nursing uniform: her black shawl trailed along the floor as she walked, a ruby glittering in the hollow of her high-necked dress. "He is compromising our family—leading the dynasty to ruin. I know I'm not the only one to raise such concerns, Nicky, if you'd only *listen*—"

"Listen to your conspiracies?" Mamma looked at Aunt Olga, her blue eyes as hard as chips of ice; beside her, Papa stared, stone-faced, into the fire. "First your mother's meddling, then Sandro, sending his poisoned letters… I see how it is! Your family never loved me—never *trusted* me. You've never believed in Nicky's ability to lead, and you always thought you'd be the ones to make his decisions. You can't stand the fact that you're no longer relevant in this court, can you? You can't stand the fact that we've got better advisors, more *trusted* advisors, who know the will of the people, the will of *God*—"

Aunt Olga snorted. "It's the will of the people, is it, to have uncertainty in their ministers? To have no food in their stomachs; no bullets in their guns? You've never understood us, Alix, and you never tried to. You've only cared about power—it's the only thing you have, given the glaring lack of affection you've cultivated in anyone but your children. What a pity you've given it all up to a *khlyst*."

"You have no idea what you're saying," Mamma breathed. She reached for Papa's hand and he took it in both of his, covering her wedding ring as he closed his fingers around hers.

Aunt Olga exhaled. "I can't know what you don't tell me," she said, "but I can see there's no further point in discussing this with you." She turned to Papa, her hands clasped with businesslike tact. "If you cannot remove Rasputin from your wife's influence, you must at least protect yourself from it," she said. "I'm sorry to be so blunt, but someone has to be. If you continue to ally yourself with him, it will be to the ruin of us all."

Papa didn't look Aunt Olga in the eye as he got to his feet. "I'm sorry it's come to this," he said quietly. "I don't believe this conversation is to anyone's benefit any longer. I wouldn't want you to say anything else you might regret."

Aunt Olga's expression crumbled as she stared at her brother. "I see. And you have nothing more to say on the matter?"

"I'm afraid not."

A deep flush rose in Aunt Olga's face as she gathered her shawl around her shoulders. "Very well. I suppose—I suppose I will take my leave." She curtsied deeply before turning on her heel. "Nicky, please know that I love you. We all love you."

Olga stood away from the door, panicking—but before she could hide in the next room, Aunt Olga came out. Red-faced and red-eyed, Olga could see the toll the conversation had taken on her aunt; quietly, she stepped forward to fuss with Olga's necklace, which had turned clasp-down. "The double-eagle clasp… Fabergé, I suppose? I remember my own papa giving me my first set of Romanov pearls… You know, your father and I used to say that if the clasp fell to the front, it meant someone was thinking of us." She looked up, her smile falling just short of convincing. "I hope that means someone's thinking of you, my dear."

Olga glanced down. "I hope so, too," she responded. "Aunt Olga…is everything all right?"

Aunt Olga sighed. "I suppose you heard it all, didn't you? Well, I'm sorry it's come to this. That man is a charlatan and a liar, and your parents must know the truth." She kissed Olga on the cheek, a lingering embrace that felt, in Olga's reeling mind, somehow final. "I love you, my dear. Please take care of your sisters."

When Olga entered the Mauve Room, the color was still high in Mamma's cheeks as she worked at embroidering a pillowcase; Papa held a book open in his lap, but his eyes didn't move as he stared down at the page.

"Was that Aunt Olga I saw just now?" Olga asked carefully.

Papa looked up; behind him, a fire crackled in the grate. "Hm? Yes, it was. She came to ask me for permission to divorce her husband." He looked back down at the book, running his thumb along the page edges. "I granted it."

Olga sat down, glancing at the half-drunk wineglass next to her seat, a smear of lipstick visible on the rim. "What a pity," she replied. "But she'll be able to marry again, won't she? One day?"

Papa nodded. "One day," he muttered, getting up to put a fresh log on the fire.

"You would think she'd be grateful for it, instead of throwing our generosity back in our faces," Mamma remarked, stabbing her needle and thread into the fabric.

"That wasn't the only reason she came, though, was it?" Olga said as Papa, knocking ash from his hands, circled to Mamma's dainty secretary desk. "Only, I heard through the door..."

"She has no idea what she asks of us, the stupid woman," Mamma muttered. She threw the pillowcase down in her lap, pressing her fingers against her temples. "She has no *clue*—"

"Then why not tell her?" At the secretary, Papa pulled out Mamma's bottle of veronal and dropped a pinch of the crystals into a glass of water. He stirred the water cloudy before passing it to Mamma. "Alicky, perhaps it is time to send him away."

Mamma gripped the glass, appalled. "And leave our son in peril? You know what he has foreseen."

Papa sank onto the cushion beside her, his lined face slack. He looked impossibly worn-out, as if he regretted returning from Stavka; as if he'd had this argument too many times before. Without his name even being mentioned, Father Grigori's presence in the room was palpable, the power he held over Mamma absolute. Saint, satyr, *khlyst*...which truth lay at the heart of the man?

"Mamma," Olga whispered as Mamma downed the veronal. "Mamma, please. What has he told you?"

"What do you think, Olga?" Mamma whispered. "He's the only one who can heal Alexei. You've seen for yourself the miracles he's capable of. If he's removed from court, it will mean Alexei's ruin. The end of the tsarevich; the death of my son."

"He's said this?" Olga asked, looking to Papa for confirmation.

Mamma's glassy eyes filled with tears. "You don't think I know what Alexei's disease can do to a family—to a dynasty?" She bowed her head, firelight glinting in her blond curls. "He's the heir to your throne, Nicky—and Father Grigori is the only one standing between us and chaos. My darling, the vultures are circling. Any sign of weakness and they will strike."

Olga's heart plummeted. So that was it: the reason for Mamma's angst. Fear for Alexei; fear for Russia's future. Father Grigori was holding Alexei's illness over Mamma's head, wielding her fears as surely as a blade, his logic ruthlessly simple: without him, Alexei would die. Father Grigori had foreseen it; Mamma believed it, as clearly as she believed right from wrong. Olga thought back to the first time she'd met Father Grigori: Mamma's desperation, her knuckles curled white over the hem of his cassock. Had it been his goal from the start, to tie himself so closely to the tsarevich that no man could cut him loose?

Mamma opened her eyes, fixing Papa with glassy desperation. He lifted his arm and Mamma leaned into his chest. "You mustn't pass a broken throne on to Alexei; you mustn't give the Duma the fodder it needs to bleed more power from your crown. Father Grigori understands this. He understands, better than anyone else, the importance of what we must achieve.

"Alexei needs him; I need him," Mamma whispered, and it was clear in Papa's tortured face that he would never send Father Grigori away; that Aunt Olga had lost the fight before it had ever begun. "You must understand, Nicky. You must trust in Our Friend, over everything else."

36

June 1918
Ekaterinburg

Olga walked out into the courtyard, breathing in the fresh, cool scent of the summer air. Life indoors was taking its toll on her: in her newfound inability to withstand bright light; in her exhaustion after climbing a single set of stairs.

In the sloped garden at Ipatiev House, tangles of weeds choked the wrought-iron staircase that led down from the second floor, wrapping around the balcony they'd been forbidden from using. Olga picked through the overgrown brush, careful not to lose her balance. Given his affinity for gardening, why hadn't Papa asked the guards for a machete so he could start taming the lawn? But then, perhaps he already had.

She walked toward the swinging bench—left over from the previous owner, the guards hadn't seen fit to remove it, though they had carved rude words into its wooden seat. The profanity didn't bother Olga; it didn't seem to bother Papa, either, who had merely covered the seat with his jacket. As Olga walked down the sloping lawn, Papa pushed the swing lazily back and forth with one foot, shielding his lighter from the breeze as he lit a cigarette.

She sat down, wrapping her hand around the swing's chain.

"So, it wasn't the Treaty of Brest-Litovsk after all." She looked up, squinting in the sunlight as she took in their limited view: guards had taken refuge from the summer glare beneath the balcony, giving her and her father a rare moment for private conversation. On the roof of the house next door, the little boy had reappeared, and was testing the quality of the wind before setting his kite adrift. "I keep wondering why they moved us from Tobolsk. I thought it might have been an attempt to make you ratify Lenin's treaty with the Germans, but they would have taken you to Moscow if that had been the case. So what was the point?"

Papa sighed. "I'm just relieved it was a fight your mother and I didn't have to endure," he replied. "I would have never put my name to such a thing—not if they'd threatened to cut off my hand. But I suppose it makes sense. Why should they ask me to ratify a treaty if they no longer recognize my authority?" He followed Olga's gaze; together, they watched the kite catch on an updraft. The little boy tugged on the string, making the flash of scarlet dance in the breeze. "Though I must confess, I'm disappointed that Cousin Wilhelm was willing to work with Lenin. I always knew him to be odious, but it seems beyond the pale, even for him."

"Well, we never liked Cousin Willy anyways," she said, trying to coax a smile from Papa. Olga knew what he meant: the German emperor had never been a favorite relation. His grasping insistence on his own importance made him difficult to respect—but Olga would have expected him to defend the divine right of kings, rather than break bread with socialists. But the conversation raised a new worry in Olga's mind. If the Germans were willing to recognize the legitimacy of Lenin's treaty, they were willing to acknowledge the legitimacy of his government. How many other countries—allies and enemies alike—had accepted the revolution as a *fait accompli*?

Beneath the balcony stairs, the soldiers began to stir; they shifted upright as Matveev rounded the corner.

Olga tightened her grip on the swing: whatever Matveev wanted, it wasn't good. He stormed down the yard, trampling the tall grass beneath his shining boots; behind him, no fewer than five guards jogged in his wake, their rifles held at the ready.

"Romanov!" he barked. "Up to the house, now!"

Papa picked up his jacket and stubbed his cigarette out on the swing's seat, neatly marring the carved expletive with his ash. Slowly, deliberately, he pulled his jacket back on—as he turned, Olga was struck by the look of fear marring his usually sanguine expression.

"Whatever happens, know that it was all for you," he muttered. "Everything—for you children. All of it—"

"Now, Romanov." Matveev stopped halfway down the garden and unholstered his pistol, holding it loose at his side.

"Is this not a matter you can discuss with Dr. Botkin?" Papa asked. Alongside his duties tending to Mamma and Alexei, Dr. Botkin had become something of the go-between for Papa and the Bolshevik guards. He'd taken up an apartment in the city, and paid calls to Olga's family on a near-daily basis. "I've only been outside for ten minutes or so; I believe I'm to be afforded at least another twenty minutes of fresh air."

"Absolutely not." Matveev's pistol twitched. "We will discuss it inside."

"Only if Dr. Botkin is present," Papa replied. "I'm afraid I must insist on a witness to our conversation."

"Botkin is not on the premises at the moment, as you well know," Matveev shot back. His small eyes darted from Papa to Olga; she could almost hear the gears whirring in his head. "Very well, your daughter may join us. But I'm in no mood for your obtuseness, Romanov, nor your temper, Grand Duchess."

Matveev's guards flanked Olga and Papa as they followed him back into the damp heat of the house: the windows had been sealed shut for weeks, ever since the guards accused Anastasia of signaling out the window at night, and the home had developed a humid, greenhouse heat that slowed Olga's steps as she climbed the stairs. She could all but feel the rifle pointed at her back, but she resisted the urge to turn around: what signal would it send, to let the guards know that such a thing unnerved her?

At the top of the stairs, Matveev led them into a small room off the landing, stowing his pistol back beneath his greatcoat. Used as an office for the on-duty guards, the room was flooded with light from crystal-clear windowpanes, and Olga looked out, her heart lurching at the sight of the harbor stretching long beyond the double fence, the water sparkling impossibly blue. Was such a view so precious that the Bolsheviks couldn't stand the thought of sharing it?

Clearly, however, it was too banal a sight for the man seated at the desk, facing the door. He didn't look up as Matveev ushered Papa and Olga inside; rather, he continued poring over his documents, allowing Olga to take stock of the room: the taxidermied head of a stag; the pictures beneath it, too small on the expanse of patterned wallpaper. She guessed that the room had been a study for Ipatiev House's previous owner, but the guards had filled the space with their little luxuries: bottles of vodka and whiskey, slotted into the bookcase alongside dirty glasses; bars of chocolate, no doubt pulled from packages meant for Olga and her siblings.

The man looked up from his papers, unsmiling. Unlike Matveev, who was still seething at the door, this guard was neither overawed at the sight of Papa nor apologetic; neither welcoming nor hostile. He stood, his gray jacket banded with red around his upper arm. His shoulders were rounder than Olga had expected, as though he spent his life bent over books rather than the barrel of a gun. To Olga, this man, with his thick goatee and arched eyebrows, exuded calm: a professional, unlikely to flinch under pressure, rather than a brute-strength soldier.

He circled the table. "Nicholas Alexandrovich, we've not had the opportunity to speak to each other before now. Your doctor has done an admirable job conveying your needs to me thus far, but in light of recent discoveries, I thought it best to meet directly. My name is Yakov Yurovsky. I am Commandant here at the House of Special Purpose. Please," he said, motioning to the chairs.

Papa eyed the chair, but made no move to sit down. He didn't seem surprised by Yurovsky's words, but Olga looked from man to man, unease twisting her stomach into knots. *The House of Special Purpose?*

Wordlessly, Yurovsky pushed a yellowed sheet of paper he'd been reading across the table. Ripped from the flysheet of a book, it had been folded on itself so many times that, now open, it refused to lie flat: Olga pictured what it would look like creased, smaller than a sugar cube.

Yurovsky tented his fingers atop it, the paper protesting as he pinned it to the table. It contained a hand-drawn map of Ipatiev House: bedrooms, clearly marked; staircases. Corners where the guards tended to stand, noted with small black crosses.

Papa, she thought, her heart sinking. *What did you do?*

"Do you recognize this?"

Papa hinged at the waist, looking down at the map with only the mildest expression of surprise, as if he was speaking to a minister whose portfolio was only glancingly familiar. "Should I?"

Yurovsky pushed it farther along the table with a blunt finger. "It's your handwriting."

Papa looked up. "What of it?" he asked, shrugging. "It's a drawing of the house. Meager as they may be, I didn't think our artistic offerings were under surveillance, too."

Yurovsky's glacial expression became almost pitying. "Please don't insult my intelligence." He pulled a similarly crumpled sheet of paper from his breast pocket, unfolding it square by square before reading it aloud.

"The orderly officer makes his round of the house twice an hour at night…one machine gun stands on the balcony and one above it, for an emergency. Opposite our windows is the outside guard house, which consists of fifty men… Inform us when there is a chance and let us know whether we can take our servants," he read, holding the paper at arm's length. He looked up; Papa was staring back, a deep flush rising in his cheeks. "Surely you must have known we would uncover such a ham-fisted attempt at escape. You don't think we inspect every item brought into this house? You don't think we comb over each piece of rubbish and dinner plate once you're finished with them?"

Olga listened, too terrified to move. Behind her, she could hear Matveev breathing heavily.

"After all we've done," Matveev said bitterly. "We ought to haul you to Moscow."

Olga willed Papa to be sensible. She'd goaded him into this; it had been her cutting words in Tobolsk that had led him to this futile show of bravery. The guards at Ekaterinburg were more ruthless, more dangerous, than their counterparts in Tobolsk—even Matveev seemed to have stiffened his resolve in these new surroundings.

You could have saved us all, if only you'd been brave enough to do so.

Now that it had come to it, Olga could see how reckless Papa's actions had been; she could see how naïve she'd been in her own expectations, her own hope of escape.

Yurovsky spoke again. "We could have you shot for this, you know," he said, and Olga could see that Matveev, with his cowboy petulance and his pistol, wasn't the danger in the room—it was Yurovsky himself. His calm demeanor was a mask for his bloodless efficiency; his measured reason, ruthlessness.

The commandant looked at Papa a moment longer, letting the terrible silence speak its volumes.

"You must recognize the peril you've put your family in," he said. "As you so accurately point out in your letter, I've fifty armed guards outside this house at all times, and thirteen within. We have the tactical advantage in terms of location, terrain, logistics. If I've not made the point sufficiently clear before, I will do so now: should the need arise, we will not hesitate to eliminate the threat you pose to our government."

He tucked the paper back in his breast pocket. "So, the question remains: what to do with you? I could have you sent to prison," he said, and Papa looked up in alarm. "Remove you from your family, for your safety and theirs. I would be well within my rights to do so."

Papa bowed his head. "Please," he said, and it broke Olga's heart to hear him plead. "Please, don't. I will endure any punishment you see fit…but please don't separate me from my children."

"Do I have your word as a gentleman that you will desist from any further attempts at escape?"

Papa nodded, once, the muscles in his jaw working with the strain of maintaining his composure. "You have my word."

Yurovsky glanced at Matveev. "Then we'll take this matter no further." He returned his attention to his desk, folding the map along its well-worn creases. "You may return to your family."

Olga offered Papa her hand as they turned to leave; Papa squeezed it, and though his eyes were dry Olga could feel his word weighing on him, as heavily as the accusation she'd leveled against him months before. Papa's word was his bond: he would hold to the promise he'd made to Yurovsky, though it might tear him apart to do so.

As they reached the lintel, Papa turned to face Yurovsky once more. "Tell me one thing, Commandant," he asked as Yurovsky, silhouetted by afternoon sunlight, lit a cigarette. "The letters I received…the rescue attempt. Was it genuine?"

Yurovksy snapped his lighter shut, a thin ribbon of smoke rising from the end of his *papirosy*. Despite his outward froideur, Olga could see the gleam of triumph in his eyes as he lowered the cigarette, knocked ash into a teacup on the desk.

"Of course not," he replied, and turned to face the spectacular view.

37

December 1916
Moika Palace, Petrograd

Felix stood in the entrance hall of Moika Palace, the marble room as ornate as a wedding cake. He passed the box Olga and Tatiana had brought to a waiting attendant, the vials of morphine tinkling as the attendant carried them up the stairs.

"This was awfully kind of you. I'm sure our nurses will put those medicines to good use." He smiled, twisting a gold-and-ruby ring around his finger; in the alcove at the top of the stairs, two marble figures stood in alcoves, one over his left shoulder, one over his right.

"It was no trouble at all," Olga replied, clasping her hands to ward off the lingering chill of the afternoon. "We're only too happy to help."

Tatiana cocked her head, peering up the stairs. At the top, a Sister of Mercy wheeled a trolley into the ballroom that Felix had converted into a ward; they could hear the sound of the patients within, their conversation as loud and indistinct as the noise of a beehive. "We've a few hours to spare before our shifts at the Annexe," she offered. "We could help here, if you like."

Felix hesitated. "I would invite you up, of course, but I don't know that it's the wisest idea. The men seem…a little out of sorts today."

"Out of sorts?" Olga tugged her collar closer around her neck. "How so?"

Felix glanced from her to Tatiana, an uncharacteristic flush rising in his cheeks. "I don't know how gentlemanly it would be to spell it out for you," he muttered, "suffice to say, there are—rumors they hear at the front. We do our best to quash them, of course, but…"

"Of course." Olga touched Tatiana's elbow. "Say no more, Felix. We wouldn't want to do anything to put our brave soldiers off their convalescence."

"I do hope you understand," Felix said as he led them out into the fading white of an afternoon caught in the grip of a snowstorm. Outside, Papa's motorcar idled between two snowbanks, a carpet helpfully laid atop the snow between the palace steps and the chassis. "It's a difficult time for all of us. The strains of war, Irina says…"

"And Irina is quite right." Olga stepped into the car, settling a fur blanket over her knees. "Please pass along our regards."

Felix shut the door as the chauffeur rolled up the carpet. "And pass mine along to your mother. She's well, I hope?"

Tatiana leaned past Olga to meet Felix's gaze. "I'm sure Mamma will be pleased to hear you asked after her."

Felix looked miserable as he waved them off the curb, and Tatiana twisted in her seat to watch him through the back window.

"Goodness," she said. "What do you suppose all that was about?"

"Mamma's furious with the rest of the family for their treatment of Father Grigori—I suppose word has trickled down to Felix," Olga replied. She stared out the window at the colorful palaces punctuating the relentless white: apricot and ochre, sunset colors lined along the canal.

"It's not Felix I'm worried about," Tatiana replied. "If the enlisted men feel they're able to discuss Father Grigori so openly in the hospitals, what are they saying about him on the streets?" She leaned forward to tap on the glass divider and the chauffeur opened it with a gloved hand. "Kegresse, would you please drive us past the Winter Palace?"

The chauffeur nodded and slid the divider shut; Tatiana settled back against the seat cushions, leaning against Olga's shoulder.

Olga looked out the window as the motorcar changed directions. Given the weather, they were the only motorized vehicle on the street—most motorcars couldn't handle heavy Russian winters, but Kegresse had adapted several of Papa's Rolls-Royces by attaching heavy rubber tracks to the back wheels and skis to the front. It was a curious enough sight for the people of Tsarskoe Selo, but in Petrograd the car was a marvel—onlookers standing in long lines outside the bakeries watched them pass, openmouthed. From force of habit, she lifted her hand to wave; to her surprise, the onlookers didn't wave back as Kegresse shifted gears to pass them.

Her cheeks burned as she turned her attention back to the road. Everything felt different—Petrograd felt different, this long winter.

They turned onto Palace Square, and despite the deepening twilight the square was alive. Bonfires illuminated pockets of activity where people were huddled together to ward off the biting cold. Many held placards as they faced the Winter Palace's dark windows, and in the flickering firelight Olga could catch glimpses of what the placards showed: crudely drawn illustrations of Father Grigori, dark-eyed and menacing; Mamma and Papa dancing on the end of puppets' strings.

Farther from the firelight, a makeshift village had cropped up on the square: cobbled-together shacks made of canvas and wood, too sturdy to be temporary, but too pathetic to be actual homes. Once or twice, Olga made out the small figure of a child staring, hollow-eyed, into a trash-can fire.

"Good Lord," Olga breathed. Three years ago, she'd circled this square in an open landau, awed by the intensity of the people's love. How had so much changed?

Kegresse shifted down-gear and opened the divider once more. "I'm not sure it's wise to get much closer to the palace, Grand Duchess," he said uneasily. "I don't feel we should linger."

Tatiana cleared her throat. "No," she said, and Olga could feel her sister's shock. "Drive on, please, Kegresse."

Neither Olga nor Tatiana spoke for the rest of the trip: not on their way to the train station, nor in the train on the short trip back to Tsarskoe Selo. Her parents wouldn't believe what she'd seen at Palace Square—but for their visit to the seer, Mamma hadn't left the grounds of Alexander Palace in weeks, while Papa shuttled back and forth between Alexander Palace and Stavka too frequently to tour his capital city. Mamma had spent months fighting the Duma, cycling ministers in and out of office so that Papa could maintain his hold over Russia. But who among them had been caring for Russia's people in their struggle for power?

By the time the train pulled into the station at Tsarskoe Selo, night had fallen. Tatiana stared out the window onto the platform, steam fogging the windows as Olga reached for her gloves.

"What do we say to Mamma?" She looked up at Olga, her eyes wide. "About the soldiers—the placards?"

"It's nothing she doesn't already know." Olga handed Tatiana her handbag, wishing she had more she could offer her sister than emptiness. "It's nothing she wants to hear."

When they arrived at Alexander Palace, Olga's heart leapt at the sight of a familiar silhouette waiting in the hall.

"Mitya!" She leapt into his arms, not caring how he got through the palace gates—he was here, home from the front, solid in her arms. Alive. She rested her cheek against the serge of his overcoat, breathing in his familiar scent; tactfully, Tatiana slipped up the stairs, beckoning the nearby footman to follow. "I didn't realize you were coming. How did you…?"

"I went to the hospital, first; Dr. Gedroits was able to call ahead and make the necessary arrangements." He pulled away from Olga and bowed, smiling. "I hope you don't mind the surprise."

"I'm thrilled about it." She took Mitya's hand and led him back out beyond the courtyard, into the grounds of Alexander Park where they could talk properly. After the crushing lows of her afternoon, Mitya's unexpected arrival was a dizzying high. Though he still walked with something of a limp, Mitya had gained muscle in his months at the front: he looked healthy, strong. His fingers twitched in hers and she smiled, thinking of their countless chess matches. Had he found someone with whom to practice in his regiment, perhaps? "When did you arrive? How long are you here?"

"I arrived last night; I'm on leave for two weeks. I needed to see you, Olga, I—"

They passed beneath the white columns that separated the courtyard from the drive, and Olga pulled him into the shadows, pressing her lips against his; he responded, so enthusiastically he lifted her off her feet.

Mitya was here. Safe and warm in her arms.

She pulled away, feeling light-headed as they resumed walking along the path toward the pond. "Tell me about the front. Tell me everything you've done since I last saw you."

"How has it been so long?" Mitya smiled; just off the footpath, untouched snow glittered in the moonlight, stretching long into the darkness. "I've missed you."

Olga stopped walking and tilted her lips to meet his. She was thrilled—relieved—that his feelings hadn't changed; that he was still here, still alive. Solid; dependable. So undeniably the man she'd fallen in love with. Even with the spilled light of the palace behind them, Olga wasn't worried that someone might see them: here, in the dark, they were a couple in love. Two young people, alone in the buffeting snow.

Too soon, Mitya ran his hand down Olga's arms. "Believe it or not, I came here with a purpose," he said.

Olga laughed. "A better purpose than this?"

"A more critical one." Mitya's gentle smile dimmed. "Your last letter. About your visit to the seer."

"You received it?" Olga took Mitya's hands in hers; in the long light from the palace, she could see the bloom in his cheeks from the cold; the clouding of his breath in the air. "It was an odd experience, I must admit. She was not what I expected."

"Olga, my darling..." He tucked a lock of her hair behind her ear. "I'm scared for you. The things people are saying at the front; in the villages. What the seer told you...none of it bodes well."

She thought of the placards in Palace Square; Felix's uncharacteristic gracelessness. Aunt Olga, storming out of the palace; Mamma's veronal, Papa's growing lethargy. "I'm worried too," she said. "Mitya, tell me the truth. What are people saying about Father Grigori? All I hear is innuendo."

He hesitated. "I don't know that it's for me to say."

"Someone has to. If you're worried for me, then please don't treat me like a child. Please. You're the only one who will tell me the truth."

Mitya cleared his throat. "There are...rumors that your mother is controlled by Rasputin. That he's—seduced her, somehow; that he's seduced most of the noblewomen in Petrograd, in order to wield influence over their husbands." He closed his eyes, relaying the next few words in a rush, too distasteful to linger over them. "That he's seduced you and your sisters too, and that Tatiana is carrying his child to be next in line to your father's throne."

Olga stared at him for a long moment. "But that's ludicrous," she said finally. "There's not a word of truth to it. He's a *priest*!"

"A priest whose drunken exploits are legendary in Moscow and Petrograd; a priest whose visits to—to fallen women are well documented. Surely your father is aware of it all, even if he shields you and your sisters from such truths. But that's not the worst of it, Olga. They say he's a German spy, that he and your mother are passing state secrets to Berlin. They say the emperor's mind is no longer his own, and that Rasputin has bewitched him."

"Is that it, then?" Olga let out a mechanical laugh that belied her growing panic. "Are there any more crimes he could possibly commit? You can't possibly believe it, Mitya."

Overhead, wind rattled through the trees, clattering bare branches against one another. "Of course, I don't, but you must see the danger it poses," Mitya replied. "They're saying it in the trenches, in the streets and the newspapers. Soldiers are calling for a revolution to save the country from the mad monk. You must understand how much peril your family is in. Your father must dismiss him. For your sake—for your brother and sisters—he must see reason."

Rivers of blood, she thought, her veins running cold. The young, withering to dust. Alexei, his life inextricably bound to Father Grigori's.

"He won't," Olga replied, knowing in her heart that even if Papa were to send him away, it might still be too little, too late. "He's too important to Mamma, to our family. He will never dismiss Father Grigori."

"Then Father Grigori must be removed," he shot back. "Whether by your father's hand or another's, the monk must go. Surely you can see it, Olga." He drew close, despair steeling his expression as he pressed his forehead to hers. "If you want him gone, say the word," he murmured. "Simply say it and I will make it so. I'll kill him if you ask it of me—for you.

For Russia." He kissed her lips, her cheek. "Please, Olga. Say the word, and I'll do it."

"I know you would," Olga whispered, resting her hands against Mitya's chest to feel his beating heart. "But I do not ask it of you—I will not ask it of you. Not now, not ever. Please understand."

He pulled away, his boots crunching in the snow. "Then *make* me understand! Please, Olga, because from where I stand all I see is peril."

She closed her eyes, the weight of her family's secret threatening to crush her, suffocate her if she didn't say it aloud. "My brother is ill," she said, and though she was trembling it wasn't from the cold. "He's been ill his whole life, and Father Grigori is the only one who can heal him."

Mitya was so silent they could hear the falling snow. "What?"

"It's a disease of the blood. Only Father Grigori knows how to manage it." Olga squeezed her eyes shut, striving to ward off the tears that threatened to fall. "He's the only one who can help Alexei. The only one who stops the bleeding."

Mitya stepped back, running a hand across his jaw. "I think most people suspected the tsarevich isn't well," he muttered, "but surely doctors…?"

"They've tried, and they've failed." She looked up at the palace windows. "It's only Father Grigori. It's only ever been Father Grigori. Whatever he's done, whoever he's wronged…none of it matters, don't you see? Whatever price he asks, my parents will pay. So long as he cares for Alexei, none of it matters."

She stepped away, wishing she could wash away the look of incredulity on Mitya's face. Mystics and prophecies; rumors and myth. How did any of it hold such sway in a world of medicine and electricity, steel and steam engines? Outside the palace gates, guns were massing along rivers already choked with the blood of millions, young men who'd laid down their lives in service to the tsar: how could Olga tell them her parents, shut away in their fairy-tale palace, were steering the fate of Russia on the promise of a prophecy?

Their faith in fairy stories died long ago—died along with their comrades in the dust and mud of the Polish front.

Mitya took her hands in his. "Come away with me," he said. "We can leave, right now. You and me. We can go, just the two of us, escape—"

Olga shook her head, her throat aching with the strain of trying to keep her composure. "Escape how? You have your duties at the front—my family—"

"Damn the front!" Mitya released his hold, stepping back; he ran his hand through his hair, looking as desperate as Olga felt—then he knelt. "Marry me, Olga," he said. "I can't save your family, but I can save you. Marry me, and we'll leave, tonight. We'll run away, leave the country—"

Olga closed her eyes. They were words she'd one day hoped to hear but they fell, bittersweet, on the wind. "I won't leave Russia—I can't leave Russia," she said, her voice breaking. "If things are truly as dire as you say, I can't abandon my family."

Mitya got to his feet, his knees brushed with snow. "It's revolution, Olga," he whispered, gripping her hands. "The call is getting stronger by the day. Revolution. Civil war. Do you really think your family can withstand it? I would take you all with me if I could, but if you stay—"

"What? If I stay, what?" She could feel the tears freezing dry on her cheeks; her heart hammering, protesting, in her chest. "Say it, Mitya. No special treatment. Say it out loud."

He hesitated. Around them, the snow was falling faster, deeper than before, eddying in wind caught between the bare trees; it piled on his shoulders, in the dark brush of his hair. "If you stay," he said finally, "I cannot imagine there is any future awaiting you other than death."

She closed her eyes. Something about hearing him say it aloud strengthened her resolve.

Blood in the rivers; young bones, ground to dust. When did rumor become prophecy; when did prophecy become truth? She saw, once again, the placards in Palace Square; the shying away of soldiers as Mamma sought to bring them comfort.

Who would stand in defense of her family? The government, belittled and alienated by Mamma? The army, already deserting their posts? If Mamma and Papa had lost the love of the people, revolution had already reached Russia: her family was already doomed.

She could run with Mitya to some foreign country, but revolution would be uncontrollable, unstoppable. She wouldn't be able to live with herself if she left her family to her fate, nor would she be allowed to survive. As a grand duchess—as a symbol of her father's regime—she would be hunted down, no matter where she was. What she represented would be too dangerous for the revolutionaries to allow her to live.

And the man who'd spirited her away to safety? Escaping with Mitya would mean signing his death warrant as well as her own.

"If that is the case, then I die," she said finally. "I am a daughter of Russia. A daughter of the tsar. I will not abandon my family. If death awaits me, then I will die on Russian soil."

Mitya brushed his fingers across Olga's cheeks, drying her tears with the pad of his thumb. He opened his mouth, but couldn't bring himself to speak; instead, he stared at her as if committing her face to memory. He accepted her decision—of course he did, for what sort of man would he be if he didn't? He wouldn't ask her a second time, nor would he question her judgment. She'd earned, over the course of her short life, the strength of her conviction, and Mitya understood it: he wouldn't have been the man she loved if he didn't.

Olga memorized the curve of his cheekbones, the warmth in his dark eyes. The streak of gray at his temple, an indicator of the older man she would never see him become.

She closed her eyes, savoring the feel of his hands as they

drifted down to her shoulders, to her waist. "If it all comes to pass, you must leave. Promise me, Mitya. Promise me you'll leave Russia. A revolution won't stop with us; they'll hunt down everyone loyal to the tsar."

"No," he said fiercely. "Not so long as there's a chance I can rescue you. I'll form a regiment; I'll find you—"

"No, you won't." Olga looked up, knowing that agony would come; that she only needed to maintain her composure a little longer. "I will do everything in my power to protect my family, but you must survive, Mitya. For me." She reached up and twisted the double-eagled clasp on her necklace; she let it slide down her chest and into her hand. "A Christmas present," she said, attempting to smile as she bundled it into his hand. The pearls glinted silver in the moonlight, still warm from the heat of her skin. "Take it. It's small enough for you to conceal, if you need to flee—it will fetch enough for you to start a new life, somewhere. England, maybe. America." Her breath hitched over her final words; she took a breath and looked up at Mitya once more. "Take it and live the life we would have wanted."

He wrapped his hand around hers. "I love you, Olga," he whispered.

She pulled him close, her beating heart reminding her that she was alive; that she was more than the pinprick princess people thought her to be: more than her grief, more than her pain. "If I die, I die with them," she whispered. "If I could have lived, it would have been with you."

38

December 21, 1916
Alexander Park, Petrograd

The sun shone brightly on the day of the funeral, transforming the freshly fallen snow in the empty churchyard into a blanket of diamonds. Mamma had chosen this spot as Father Grigori's final resting place—this secluded corner of Alexander Park, near the skeletal bones of a half-built church commissioned by Anna Vyrubova. Here, Mamma had gathered only those she considered most loyal to pay their respects to her fallen priest.

The chaplain finished his reading beneath the swaying branches of a larch tree and Mamma knelt before the zinc casket, her black veil billowing in the breeze. Though Mamma had insisted on seeing the body earlier, the casket was now sealed and Olga was thankful for it. Father Grigori had died in pain, bullet holes riddled throughout his torso; one arm still raised, frozen, in an agonized benediction. And though the morticians had done what they could to prepare his body for burial, nothing had prepared Olga, when she placed a signed icon atop his chest earlier that morning, for the sight of his frostbitten face, haggard and contorted in a grimace of dismay.

Mamma pressed a kiss to the casket's lacquered lid. Behind her mourning veil, she wept as Papa, his greatcoat banded with a stripe of black, helped her to her feet. He nodded, and the undertakers began lowering Father Grigori's coffin into the hole they'd chipped in the frozen ground.

He led Mamma back into the thicket of trees where Olga and her sisters stood, Tatiana's arm wrapped around an inconsolable Anna Vyrubova. It was murder—that much had been evident from the outset, when Father Grigori's daughter, who'd moved to the capital to act as a social secretary for her father, had called the palace to tell Mamma that he'd not returned after a night out.

Father Grigori had survived many attempts on his life over the years, Tatiana had reassured Mamma as they waited for news. He was a survivor with the luck of an alley cat. But as they kept a silent vigil with Mamma throughout the day, Olga was certain that Father Grigori's luck had run out, a suspicion that became ever more undeniable after she learned that Father Grigori had been bound for Felix Yusupov's palace on the night he disappeared.

The undertakers finished lowering the coffin; Papa held out a handful of earth over the grave. He let it fall, the dirt hitting the coffin with a hollow thud before turning away: Olga flinched with the horrendous thought that the noise was Father Grigori himself, clawing to get out. According to the coroner, he'd survived even this assassination attempt, at first: he'd lived through the poisoning, then the gruesome shooting that followed. Frostbite, it was said, had killed him in the end, after the conspirators had dumped his still-breathing body into the canal.

Papa turned away as the priest recited the Trisagion, rubbing his wearied eyes. Father Grigori's death had been a shock for Mamma, and a betrayal to Papa: he would never have believed his own blood capable of such a vicious crime. The news had ripped Olga's extended family apart as they tried to plead for clemency: clemency, for Felix Yusupov and Dmitri Pavlovich, who'd lured Father Grigori to Felix's home; clemency, for the princes who'd murdered a priest. But Mamma had been set on vengeance. Papa, caught in the middle, had exiled Felix from the capital, and sent Dmitri to serve on the Persian front.

Dmitri. Olga still couldn't quite believe the role he'd played in it all. Dmitri Pavlovich, capable of murder? She tried to picture him wielding the pistol, shooting Rasputin in the lamplight glow outside Moika Palace's buttered walls; carrying the body to Kretovsky Bridge and throwing it over, with no sympathy, no remorse for Father Grigori or his family. Was Papa's favor worth so little to him? Was Olga's friendship so easily thrown aside?

And yet, Dmitri hadn't been alone in his bloody convictions. Hadn't Mitya, too, seen no way forward but Father Grigori's demise? He'd offered such violence out of loyalty, out of love, viewing his actions as the service of a soldier, rather than a murderer.

Perhaps Dmitri viewed his own deeds in a similar light.

She thought back to her last conversation with Dmitri: his increasingly despondent outlook on the war; his frequent allusions to Father Grigori. He'd always known more than he let on, it seemed: had he resolved to do it, that night she danced with him at Alexander Palace? Had he already been making plans to murder the one man who could save Alexei from himself? Perhaps if Olga had spoken to him more directly—if she'd listened, if she'd looked a little closer—she might have been able to warn Dmitri off his destructive path.

Mamma let out a ragged sob; beside her, Alexei took his hand in hers as he stared down at the grave. At twelve years old, he'd begun to grow out of the chubbiness of childhood. With his newly hollowing cheeks and lanky frame, he'd begun to resemble Papa.

Alexei's face tightened, and Olga could tell he was trying not to show the grief he felt for the man who'd been his friend as well as his healer. Whatever Father Grigori was to the rest of the world, he'd been important to Alexei. Olga thought of the priest smiling at her little brother, lost within the white expanse of his sickbed; telling him that such agony was a test to bring him closer to the people he would one day lead.

Had Father Grigori told Alexei what he'd told Mamma: that his death would mean Alexei's ruin in turn?

They'd done it for Russia, Dmitri had said in the feeble letter he'd sent to Papa from the front: they'd murdered Father Grigori to keep Russia from tearing itself apart.

Little did he know they'd assured the end of the Romanov dynasty.

The burial ended shortly afterward, Mamma letting fall a small bouquet of baby's breath into the grave.

"My dearest martyr," she murmured. "Forgive us."

"It's an awful business," Tatiana murmured as the gravediggers began to cover the casket in frozen earth. From the other side of the burial site, Anna Vyrubova watched the casket disappear, suddenly, curiously stoic. "Awful. I hope this puts an end to the anger. Perhaps there's some peace that will come from it, in some way."

Olga watched Mamma, her pale face set beneath the black of her mourning veil. The myth of Father Grigori—the myth of Rasputin—had grown in recent years, grown so large that it had eclipsed the glittering legends of tsars and heirs, grand duchesses dancing beneath the glow of a chandelier.

Her family had survived this long on a myth of their own: a myth of their power, a myth of their divine right to rule.

That myth was no longer enough to sustain itself in the real world. It had faded beneath the unstoppable tide of the all-too-real struggles that plagued Russia and its people.

Whether Olga believed Father Grigori's final prophecy or not, that much, at least, was true.

"No, Tatiana," she murmured. "Whatever comes next, I'm afraid it isn't peace."

39

July 16, 1918
Ekaterinburg

Laughter spilled through the open window at Ipatiev House, carried in on a breeze scented with wildflowers. Sitting indoors with Mamma, Olga looked up at the opaque windows, the noise as uncommon and familiar as joy itself: it had been weeks since her family had had anything to laugh about.

She shifted closer to the window, glancing up at the guards that lingered on the opposite side of the room: one watched, but didn't object as she pushed the window open and looked out. Below, Olga's siblings were playing with Papa in the garden, some game that involved chasing each other through the tall grass. Soldiers flanked the yard, their knuckles tight over their rifles as if worried that Papa might dodge beneath a gap in the fence and break for freedom, but Olga knew that their vigil was in vain. When would the guards learn that not a single member of this family would leave the others behind?

Olga turned her attention back to Mamma, who was dozing on the sofa, her basket of mending nestled beside her. She blinked awake as one of the guards coughed, and reached automatically for one of Alexei's shirts, settling it in her lap.

"It's nice to hear them enjoying themselves," she said, locating a rip beneath the shirt's arm. Olga stood, and circled to the tea service set on a nearby coffee table. "It's been so quiet, here. *Shvybzik* needs something to amuse her."

"She's not so little anymore," Olga pointed out, setting down two cups of tea.

Mamma closed her eyes. "Seventeen." She looked down at the shirt, finding the seams she planned to stitch together. "And Alexei: thirteen already. It's hard to believe they're not children anymore."

Olga returned to the sofa, stretching long across the cushions as she let the heat of the day lull her eyes shut. Outside, she could hear Tatiana berating Alexei for some misstep in their game; from down the hall, she could smell cigarette smoke, hear the shifting floorboards creak beneath the heavy sole of a boot.

She started at the sound of breaking china and looked up to find Mamma staring at her smashed teacup as blood pooled scarlet in her palm.

"Foolish of me," said Mamma as Olga grabbed a clean napkin and a bottle of vodka from the sideboard. "My hand must have slipped... I was miles away."

Olga twisted the napkin around Mamma's hand, watching the white linen turn red. She met Mamma's glassy gaze, and realized she must have taken more veronal from her dwindling supply.

"It's nothing," she murmured, inspecting the cut. Compared to what she'd seen at the Annexe, it was nothing, indeed—but a shard of china had sunk deep into the fleshy mound at the base of Mamma's thumb, leaving a wound that wouldn't knit together without the intervention of stitches.

Olga splashed vodka over the wound before passing Mamma's needle through an open flame. Dr. Botkin wasn't due until tomorrow, and the procedure was nothing she hadn't done before. Quickly, carefully, she delved the needle into Mamma's hand, tying a stitch in a clean knot. Despite the lack of proper supplies, this abbreviated version of nursing felt comforting: a reminder of the everyday miracle that was the human body, healing.

Mamma barely winced as Olga tugged her flesh together and Olga paused, disturbed by the realization that her mother was so heavily sedated that she barely registered the pain.

"That ought to do," she said, tying a final stitch. She poured one final splash of vodka over Mamma's hand before binding it up with a clean napkin.

Mamma lifted her hand, squinting to inspect Olga's handiwork. "Yes," she murmured, before lying down on the sofa. "Thank you, my dear."

Olga propped a pillow beneath Mamma's head. "You're welcome," she said, but before she could turn away Mamma gripped her wrist with her good hand.

"I've been a good mother to you, haven't I?" she asked, staring up at Olga with sudden clarity. "To you and your sisters? To Alexei?"

Olga smiled, brushing a stray lock of hair from Mamma's cheek. "You did the best you could."

The sentiment seemed to comfort her: she lay back on the pillow, her eyelids fluttering shut. "I did," she murmured. "I did the best I could with you all."

That evening, Olga lay awake, listening to the creak of boots against the floorboards. She'd grown used to the sound of the guards, coughing and whispering even in these witching hours: though they never disturbed Olga and her sisters, the knowledge that they were there, on the other side of the door made for fitful sleep even on the most peaceful nights. Tonight, they were less inclined toward silence than usual. She could hear them talking, pacing the hallway as if they were manning a watchtower.

She'd done the best she could, Mamma had said: wasn't that all anyone could ask of themselves, in the end? But anyone's best was determined by circumstance: it required an understanding of a thousand small decisions, those everyday choices that echoed, like the ripples of a pebble thrown in a pond, down through the days, the months, the years. How would Mamma's life have turned out if she'd had more sons; how might her life have been different if Father Grigori had never set foot in the palace? If she'd been able to address Alexei's condition without the added pressure of politics: as a mother, as opposed to an empress?

But then, her role as a mother wasn't the one Mamma would be remembered for, no more than Olga would be remembered as anything other than the last of Russia's grand duchesses. In the minds of the world, Olga and her family were the titles they'd never asked for, the positions they'd never sought. They were symbols of a world already long gone before the revolution: that fairy-tale life of glittering ballrooms and sweeping gowns, of tsars and prophets and snow-sparkled carriage rides along the Neva.

Perhaps that world had never truly existed in the first place.

From beyond the bedroom door, the sound of voices grew louder, ripening in the late-night stillness. Olga sat up, her heart thudding. A rescue attempt, perhaps? Her sisters stirred in their sheets, their slumber interrupted by the noise of boots clattering down the hallway: Tatiana scrambled out of bed; Anastasia grabbed a shawl as Maria hunted in the darkness for her camera.

No, Olga thought as she got to her feet. This was no rescue attempt. She'd given up faith in their rescue long ago.

But faith in her family—faith in God. Those things still remained. The door slammed open, and Olga and her sisters were pushed into the hallway, but in that moment, Olga thought not of the hard looks on the guards' faces, nor of the terror that had gripped her heart, ice-cold, in her chest. She thought of her faith in Papa, as he marched ahead of her, one arm holding Alexei upright, his other protectively over Mamma's shoulder as she knotted her house robe around her waist; her faith in her sisters, in Anastasia, Maria and Tatiana, even as they all huddled together before Yakovlev.

Her faith, too, in Mitya. Mitya's love, Mitya's goodness.

As Yakovlev barked instructions, those thoughts gave her the courage to stand, straight-backed and dry-eyed, to hold her head high as the guards chivvied them, rifles drawn, down the staircase. She gripped Tatiana's hand as they descended into the unfamiliar cellar of Ipatiev House. She knew what awaited them at the bottom of the stairs: she'd known it for months, now. Theirs was a tragedy centuries in the making, their fate bound up in the lives and deaths of the millions who'd lived in their shadow; in the casting of chicken bones and the roll of dice, in the fateful lay of painted cards.

Armed guards stood waiting by the double doors to a small cellar, a single bare bulb illuminating the papered walls within.

Their destiny had been clear, to all but those who had refused to see it. The ghost of a fragrance left in an empty bottle. Portents of disaster, written in fire on a moonless night.

All that was left now was to face it with grace.

EPILOGUE

June, 1952
Campbellville, Ontario

Olga Alexandrovna finished kneading the dough for her scones, wiping her forehead with the back of her palm. As she patted the dough into plastic wrap to chill, she glanced out the kitchen window. Outside, Nikolai was herding the sheep into the barn. Though his dogs did most of the work, he preferred to walk the fields when he could, leaving their sons, Tikhon and Guri, to the shearing. He whistled, his gnarled hand curled over the fencepost, and Olga knew he wouldn't be long in the fields: he felt the damp, these days, settling in his knees, in his back.

She set a kettle to boiling and rummaged beneath the sink for a hot water bottle. The instinct to nurse—cultivated so long ago, in such terrible times—hadn't left her; not when it came to her beloved husband. She looked out the window once more, smiling: though his dark mustache had long since faded to gray, he still carried himself with the disciplined bearing of the soldier he used to be; the aide-de-camp who'd brightened the echoing halls of her St. Petersburg mansion.

She sighed. Nikolai was spending fewer and fewer hours in the fields these days. His old back injury—sustained in the Great War—made it increasingly difficult for him to work; their sons, meanwhile, had never expressed much enthusiasm in taking over the farm. No, their boys craved the excitement of city life, never truly understanding Olga and Nikolai's preference for a peaceful country existence. But then, she'd once scoffed at her brother's longing for a country life, too. In the long years since, marked by heartbreak and horror, she'd learned to value the simple pleasures of a simple life.

She set the dough in the icebox, allowing herself a rare moment of nostalgia. Life had been too cruel for her to regularly dwell over reminiscences of her brother and his family—too cruel for her to think about the unknown fate of her four beautiful nieces, her handsome nephew. But moments like this were undeniable: how could she not think of her brother Nicky, when she was living the life he'd wanted to lead from the outset? No, she thought, looking out over the farm that she and Nikolai had cultivated since moving across the Atlantic—Nicky had never been cut out for what fate had destined for him. It would have been far better if Nicky had been dealt a hand like hers: a quiet life, even if she'd had to fight him for the privilege of spending it with the man she loved.

Still, she couldn't begrudge Nicky for his stubbornness, no more than she could begrudge herself for marrying a man so impossibly ill-suited to her in the first place. Nicky had warned her off of Petya when he'd first proposed marriage—it had been Olga, with her headstrong manner, that had insisted upon the union, only finding out weeks later that Petya was fundamentally unsuited toward the duties of a husband. She still recalled her wedding night: handsome Petya, leaving her bedchamber with a bottle of wine in one hand and a glass in the other, smiling his reassurance that he'd breakfast with her in the morning.

Thank the Lord for Nikolai. As Petya's aide-de-camp, he spent more time at their home than anyone else—they'd gotten to know one another through the long days of her estrangement from her husband, while Petya spent his evenings pursuing handsome soldiers. It had taken her a few short months to fall in love with Nikolai; years to convince her husband to divorce her.

Years longer, still, for Nicky to agree that her marriage had been a failure. Granting divorces had been within the sole purview of the tsar back then, and Nicky had been bound by the strictures of Russian Orthodoxy to deny her the one thing she'd ever desired. For fifteen years her own happiness had been a lamb upon the altar of her faith.

It was only when Nicky could admit to his own failures as tsar that he'd finally granted Olga's wish. She thought back to the last time she'd seen her older brother: the harsh words they'd spoken to each other; Alix's blind refusal to see reason. Though they'd parted on poor terms, Nicky had still given her the divorce she'd yearned for; he'd allowed her to marry the love of her life.

It had been a last act of love, from the brother she'd mourned every day since.

Olga watched Nikolai out the window. Nicky had made his choices, but the choices he'd made on behalf of his daughters—Olga's nieces—still pained her. She'd thought about the demise of his family a thousand different ways and seen a thousand different roads her brother hadn't taken: but still, her imagination couldn't count for fact. There were no guarantees that another path might have led to a different end. She had faith enough to know that her brother had done what he'd thought best under circumstances of his own making.

She filled the sink with soap and water, hardly noticing when the water splashed on the countertop—were Nikolai in the room, he would have noticed her distraction and pulled her back from the brink of memory. He'd lived with her long enough to know that the ghosts that haunted her would never leave. How could they? Lenin's government had never admitted what they'd done to her brother, but the silent disappearance of Nicky's family—of Olga and Tatiana, Maria and Anastasia and sweet

Alexei—carried its own admission. The last anyone had heard of them was in the letters Maria had sent from Ekaterinburg; letters that had ceased, without explanation, in 1918. Regardless, the whispers still regularly captivated Europe—rumors that Olga's mother, the Dowager Empress Maria, had believed to her dying day.

It rankled Olga to think of the impostors who'd shown up at her door, stalking her from Denmark to London, trying to prove, through an errant birthmark or the unique structure of their feet, that they were one of Olga's nieces. Those charlatans spent their lives torturing Olga with the hope that someone in her family might have survived: that one of her nieces might have outlived their parents.

Such hope didn't sustain her anymore, but she still yearned for the beautiful serendipity that could never be: the survival of Nicky's line; the survival of the remarkable girls that Olga had loved so deeply.

She finished cleaning the dishes and opened the half door to air out the kitchen. She recalled, with a smile, the tea parties she used to host for Olga and Tatiana—would they recognize her now, with her penchant for dishwashing; with her Canadian farmhouse, half the size of her ballroom in St. Petersburg? With a smile, Olga realized she didn't mind if her nieces wouldn't have recognized her new life; in fact, she thought they would have enjoyed it, along with the opportunities it would have afforded them, outside their parents' cloistered world. Olga and Tatiana had yearned for nothing more than the chance to live their own lives.

She crossed the kitchen—the chickens would need tending to, she knew, before too long, but if she could get the laundry on first it would be all the better for tomorrow. She dissolved lye in boiling water, but before she could add her husband's shirts, a knock came at the door.

It was a tall man with a narrow face and salt-and-pepper hair.

With his unkempt shirt and cardboard suitcase, it was clear he'd been traveling for quite some time; she smiled, noting that, beneath his trimmed mustache, he was a handsome man.

"Olga Alexandrovna?" He bowed at the neck, and Olga tensed, recalling so many impostors who'd come to make some claim of friendship to her nieces—some story intended to wound, to draw out whatever remaining money they thought she might have had.

The man rummaged in his overcoat, and Olga couldn't help but notice that the fingers on his left hand curled in on themselves, as if over the ghost of a chess piece. She leaned against the door, not quite allowing it to open: she'd had too many of these pilgrims to her door.

"I… I knew your niece, Grand Duchess," he said. He met Olga's eyes, and something within his gaze caused her to hold back her half-formed rejection. "Olga—your namesake. I… I suppose we were friends—more than friends—long ago."

Olga found her voice, somewhere deep within the pain that, at seventy, she still carried. "What makes you think you were friends?"

He pulled his fist from his pocket and held it out. Between his fingers, Olga could see what he carried: a pearl necklace, the clasp an undeniable Fabergé, still luminous, bearing the double-headed eagles of the Romanov family. "You might have heard of me, from her… She used to call me Mitya."

Olga reached for the necklace, almost involuntarily. The pearls were warm, still carrying, she fancied, the long-lost warmth of their beautiful owner.

"Well," she said, clearing her throat with sudden emotion, "I suppose you ought to join me for tea."

★ ★ ★ ★ ★

AUTHOR'S NOTE

The imperial family of Russia died in the early hours of the morning on July 17, 1918. Summoned from their beds by Yakov Yurovsky, the family was told that they were being moved to a more secure location following reports of Czechoslovakian forces advancing on Ekaterinburg. They were led down to the cellar of Ipatiev House (known as the House of Special Purpose), where two armchairs sat empty, brought in for the comfort of the tsarina and the tsarevich.

Flanked by a firing squad of twelve men, Yurovsky read out the order, given to him by the Ural Regional Soviet Executive Committee, that condemned Nicholas II to death. Nicholas, who had been helping Alexei into his chair, turned.

"What? What?"

Yurovsky repeated the order, and the firing squad lifted their revolvers.

Nicholas died first—shot, according to most reports, by Yurovsky himself. The rest of the firing squad aimed for the family; however, uneasy at the prospect of killing children, many closed their eyes when pulling their triggers. According to some reports, when the smoke cleared, Olga and her siblings were still alive. The jewels they'd sewn into their corsets and coats had saved their lives, leaving the executioners to finish their grisly job with bullets and bayonets. In a tragic twist of irony, Alexei was the last member of the imperial family to die—shot, like his father, by Yakov Yurovsky.

Alongside the imperial family, the slaughter in the cellar claimed six more lives: Dr. Eugene Botkin, the family's physician; Anna Demidova, Alexandra's maid; Ivan Kharitonov, the imperial cook; Alexei Trupp, Nicholas II's head footman; and Ortipo and Jimmi, Tatiana's and Anastasia's faithful dogs, who died defending them from the onslaught of bullets.

Questions still abound as to who passed the final sentence on the Romanovs. Was it a direct order from Lenin, or had the Ural Regional Soviet Executive Committee taken the initiative to execute the family without Moscow's knowledge? Despite a lack of concrete evidence linking Lenin to the murders, current scholarship, corroborated by Leon Trotsky's diaries, suggests that Lenin at the very least sanctioned the executions, if he didn't order them outright. Whatever the case, although the revolutionary government admitted to executing Nicholas, they never confirmed what they'd done to the rest of the imperial family. Admitting to the murder of the children would spark international outrage, so they allowed rumors to flourish. Over the next several decades, many impersonators came forward, alleging that they were one of the grand duchesses. Most frequently, pretenders claimed to be Anastasia, who was the youngest at the time of the murder—impersonators could simply say that her looks had changed with age. But the sad fact of the matter is that the entire imperial family died that day, their bodies disposed of in two mine shafts in a nearby forest. The first mine shaft, exhumed in 1991, contained Nicholas, Alexandra, Olga, Tatiana, Anastasia, and the four retainers; the second, discovered in 2007, contained Alexei and Maria.

The Romanov family has captivated generations of armchair historians, the myths and mysteries surrounding them too many to list here. As history's most documented family, the last Romanovs have become symbols of a lost era, glossed to a high shine by the sensational events surrounding their lives and tragic deaths.

In writing this book, I aimed to look beyond the shine and see the Romanovs not as symbols, but as a family, flawed and fallible. In the most fundamental way, theirs is a story about people ill-equipped for the roles that fate saw fit to give them. Naive and insular, with a stubborn refusal to move with the times, Nicholas and Alexandra would have been better suited to the quiet family life they craved rather than to life at the apex of the Russian court.

In this work I chose to focus on Nicholas II as a father, but I would be remiss if I did not mention some of the worst atrocities committed during his reign. The Romanov dynasty, and Nicholas II, were active participants in the oppression of the peasant class, not only through the lingering aftereffects of serfdom (abolished in 1860), but also through their appalling treatment of Russian Jews. Encouraged by members of his government, Nicholas II viewed revolutionary sentiment as stemming from his Jewish citizens—an entirely baseless claim, but one which led to the repression of Jewish people through violent pogroms and discriminatory legislation. Little did Nicholas realize that the revolutionary sentiment among all his people was widespread and growing.

The Russian revolution did not occur overnight. Indeed, some historians see the 1917 overthrow of Nicholas II and his imperial government as a continuation of the earlier 1905 revolution—Bloody Sunday—that resulted in the formation of the State Duma. The reasons for the revolution were wide-ranging and too numerous to mention here, but it's true that Grigori Rasputin's outsize influence at the imperial court severely eroded confidence in the tsar's and tsarina's abilities to rule, and that Nicholas II's decision to take personal leadership of Russia's armed forces, both in victory and (more frequently) defeat, was a critical body blow to his already-tarnished image.

As Father Grigori predicted, the war was a disaster in terms of casualties, logistics, and morale. With over twelve million poorly equipped troops to feed on the front, food shortages quickly swept through Russian cities, leaving a population desperate for change. Socialist groups, including the Bolsheviks and the Mensheviks, saw opportunity in the unrest and toppled three hundred years of Romanov rule, replacing the autocrat with a short-lived Provisional Government that soon ushered in the advent of the Soviet Union.

The job of the historical fiction author is to tell a good story rather than provide an entirely accurate recounting of facts, and there are many moments in this book where I've had to sacrifice historical accuracy for the sake of plot. While I've done my best to address the most notable instances here, rest assured that deviations from the historical record were deliberate and done with a mind to telling a compelling story.

On the night of the abdication, Olga was in the sickroom with her siblings, suffering from the measles—it was Maria, rather than Olga, who visited the Cossacks on duty alongside her mother. I gave Maria's role as a witness to Olga in order to contextualize the abdication from the perspective of the book's protagonist. During the family's imprisonments in Tobolsk and Ekaterinburg, the guards and overseers in charge of the family's welfare changed frequently. Before the arrival of Yakov Yurovsky in July 1918, the House of Special Purpose in Ekaterinburg was overseen by Aleksander Adveev. For brevity's sake, I chose to have Pavel Matveev accompany the imperial children to Ekaterinburg instead of introducing Adveev as a new character. Finally, though the content of Rasputin's July 1914 warning to Nicholas II about declaring war on Germany is accurate, historically it was delivered by telegram—at the time, Grigori Rasputin was convalescing in Pokrovskoe following an assassination attempt.

Father Grigori's first meeting with the imperial couple took place in 1905, arranged by the Montenegrin Princesses Stana and Militsa (known in court circles as the Black Crows). While Rasputin didn't seem to have made much of an impression on Nicholas and Alexandra during those first few encounters, he became indispensable to them after healing Alexei of a hemophiliac attack in 1907. Scholars still debate exactly how Rasputin managed to alleviate Alexei's pain—several theories have been put forward, including hypnotism, the power of suggestion, prayer, and breathing exercises. Whatever the case, Rasputin's calming influence, not only over Alexei but over the frantic empress, undoubtedly soothed the young boy and helped to facilitate conditions for recovery. According to Douglas Smith, author of *Rasputin: Faith, Power, and the Twilight of the Romanovs*, "Rasputin's assurances calmed the anxious, fretful mother and filled her with unshakeable confidence and she, in turn, transferred this confidence to her son... He relaxed, his blood pressure most likely dropped, his pain eased, and his body mended."

Rasputin's influence at court soon extended beyond Alexei. As a religious, rough-spun peasant, Rasputin represented the Russia that Nicholas and Alexandra thought they ruled: humble, God-fearing, and devoted to the patriarchal image of the tsar as the "Little Father" of its people. For his part, Rasputin told Nicholas and Alexandra what they wanted to hear: he preached faith in God and in the tsar as God's representative on Earth; and he reminded Nicholas to care for the poorest among his people.

But behind Grigori Rasputin's gentle façade lay another man entirely. Though he presented himself to the tsar and tsarina as God's intermediary, Rasputin's exploits outside the palace walls soon became the stuff of legend. Leveraging his proximity to the reclusive imperial family, Rasputin became an object of fascination to St. Petersburg's society set. Preaching sin as a pathway to redemption, Rasputin drank to excess, made obscene advances on women of the court, and boasted of his connection to the empress. While rumors that Rasputin shared Alexandra's bed—or indeed, those of her daughters—are undoubtedly false, it's very likely that he took advantage of women who sought him out for religious guidance. Rasputin himself admitted to having a "weakness" for women, twisting the teachings of the Bible to suit his purposes:

> Rasputin made it easier for the ladies by preaching his personal doctrine of redemption: salvation is impossible unless one has been redeemed from sin, and true redemption cannot be achieved unless sin has been committed. In himself, Rasputin offered all three: sin, redemption, and salvation. (Robert K. Massie, *Nicholas and Alexandra*)

Though Rasputin's shortcomings were repeatedly raised to Nicholas and Alexandra—so much so that Rasputin was put under surveillance by the secret police—the imperial couple refused to see anything in their "Friend" other than his virtues. "A prophet is never acknowledged in his own country," Alexandra wrote, staunchly defending Rasputin from his detractors. Nicholas, it seems, was less convinced, but Rasputin's results spoke for themselves: when Alexei was in peril, Rasputin alone seemed able to bring him back from the brink. What else mattered if he could cure their beloved son?

Olga and her sisters led notoriously sheltered lives, due, in large part, to Alexandra and Nicholas's fears that someone would learn about Alexei's condition. Except for official functions and tea parties thrown by their aunt Olga Alexandrovna, Olga and her sisters were kept behind the walls of Alexander Palace, relying on each other—and on the family's courtiers—for friendship and amusement. As a result of their sheltered existence, Olga and Tatiana in particular were quite immature. Whereas other twenty-year-old women in the early 1900s were getting married and having children, Olga's and Tatiana's early romances read as schoolgirl crushes. Olga's hopeful diary entries describe the objects of her infatuation as flawless, as though she'd not yet learned that flaws are inherently human.

In the years in which this novel takes place, Olga had three, not two, romances. The first, with a soldier named Alexander Konstantinovich Shvedov (known in her diaries as AKSH), began in February 1913, when she met him at one of her aunt Olga's tea parties. The attraction faded after Olga met Pavel Voronov in June 1913 aboard the Shtandart, the imperial family's yacht. Dashing and discreet, Pavel became the all-encompassing object of Olga's affections as their innocent romance played out beneath starlit skies in Crimea.

As the cast of characters for this book is already quite extensive, I combined Olga's experiences with AKSH and Pavel into a single character. What is undeniable is that Olga's feelings for Pavel extended beyond infatuation. In her diaries, she calls him her "happiness," her *schaste*, and describes watching for the glint of his binoculars aboard the *Shtandart* from the balcony at Livadia Palace in the hopes that he, too, was thinking of her.

Pavel's marriage to Olga Kleinmichel (called Anya in this book to distinguish her from the other two Olgas already present) was a seminal moment in Olga Nikolaevna's life. In her diary, she recounts the day with a dignified resignation, but it's clear that her heart was breaking: "I learned that [Pavel] is to marry Olga Kleinmichel. May the Lord grant happiness to him, my beloved."

And what of Dmitri Shakh-Bagov? Dmitri, referred to as *Mitya*, "darling," in her diaries, was undoubtedly an important figure in Olga's life. Historically, we know little of Mitya himself. Born in Georgia in 1893, he was an adjutant with the Imperial Life Erevan Grenadier Regiment, and was wounded three times in service to the tsar. What else we know comes from Olga's diaries, in which she breathlessly describes his virtues: his "sweetness" and his "cheerfulness"; his bravery and his thoughtfulness. During his periods of convalescence, Olga's diaries become records of nothing but her time spent with Mitya—so much so that other nurses and doctors at the Annexe, including Dr.

Vera Gedroits, took notice. According to Valentina Chebotareva, a senior nurse at the Annexe Hospital, Olga's attachment to Shakh-Bagov, while "pure," was also "naïve and hopeless."

Given her rank and position, Olga was meant to be married off to a foreign prince—something that she resisted, even as a young girl. According to Helen Rappaport, author of *Four Sisters: The Lost Lives of the Daughters of Nicholas and Alexandra*, Olga vowed that she would never become a princess in a foreign court: "'I'm Russian, and mean to remain Russian,'" she told her parents. To their credit, Nicholas and Alexandra told her that she would be allowed to marry for love, though it was certain that love, in their minds, did not extend to the affections of a lowly adjutant.

One particular historical note pertaining to Mitya stood out to me, and it ultimately became a seminal moment in *The Last Grand Duchess*. According to Valentina Chebotareva, Olga's love for Mitya was reciprocated, so much so that Mitya once declared, "Tell me, Olga Nikolaevna, that Grigori Rasputin is disgusting...tomorrow he will be gone, I will kill him." This, combined with Olga's statement in her diary about Rasputin after his assassination by Felix Yusupov and Dmitri Pavlovich—namely, that she understood why they did it—indicated to me that despite her sheltered upbringing, Olga was more politically aware than many gave her credit for.

The historical record is unclear about whether Shakh-Bagov survived the First World War and the Russian Civil War that followed. We do know that a Shakh-Bagov led a White Army detachment in Echmiadzin (now Vagharshapat) in 1920, narrowly defeating Red Army forces in the South Caucasus—whether it was Olga's Mitya has never been confirmed. Given Olga's clear affections for Mitya, I chose to give him the happier ending that she would have wanted.

To Nicholas and Alexandra, Prince Carol of Romania would have been a more acceptable suitor for Olga's hand, but despite multiple efforts to bring them together, Olga and Carol despised each other on sight. Conscious of Alexei's illness, Carol's parents were already wary of marrying him off to a Romanov; Carol himself, meanwhile, set his sights on a different sister. At the final meeting of the families at a state dinner in January 1917 (which takes place a year earlier in the novel in order to set up Dmitri's role in Rasputin's assassination),

Carol asked Nicholas for Maria's hand. Nicholas, however, laughed away the suggestion: at eighteen, "fat Marie"—Nicholas's favorite daughter—was too young to marry. The proposal does raise one of those unique what-if moments in history: What if Maria had married Carol and survived the revolution? Would she have become a rallying point for the monarchist White Army? Would she have been able to leverage her position in Romania to rescue the imperial family?

Grand Duke Dmitri Pavlovich had been another proposed suitor for Olga in her younger years. On paper, Dmitri appeared to be all that she could have wanted: Russian, wealthy, and titled; charming and strikingly handsome. Nicholas II seemed to have initially encouraged the match, adopting Dmitri as a sort of son from the outset. However, Dmitri's racy lifestyle may have been too fast for Olga, who disapproved of his bawdy jokes and long nights out with his closest friend, Felix Yusupov.

Felix was a handsome and magnetic individual, prone to excess and a degree of hedonism: in his memoir, he writes that he was a "most undisciplined" young man who "flung [himself] passionately into a life of pleasure." In his adolescent years, Felix borrowed his brother's mistress's dresses to perform as a woman in a cabaret, gaining such attention that his father, outraged, threatened to send him to a Siberian convict settlement. As a bachelor, he and Dmitri were playboys of St. Petersburg's high society set, known for drinking with ballerinas and gambling their vast fortunes.

Scholars are divided on whether Dmitri and Felix were lovers or whether, perhaps, Dmitri harbored unrequited feelings for Felix. Whatever the case, the two had such an intense bond that even Nicholas and Alexandra took notice and tried, unsuccessfully, to convince Dmitri to distance himself from his friend.

To all who knew them, Dmitri was entirely in Felix's thrall, willing to follow wherever he led. However, when it came to Grigori Rasputin's murder, Felix tells us in his memoirs that Dmitri had been the instigator. Felix and Dmitri both concluded that Rasputin represented an unavoidable threat to the already-tarnished monarchy. In the trenches and the streets, stories about Rasputin were viewed as solid fact rather than rumor: that Nicholas was a puppet of the Mad Monk, allowing Rasputin to take the empress and the grand duchesses to his bed; that Rasputin and Alexandra were German agents, deliberately destabilizing Russia through bad policies that affected troops and citizens alike.

Felix's and Dmitri's fears for the monarchy were well-founded and widely shared. Given Alexandra's unshakeable faith in Rasputin, dissuading her and Nicholas was a job for family alone. In November 1916, Grand Duke Nikolai Mikhailovich, Nicholas's second cousin, wrote to Nicholas, warning him that Alexandra was being "led astray by an evil circle," and concluding that if Nicholas was "not able to remove this influence from her, at least protect [himself]." In December of that same year, Ella, Alexandra's sister, traveled to Alexander Palace in a last-ditch effort to deliver a warning that Rasputin was "compromising the imperial family and leading the dynasty to ruin." For the sake of not overloading an already-heavy cast of characters, I gave both of these warnings to Olga Alexandrovna, Nicholas's sister, but the result of the family's efforts was the same: silence from the imperial couple.

Knowing Rasputin's weakness for beautiful women, Felix lured Father Grigori to his palace on the night of December 16, 1916, with the promise of an introduction to Irina, Felix's wife. Alongside their third conspirator—a monarchist politician named Viktor Purishkevich—Dmitri and Felix plied Rasputin with cyanide-laced cakes and poisoned wine before shooting him and dumping his body in the Neva River. Nicholas and Alexandra were horrified by Felix's and Dmitri's involvement, seeing their actions as a betrayal rather than a sign of allegiance. Their horror was twofold. First, there were the undeniably bad optics of two of the country's wealthiest men—Nicholas's own relatives, Dmitri by blood and Felix by marriage—murdering a peasant in cold blood. Second, Rasputin had recently issued a chilling warning. Sensing, no doubt, that his good fortune was turning, Rasputin had written a letter to Nicholas, warning him about his impending death. Should he be killed by Russian peasants, Rasputin wrote, the tsar would have nothing to fear. Should he be killed by nobles, however—or worse, by Nicholas's own relations—then the world would know a different future.

> "If you hear the sound of the bell which will tell you that Grigori has been killed, you must know this: if it was your relations who have wrought my death then no one of your family, that is to say, none of your children or relations will remain alive for

more than two years. They will be killed by the Russian people." (Quoted in Robert K. Massie's *Nicholas and Alexandra*)

In 2000, the Russian Orthodox Church canonized the last Romanovs as passion bearers: individuals who faced their deaths with Christian resignation. Their remains are now interred at the Saints Peter and Paul Cathedral in St. Petersburg.

GLOSSARY

AIGUILLETTE—Decorative braided loops on a military or naval uniform, hanging from the shoulder

ARSHIN—A Russian unit of length corresponding to approximately two feet

CHOKHA—A traditional woolen tunic worn by Georgian men

DUMA—The Russian state government, first established by Nicholas II in 1905

GYMNASTIORKA—A light jacket worn by noncommissioned members of the Imperial Russian Army

KHLYST—Member of a Russian Orthodox sect known for self-flagellation

KOPECK—A Russian monetary unit equivalent to one hundredth of a ruble

KOZACHOK—A traditional Ukranian couples folk dance

KREMLIN—Fortified complex in the center of a Russian city

MUZJIK—Peasant

OKHRANA—The imperial secret police

PAPIROSY—An unfiltered cigarette

SANITAR/SANITARY—A medical orderly

SOVNARKOM—The Council of People's Commissars, created by Vladimir Lenin following the 1917 revolution

STARETS—A spiritual elder of an Eastern Orthodox monastery

STAVKA—High Command of the imperial Russian armed forces

TARANTASS—A low-slung horse-drawn carriage

TRISAGION—A hymn in Eastern Orthodoxy

VERONAL—Barbital

VERST—A Russian unit of length corresponding to 0.66 of a mile

SELECT BIBLIOGRAPHY

Nonfiction

Azar, Helen. *The Diary of Olga Romanov: Royal Witness to the Russian Revolution*. Westholme Publishing: Pennsylvania, 2014.

Azar, Helen. *Journal of a Russian Grand Duchess: Complete Annotated 1913 Diary of Olga Romanov, Eldest Daughter of the Last Tsar*. Helen Azar: 2015.

Azar, Helen, Eva McDonald, and Dan McDonald. *Russia's Last Romanovs: In Their Own Words*. Helen Azar: 2016.

Bykov, PM. *The Last Days of Tsardom*. London: Martin Lawrence, 1934.

Farmborough, Florence. *With the Armies of the Tsar: A Nurse at the Russian Front in War and Revolution, 1914–1918*. Cooper Square Press: New York, 2000.

Figes, Orlando. *A People's Tragedy: The Russian Revolution, 1891–1924*. Pimlico: London, 1996.

Hallett, Christine E. *Veiled Warriors: Allied Nurses of the First World War*. Oxford University Press: Oxford, 2014.

Massie, Robert K. *Nicholas and Alexandra: The Classic Account of the Fall of the Romanov Dynasty*. Ballantine Books: New York, 1967.

Massie, Robert K. *The Romanovs: The Final Chapter*. Random House: New York, 1995.

Montefiore, Simon Sebag. *The Romanovs: 1613–1918*. Alfred A Knopf: London, 2016.

Rappaport, Helen. *Ekaterinburg: The Last Days of the Romanovs.* Windmill Books: London, 2009.

Rappaport, Helen. *Four Sisters: The Lost Lives of the Romanov Grand Duchesses.* Pan Books: London, 2015.

Rappaport, Helen. *The Last Days of the Romanovs: Tragedy at Ekaterinburg.* St. Martin's Griffin: New York, 2008.

Rappaport, Helen. *The Race to Save the Romanovs: The Truth Behind the Secret Plans to Rescue Russia's Imperial Family.* Windmill Books: London, 2018.

Rounding, Virginia. *Alix and Nicky: The Passion of the Last Tsar and Tsarina.* St. Martin's Press: New York, 2011.

Service, Robert. *The Last of the Tsars: Nicholas II and the Russian Revolution.* Pan Books: London, 2018.

Smith, Douglas. *Rasputin: Faith, Power, and the Twilight of the Romanovs.* Picador: New York, 2016.

Stone, David R. *The Russian Army in the Great War: The Eastern Front, 1914–1917.* University Press of Kansas: Kansas, 2015.

Stouff, Laurie S. *Russia's Sisters of Mercy and the Great War: More than Binding Men's Wounds.* University Press of Kansas: Kansas, 2015.

Zygar, Mikhail. *The Empire Must Die: Russia's Revolutionary Collapse, 1900–1917.* PublicAffairs: New York, 2017.

Memoirs

Buxhoeveden, Sophie. *The Life and Tragedy of Alexandra Feodorovna, Empress of Russia.* Longmans, Green and Co: London, 1928.

Dehn, Lili. *The Real Tsaritsa.* Little, Brown: Boston, 1922.

Yusupov, Felix. *Lost Splendor: The Amazing Memoirs of the Man who Killed Rasputin.* Helen Marx Books: New York, 2003.

ACKNOWLEDGMENTS

I started writing *The Last Grand Duchess* in 2019, shortly following the publication of *The Woman Before Wallis*, but it had existed in my head, in one form or another, for many, many years before I put pen to paper. Naturally, that means my list of acknowledgments could span the length of a city block, but after writing the behemoth that was my author's note I'll do my best to keep it short.

First and foremost to my agent, Kevan Lyon, and my editor, April Osborn, for believing in this novel and giving me the time, space, guidance, and confidence to write it. I couldn't ask for better partners to help me reach my potential as an author.

To my team at MIRA and HarperCollins—Heather Conner, Nicole Brebner, Randy Chan, Ashley MacDonald, Lindsey Reeder, Lia Ferrone, Rebecca Silver, Elita Sidiropoulou, Kathleen Oudit, my authenticity readers, and everyone else at HarperCollins who have been such supporters of my books: thank you for your hard work and dedication to telling great stories.

I am heavily indebted to Bob Atchison's *Alexander Palace Time Machine*, which provided me with invaluable access to palace floor plans and photos, eyewitness accounts of the revolution, and so much more. It is an endlessly fascinating resource into the lives of Nicholas II and his family and is well worth an afternoon of browsing. My thanks as well to Helen Azar for translating the private diaries of the Romanov family, the University of Toronto Libraries, and all of the historians referenced in my bibliography for providing the historical foundations to this book.

I wrote this book during the 2020 pandemic, which threw off my long-awaited plans to travel to Russia's grand palaces. As a result, I could not have brought this book to life without the generosity of people who posted their travel videos of Alexander Palace, the Winter Palace, Ekaterinburg, and Tobolsk online. I hope that I've managed to capture some of the magic of Russia as shared through your travelogues.

My endless gratitude goes to my family for their support, encouragement and love—particularly my mom, Dana Turnbull, who typed out my handwritten edits to the manuscript over a frenzied nine-hour day that had been advertised to her as "a few hours' work." My thanks as well to Margie McCain, Derek Plaxton, Brenda Doig, Josh Nehme, Kate Atkinson, Louise Claire Johnson, Ben Ehrensperger, Mandy Bean, Natasha Campbell, Nastasia Nianiaris, Rachel Thorne, and Pierce Cassidy who—bless him—listened to me recount the entire saga of the Romanovs over a bottle of wine in Berlin in 2016.

Over the past two years, my network of author friends has become, bar none, the most wonderful and supportive group of colleagues. Kaia Alderson, Kristin Beck, Janie Chang, Chanel Cleeton, Natasha Lester, Jennifer Robson, Erika Robuck, Kate Quinn, Rachel McMillan, Louise Claire Johnson, and so many others—thank you for your words of wisdom and support. To the booksellers who've shared my work with their community of readers, and to everyone who's picked up *The Last Grand Duchess* or *The Woman Before Wallis*: thank you for reading. It means the world.

Finally, my thanks to Olga, whose remarkable life was cut far too short.

THE LAST GRAND DUCHESS

BRYN TURNBULL

Reader's Guide

QUESTIONS FOR DISCUSSION

1. Why do the last Romanovs hold such a fascination for modern audiences?

2. Despite sharing a sheltered upbringing, Olga believes her sister Tatiana to be more "worldly" than her. Why do you think she feels her younger sister is more equipped to handle the nuances of high society?

3. Dmitri Pavlovich describes himself as a "lonely fool" who hopes that someone might "take him seriously one day." How does Dmitri change over the course of the book, and how do those changes result in his participation in Father Grigori's assassination?

4. In the prologue, Grandmamma Maria Feodorovna tells Olga that courage means "meeting whatever the future may hold with grace." How does Olga exercise courage—or a lack thereof—throughout the book?

5. How do Olga's experiences during World War I open her eyes to the inequities in Imperial Russia?

6. Nicholas and Alexandra view themselves as parents, first and foremost. How do they attempt to reconcile the duties of ruling with caring for their children?